CHASING REDEMPTION

Don't miss any of Doc Ephraim Bates'
exciting comedic action thrillers

Chasing Black Ice
Chasing Revenge
Chasing Liberation
Chasing Redemption

CHASING REDEMPTION

Boom!!...Killers.
SERIES BOOK #4

Doc Ephraim Bates

Golden Alley Press
Emmaus, Pennsylvania

Golden Alley Press
37 South 6th Street
Emmaus, Pennsylvania 18049

www.goldenalleypress.com

Golden Alley Press books may be purchased for educational, business, or sales promotional use. For information please contact the publisher.

Printed in the United States of America

1 3 5 7 9 10 8 6 4 2

Chasing Redemption: Boom!!...Killers. series book #4 / Doc Ephraim Bates.

This book contains an excerpt from the forthcoming book *Dragon's Men: Domestic* by Doc Ephraim Bates. This excerpt has been set for this edition only and may not reflect the final content of the forthcoming edition.

ISBN 978-1-7333055-5-6 paperback
ISBN 978-1-7333055-6-3 ebook

Back cover photograph of the author ©Starr Belle Photography

Cover design by Michael Sayre

Worst Morning Ever

<pre>
MINNEAPOLIS, MINNESOTA -
THE BRADLEY RESIDENCE
JANUARY 5TH
7:09 A.M. (UTC-5)
12 DEGREES F
</pre>

Any person from the Minneapolis area on the morning of January 5th would have scoffed at the idea of global warming.

It was cold and bitterly so. Winds were steady at 25 mph with gusts up to 40, wind chills in the negative teens. And it was snowing. Again.

According to the calendar, it had been winter for only two weeks. But the second snowstorm of the season was already pounding the area, dropping another 10 to 12 inches on top of the 8 inches already on the ground.

Most people were being urged to stay home. But some people *had* to go to work. Erica Bradley was one of those people. She was not a doctor – at least, not the medical kind. She was not an officer of the law. She was not a snowplow driver. She was, in fact, an astrophysics engineer.

Bradley led a team of experimental theorists at an organization called OMGlobal, which was nothing more than a front for one of the many secret government test labs all across the United States of America.

Erica was paid millions to do the kind of work that she did. But on a day like today, she would gladly have given half a million back just to have someone send a car to drive her to the lab.

Just a few years back, Erica had been a mid-level lackey at NASA's Kennedy Space Center in Orlando, Florida. Little did her superiors recognize the genius they had in their midst. Little did they know that when Erica Bradley went home after work, she was configuring a spacecraft that could advance the human race by light years. Little did they know that one day Erica Bradley's name would go down in the annals of history alongside the likes of Benjamin Franklin, Thomas Alva Edison, and Percy Spencer.

At least, that's how it should have been.

What someone did know was that Erica Bradley was a great mother to her two kids. Kids that her ex-husband had given not two craps about when he walked out on them, leaving her on her own to raise a son, Brady, and a daughter, Johnica, who at five years old was the spitting image of her mother at the same age.

Some three years ago, Erica had shown her off-time project to her superiors. Instead of public recognition, they rushed to cloak her idea in secrecy. To keep her on the hook, they rewarded her with her own team at a secure state-of-the-art facility in Minneapolis, where she was to produce a working model of her space shuttle idea. Plus $1.3 million annual salary, twelve weeks' vacation, free college tuition for her kids, a luxury condo, and the company car of her choosing.

Erica knew, had she pressed the point, that she could have become famous for all time. But what good would that have done her and her kids? Given that she was already in her mid-thirties, getting a patent would probably have taken longer than she had left to live. Best to grant it to NASA, the people that could do the most good with it. Their offer was everything she needed. So she took the deal and never regretted it. Although on snowy Minneapolis mornings, she considered regretting it.

In theory, with a Bimmer like hers, all she had to do was press a button on her key fob to melt off the snow and ice and start the car.

But, of course, of all days for the thing to not work...it just had to be today.

Erica hit the button over and over again only to get the same result: nothing.

"Ugh, you stupid piece of crap," she said out loud to no one. Still in her pajamas, she pulled on her puffer coat and trudged through the swirling snow to her vehicle.

Sticking the key in the lock to manually unlock the door, Erica slid in and shut the door behind her. Shivering, she pressed the ignition button. The engine made a horrible sound.

Erica was about to panic when she noticed that the auxiliaries were all working. The gauges were reading properly, the fan was blowing, and the radio was playing a promo for Senator Brenda Cobb-Schmidt for president.

"Good Lord, it's only January and they are already playing campaign ads." She shook her head in disgust. "I just recovered from Christmas carols twenty-four hours a day...and now this nonsense. Come on, November." She raised her eyebrows.

And that was the last thought Erica Bradley ever had. When her finger hit the ignition button this time, the explosion woke the entire neighborhood, and for a few minutes, took their minds off the weather outside.

Headed Home

Bairre Dolan did what he said he would do.

He kept the snow from building up around the plane's wheels, kept the plane's wings de-iced, and had the bird ready for takeoff when Kinley Devereaux and Harper Rowe returned. He did not even mind that they had brought their friend Taralyn Tharp.

Once the trio boarded, the pilot had the plane rolling through the snow and headed back to the States. He flew below the radar until they were over the ocean.

In the rear of the plane, Kinley, Harper and Taralyn discussed what they had just been through in Prague.

"I don't think I will ever get those images out of my head," Tara said.

"Me either," Kin lamented.

"You guys," she said. "You guys were amazing. The things you did...I knew I made the right decision coming to you to get this job done."

"I'll probably see them in my dreams for a while, but for what it's worth, I know those boys and girls are so much better off now. Constance will make sure of that."

Tara was lost in thought for a moment. "If ever there is anything that the two of you need, I will do it. I owe you both big time. I know you're headed back to the States to get some clarity about Mexico City and the fallout from that. So if there is anything I can do to help further that along, please, let me know."

"Tara, you're golden, baby," Kinley said. He was feeling the effects of the pain meds that Constance Ondracck had administered to lessen his utter discomfort from being shot while liberating the children from the orphanage back in Prague.

"Yeah, Tara, you're golden...like a properly cooked waffle. Can't believe I got shot," Kin laughed. "The stupid guys got two shots off before we put them down, and one of them happened its way right in and out of me."

"How ya feelin' right about now?" Harper asked.

"Kinda feelin' a little higher than the plane. Kinda feelin' like I can look down on the plane and guide it safely home," Kin said, a glazed look in his eyes.

"I think you need to lay down on that couch you're sitting on."

Without arguing, the wounded man lay down and closed his eyes. "Wake me up once we're home. And try not to kill anybody, Harper...I need to call Laurie. I miss her..." and Kinley was out.

Harper looked at Taralyn. "We need to call Kelly Campbell."

"Why is that?"

"She's the only one that knows what's going on. We're supposed to meet some senator who has an idea about how to clear our names. Kelly is our only connection to her."

"Do you have her number?"

"I sure do. Kin can call her when he wakes up. She likes him better anyway." Harper picked up his cell phone and began flipping through his contacts. "It's a long flight. You must be tired, too. We'll figure out the finer points of this plan once we've all gotten some sleep."

"What are you going to do?" Tharp asked, pulling up her footrest and leaning back.

"I've got one call to make. Then I'll join you guys in Slumberland."

After only one ring, Harper heard her answer.

"Harper Rowe, please, tell me that it's you, and you're okay!"

"It's good to hear your voice, Mercedes."

FRUSTRATION

Tenente **Aline Rapido was** there, waiting for her catch.

Laurie Chase, Big James Gray, NSA Agent Jeb Crool, Agent David Baldwin, Tito del Fuento and his wife had all been brought up from the basement of Tito del Fuento's safe house where Tito and his wife had been stashed after their arrest on more charges than Crool could count.

Jeb Crool handed Tito del Fuento and his wife over to Tenente Rapido, promising her that if she needed anything at all, he would be more than happy to oblige.

For himself, he kept the larger catch: former DEA Agent Laurie Chase, big time gun runner James Gray, and their knowledge of where Kinley Devereaux, Harper Rowe, and Senator Brenda Cobb-Schmidt might be showing up.

Agent David Baldwin, for his part, followed through on Jeb Crool's earlier promise to Laurie Chase. He brought her over to a laptop, and the two of them were able to find her boyfriend Kinley Devereaux's cell phone number.

Using a spare burner phone from Agent Baldwin, Laurie tried Kinley's number over and over again, only to get the same result: the call went directly to voicemail.

"Unbelievable," Chase finally gave up. "How can he have his phone turned off at a time like this?"

"Could be a lot of reasons," Baldwin tried to encourage. "He's coming out of a huge adventure. I mean, give me a chance to save orphans from becoming sex slaves, and I would definitely want some down time."

"Do you think that's it?" Chase asked. "He's just spent, and he will call me later?"

"Absolutely," Baldwin smiled. "I can't imagine any other reason why a guy wouldn't call you."

"All I know is that until I can talk to him, my stomach is going to be in knots."

Agent Jeb Crool quickly finished his conversation with Tenente Rapido, squaring up the situation with James Gray and Laurie Chase. It was easy to do, as Tito del Fuento and his wife, Mitra, were the biggest arrests of Rapido's career. In trade, she willingly allowed Crool to take James Gray into custody.

Crool and Gray made their way from the center of the busy scene to where Laurie Chase and Agent Baldwin were sitting.

"How's things going over there?" Dave asked.

"As far as we're concerned, everything's great. I signed off on a few things to get you and Mr. Gray here free and clear of all this. I told Tenente Rapido that we would make ourselves available in the future in regards to del Fuego's case. She was good with that."

"What about Diego and his being able to keep Tito's kids for now?"

Crool let out a little laugh and looked at Laurie. "I'm going to go out on a limb here and guess that you knew that your little friend has been 'dead' for a couple of years now?"

"I did. Tito killed Diego's wife and children, and he thought he had killed Diego, too."

"So, how did you end up with him?"

"It's a long story," Chase said.

"It's a long plane ride," Jeb countered. "Still, being able to put away the man who killed your entire family and save *his* kids in the process...not the worst ending to a story that I've ever heard."

"Are they going to let him keep Tito's kids?" Baldwin repeated.

"Rapido is working on it. She's got some people in the child services division that can pull a few strings. According to Diego, he has a lot of money. Apparently, being dead is a pretty lucrative undertaking," Crool punned. "He says he can get a house for the four of them within the next week or two."

"He'll be fine," Chase commented. "He's just what those kids need."

Aline Rapido came over to the quartet. "Give you and your people a ride somewhere, Agent Crool?"

"Oddly enough, we are both parked about a half mile over that way," Jeb pointed in the appropriate direction. "If you can give us a lift there, we'll be on our way and out of your hair."

"Right this way then," the tenente began walking. "I will say this, Agent Crool. Things certainly have gotten a lot more interesting for me since you got into town."

"It's been a pretty wild ride, some of it a bit more wild than I would have liked," Crool said, alluding to the car wreck that he and Baldwin had suffered the night before, compliments of Laurie Chase and Big James Gray. Chase and Gray looked at each other, then back to Jeb.

"Well," Big Time smiled, "the important thing is that we're all okay so we can laugh about it now."

The Senator and Kent McCleary

His burner displayed "Unavailable." Kent McCleary normally would have disregarded the call altogether. But since only one person had the number, he answered.

"Hello, Senator," he said. "Are you calling me with an update about Harper Rowe and Kinley Devereaux?"

"No update. Just calling to see how our package is doing."

"The package is fine," assured McCleary. "It's downstairs in the basement all tied up."

"How many men do you have there at the house?"

"Seven, counting me."

"And how many men will you have at the exchange?"

"I could have seven there, too, Senator. I mean, it's just two guys, but since I know how important this is to you, I will have twelve men at the exchange."

"Mr. McCleary, let me make myself perfectly clear. If anything goes wrong at the exchange, it's going to get messy. My political career will be over, and I promise you that if I go down, you go down. So, I don't care if it is *just two guys* that you're going to be dealing with. Just be sure you have more than enough men to take care of this situation properly."

"Senator, please," Kent said, "don't spend even one second

worrying. The exchange will go just the way we planned it. You're going to look like a hero *and* a victim. The country will feel your pain but love your power and resolve. What we are getting ready to do is going to get you elected president of the United States, Senator."

"Yes, it will. I know you and your team will be able to pull this off. I just need to make sure you understand the gravity of the situation," Brenda paused and took a deep breath. "Tell me that you – without the slightest misgivings – understand the gravity of this situation."

"Boss, I – without the slightest misgivings – understand the gravity of this situation."

"And your team?"

"And my team," McCleary affirmed. "We are just waiting for the go from you, Senator, and a few hours later you'll be the number-one news topic all around the globe. You'll shine like the leader that you are, and your poll numbers will jump through the roof."

"One last thing, Kent."

"What's that, Senator?

"Other than you and your men...no survivors at the exchange."

Catching Up

It was good to hear her voice.

Sure, it had been less than 48 hours since they had said goodbye, but ever since that moment, Harper Rowe's world had been a nightmarish blur. He was just finishing up telling Dr. Mercedes Lara all about it.

"...and now the kids are in very capable, very loving hands. And Kinley, Taralyn, and I are on a plane heading back to the good old U.S. of A. Those two are sleeping, by the way," Rowe smiled. "But, enough about me. What have you guys been doing? How was your flight back from Rio?"

"Hawk flew while the rest of us slept. When we woke up, Danny took over flying for a while, Hawk slept, and Johnny and I started going through the insane piles of cash that we had in the back of the plane. Ever since we've landed, we haven't even opened back up for business because we've been working on laundering all that cloth."

"Best guesstimate, how far into the pile are you?"

"Best guesstimate?" Mercedes asked both herself and Harper. "I'd say at our current rate – which is really quite nice, actually – we might be able to finish the wash in just about a year from now. And that's only doing half the load."

"Sounds like the four of you will be keeping the Tide company in business for a while."

"Sounds like you'll be needing a better joke book," she mocked. "So, you know how people say that bad things always happen in threes?"

"I do believe I've heard bad people say that. Yes."

"Do you think that good things happen in threes, as well?"

"Like?"

"Like, I think I just had the adventure of a lifetime, met the man of my dreams, and struck it rich all in about a twenty-four-hour period of time."

"Really?" Harper asked.

"Yeah, really."

"Well, okay, I am comprehending what you're saying, but let me ask you this…"

"Yes?"

"If you had to drop one of those three things that you just named, just to be sure that the other two would come true…which one would you drop?"

"Oh, I'd definitely drop the man of my dreams in lieu of having the adventure of a lifetime and lots of money. It would be ludicrous if I didn't, wouldn't you say?"

"If you had said anything else, I would have called together a board of your peers to convene an investigation into your mental well-being, is what I would say."

Dr. Lara laughed. "So, we're agreed then?"

"Absolutely. As long as the board of your peers is Charlie Manson, Ted Bundy, and Pol Pot, then we are very much agreed."

"Well, you've met John, Danny, and Sam, so you know that you're not too far off with those comparisons," Mercedes said warmly. And then, from out of nowhere, "I miss you a lot."

She halfway expected him to fumble around with his comeback, but Harper came back smooth and clean. "It would be a shame if ya didn't, as much as I've been thinking' about you."

"Oh, is that a fact?"

"Without a doubt or a shadow thereof."

"Well, that makes me feel better."

"Did you think that I *wasn't* thinking about you?"

"Part of me thinking about you was me wondering if you were thinking about me. Of course, now that you've told me what you've been up to for the last day, day and a half, I'm amazed that you had any time to think about anything at all."

"I was thinking about getting those kids to a better state in life, but in between the nooks and crannies of that English muffin...I was thinking about you."

"I'm glad you're okay. I mean," Mercedes suddenly found herself at a loss for words. "I mean that I'm really...well, I think you know."

"I do know," Harper said. "I definitely know."

He heard her smile on the other end of the line.

"You all are headed back to the States, then, yeah?"

"Yes, we are."

"Where will you be landing?"

"Best of my intel, we'll be landing around Minneapolis, Minnesota."

"And what's there?" Mercedes asked.

"Hope," Harper answered.

CONFESSION

They had stopped by Big James' place on their way to the airport so that the big man could pack a few things for his trip to the States. It was a little past 8:00 p.m. by the time everyone was on board, settled in, and ready for take-off in the government jet. Crool's men were in the back of the plane, most of them planning to get some sleep since they had been going non-stop since their arrival in Rio 40 hours earlier.

In a lounge area toward the middle of the plane, Agents Crool and Baldwin sat next to each other on a very nice couch. Laurie Chase and James Gray sat across from them, each in a comfortable recliner.

"We really could have gone by your place to pick up some clothes for you, Miss Chase."

"No," Big James answered in her stead, "because if we had, we would still be driving there. The location of her home is, without a doubt, the epitome of *out of the way*. When you travel to where she lives, you literally run out of road."

"So, you live in the middle of nowhere?"

"Let's just say that Lewis and Clark would have a hard time finding it," she joked.

Crool's phone signaled the arrival of a message in his voice mailbox.

"Baldwin, did you hear my phone ring?"

"Can't say that I did."

Jeb entered his password and listened: *"Hey, Jeb, it's Susan Lincoln from Justice. Wanted to let you know that we have had eyes on Kelly Campbell since she landed in Minneapolis. Last night she had a late dinner with none other than Senator Brenda Cobb-Schmidt. My guy wasn't able to get close enough to hear what they were talking about, but he said they were talking for well over an hour. She went back to a hotel from there, and she hasn't gone anywhere since. Just wanted to call and let you know. Hope you're having some success down in Rio. Hope to see you soon."*

Jeb hung up the phone and smiled.

"Anything good?" Baldwin asked.

"Plenty," Jeb replied, looking over at Chase. "Seems your boys' former handler met up with Senator Brenda Cobb-Schmidt last night. According to that message, they were together for a pretty long time."

"I guess their former handler – what was her name again?" Chase asked.

"Kelly Campbell."

"Right. So, I'm guessing that she's as clueless to the intentions of the senator as Kinley and Harper are."

"Do you have her number?" Baldwin asked Laurie.

"Dude, I didn't even know her name," Chase scolded. "Why would I have her phone number?"

"Right, right," he shook his head. "I'm kinda running on fumes here."

"Why don't you head on back and getcha forty. It'll be a while before we land, but once we do, you're gonna need to be ready to roll."

"Sounds good to me, boss." Baldwin stood wearily to his feet and shuffled off toward the back of the plane.

"Me, too," Big James said, kicking out the footrest of his recliner and leaning back. "It's been a hard day's night, kids, and

Mr. Sandman – he's got me down for a reservation of one."

"What about you?" Laurie asked Jeb.

"I'm good for now. What I would really like to do is listen to your story about what happened a couple of nights ago at Tito del Fuento's drug plantation. It might help me to understand a little better everything that happened just a few hours ago at that safe house."

"Well, Agent Crool, that would be quite the confession on my part. So before I even utter one fraction of one syllable about any of it, I need to know just how on the record this is going to be?"

"Just consider me your very own government-appointed priest. I'm not looking to jam you up. I'm just looking for some understanding, is all."

"Did ya hear that, James?"

"Do I need to break out my steno machine for this?" Gray asked without opening his eyes.

"We'll be fine," Jeb affirmed.

"Fine," Chase agreed, "but if we're going to do this story justice then I'm going to have to go all the way back to Mexico City, and the events that took place there."

"Fine by me. I love a good backstory."

"Alright," she shrugged, and began telling Jeb Crool the details that had led to the events at Tito del Fuento's safe house just a few hours ago.

Beginning with why she had become a member of the DEA in the first place, Laurie sprinkled in details about the other members of her unit, then progressed to the reason her team had been in Mexico City: Tito del Fuento.

She described all the work that her DEA team had done to uncover solid evidence against del Fuento. How, when they found out that the man himself was going to be in town, it was all supposed to come together in one final raid to bring this dirtbag down, once and for all.

Laurie recounted the events of the night of the raid, going into gruesome detail about the set-up and slaughter of her whole team. And though months and months had now passed, she still had to fight to keep back the tears as she told the story.

Jeb Crool was completely enthralled by the tale. But what really got his attention was how Laurie Chase's face began to beam when she got to the part where she met Kinley Devereaux and Harper Rowe.

As Laurie related how she and the two assassins tracked the infamous thief Black Ice and smoked out Secretary of Defense Paul Michaels, Jeb found himself sitting on the edge of his seat. When she described the events surrounding the assassination of Paul Michaels, Jeb was simply astounded.

"So, what you're telling me is that the Secretary was the one pulling all the strings?"

"I am," Chase answered, "and I'm pretty sure that you were one of the strings."

Jeb shook his head in disbelief. "Then what you're saying is that it was Kinley Devereaux that shot Secretary Michaels?"

Laurie shrugged and smiled, "I wasn't actually present for this particular part of the story. This is just what I was told."

"Yeah, but it was told to you by Kinley Devereaux. Right?"

"To put it in government-speak, I can neither deny nor confirm that."

"Right."

Laurie continued by telling how she, Kinley, and Harper were forced to go on the lam, and how she set up shop just outside Rio de Janeiro to pursue her vengeful plot against Tito del Fuento. She told him about the abandoned warehouse, and finding Diego, and using him to further her plan to destroy the Brazilian drug lord.

Next, Laurie described her reunion with Kin and Harp; their friend, Big James Gray – who supplied all the munitions for the attack; and his friends, Dragon's Men – the former Delta Force squad. She told him about the terrorist attack they had thwarted at the Espetto Carioca. Laurie detailed the plan to take down Tito, the execution of it, and the ultimate results. She did, of course, omit the part about the millions of dollars that they had taken for their troubles.

She described how the group went their separate ways at this point, with Kinley and Harper heading to Prague while she and James Gray and Diego stayed behind in Rio to finish up with Tito del Fuento and his family.

All told, it took Laurie Chase just over an hour to give Special Agent Jeb Crool the complete picture of what had happened over a year and a half ago in Mexico City and the resulting fallout.

"I gotta say, Miss Chase, that in all my almost thirty years of experience doing this job, I have never heard or seen or known anyone that has been a part of anything like this."

"But now you see why we had to go into hiding, yes?"

"Of course. I mean, if I hadn't just seen you and Mr. Gray and your little friend Diego in del Fuento's house, there's no way I would have ever believed any of this."

"Tell me about it. I've been living this reality, and I can hardly believe it myself."

A dour look suddenly passed over Jeb's face.

"What's wrong?" Chase asked.

"I was just thinking. When this is all finally wrapped up, I'm going to be a month of Sundays filling out all the paperwork."

"Don't you have a secretary for that?"

Crool snickered. "Sure I do. She also doubles as a Playboy Playmate and always comes to work in a French maid's outfit."

Laurie gave him a perturbed look. "You could've just said no."

"Could've," the agent nodded in agreement. "Didn't."

Pockets Full of Hands

"What a cluster bomb this is"

Field Agent Sandy Wyrick, head of the Minneapolis Anti-Terrorist Unit, had been summoned to the scene of the crime, along with the Special Crimes Unit and the FBI.

"Anybody want to step up and take charge of this bullshit? Because if it's me...I'd gladly give it up to whoever it is that might be next. I have no problem letting someone make a name for themselves on this one. FBI? SCIU? Anyone? Bueller? Anyone?"

After several seconds of nothing, Wyrick asserted herself. "It could've been any of you, but now it's me, ya bunch of dicktards. I'm in charge, and you all get to report to me. And if any one of you tries to pull rank, I've been recording this whole conversation. So down the road, when it becomes clear that my investigation brings whoever it is that is responsible for all this foolishness to justice, you'll have a whole lot of nothing to stand on."

She took a breath. Still no one made a move to challenge her taking charge.

"Ugh, really?" She looked around at the representatives of the different law enforcement agencies peppering the crime scene. "Okay, well, somebody better start giving me something to go on because if I've got nothing to work with, I will start firing people just out of pure boredom. Let's go, let's go, something, people!"

One of the Minneapolis PD investigators started reading to her from his flip notebook. "Family says that the deceased—"

"Hey, officer," she interrupted.

"Yes, ma'am?" he looked up.

"Do you write your notes in English?"

"Yes."

"Are they legible?"

"I think so. Why?"

"Because if all you're going to do is read them out loud then just give them to me. I assure you the reading voice I have in my head sounds a sweet sight better than yours."

"I'm sorry. What?"

"Am I stuttering?" she reached her hand out. "Come on, officer. Fork 'em over. Your notes."

The officer meekly handed his notebook to Wyrick and began walking away.

"Whoa. Where are you going?" Sandy asked.

"Back to my squad, ma'am."

"Yeah, I don't think so. These are your notes. What if I have questions?"

"Umm—"

"Yeah, you bet your stupid ass 'Umm.' Don't walk away from me until I tell you that you're dismissed."

"Umm...okay, ma'am."

"Stop saying 'Umm,' will you?" she said, skimming down through his notebook. "This is good. These are good notes. Complete, thorough." She looked up at him. "What's your name, officer?"

"Investigator Sam Bergman, ma'am."

"Who do you report to, Sam?"

"Well, my captain is—"

"I don't really care, actually. What I need you to do is go report to them that you no longer are under their command. You're mine now. Can you do that, Sam?"

"Actually, I'm not even sure that you can do that."

"I can. And I am."

"Okay, well, what would I be—"

"Sam? Was it?"

"Yes, ma'am."

"This case will make or break you. Now you can go back to your little investigation troupe and hang out with them drinking coffee, watching how me and my team break this case like a Triscuit, or you can go back to your little investigation troupe and tell them you're moving on to the big time. So go. And if I don't see you back here within three minutes then I'll leave your little notebook with the duty officer back at your precinct." She cocked her head and looked him right in the eye. "Am I clear?"

"Message received and understood. You'll see me back here in less than two, ma'am."

Wyrick was already back to reading Bergman's notes.

Interview with neighbors:
- Four neighbors confirmed that Erica Bradley got into her car (black 2008 BMW S-series) at or about 7:10 a.m. Car exploded within a minute later
- All neighbors interviewed saw nothing or no one suspicious in the area prior to or after the car exploded
- All neighbors interviewed were of the opinion that Erica Bradley, husband Ken, and children, Brady (7) and Johnica (5), were great neighbors and never caused a disturbance, neither publicly nor domestically. Often, if not always, participated in neighborhood gatherings, projects, charity events. Abided by all HOA standards

- All neighbors confirmed that both children attended Grayson Christian Elementary School
- All neighbors confirmed that husband, Ken, worked as an instructor at local gun range, Locked-n-Loaded Target Shoot
- None of the neighbors interviewed knew where Erica Bradley worked, only that she left for work every M-F at or about 7:45 a.m. and returned each night at or about 6:30 p.m.
- Family regularly attended church services at Grayson Baptist Church

Interview with head of HOA – Joseph McKnight
- Confirmed that Ken and Erica Bradley had been members of neighborhood HOA for 3+ years. No reportable HOA incidents. No neighbor complaints. No domestic complaints
- Never late for any HOA dues. Often contributed ideas to better neighborhood. Also concurred on all topics of bullet point #3 above
- Never had any strange or unseemly comings or goings during their stint in the neighborhood
- Always came back with 720 or higher on the yearly credit check

Interview with husband – Ken Bradley
- Confirmed that the deceased was his wife of 4 years, Erica Renee Bradley, aged 35 years, mother deceased, father aged 77 years, two sisters – twins, aged 37 years, two children, Brady - age 9 and Johnica - age 5
- Ken Bradley, aged 44 years, both parents deceased, only child
- Confirmed his employment as a shooting instructor at Locked-n-Loaded Target Shoot at 933 Nicollet Ave S. Worked there for 3 years. Former military
- Confirmed that his wife, Erica, worked for a gov't research lab, OMGlobal, for over 4 years. Could not recall OMGlobal street

address. Could not find anything with OMGlobal address on it (odd?). Said that wife's position at company was innovations analyst. Hired to the firm straight out of high school. Confirmed that wife's schedule was same as bullet point #6 under neighbors' interview
- No known enemies. No extramarital affairs on either side. Were getting ready for their second honeymoon to Paris

Follow-up notes:
- Look up OMGlobal and what they do
- Talk to E. Bradley's co-workers/boss
- Interview members of Grayson Baptist
- Look into the Bradley's financial records
- Get the Bradley's phone records – landline and cell
- Catch up with forensics to see what kind of explosive device was used

"I'm back, ma'am," Bergman announced. "Well within the three-minute time limit."

Wyrick looked up from the notes, somewhat taken aback by Bergman's presence. "You...changed."

"Well, when I told my boss that I was moving on up and coming to work for you, he demanded that I give back my uniform before I disgrace it by joining MCTU. All I had to put on was what I wore to work this morning."

"You wore that to work?"

Bergman stood before her in a white button-down shirt and loosely tied skinny brown tie, wrinkled khaki pants, and a rumpled brown tweed jacket.

"Truth be told, while I may have shown up in time to join your squad, ma'am, I was cutting it close reporting for muster this morning. Just kinda shoved my civvies in my duffel bag, being that

I was a little short on time. Had I known I'd be wearing them on the job today, I'd've taken better care," Bergman said.

"I like it," Sandy smiled. "You've got that throwback old-school Philip Marlowe look going on." She tossed his notebook back to him. "You take good notes, Old School, but you won't be needing that anymore."

"Ma'am?"

"When we get back to the office, you'll get a tablet that will be tied into the electronics of the rest of the team. Keep your notes, findings, etc. on there. That way we're all on the same page. What one team member uncovers goes out to all the rest of the team members."

"Heck, that's a real nice way to do things, boss," Sam tucked his notebook into his pocket. "Mind if I ask you something?"

"I'll try not to."

"Shouldn't I have some sort of training to be on your team? Just seems like going from police investigator to the counter-terrorist task force...well...it's a bit of a leap, don't you think?"

"Our unit lost its lead investigator two days ago. You're the replacement, Sam," Wyrick informed him. "You still remember how to investigate stuff, dontcha?"

"I sure do, ma'am."

"You'll find the only difference between being a cop investigator and investigating for this unit is that you can wear whatever you want." Sandy Wyrick walked up to Sam and shook his hand. "Welcome aboard, Marlowe. Let's get back to work."

The Skinny on Sam

Departing from Erica Bradley's residence, Sandy Wyrick and Sam Bergman stopped at MCTU headquarters to take care of a multitude of items: the paperwork for Bergman's transfer, equipping him with proper field gear and electronics, introducing him to the team, and familiarizing him with the daily comings and goings of the agents under Wyrick's command.

Meanwhile, Agent Tony Sawyers, another one of Wyrick's men, had put a call into OMGlobal and tracked down Erica Bradley's boss, a fellow named Dr. Modra Bowsky. Sawyers informed Dr. Bowsky that Agents Wyrick and Bergman of the Minneapolis CTU would be there shortly to ask him some questions about Erica Bradley and that he needed to make himself available to them. The man assured Sawyers that he would be awaiting their arrival.

It was just after 9:30 p.m. when Wyrick and Bergman were finally able to drive to the OMGlobal facilities, Wyrick behind the wheel, Bergman riding shotgun.

"So, I'm guessing this wasn't how you saw your day going when you left your house this morning."

"I'd be lying if I said it was," Sam answered. "I'm glad of it, though."

"How long have you been an investigator?"

"Went to Stanford and got my bachelor's in Criminal Law. Joined the academy after that. Went through the usual paces for about two years in Oakland, California, before I got brought on to the homicide division out there just before my 28th birthday—"

"You worked homicide in Oakland?"

"Yes, ma'am. Almost four years."

"Holy cuh-rap!" she exclaimed. "Number one, I would've never pegged you for an Oaktown homicide dick, although I know you've got some stories, and I expect to hear some of them soon. Number two, call me boss or just call me by my name. Ma'am is what people that aren't on my team call me. Number three, why'd you leave Oakland homicide?"

"My wife was offered the Chief of Medicine position at UMMC. We couldn't say no to that so we left the comforts of the Bay Area and came here to the land of a thousand lakes and ten thousand snow plows."

"You mean to tell me that your wife is the head of meds at University? The best hospital in the state?"

"Yes, ma...uh...boss, that's what I mean to tell you. I'm really proud of her," Sam beamed.

"Well, you're just full of surprises," Sandy smiled. "I mean, you've got this Beaver Cleaver RFD way about yourself, but behind the mild-mannered persona lies an ex-homicide detective from one of the most dangerous cities in the country who's married to one of the most decorated doctors in all of Minnesota."

"Aww, now, it ain't all like that." Sam blushed slightly. "We're just Sam and Samantha Bergman, couple of high school sweethearts that were able to take advantage of a few opportunities that got tossed our way. Could have been anybody, really."

"Let me tell ya something, Sammy – may I call you Sammy?"

"As long as it's just you and me, sure. I'd rather you didn't do it when there's company around."

"Let me tell ya something, Sammy, there's a lot of people in this world that have been given opportunities to do great things, and most of those people just watch those opportunities come and go like they're at a NASCAR race. No, you and your wife aren't just anybody. You two should be proud of your achievements. I definitely made the right decision bringing you on to my team. I look forward to meeting your wife, too. Wouldn't mind comparing notes with her."

"Comparing notes, boss?" Sam asked. "I'm afraid I don't follow you."

"She's a female in a high-ranking position in a male-dominated field. I'm sure that she's let you know more than once just how tough that can be to navigate. I know all too well what that's like. So I would just like to compare notes with her sometime as to how she handles certain affairs and conditions."

"I'm sure she'd like that."

Agent Wyrick turned the government-issued sedan onto the service road leading to the OMGlobal security gate. The entire facility was surrounded by a ten-foot reinforced chain link fence topped by four lines of barbed wire. Inside the fenced area, tall streetlamps peppered parking lots extending as far as Wyrick and Bergman could see. The sterile light shone down on a myriad of vehicles in parking lots surrounding a cluster of multi-storied, well-lit buildings. Infrared security cameras attached to the light posts appeared to have every inch of OMGlobal's property under surveillance.

"Impressive," Bergman sighed. "It would appear that Fort Knox has got nothing on this place."

Wyrick pulled up to the security booth where two security guards and their German Shepherds manned the station. One of the guards and his dog approached the vehicle.

"Good evening," he said, friendly enough. "Identification, please."

Wyrick and Bergman obligingly handed him their IDs and credentials. "We're here to see a Dr. Modra Bowsky, to question him about an incident that occurred this morning with one of the employees that works here."

"Okay. Wait here and I'll check it out."

The agents waited patiently while the sentry went to verify their information.

"Have we figured out what this place is yet?" Sam asked.

"I did some digging and made a few phone calls while we were back at HQ. OMGlobal is a government research facility. And it's, apparently, a top-secret facility. Because, other than some rather benign trivial facts, I couldn't find too much else about it."

"What kind of trivial facts?"

"Like the fact that it employs around ten thousand people from all over the world. Like the fact that it brings in about ten to fifteen million dollars a year to the city Like the fact that there just wasn't very much else available as far as what they do here."

"Huh. Well, I guess we'll find out in a few minutes."

"I just hope they don't jam us up with a whole lot of 'Sorry, but that's classified' bull crap. This Erica Bradley woman seems like the perfect wife, mother, churchgoer and neighbor. I'm going to guess that the reason somebody wanted to blow her up has to do with her top-secret government research job. It's bad enough that we're out here at such a late hour, but if we have to put up with a bunch of red tape, hush-hush, need-to-know-basis foolishness then I am not going to be in a very ladylike mood. I'm sure your wife is going to be thrilled that your first night on the job has you out way past a decent bedtime."

"Ah, it's all right, boss. She works all kinds of crazy hours, too. She always feels bad that I'm usually home eating dinner and going to bed by myself. Now she won't have to worry about it too much anymore." Sam looked out Sandy's window at the German Shepherds sitting at perfect attention just waiting for their masters to give them an order.

"I wonder if the dogs are here to make sure that no contraband comes into this place or to make sure that nothing top-secret goes out?"

"Probably both," Sandy answered as she, too, looked over at the security dogs. "Just look at them though. Absolutely beautiful."

"My buddy and his family adopted one of those retired bomb-sniffing dogs. A yellow lab named Charlie. It took them a while to get Charlie used to being around regular people in non-stress situations, though. Funny thing is, dog's upbringing being what it was, it had never been around little kids. The family and their kids were all grown up. But, I'm guessing at some point, somebody came to stay with them for a few days, and they had two little girls – three or four years old, I reckon – and there was a bit of uneasiness about how Charlie was going to be around the little ones." Sam started to smile.

"Hey," Wyrick snapped her fingers, "don't give away the end of the story with facial expressions. Finish your anecdote and then you can reflect gleefully."

"Right, right. Okay, so they bring the two little girls into the room to meet the dog, and Charlie looks at them, and he starts to get closer to them, and the older people are telling the little girls not to scare him, and he gets closer to them, and the little girls are looking at Charlie and then up at their parents and then at Charlie, and the dog puts his nose right up to the face of one of the little girls and starts sniffing, and then"—Sam paused for dramatic effect— "and then he just starts licking her and he starts licking her sister, and the little girls start hugging Charlie, and the whole scene is like something right out of a Norman Rockwell painting."

"Aww, that's so cool. Cute story, Uncle Remus."

"Seemingly, yes, but here's the thing: Since this was the dog's first interaction with little kids, he immediately thought that the appropriate response to encountering children was to lick them. Now, whenever they take the dog on a walk or into some sort of public setting and there's a little kid? Or a dwarf? Or a member of the Lollipop Guild? Charlie wants to lick them. Whether he knows them or not, the dog thinks that proper procedure for little people of any sort is to lick them."

"I can see where that might make things awkward. Although, if I were a kid, I think I'd absolutely love it if a dog just came up and started licking my face. Of course, I'm a dog person."

The security guard came back to the car and handed them their IDs and badges. "Okay, agents, drive through this gate and follow the road down to building 1121. Third building down on your left. The numbers are displayed rather prominently above the entrance. Since you're here on official business, you can just park right in front of the building. A guard will be waiting there for you, and they will escort you inside and to the office of Dr. Modra Bowsky."

"Building 1121?" Wyrick double-checked.

"Yes, that's correct."

"Thank you, officer." Wyrick raised her window and slowly pulled the car forward.

"Let's go try to get some answers, Sammy."

Parking Lot Guardians

Laurie Chase was not the only one futilely trying to contact Kinley Devereaux.

Kelly Campbell, in her hotel room at the Aqua City Motel on Lyndale Avenue in Minneapolis, was stretched out beneath the blankets watching late night infomercials.

Kelly had been waiting for hours to hear from Kinley Devereaux about his and Harper Rowe's impending return to the United States. When she had not heard from him by midnight, she started calling him. The calls went straight to voicemail.

When her bedside clock read 3:41 a.m., Kelly tried calling Kinley twice more, muted the television, rolled over, and was asleep within five minutes.

As she slept, two men in a black sedan sat out in the Aqua City Motel parking lot. These federal agents had been assigned to "keep eyes" on Kelly Campbell ever since she landed at the Minneapolis airport about 36 hours ago.

The first agent, Chris Pringle, was flipping through the notes from the previous shifts.

The second agent, Mark Rose, was trying to find something worth listening to on the radio. "Gah! They should put XM Radio in these cars when they give us assignments like this."

"You're not kidding," Agent Pringle agreed. "This woman met up with Senator Cobb-Schmidt her first night in town, but other than that, her skinny ass has been parked here ever since. She hasn't even left to go out to eat. She's just been ordering-in the whole time."

Besides the other shift reports, the folder held three 8x10 photographs: one of Kinley Devereaux, one of Harper Rowe, and one of Laurie Chase.

"Well, I look at it this way: she was in hiding for well over a year. I'm pretty sure she didn't just show up to enjoy the fine accommodations here at the Aqua City Motel. She's here waiting for someone. If she's waiting for them"—Rose pointed to the three photographs— "then it's just a lottery draw as to who is here on the stakeout when they do show up. Those agents may very likely be the ones that capture *America's Most Wanted.* That's the payoff for sitting in this parking lot for all these ungodly hours."

"Why do you think she took a meeting with the senator?"

"Hey, it's no secret that the senator is the frontrunner to be the next Commander-in-Chief. Maybe she was trying to broker some kind of pardon for her people."

Pringle nodded thoughtfully. "Sure. That makes sense."

"One thing's for sure – and you don't have to be a crossword puzzle whiz to figure it out – something big is getting ready to break. And it looks like it's getting ready to break right here in our Twin City."

She Can Be Hard to Talk To

Kinley Devereaux opened his eyes in uncomfortable shock. He had been sleeping soundly – for how long he was not quite sure – when the pain meds he had taken for his gunshot wound wore off. The pain jarred him awake prematurely, causing him to wince and involuntarily cry out.

Taralyn slept through the disturbance, but Kinley's outcry pierced through Harper's veil of unconsciousness. He immediately sat upright and scanned his surroundings through sleepy eyes to see what had snapped him awake. It did not take him long to find out.

"Harper," Kin moaned.

Rowe sprang to his feet. "You all right? What can I do?"

"Constance sent some of those pain meds. I'm going to need one, like, five minutes ago."

"No need to fret, chief. I have them right here." Harp removed a plastic pill box from his pocket, pulled out two pills and handed them to his friend.

"Am I supposed to take two?"

"Yes." Rowe found some bottled water and opened it up. "Wash 'em down, champ."

Still horizontal on the couch, Deveraux put the pills in his mouth and swilled the bottle of water until it was gone. "Help me sit up," he instructed his friend, letting out a small belch. "Ugh, it even hurts to burp."

With one hand behind Kin's head and the other around his waist, Harper carefully sat him up on the couch. Kinley gingerly swung his legs down. "Aww, Mother Russia, that hurts."

Harper moved away slowly. "You okay like that?"

"Yeah, I think so."

"Want some more water or something?"

"Sounds good."

He retrieved another container of water from the plane's mini-fridge and gave it to Kinley. A pained expression crossed his friend's face when he lifted the bottle to his mouth.

"Those pain meds will kick in any time now," Rowe assured.

"How long have I been asleep? Any idea what time it is?"

"I don't know what time it is because I really have no idea what time zone we're in. But I did start the timer on my watch when we took off because I know this flight should be just under fourteen hours." Harp looked at his watch. "Right now, we are at a cool nine hours and forty-two minutes into the flight. Which means you were asleep just over eight and a half hours."

"Really? It felt like I was only asleep for a few minutes."

"That's the pain meds. They've got you sleeping pretty hard."

"I guess so."

"And speaking of pain meds, how ya feelin' now?"

Kinley took a few seconds to assess. "Not too bad right now."

"Well, good. Good. In that case, I think now might be a good time to go over what our situation is and what we'll need to do first once we land."

"I don't know what to do. I can't get in touch with anybody because my stupid phone is shot. Literally shot."

"Let me ask you what might be a really stupid question…"

"Go ahead. It's not like you haven't done it before."

"What do you think the chances are that Kelly still has the same number after all this time?"

"The same number as what?" Kinley asked.

"The same number as when we were doing proper jobs for the NSA. You know, back before Mexico City. Do you recall if her current number is the same as before?"

"I – I really don't," Kin slowly shook his head. "Between the sleepiness and the pain pills, my recall ability is pure mush. I'm rather impressed that *you* can remember her number after all this time."

"Hey, don't forget that she used to be my handler, too. I had to commit that number to memory because, as much as I hated to admit it, I knew that in certain given situations that particular number was my only lifeline. You don't soon forget a number like that."

"Apparently."

Harper walked back to his recliner and grabbed his phone. He dialed the number. There was a long silence.

"It's ringing," Harper finally said.

Five rings.

"Hello," answered a sleepy voice. A *woman's* sleepy voice.

"Holy Malone," he said to Kinley. "It worked."

"You're kidding."

"Not even a little bit."

"Hello?" the woman's voice came again.

Harper suddenly realized that he was supposed to be talking to the person on the other end of the line. "Uh, yeah...Kelly?"

"Who is this?" she asked, sitting up in bed.

"Harper. Harper Rowe."

"Wait, what? This is...is it...Harper?" In her excitement, Kelly threw the covers off and tried to stand up so quickly that her feet got tangled, sending her headfirst onto the floor. She laid there laughing uncontrollably. Devereaux could hear her all the way at the other end of the couch.

"Is she okay?"

"You okay there, princess?" Harper asked.

Taking a deep breath, Campbell began asking rapid-fire questions. "Are you okay? Is Kinley with you? Is he okay? I thought I would have heard from you guys by now. I was worried. Where are you? Are you headed back to the U.S. yet? And if you are, when do you expect to arrive?"

Silence. More silence.

"Hello? Harper?"

"Oh, I'm sorry," Harper Rowe finally said. "Were you finished?"

"Harper, sweetie," she sighed. "For the first time in my life I am actually glad to hear from you. Please don't ruin it by being a jackass."

Harper was preparing to smart off to his former handler in a fashion that would make up for all the days gone by that he had not been able to smart off to her. Then he saw the look on his partner's face.

"Don't," Kinley whispered. "Just...just don't. We've got too much riding on this, buddy. Once we get through this and finally get things back to good, you can make a three day weekend of it. Just not now."

Harp took a deep breath and let cooler heads prevail.

"Sorry about that," he said sincerely. "Let me see if I can answer your questions. First and foremost, I'm okay. Yes, Kinley is with me. You haven't heard from us because there was a communications snafu. But fortunately for us, you never changed your number."

"Kinley usually calls me on the other phone – the one he gave me a while back."

"Yeah, but as it turns out Kinley won't be calling anyone in the immediate future."

"What? Why? Is he okay? What's wrong?"

"Okay, let me rephrase my last statement. His *phone* won't be calling anyone in the immediate future. His phone, which has all of his contacts and contact numbers on it, is currently defunct. I happened to remember this number because I called it so many times back when you were my handler in hopes that you wouldn't give me another crappy assignment in a country that sucks more than the average black hole. You always did, but my relentless habit of dialing your number finally paid off today."

"So you're saying that Kinley's phone is dead, but he's okay, right?" Campbell asked. Shaking herself free of the covers, she got up off the floor and turned on a lamp.

"We'll come back to that one. Let me answer your other questions first. Where are we? On a plane. Are we headed back to the States? Yes, we are. When do we expect to arrive? Well, let me answer that question with this question: What time is it where you are?"

"It's about twenty past four."

"Okay," Harper looked at the timer on his watch. "We should be landing in Minneapolis between 8 a.m. and 9 a.m. your time. Where do you want us to meet you? Do you know where you'll be about that time?"

"Yes, I'm staying at the Aqua City Motel. The address is 5739 Lyndale Avenue. I'm on the first floor in Room 11. Call me when you land and are on your way here. Did you get the address, Harper?"

"Yes, 5739 Lyndale Avenue, Room 11," he repeated. "We'll land, get a car, and head to you. We'll talk to you when we do. Get back to sleep, and we'll see you in a few hours."

"Wait! You didn't tell me what's going on with Kinley?"

"Eh," Harp hesitated. "There's really no good way to say this without you going into complete hysterics, and you shouldn't do that."

"Harper, just tell me.

"He's okay."

"But?"

"There was an incident that occurred while we were in the

process of rescuing the children from the orphanage in Prague."

"Will you just tell me what's going on? Now!"

"Hey, will you let me break this to you gently? I'm trying to think about your feelings here."

"Okay, fine."

"So, we got the kids out and off to a better place, but during the operation some of the people that were responsible for the whole atrocity showed up. Kinley and I took it upon ourselves to let them know that we did not approve of their actions. So…," and Harper took a moment to think about how to tell Kelly just what had happened.

"Good Lord, Harper, I'm putting my neck on the line for you and Kinley. I think I deserve to know what is going—"

"Kinley got shot," he finally came clean.

He got the response he knew he was going to get. A gasp, a stutter, and then, "What? What? Shot? Where? Is he okay?"

"Just calm down, Kelly. He's fine. I mean, for the most part."

"For the most part? What does that mean?"

Harper pulled the phone away from his ear and looked at his friend. "You wanna talk to her? I can't talk to her when she's like this. I tried, dude. I really did. But you know how she gets."

Kinley motioned for Harper to hand him the phone.

Kelly Campbell was still in the process of yelling at Harper. "Kell?"

"Kinley?" she stopped mid-rant. "Kinley, baby, are you okay? What's going on? Where are you? When—"

"Kelly. Everything Harper told you is accurate. We're on our way back. I'm fine. I got shot, but it's nothing serious."

"Nothing serious? Nothing serious!"

Kinley handed the phone back to Harper. "Hey, I tried," he shrugged gingerly. "Sometimes she can be hard to talk to."

Harper scowled at his buddy as he took the phone back. Not bothering to put it up to his ear, he spoke into the microphone.

"Okay, Kelly, we got the address. We'll see you soon. Get some sleep now because you're probably going to need it." He disconnected the call and looked at his ailing partner. "I'm probably going to regret doing that."

"Yep, I'd say that you are 100% accurate with that statement."

ALL ABOUT ERICA

Dr. Modra Bowsky met Wyrick and Bergman just outside of building 1121. He was a tall, lanky man of Indian descent, a bit quiet when he spoke.

"I just figured that it would be better for me to come out here and walk the two of you in. Letting security hand you off in some sort of hallway relay would have just been dreadful for all involved." Sliding his ID through a digitized reader next to the door, Dr. Bowsky led the way inside the building.

He repeated this maneuver several times as he, Sandy, and Sam made their way through the building, down countless halls, an elevator or two, more hallways, and then, finally, into Dr. Bowsky's office.

"So, what can I help you with?" Bowsky asked once everyone was seated in his nondescript office. Bowsky sat behind a rather large mahogany desk, with Wyrick and Bergman across from him in two cafeteria chairs.

"I'm sure you've heard by now that there was an incident this morning with one of your employees," Wyrick began. "A member of your team named Erica Bradley."

"I am aware of what happened, yes. What I am wondering is why are Minneapolis CTU agents here asking me questions instead of the regular police?"

"Regular police?" Wyrick furrowed her brow.

Sam leaned over in his chair and whispered to Sandy, "I think he's wanting to know why we're here and not the Metro Homicide Division."

"Oh." Sandy looked back at Dr. Bowsky. "Did you happen to hear how your employee was killed? Because I assure you it wasn't a simple stabbing or a drive-by shooting or road rage or anything like that." Wyrick locked eyes with the doctor, making sure she had his attention. "It was a bomb, and a very effective one at that. It blew her and her car to pieces. The only difference was that her car was made out of metal, and Erica Bradley was made of flesh and bone and blood. We were able to pick up the pieces of one but not the other."

"I see," Bowsky answered flatly. "So, you think Ms. Bradley's death was the work of terrorists, and that is why you are here?"

Sam noticed his boss's breaths coming a little faster. The hour was late and here was this joker trying to play dumb by captioning the obvious and asking dopey questions. Not knowing if it was the right thing to do or not, Sam jumped in.

"We're here because she worked in a place like this – security clearance out the yin and the yang, am I right? So, it wouldn't matter if she was the head of janitorial services or the head of technological sciences, CTU gets first crack in circumstances such as these."

"I see," Modra replied without changing his expression. "So, should I expect the regular police to come by later?"

"I don't know," Sandy said, gathering her wits. "This may be the beginning of something much greater and more dangerous, or it might just be a huge scare that is getting – no pun intended – blown way out of proportion. Regardless, we are here, and we would just like to ask you some questions. Are you okay with that?"

"I can only tell you what I am able to tell you. You must understand that this facility is under constant lock and key and the watchful eye of many government agencies from all over the world twenty-four hours a day, seven days a week. Like you said, Agent Bergman, security clearances out the yin and the yang...every day, everywhere, for everyone."

"So," Wyrick continued, "with the amount of security that you have here at OMGlobal, it makes sense to us that this is an outside job. With Erica Bradley working for you and this facility, she was potentially privy to unknown amounts of national security secrets. Maybe when she was off the OMGlobal campus, she was approached by the right faction with the right offer. Then again, maybe she was being extorted or blackmailed. Regardless, when a bomb goes off in a major city in this day and age, the first thought on everybody's mind is terrorism. It didn't used to be this way, but it is now, and because that's the case, CTU is here first. The regular, ordinary police will be stopping by later."

"Okay," answered Bowsky. "Where do we start?"

"Let's start with an easy one. What was Erica Bradley working on that may have gotten her killed?"

"What you may not understand is that my being her supervisor is strictly in name only. She headed up her own team of scientists, physicists, and engineers. The only reason that I am her supervisor is because I just happen to be the guy on the next rung up from her. Up until two months ago, Dr. Bradley and her team were working on a project outside of this facility. I never saw her or them."

"What happened two months ago?"

"They finished the project."

"Any idea what that project was?" Wyrick asked.

"I have no idea. Whatever the project was, it had government clearance, but the security level on it was above my pay grade."

"Was it normal for an entire team to be working at another site?"

"Normal? No. Did it happen on occasion? Yes."

"Any idea how long they were working on the project?"

"Dr. Bradley has been employed at OMGlobal for just about

four years, so I would guess that they were working on the project for over three years."

"In the two months since she's been back, have you had much contact with her?" Bergman asked.

"The only contact that I really had with her was delivering her the assignments that those in charge wanted her team to work on."

"And who were 'those in charge'?"

"I do not know."

Sandy Wyrick ran the tips of her fingers across the bridge of her nose and sat back in her chair.

Bergman leaned forward. "Dr. Bowsky, if you were the one delivering Dr. Bradley her assignments, then you must have had some idea of what she was working on."

"Nothing," the doctor answered, his face once again unreadable. "Sometimes when I come into work, there is a sealed envelope on my desk. I take it to her office, and someone from her team takes it from me. Other days, I come into my office and there is nothing, so I do not even see her or her assistant or whatever she is. That is all."

"Okay," Sam said, "besides Erica Bradley and her team, how many other employees do you supervise?"

"Thirty-one," he answered without hesitation.

"And you see them and talk to them...like in a regular supervisor-employee relationship?"

"Yes. Yes, I do."

Bergman and Wyrick exchanged looks. "Surely, you must have said something to somebody. Asked *someone* what the blazes was going on with Erica Bradley and her team?"

"Look, agents, she was assigned to me two months ago. I was told nothing except that she would be given assignments through me, and if anyone came around asking questions, I was told not to answer them. When I asked what she was working on, the only thing they told me was that she and her team had just wrapped up a very classified project that I was not to ask her about."

"Come on, Dr. Bowsky," Bergman continued to grill. "You expect me and my partner here to—"

"I will tell you this: I am retiring in four months. Two months ago they sent me Erica Bradley. They told me that she would be the one to take my place, and I did not need to train her."

"Seems...odd...doesn't it?"

"I thought the same thing," Modra Bowsky's voice dropped to a whisper. "I went to look her up, and, virtually nothing for the last three years. I was shut down at every turn."

"So..." Sam asked, "did you find *anything* out about her?"

The doctor hesitated. "Yes. One thing."

"What was that?"

"I have worked for this facility for over two decades. I have a very, very high security clearance. But when I went to look for Erica Bradley's background, I found only one thing of importance."

"And what was that?" Wyrick asked.

"The only thing I could find out was the name of the project she spent the last three years working on. It was called Space Frequency."

"Space Frequency?"

"Before you even ask, I can tell you right now that there is nothing to be found about it. I promise you. I looked and looked again. Regardless of my security clearance, I found nothing useful to help me with Erica Bradley or her involvement with Space Frequency."

"Okay, okay," Bergman obliged. "Well, let me ask you this. Did you ever actually meet Erica Bradley?"

"Never."

"But...didn't you just say that she was handed over to your supervision two months ago?" Sandy asked. "And that she was going to be taking your place when you retire? Wouldn't she – I don't know – need to talk with you about the hours or the pay or if she had to work from this crappy office?"

"I did."

"And you never met her?"

Bowsky took his time before answering. "I've told you all that I know. All that I can." He locked eyes with Agent Wyrick to make sure he had her attention. "I may have already told you too much."

Agent Wyrick stood up from her chair and touched Bergman on the shoulder, signaling that it was time to go. Sam had a few more questions in mind, but Wyrick was the boss. He got up and waited to hear her exit strategy.

"I think we have all that we need. My partner and I thank you for your time, Dr. Bowsky. And don't worry, what you have told us here tonight will be kept in the strictest of confidence. I'm guessing that you'll need to escort us out?" she stated.

Dr. Bowsky stood up from behind his desk and led Bergman and Wyrick back through the complex. The trio walked in uncomfortable silence until they were a few feet from the exit. Agent Wyrick stopped short, handing Bowsky her business card.

"If you think of anything else, call me," she said quietly. "If you hear anything that might shed some light into our investigation, call me. Most importantly, if you get scared and feel like what happened to Erica Bradley might happen to you – if you fear for the well-being of anyone around you: friends, family, co-workers – don't wait until it's too late, Dr. Bowsky. We can protect you, sir."

Modra took her card and nodded.

Agent Bergman reached out and shook the doctor's hand. "We appreciate your time, Dr. Bowsky."

With that, Agents Wyrick and Bergman left Building 1121 – one agent pleased with what they had learned, the other wondering if they were leaving with more questions than they had arrived with.

A Quick Call to the Senator

After Harper Rowe hung up on her, Kelly Campbell lay in her bed for half an hour debating whether or not to give Senator Cobb-Schmidt an update on Kinley and Harper's arrival. On the one hand, it was very early to be calling someone. On the other hand, she knew that the senator was eager for news.

Kelly finally gave in and picked up her cell phone. Butterflies stirred in her stomach as with each ring she hoped the call would go straight to voicemail if Senator Cobb-Schmidt was still asleep.

No such luck. At the sixth ring, a woman's voice answered. "Miss Campbell? Is that you? Is everything okay?"

"Senator," Kelly began uneasily, "I apologize. I do realize the earliness of the hour. But I have an update on the arrival of Mr. Devereaux and Mr. Rowe."

"Really? What's going on? Are they on their way?"

"I just got off the phone with them a little bit ago. They *are* on their way, and will be landing in Minneapolis around 9:00 a.m. Central Time. I don't know exactly where they will be landing, but I do know that they will be traveling by car and coming here to meet me at my motel. Shortly after that, we will be ready to come and meet up with you."

"That is fantastic news, Miss Campbell."

"Well," Kelly said, trying to sound modest, "I did tell you that I would get them here."

"That you did," the senator admitted. "I can't help but feel that this is going to be so fantastic. If I may, Kelly, would it be okay if I send one of my staff to collect the three of you? We can't meet at my office in the Capitol – with Harper being America's most wanted man, we don't need that kind of publicity. The place that I've reserved for us to meet instead is a bit out of the way. If you're not familiar with the landscape, you could very easily end up in Canada by mistake. I'd just feel much more at ease if one of my people could be there. And you could easily follow them to where we will be meeting. Would that be okay?"

Campbell hesitated for a moment, unsure how Kinley and Harper would feel with having a stranger in their midst upon returning to the States for the first time in almost two years. But then, why would they be upset? After all, Senator Brenda Cobb-Schmidt was the one that was giving them the chance to get their freedom back again.

"Absolutely, Senator. That would be a most gracious gesture on your part."

"Did you say that you were staying at the Aqua City Motel?"

"I did, yes, Room 11."

"I will send my aide over between 9 and 9:30 this morning to meet you there. Her name is Stephanie Cash. I'll tell her to call ahead and also identify herself at your door. We certainly don't want any miscommunication this late in the proceedings. We've come so far."

"Absolutely, Senator."

"Please, call me Brenda. We're getting ready to do some very good things for this country."

Urgent Message

Only the pilot was awake.

As if the rest of them were in a time capsule set to awaken in the year 2599, the co-pilot, Big James Gray, Laurie Chase, Jeb Crool, David Baldwin, and the NSA agents all slept as the plane hurtled on its course from South America to the Twin Cities.

At about seven hours from touchdown, Jeb sat bolt upright in his recliner.

"Mother of Pearl!" he exclaimed. Looking around, he saw that everyone else was still asleep. His hand flew to his pants pockets, looking for his phone.

Not there.

He looked down to the right of his seat. Nope.

He looked to his left. No phone.

"Dang it. Where are you?" he said aloud. Crouching down to look under his seat, he found nothing but a few cracker crumbs. He lifted his head – and there it was. He had been sitting on it.

Grabbing it, he quickly looked up the number he desperately needed.

"Hello?" she answered on the second ring.

"Susan, it's Agent Jeb Crool."

"Jeb?" Susan Lincoln yawned, glancing at the clock on her nightstand. "Kinda late, so this must be important."

"It is, yes. You said that some of your boys had eyes on Kelly Campbell. Is that still accurate?"

"Yeah, as far as I know. Why?"

"I need you to get a message to them. Can you do that?"

"Yes, of course."

"I think there's a good chance that Kinley Devereaux and Harper Rowe are going to contact her and soon. I need to make sure that your guys leave them alone. Do not pick them up."

"Okay. Why?"

"It's kind of a long story, and by the time I tell it to you, your agents may have already picked them up. I just need you to get them that message asap."

"Okay. I'll call them right now."

"Good. Thank you. Oh, and Susan, do you have a dossier on Senator Brenda Cobb-Schmidt from Minnesota?"

"Yeah, I'm sure we do. Why?"

"When you get to work in the morning, can you email that over to me?"

"Absolutely. I'll do it first thing."

"Great. Thank you. I appreciate it. And…sorry to have called so late, but it's urgent that you get your guys that message immediately."

"Going to do it now."

"Oh, one more thing real quick. You don't happen to know off the top of your head what motel Kelly Campbell is staying at, do ya?"

"No, but I'll get it to you as soon as I get in. I swear."

"Very well. Good night, Susan."

Sometimes Bad Things Happen

It had been a long night of sitting in a car doing surveillance on a subject that did absolutely nothing.

"Almost eight o'clock in the morning," Agent Mark Rose scribbled in his notes, "and the skies are just starting to brighten. No change in the situation."

Then there was a change in the situation.

A beautiful woman pulled into the parking lot. Ignoring the painted lines, she slammed her car into park and jumped out, looking lost and exasperated. And good. A fine distraction as far as this mundane assignment was concerned.

"Pringle, wake up. We have company."

Chris Pringle woke up just in time to see the attractive woman approach their car. Her skirt was short and her blouse was about two sizes too small, but it did its job. When she was within about four feet of their car, she waved her hands.

"Hello. Hi. I'm so lost. Can either of you maybe help me?"

Agent Rose had already rolled the window down. "Where are you trying to go?"

Walking up to the driver's side window, she leaned in. Her cleavage, enough to distract an autistic savant, distracted Agents

Rose and Pringle to the point that they never saw a man walk up to the passenger's side of their car and shoot both of them dead.

Stephanie Cash looked at her cohort. "You and your team clean this up. I'm going after our mark in the hotel room."

LANDING

Snowy Minnesota.

Bairre Dolan had landed in worse places, but this would rank right up there with the worst of them. The tarmac was slippery, the snow was heavy, and the landing strip was shorter than most. Still, he got his souls to where they needed to be.

From their seats in the plane, a sore Kinley Devereaux was giving his partner the third degree.

"Did you make the call?"

"Yeah, I made the call. One of his people will be picking us up when we land," Harper answered.

"Your boy gets around, doesn't he?"

"Oddly enough, he says the same thing about me and you. He's just glad to have us back in the States again. He's got people everywhere. You got people, I got people, he's got people. One of his people will be picking us up."

"I'm looking out the window...I don't see one of his people."

Kin looked at Harper.

Harper looked at Kin.

Taralyn looked at both of them.

"Give it a minute," Rowe said. "Someone will be here. Rob Perry does not disappoint."

All three moved to a window and looked out for somebody, anybody, to come pick them up.

Sure enough, within the minute, a black four-wheel drive SUV came plowing through the snow.

Harper looked at Kinley and Taralyn. "I do believe our chariot awaits."

KILL SHOT

Stephanie Cash returned to her car and parked it responsibly. Then she got into the back seat and changed into something much more business appropriate.

Satisfied with the effect, she straightened her hair, got out of the car and headed toward Room 11.

Kelly Campbell was still asleep when the knock came at her door. She opened her eyes and looked at the clock. Just a few minutes past eight o'clock. She sat up and shook the cobwebs loose from her head.

A second knock came before Kelly was presentable enough to answer the door. "Miss Campbell? My name is Stephanie Cash. I'm from Senator Cobb-Schmidt's office. Are you awake?"

Kelly cracked the door wide enough to pull the security chain taut. She did a quick visual of what she could see of Stephanie Cash. Everything looked kosher.

"Sorry. It was a long night. Still waking up." Kelly pushed the motel room door shut long enough to remove the safety chain, then opened the door for Cash to enter.

"I'm sorry to be here so early, but the senator is anxious to meet you and your boys." Cash shut the door behind her. She pulled a

Beretta Pico pistol from her waistband. "Sadly enough, you'll never make that meeting."

Campbell, who had her back to Cash, began to turn around. "What is that supposed to mean?" Her eyes widened as she suddenly realized that her end was coming.

Cash fired one bullet through Kelly's forehead and deftly caught her corpse before it had the chance to hit the rug and make a huge mess. She laid her down and grabbed some towels from the bathroom to wrap Kelly's head. Once she had the scene contained, she returned to the Aqua City parking lot and signaled for some of the men to come and clear the corpse from the premises.

Within ten minutes, the corpses of Agents Pringle and Rose, their car, Kelly Campbell's body, and any physical remnants thereof had been removed from the scene.

Stephanie Cash sat on the bed in Room 11 and waited a bit before deciding to go back out to the parking lot and wait in her own car.

Kinley Devereaux and Harper Rowe would soon be arriving.

LANDED

The small airstrip that Bairre Dolan finally touched down in was not as remote as Kinley and Harper had feared. They could see the tall buildings of the northern Minneapolis skyline from the plane's window. They could also see the snow that covered almost everything in the immediate area.

"Are we sure we left Prague?" Devereaux asked.

"Things have been going so insanely fast the last few days, I'm not sure we were ever in Prague."

"Unfortunately, I've got the irreplaceable mental images that prove all too well that we were. Not to mention this gunshot wound in my hip."

"Don't worry, brother." Harper patted his friend on the shoulder as the two of them looked at America the beautiful for the first time in a long time. "We're home now."

Bairre Dolan came barreling out of the cockpit and into the cabin, his normal spirited self. "Ay'm guessin' that SUV out there is fer the lot of yas?"

"We'll be getting to that, actually. We were just taking in the morning view."

Dolan bent down to take a gander at the landscape. "Shay is a beaut, aren't shay?"

"We're liking it."

"Nevertheless, me buys," Dolan stood up straight, "this has been a foon tame, but I've been summoned fer may next job. I really have enjoyed my stay, boot I must bay movin' on."

Kin looked at Harper and Taralyn. "You two go on. I'm going to settle up with our pilot friend here."

Harper and Tara shook Bairre Dolan's hand appreciatively, Tara first, then Harper. "See ya 'round downtown, my good man," Harper was smiling as he and Tara exited the plane, bundled up in the nice warm clothes that Constance Ondracek had given them for their journey home. They took their time climbing down the steps. By the time they reached the bottom, Kinley had already caught up to them.

"Wow, this feels like Cleveland compared to Prague."

"I know what you mean," Kin laughed, ducking his head into the cold Minneapolis wind. "I'm already looking for the nearest tiki bar."

Like synchronized swimmers, the trio moved through the windy air and across the snow-covered tundra. As they approached the SUV, the driver jumped out to greet them.

"Is one of you Harper Rowe?"

"That'd be me," Harp stepped up.

The driver flipped him the keys. "Compliments of Mr. Perry with the message, 'Welcome home, puddin' pop.' And also he's sorry he can't be here himself."

"Wait. This is ours? Mr.—?"

"To use. Not to have. It's a rental. And my name's Scritchfield."

"And what about you, Mr. Scritchfield? Need us to drop you somewhere? Or will you be hanging out for a while?"

"Mr. Perry called me this morning, had me rent this vehicle for you guys and drive out here to pick you up. If it's not too much trouble, would you mind dropping me back at my car at the rental place?"

"We don't mind if you don't mind."

"What does that mean?" the driver asked.

"It means you get to drive," Rowe answered, flipping the keys back to the guy. "We're not really too familiar with the lay of the land. So maybe on the way to your car, you can give us the directions to the Aqua City Motel."

"Absolutely. That's just a couple of blocks away from where we'll be—"

"Then let's go," Taralyn shivered as she opened the back door of the SUV. "It's colder than moonlight on a tombstone out here."

"Got any luggage?"

"Other than a Kimber 1911 that I bought off of a cabbie in Prague, and a rather expensive infrared scope that my man Kinley here has, all that we've got is just what we got on."

"Speaking of weapons," Scritchfield said, "there's a small suitcase in the rear of the vehicle – compliments of Mr. Perry, again. He wasn't sure what you might need, so he put a few things in there just in case."

Harper was barely able to muster a smile across his shivering lips. "That's our Mr. Perry. Always thinking of others."

Rain Sam

Sandy Wyrick hated winter.

She hated the cold, hated the snow, hated having to bundle up every time she had to go somewhere, hated having to unbundle whenever she got to that somewhere. But most of all, she hated how it always seemed to be dark. Dark when she went into work, dark when she came home. Dark when she eventually found her way to bed, and dark when she woke up.

This morning on her dark, cold, and snowy drive to work, Christoph Devine, the overnight shift commander, was on the phone giving her the rundown on developments in the Erica Bradley investigation.

"A rather large chunk of my night was taken up by the Chief of Ds for Minneapolis Homicide-Robbery. He wanted to talk to you about how you had no right pilfering his best detective the way you did, but since you weren't available, he took it out on me instead."

"Ah, gosh. Sorry, Christoph. I owe you one, for sure."

"One? Oh, I don't think so. For what I had to endure last night because of you, you now owe me dinner, a car wash, and a gift certificate for at least $40 to Bass Pro. Plus, my kid's school has him shucking some kind of crap to raise money for new playground equipment, so I'm putting you down for two of whatever he's selling."

"Okay," Sandy laughed. "And I'll talk to the Chief of Ds."

"Will you?"

"If I get time."

"Yeah, that's what I thought." Devine rolled his eyes.

"Did your guys make any headway with the Bradley case? Any new developments there?" Wyrick inquired.

"My team's been tracking down leads all night long, but this case seems to have more dead ends than a multicursal maze. For one thing, we have been trying to track down the other members of the Space Frequency project that Bradley was working on, and up to this point...nothing. For two, I guess once the news that our victim was a government worker with an incredibly high security clearance got out, every Shai, Basim, and Aram terrorist group is trying to say that it was them that's responsible for Mrs. Bradley's murder. So far, we've been able to rule out just about all of them."

"What about domestic suspects? Maybe someone a little closer to home?"

"Eh, there aren't a lot of sure things in this line of work, but we've got the next closest thing when it comes to the husband not being involved. The financials are solid, no one in the family has any dirty little secrets like a hidden addiction or any off-the-books dealings with mysterious third parties. The Bradleys' marriage seems just about as strong as any I have ever seen. Spic and span as far as that goes. No," Devine sighed, "if you wanna know what I think, my money's on that job of hers holding the key as to whom the culprit is on this one."

"That's what I'm thinking, too, but when Agent Bergman and I went to interview her supervisor last night, all we got was a big old helping of Shutdown Stew. In trying to find the other members of her Space Frequency team, were you able to find out anything more about what Erica Bradley was working on up until about two months ago?"

"Well, the cell phone records for her and her family just came in about an hour ago. Your boy, Agent Bergman, is already in here going through them. How far out are you?"

"Just got on 35 West. Traffic is moving at a crawl, but I should be in-office within the half hour."

"I'll tell him to give you a call if he finds anything."

"Don't bother, Chris. He's beeping in now. I'll see you in a few." Sandy clicked over to Bergman on the other line.

"Whaddaya have for me, Sammy?"

"Erica Bradley's phone records for the last three years, boss. I think I may have found something."

"Really? Like what?"

"I found a bit of an irregularity. I can show you what I'm talking about when you get in."

"No, tell me about it now. I'm stuck in traffic and need something to pass the time."

"Well, heck, all right then." She heard the rustling of papers in the background. "Okay, boss, I was looking for some sort of pattern to the numbers that she was calling. Starting at the beginning of all this – just about four years ago – she has a pretty regular pattern: calls to home, calls to friends, calls to work, calls to her family's cell phones. During this time she and her family are living in the Chattanooga, Tennessee, area. Everything fits that pattern for a while...about a year, give or take...and then she moves to Minneapolis, and things get different."

"Different? Different, how?"

"The call patterns are pretty much the same: calls to home, calls to friends, looks like some local calls to the Minneapolis area – probably some new friends – calls to her husband's cell phone. However, there are two things here that are worth mentioning. Number one, she's the only one that has moved. The rest of her family, at this point, is still living back in Tennessee."

"Must have been a work-related move," Agent Wyrick noted.

"And that's thing number two. Upon her move to Minneapolis, Erica Bradley stops calling work altogether."

"Maybe the job she had there gave her a business cell."

"Could be," Sam concurred, "but I checked the phone records for the husband and the sisters at that same time, and there's no different numbers coming in. You'd think that if she had a separate work phone number that one of them would've called it during that time...even if by accident."

"So, what do you think that means?"

"I think she was under strict orders from whomever it was that gave her that business cell – whomever it was that she was working for in Minneapolis – not to call or give out that number to anyone, at all, whatsoever."

"What do you think that means?"

"Whoever it was that she was working for wanted everything to be completely hush-hush."

"Which fits considering we can't seem to find Jack Sprat as far as the whole Space Frequency project is concerned."

"A whole lotta secrets goin' on here, boss."

"So, where would you go from here?" Sandy asked.

"The husband. I think we need to take a run at him again. I questioned him at the scene, but that was before I knew what I know now."

"Why the husband?"

"Simple," Sam replied. "Pillow talk. I can tell you this: As a homicide detective, I've broken more cases from pillow talk than I have from scrounging around in dumpsters, alleys, crime scenes, bars, or churches. I think we can do the same thing here."

"You know, the night shift commander told me that those phone records had just gotten there about an hour ago."

"Mm-hmm, that's right."

"And you found all this stuff out in the last hour?"

Yes, I did."

Geez, no wonder the Chief of Ds was so irked about losing this guy.

"Boss? You still there?"

"Yeah...yeah, Sam. Uh, that's good work. I'll be in shortly. In the meantime, why don't you go back through those phone records and highlight some of the main numbers for me."

"I already did that, boss."

Sandy shook her head. "Yeah, of course, you did. Okay...well... go get some coffee or something. I'll see you in a few."

The Long Flight Home

The flight seemed to last forever. Now that everyone was up and around and the hours until touchdown in Minnesota were dwindling, Jeb Crool was more on edge than ever.

"You look a little green, Agent Crool," Laurie Chase noted. "Long flights make you a bit nauseated?"

"Not nearly as much as placing the hopes of my future career in the hands of a wanted felon and an international arms dealer. Oh... and people that try to tell me that Coke and Pepsi taste the same. That also makes me a bit green in the face."

"So, once we land, any idea where we're going to go?"

"We still have some time before we land, so I'm hoping to have an answer for you before we do."

"What if you don't? Then what?"

Crool furrowed his brow. "I'll think of something. I always do. I've got the backing of the entire United States government behind me. I'm sure the lot of us can think of something."

"Yeah, I wonder about that," Chase said under her breath.

"Don't do that."

"Do what?"

"Do that thing that women do where you say something just loud enough for someone to hear but not be able to understand so that when they say, 'Pardon?' you give them all kinds of attitude for not being good listeners. If ya got something to say, just go ahead and say it already."

"Fine. I'll say it. You get my boyfriend killed because of you or your government's ineptitude then you better hope I die with him. Because if I don't, I'm gonna come after you with such a ferocity that it will make a pack of rabid dogs look like a CPA convention."

"I'm sure you'll be fine." Jeb closed his eyes. "I'm gonna try to get some sleep. Wake me when we get close."

Chase grabbed the pillow that was behind her head and fired it at Jeb's face.

"Good Lord, woman!" he clambered like a fish out of water. "What the he—"

"I don't think you understand, Agent Crool. The part of the deal where I give you Kinley, Harper, and the senator? Yeah, that entails you getting me to Kinley and Harper before they get killed *because* of the senator. I need you to pay attention to what's going on here."

Just then Jeb's phone rang. Susan Lincoln was calling him from her office.

"Susan, whaddaya got for me?" he answered.

"Not sure."

"*Not sure*? What exactly does that mean?"

"I called Todd Adams. He's with the FBI. The Bureau and the DOJ are working in tandem on this one, but he's the one heading up the team that's been keeping tabs on Kelly Campbell. I relayed your message to him to tell his guys that if Harper Rowe or Kinley Devereaux showed up at that hotel that it was to be a total hands-off situation."

"Great. Thank you for that. So, what's the problem?" Jeb asked, worried that the message had gotten to the agents too late and they had already picked up the wanted duo.

"We can't get in touch with them."

"With who? The agents?"

"Yes. There were several attempts to reach them but...nothing. No answer. No call backs. Can't get in touch with them," Susan said with a great deal of concern.

"So, what are they doing about it?"

"Todd is sending a second team out to see what's going on. Hopefully they're okay, and this is all some kind of communications glitch."

"Hey, make sure that the second team also knows it's *hands off* on Rowe and Devereaux."

"Already taken care of."

"Quick question before you go: Did you have a chance yet to find out the name of the motel where Kelly Campbell is staying?"

"Oh, right," Susan said. "Give me a minute, and I'll look that up for you. I'm going to put you on hold for a moment."

Before Jeb could object to the idea, the hold music was playing. Crool looked over at Laurie Chase. "Can you believe it? I've been put on hold."

"What's going on?" Laurie asked. "Did they get the message to the agents to leave Kinley and Harper alone?"

"Yes, of course, they did," Jeb lied.

"Oh, good," Laurie breathed easily.

"They've already deployed some more guys to go out there and double things up."

"Well, that's...weird."

"It's something," Jeb acknowledged.

"Jeb, you there?" Susan Lincoln was back. "I got the name of the place."

Crool pulled the phone away from his mouth. "Hey!" Jeb yelled out to no one in particular. "Someone write this down." Putting the phone back up to his mouth, he said, "Okay, Susan, go ahead."

"The name of the place is the Aqua City Motel."

"Aqua City Motel," Jeb called out.

"The address is 5739 Lyndale Avenue South." Lincoln listened as Jeb repeated it on the other end of the phone. "Need the phone number?"

"No, I think we're good here. Thank you, Susan. Appreciate your help. Call me when you know something about that other situation." Jeb ended the call and said to Laurie Chase, "You wanted to know where we're going when we land? We're going to the Aqua City Motel."

INTERCEPT

Stephanie Cash sat in the front seat of her government-issued sedan, nervously awaiting the arrival of Kinley Devereaux and Harper Rowe. She was on the phone with Senator Brenda Cobb-Schmidt.

"When they get there you have to make sure you convince them to come here. And do it fast. I've just received word that the FBI is getting ready to send over more agents to check on the ones that we took care of."

"Well, what if they get here before Rowe and Devereaux do?"

"You better pray that they—"

"Never mind. I think our boys just pulled in."

"Who? The feds?"

"No, Kinley and Harper...and it looks like a woman is with them. I'm going to go check it out. Call ya right back."

"Don't hang up!" the senator ordered. "Put your phone on speaker!"

Disregarding her boss's command, Cash disconnected the call and watched a black SUV pull slowly through the Aqua City Motel parking lot. She checked her weapon and exited her car. Knowing that she was on a tight time schedule, Cash held back as she watched the SUV come to a stop and its three occupants get out and make their way toward Room 11. Pulling out her credentials, she moved easily toward the trio.

"Hello," she called out.

Kin, Harper, and Taralyn turned towards her.

"Hi," she said again and held up her I.D. as she strolled toward them. "Harper Rowe? Kinley Devereaux?" She looked at Tara. "Laurie Chase?"

"One of my favorite entrées once said, 'Two outta three ain't bad,'" Harper quipped. "You seem to know who 66.7% of us are, so who are you?"

"My name is Stephanie Cash. I'm from Senator Brenda Cobb-Schmidt's office." She let the three of them look at her identification as she continued, "We know that you are here to meet Kelly Campbell, but about an hour ago Kelly Campbell was arrested."

"Arrested?"

"What?"

"Arrested by whom?" Harper asked.

"And when?" Kin added.

"Some Department of Justice guys apparently had their eyes on her from the time she landed here yesterday. They put in for the paperwork, and I guess it came through a short time ago. When Miss Campbell realized what was happening, she called the senator to let her know that you were en route and were planning to meet her here at this time. Senator Cobb-Schmidt already has people working on getting Miss Campbell released, and she sent me here to meet up with all of you. The senator has it on good authority that there are more agents on their way back here now."

"Well, that's all fine and swell, Ms. Cash," Kinley said, "but we were supposed to meet her here – in Room 11. I'm sure you won't mind if we go in and take a look around real quick."

"Point of fact, I will mind," Cash said adamantly. "Senator Cobb-Schmidt has taken great lengths to secure your safe return to the States. If *any* of you are picked up by law enforcement, she would be forced to deny dealings with all of you. I really don't know how to make it much clearer than that."

Kinley, Harper, and Taralyn took a moment to consider.

"No one else knew we were meeting her here," Harper said. "Kelly said Senator Cobb-Schmidt was her contact person, so I'm inclined to believe this Cash woman here is legit."

"I guess," Devereaux said.

"I don't see as we have much of a choice," Tara rang in.

"Thank you," Cash sighed. "By the way, if you're not Laurie Chase…?"

"Oh," Taralyn said, suddenly realizing that she had not been introduced. "I'm Taralyn Tharp."

"Pleasure," Cash smiled courteously. "Okay, my car is right over there. We can all ride together, so that way—"

"I hate to be a ball-buster, ma'am, but I can't go anywhere until I use the bathroom. It was a long flight, and since we've landed, no one has given me the opportunity to use any sort of facilities. I mean, if it's an issue, you can come in there with me. Make sure I'm not leaving any sort of secret messages on the toilet paper roll or something. Don't worry…I'm not shy."

"We really need to go now, so—"

"I know, right? Me, too," Harper smiled. "I *really* need to go now."

"I really must insist—"

"Yeah, me, too!" Harper walked past Stephanie Cash. "Do you have the keycard?"

"I do, but we really don't—"

"Give him the daggone keycard, lady!" Kinley insisted.

Flustered and defeated, Stephanie Cash took out the keycard and unlocked the door, granting Harper admittance into Room 11. He was halfway through the door when he turned back around. "Again, feel free to come on in with me. I don't want to break any rules or do anything that's going to be out of bounds with you or your boss. I really just—"

"Harper, just go already, will ya?" Kinley snapped.

"No, he can't—"

"Oh, gosh, Miss Cash." Devereaux stepped in between her and the motel room door. "My partner – all he does is think about himself. He doesn't give a tinker's damn about anyone else or their time schedule. I was just saying that to Taralyn here."

"He really was, ma'am," Tara said, taking her cue from Kinley. "He was saying that to me just before we walked up here and started talking to you. All Harper Rowe does is think about himself. A lot."

"Look, I don't really care how much he does or doesn't think about himself." Cash tried to push past Kinley "I need to make sure that he's—"

And just like that, Harper reappeared out of the motel room door.

"So, you were saying that we could all ride together in your car?"

"Yeah," Cash answered, confused. "Hey...are you done already? Didn't you—"

"Well, no, that's not gonna happen. The three of us will ride in the vehicle we came in. A good friend of mine entrusted that ride to us, and I'm not going to just leave it here in the middle of a hot zone like this. We'll follow you, Ms. Cash. It'll be fine."

Stephanie considered pushing the issue, but she knew that with an ever-diminishing timeframe, having the trio agree to follow her was probably the best scenario she was going to get.

"Very good," she said pleasantly. "I'm in the conspicuously government-issue-looking dark blue sedan over there. Follow me out the side exit. I promise not to go too fast or run recklessly through any yellow lights, and I swear to use my turn signals responsibly."

"That's all we can ask for," Kin forced a smile.

APPREHENSION

Once in her car, Cash immediately dialed Brenda Cobb-Schmidt's number.

"Cash!" the senator answered. "You better have them on your way back here or don't bother coming back here at all."

"They're right behind me, Senator," Stephanie said flatly. "We're on our way to you now."

"Do they suspect anything?"

"There really wasn't much time for them *to* suspect anything. I told them that Kelly Campbell had been arrested, and that at any moment someone might be coming to arrest them, too. I'm sure if they were suspicious of anything, I wouldn't be seeing them in my rearview mirror as we speak."

"I suppose that's right. Sorry I doubted you. Sorry I yelled. That's good work on your part."

"Water under the bridge, ma'am. I only ask that you keep me in mind once you're president and putting together your cabinet."

"Consider it done, Cash. Consider it done."

Cash's blue sedan, followed by the black SUV hauling Kinley, Harper, and Taralyn, exited the Aqua City Motel's parking area and headed towards their rendezvous with Senator Brenda Cobb-Schmidt.

Within thirty seconds, a fleet of FBI vehicles infiltrated the motel parking lot.

*　　*　　*

Tara was driving. Kin was in the passenger's seat. Harp was positioned in the middle seat behind them.

"I already have a bad feeling about this," Harper sighed.

"Why?" Tara eyed him up in the rearview mirror. "You were the one that said you thought this chick was legit."

"Really?" Harp asked. "If I thought she was all that legit, we'd be riding with her in her fed-mobile up there."

"Why is it you think something's wrong?"

Rowe waited for Kinley to clue Taralyn in on just what exactly was *not* sitting right about this specific sequence of events. When Kin remained silent, Harper took it upon himself to reveal the reason for his skepticism.

"She said that when Kelly realized what was going on – that she was being arrested – she called the senator. She said Kelly called the senator and told her that we were going to be meeting her at her motel room...at nine o'clock-ish."

"And you don't think that rings true?"

"Tara-my-lyn, there ain't a whole lot o' things in this world that are for certain, but I'll tell ya three things that are: water's wet, toothaches hurt, and if Kelly Campbell had one phone call to make in her time of need, it would be to my man Kinley Devereaux." Harper reached up and patted Kin on the shoulder. "I know it, he knows it, and now you know it. Granted, his phone isn't working, but she knew that calling me would get her to him. She would most definitely have done that."

"So then why are we following this woman? And what do you think really happened to Kelly Campbell?"

Kin finally spoke up. "We're following this woman because

it may very well be the *only* way to find out what really happened to Kelly Campbell."

"One thing this Stephanie Cash woman said that does ring true is that the senator has gone out of her way to secure our safe return here to the States. Question is: why?" Harper leaned forward in his seat. 'Is it for our benefit – like we're being led to believe? Or does she have some ulterior motive that we have yet to find out?"

"Only way to find out is to keep following this woman back to the senator. Hope for the best; prepare for the worst. I have learned one thing in our time together, Harp, and that is doing anything less will most certainly get us killed."

"I hope one day we can look back at this and laugh," Tharp joked.

"I hope one day we can look back at this," said a very stone-faced Devereaux.

The trio followed Stephanie Cash in silence for some time before Harper finally spoke up. "Ever notice that we are often in this same position?"

"Down on our luck and our backs against the wall?" Kin offered.

"No, not that, goof," Harper shook his head. "I mean that someone is always driving us, you're always in the passenger's seat, and I'm always in the back."

Kin turned and gave his friend an incredulous look. "Why would I notice that?"

"How wouldn't you? I mean, if our lives were a book, a good reader would have noticed it by chapter twelve, is all I'm saying."

"Really? And if our lives were a book, pray tell, what chapter are we on now?"

"Hmmm," Harper went deep in thought. "I guess if this were a novel – like – *Of Human Bondage*, we'd be on Chapter 116...of a 122-chapter book."

"So, you're saying we're coming to the end of our story?"

"Yeah, one way or another. Good or bad, happy or sad, I feel our story is getting ready to end here soon."

"Think we'll make it out alive?"

"Well, they say that only the good die young. So, yeah," Harp yawned, "we'll probably be fine."

"Very funny, William Joel. Hey, why don't you see if you can find that suitcase Scritchfield was telling us about. See what kind of hardware the good St. Perry has bestowed upon us for our return to the land of the free and the home of the second amendment?"

"Roger that, rabbit." Harper turned in his seat to peer into the back of the transport.

The small suitcase was leaning up against the back hatch. "Don't hit the brakes, Taralyn. I'm getting ready to make myself vulnerable." With that, Harper extended himself over the back seat and retrieved the bag and the weaponry contained therein. He set the case on the seat next to him, unzipped it, and flipped the top open.

"Ah, the mother lode."

"Whaddawe got?" Kinley asked.

"The man knows how to pack a bag." Harper picked through the contents of the suitcase. "Not only does he have various and sundry firearms, but he also packed small items like stilettos, daggers, piano wire...things that would easily get past the most fervent of pat downs. I like that."

"Indeed," Kin nodded. "I hope we won't need them, but it's good to know that they're there if we do."

"I hope we're not traveling too far. This snow is getting intense," Taralyn said. Loosening her grip on the steering wheel, she tilted her head back against the headrest.

"Harper and I are getting ready to meet with a U.S. senator that might be our only chance to clear our names and finally call America our home again. So," Kinley too, leaned back and rested his head, "the snow's not the only thing that's getting intense around here."

LANDIN' AND SCRAMBLIN'

"Harper Rowe and Kinley Devereaux are in this town, and I want to make sure that it stays that way."

The plane carrying Laurie Chase, Big James Gray, Special Agent Jeb Crool and his agents had barely landed in Minneapolis, and Jeb was already yelling out instructions.

"Agent Mathis, you and Agent Perelli head over to the Metro Transit Police Station. 2425 Minnehaha Avenue. Coordinate with them so that they have men here at the airport, men on the bus lines, a team on the trains, and a team monitoring the taxicab lines. Are we clear?"

"Roger that, boss," Agent Mathis was quick to reply.

"Agents Fielder and Marist, front and center, please."

Agents Jamie Fielder and Nicolette Marist hustled up from the back of the plane. "I need the two of you to find Senator Cobb-Schmidt and keep eyes on her at all times. She shouldn't be too hard to locate. She is running for president, after all. Contact me the minute you have her location."

The two female agents nodded their understanding and were quickly out of Crool's sight.

"Everyone else, you are with me and Agent Baldwin. Grab your gear and let's get going."

The agents dispersed to their assignments without questions.

Baldwin advanced to Jeb. "I've got government transports waiting on the tarmac, boss. Three rides – one for us and Miss Chase and Mr. Gray, and two for the remaining seven agents. Already to go now."

*   *   *

The three black SUVs, flashing lights and all, sped away from the airport and toward the Aqua City Motel. Crool and company were in the middle vehicle, Agent Baldwin behind the wheel.

"ETA to the motel is just under twenty minutes, Jeb."

"Okay. I'm going to give Susan Lincoln a call to see if she can give us a heads up on what might be waiting for us there."

In the back seat, Laurie and Big James were separated by their travel bags. The big man inconspicuously reached over and tapped Chase on her knee. When she looked over at him, he used his eyes to draw her attention to his bag. He quietly unzipped it and moved some clothes aside to reveal four handguns. Chase's eyes widened as she gave him an approving smile. Gray quickly covered them up and re-zipped the bag.

"Susan," Jeb said into his phone, "it's Jeb Crool. We've landed and are on our way to the Aqua City Motel. Any updates as to what is going on there?"

"I haven't heard anything, but let me text you the contact number for the AIC there, Todd Adams. You can give him a call yourself."

"Before you send me his number, give him a heads up that I'll be calling so he won't let my call go to voicemail because he doesn't recognize my number."

"I will," assured Lincoln. "Once I get an okay from Agent Adams, I'll text you his number. That will be your 'okay' to give him a call. Cool?"

"Don't take too long."

"Yeah...you're welcome."

Jeb disconnected the call and twisted around to address Chase. "We should be getting an update on your boyfriend and his villain partner in just a few minutes." He had barely finished his sentence when a text came in from Susan Lincoln.

Agent Todd Adams is awaiting your call, along with the correlating number.

"And here we go."

Jeb faced forward and punched in Agent Adams' number.

"Agent Todd Adams here."

"Agent Todd Adams, this is Special Agent Jeb Crool of the National Security Agency. It's my understanding that you were expecting my call."

"As of about 30 seconds ago, yes."

"My team and I are en route to the Aqua City Motel. We're looking for a woman named Kelly Campbell in hopes that she might be able to lead us to two of her partisans, Harper Rowe and Kinley Devereaux."

"Well, Agent Crool, my team and I are already here at the Aqua City Motel, and we are also looking for Kelly Campbell. But I have news for ya: She ain't here. On top of that, I had two DOJ agents assigned to the premises here to keep tabs on Miss Campbell, and they, too, are not here."

"Yeah, I was sort of given notice that things might be that way with your agents. But I certainly wasn't foretold about the Campbell woman. There's no sign of her?"

"Oh, there's a sign of her. Plenty of them, actually," Adams stated. "We had agents tracking her as soon as we knew she was in town. We know she was here. We know she met with Senator Brenda Cobb-Schmidt at a restaurant the night before last. We know that she was here last night at 11 p.m. when shift change for my agents occurred."

"Is that the last official time that you knew of her whereabouts?"

"Officially, yes. And I guess...technically, too."

"Your agents that came on at 11 p.m., did they check in with anyone at any point during their shift?"

"They're senior agents on an overnight shift. Unless there was some major movement that they needed assistance with, they were just babysitting and taking notes until something of substance happened. When they got off shift in the morning, they were to come back to the office and put anything that might be relevant into the case file. Other than that—"

"So, that would be a *no*?"

"Yes, that would be a no."

"What about her motel room? Any clues to her location in there?"

"Not really. No sign of a struggle. Her clothes are here, but her keys, cell phone, purse, and rental car are gone. For all intents and purposes, there are no signs of foul play at all."

"Oh, yeah, hey – what about the rental car? Don't they have LoJack in most of those things now?" Jeb asked.

"Yeah, we have a call into the rental car agency. Still waiting to hear back from them."

"And your agents' car? I thought all government vehicles were equipped with some sort of tracking system these days."

Agent Adams chuckled. "Well, in what can be called nothing short of typical government bureaucracy, the state of Minnesota found a cheaper tracking company to use than the one we had been using. Now all the vehicles have been stripped of the former tracking system and equipped with the tracking system from the new manufacturer. Except as it turns out, the car that my agents were using last night had yet to be equipped with the updated tracking system."

"Well, that's just wonderful," Jeb said.

"I feel the same way."

"I don't suppose that there's any way to tell whether or not

Rowe and Devereaux have been there yet?"

"I've got some of my men cross-checking license plates against the guest registry to see if we have any cars here in the motel parking lot that are unaccounted for. Other than fingerprinting Campbell's motel room – which will get done soon – I don't suppose there's too much else we can do to determine who has and has not been here so far."

"Okay, then, Agent Adams, my team and I will be there in just a few minutes. Hopefully we'll be of some assistance. Until then."

Jeb slid the phone into his coat pocket and turned back to Laurie and Big James. "Not sure if you caught the gist of that conversation, but not only are there no immediate signs of Harper and Kinley, but Kelly Campbell and two DOJ agents have apparently gone missing as well."

"Wait. What?" Chase responded. "What do you mean, they've *gone missing*?"

Jeb looked at Dave and then at Big James. "Did I stutter, Miss Chase?"

"No, but I just...I mean...it's a rather vague statement, is all."

"All right. Let me try to be a little more specific. The Justice Department had two agents doing surveillance on Kelly Campbell. When they tried to get a message to the two agents about the possibility of Harper Rowe and Kinley Devereaux making contact with Kelly Campbell at her motel room, they couldn't get in touch with them. Now the feds are at the motel, and they can't find the agents. Nor can they find Kelly Campbell. Her car is gone and her hotel room is empty. Her clothes are there, but according to the agent-in-charge, her purse, wallet, phone, car, and person are all *in absentia*."

"Maybe Kinley and Harper got there and she went somewhere with them, and the two agents from Justice are still tailing them."

"Then why aren't they answering their phones?"

"Because...maybe Harp and Kin discovered the agents were tailing them...and"—Big James waggled his index finger in the air— "disabled them."

"Well, let's hope not. When those two disable something, it tends to stay that way. Permanently. No, my gut instinct tells me that...well...I don't really know what my gut instinct is telling me. I know that Harper Rowe and Kinley Devereaux are here in this town somewhere, I know that Kelly Campbell holds the key to it all, and I know that I have a bad feeling about those two DOJ guys being gone because senior government agents don't just go missing for no reason, ya know?"

Baldwin slowed the vehicle and read the big purple and white neon sign to his right: The Aqua City Motel.

Crool looked over the sea of government and municipal vehicles filling the motel parking lot. "Oh, Miss Chase," he sighed, "this had better be worth it."

A Call to Mr. Bradley

When Sandy Wyrick strolled into the offices of the Minneapolis Counter Terrorism Unit, she found Sam Bergman at his desk poring over the case notes on his CTU-issued tablet. Bergman was still clad in his raincoat and fedora, an untied necktie around his neck.

"You really got that 50s noir detective look down, don't ya, Marlowe?"

"Huh?" Sam lifted his head. "Oh, yeah. Thanks. Hey, I'm trying to find the phone number for Ken Bradley."

"Planning on giving him a call?"

"Yeah. I wanna see if he can help me make heads or tails out of this cell phone issue."

Wyrick took off her coat and stood behind Bergman, looking over his shoulder as he searched for Ken Bradley's phone number. A few seconds later, they spotted it.

"There," Wyrick pointed out.

"Yeah, I see it," Sam affirmed, pulling out his cell phone and punching in the number. "Calling him now."

"So, what are you going to ask him...more or less?"

"Stay tuned and you'll find out," Sam looked at her and winked.

"Hello," the voice on the other end answered.

"Yes. Mr. Bradley?"

"Yes," was the cautious answer. "Who am I speaking to?"

"Sir, this is Sam Bergman with the Minneapolis CTU."

"CTU?"

"Yes, sir."

"Didn't I just talk to you yesterday, and you were with the Minneapolis Homicide and Robbery Unit?"

Sam chuckled. "Yes, sir. Good memory. Yesterday I was with City H&R, but that was yesterday."

"You really did a transfer of units that fast? I didn't think that was possible."

"I'd love to go into it with you, Mr. Bradley, but there are some other matters I really need to talk to you about if you have a few minutes."

"I don't, but I guess if I don't address your matters now, you'll just be calling back at an even more inopportune time, or even worse, showing up here unannounced."

"For whatever inconvenience that I may be causing, I do apologize. I promise to be as brief as possible," Sam said. "Mr. Bradley, when you and your family were living in Tennessee, and your wife moved up to Minneapolis, did she have a different cell phone for her job?"

"Yeah, she did. I never called it, though, so I don't have any idea what it was."

"Never would have written it down somewhere? Maybe just in case there was an emergency, and you couldn't get hold of her on her regular phone."

"Why wouldn't I be able to get hold of her on her regular phone?"

Sam found the question a bit off-putting. "Maybe she might've forgotten to charge it. Maybe she dropped it in the toilet. Maybe she left it in her car. There's a lot of reasons. I'm just trying to find out if there was ever a time that you called her work phone...even just once."

"Alright," Ken Bradley sighed, "let me think. Let me think."

He went silent for several moments. "There was one time. I think. You know that it's been almost four years since all this may or may not have happened, right?"

"Anything you can remember about when it was would certainly make it easier for me to track the number down through phone records."

"Why do you want to know her business phone number anyway?"

"We are trying to get some kind of idea as to what she was working on and who she was working for in regard to the Space Frequency project. We're not having a whole lot of success, and sometimes phone records can offer a decent amount of clues. I'm guessing you don't have anything that you could tell us about that, do you?"

"I wish that I could help, but like I told you yesterday – when you were a homicide detective – my wife's work was very secretive. She never talked about it, and I knew better than to ask."

"What about co-workers? Did she mention *any* names of her co-workers while she was in the Space Frequency project? Any names at all?"

"Maybe she did. Honestly, if I had some time to think about it I might remember something. It would take me some time, and I'm pretty sure you don't want to be sitting on the phone for an hour while I rack my brain over all of this. Can I give you a call back about that a little bit later on?"

"Absolutely. That would be great, Mr. Bradley," Sam smiled. "But real quick, any recollection of when you might have called your wife's work cell phone?"

"Right, right. Umm," Ken Bradley hummed in retrospection, "I remember it was when my son broke his fingers in a cupboard door. He was three, and it was the spring, too. And oh! I don't know why I remember this, but it was right after the time change when we spring forward. I also remember that. So, four years ago in the spring within a few days of having switched back to daylight savings time."

"Technically, since they reduced standard time several years back, we actually spring forward at the end of winter. Still, that would put the call sometime in March it sounds like. Any chance you may remember the time of day you called her?"

"Yeah, actually, I do remember it was evening. Probably between 5 and 7:30 or 8:00."

"And you made the call from the number ending in 4328?"

Ken hesitated for a second and then, "Yes, we had gotten rid of our house phone because the kids and I were in the process of packing up the house. So, yes, I called from my cell phone. Pretty certain that was the number I had then."

Sam went quickly to his computer and pulled up the phone records for Ken Bradley's cell phone. He found the page he was looking for and began scanning the pertinent numbers. He recognized a lot of the numbers from his earlier perusal of the call logs. But then his eyes came across a set of digits that he did not recognize.

"Mr. Bradley, if you heard the number would you recognize it?"

"Not likely, but feel free to give it a go. I'll see what I can do."

Sam rattled off the digits of the suspicious phone number and waited for Ken's response.

"Well," he hesitated again, "I wouldn't want to have to swear to it in a court of law. Like I said, best of my knowledge, I only called it once. I even remember her giving me a supreme raft of shit about it, too. To this day I still couldn't tell you what infuriated her more: our little boy breaking two of his fingers while under my watch, or me calling her on that work phone of hers. But, yeah, that number does seem to ring a distant bell."

"Fantastic! Thank you, Mr. Bradley. I appreciate your help in your tough time there, sir." Sam chucked a wad of paper at Sandy to get her attention. To her terse look of disapproval, Sam just smiled and nodded his head. "Oh, and Mr. Bradley, we really would appreciate it if you might be able to recall any of the names that your wife may have mentioned in passing or any other manner of context in regard to her recent co-workers. Please, call us at any time."

"I will let you know anything I can think of."

"Thank you, Mr. Bradley. Talk to you soon."

Sam hung up the phone.

"Proud of yourself, detective?" Sandy asked.

"Come on, boss. This could be huge."

"I don't care if you've come across the eighteen missing minutes of the Watergate tapes, you ever throw a piece of paper at my head again I'll take whatever remnants of ball sack that doctor wife of yours lets you leave the house with and put it through my paper shredder."

"I got the number for Erica Bradley's Space Frequency work phone."

"Wow, that's great. What would be even greater is if you could take that tidbit of information and use it to find out who killed Erica Bradley."

"On it forthwith, ma'am."

ODD PLACE FOR A MEETING

"Maybe we should have asked her how far we were going," Tara said.

Snow was falling in earnest again across the greater Twin Cities area, greatly compromising visibility. Tara, Kinley, and Harper had been following Stephanie Cash for a while, and now they were traversing more rural, less-plowed roads.

"Are you able to see okay?" asked Devereaux.

"For now, yes. I just hope we won't be traveling for too much longer. This snow is becoming hypnotic."

Checking the weather on his phone, Harper suddenly felt the SUV fishtail. He glanced into the rearview mirror just in time to catch a look of nervousness cross Tharp's face. He was not concerned. He would have been more concerned if she was not nervous. Nothing worse than an overconfident driver in the snow. That was how accidents happened.

"I've got the weather here. Geez, it looks bad. According to the radar, this stuff is just getting started. Looking at the five-day... snow. Today, tonight, tomorrow, the next day...good gosh. It's like the second coming of the Ice Age.

"Hey, honk your horn and flash your lights," Harper requested of Taralyn. "Get her to pull over. I want to find out how much farther we have to drive in this crap."

Tara laid on the horn and flashed her high beams until she finally saw Stephanie Cash's brake lights light up as she slowly pulled onto the snow-covered shoulder. Taralyn was still pulling the SUV to a stop when Harper slung his door open and jumped out into the snow.

"Woo, bippy, it is cold out here!" he called, pulling his jacket up tight around his neck.

Tara and Kinley watched him high-step through the snow and up to Cash's window. He stood there with his hands buried deep in his coat pockets, his shoulders hunched, and his head down, talking to her.

"Good thing Constance gave us some winter coats for this trip, or we'd all been frozen stiff as soon as we got off the plane," Kinley said.

"I gotta tell you," Taralyn laughed and shook her head, "hanging out with you guys has got to be the most amazing time of my life. I mean, the two of you have got to be the smoothest operators in the known world. With all the people you know that are willing to help you out at a moment's notice, put their lives on the line for you, give you whatever it is that you need. But then again, you and Harper do the same thing, so...I don't know why it's such a shock to me."

"It's like it states in the Bible, 'whatsoever ye would that men should do to you, do ye even so to them.' You know, the whole do unto others principle."

"You guys have introduced me to a whole brand of people that I didn't think still existed. Good people. Good, honest, moral people. I had really started to believe that those kinds of people just weren't around anymore."

"Well, keep your rose-colored glasses in check. Make no mistake about it, Harper and I and our friends, we *are* the exceptions to the rule. The earth's population as a whole, when left to their own devices, are pretty much a bunch of contemptible lowlifes and scum-sucking miscreants."

"So, how did you find so many of the good ones if they are as scarce as you say they are?"

"If you saw my list of throwaways, you'd probably wonder how I'm still alive. In my line of work, I'm usually targeting some real scumbags. If you find out who the nemeses of said scumbags are, there's a good chance that they might have some of the winning personality traits that you would look for in an ally."

"How often did that work out for you?"

Kin shook his head and laughed, "Not nearly as much as I hoped it would."

"Have you ever told anyone who you have killed?"

"Well, some people already know. For instance, my handler, Kelly Campbell, who gave me my assignments, knows everyone that I have ever had to put down. The people that gave *her* my assignments, they know, too."

"No, but I mean outside of the job. Like a therapist or a priest or even a girlfriend."

"I have not, and here's why," Devereaux took a deep breath and began his extended explanation. "You see, Tara, contrary to what you see in TV and movies, guys like me don't walk around carrying a conscience from what we do like an albatross around our necks. The people that I am tasked to put down are terrorists. Maybe not in the classic sense of the word, but these people are a threat to freedom all around the globe. These jag-offs don't want freedom. They want chaos. They want the way things are to be turned upside down and out of control so that evil people that have bad intentions can have undeserved power...for a while. These people are threats, not just to the U.S., but to countries all over the world. You want to know why you don't read about more political coups or hear about more overthrown governments in the news? It's because of guys like me.

"Next, it would be very irresponsible of me to tell anyone about what I do. If I were to tell someone about what I did on my trip to Rome or my trip to the Maldives or my trip to Azerbaijan – I don't know who, and I don't know how – but if someone were to find out that I talked about one of my assignments to a girlfriend or a priest or a therapist, those people would more than likely be dead within just a few hours. If that were to happen, *then* I would have a conscience about what I did...or should I say the *talking* about what I did. So, in summation, no, I do not talk about the people that I have killed outside the parameters of the job."

"But you tell Harper?"

"Harp and I talk about our assignments, yeah, but for the most part it's to compare notes. Or complain. Mostly from him."

"What does he complain about? Is that something you can tell me?"

Kin pursed his lips and squinted his eyes in thought for a moment. "Yeah, I guess I can tell you this," Kin said. "Harper has it in his head that our handler, Kelly Campbell, has the hots in the worst way for me, and he feels that because of this attraction, Kelly has taken it upon herself to give me the cushiest of all the assignments while he got stuck with the assignments that were hanging from the nethermost regions of the assignment tree."

"Well," Taralyn hesitated for a moment.

"Are you going to ask if there was any truth to it?"

"Yes," she laughed, "that's exactly what I was going to ask."

"I will say the answer is no, but there were times when he was sitting in a desert hideout under the torturous heat of a Middle Eastern sun, and I was eating room service and watching reruns of *Seinfeld* in the Hôtel Lancaster Paris Champs-Elysées. So, I'm sure that he just couldn't help but wonder if there weren't some kind of favors being swapped about."

Just then Harper flung open the rear passenger's side door and began dusting himself off. The snow was falling so heavily that each time he beat it off his clothes, even more seemed to supplant it.

Realizing the futility of his efforts, he tried climbing back into the SUV. Steadying one foot on the floorboard, he pushed in with the other. Unfortunately, Harper's back foot slipped on the snow and shot awkwardly out from underneath him, causing the fellow to lose his balance and grab Kinley's seat to right himself. The jolt had the unhappy effect of causing Kin to realize that the pain medication for his gunshot wound was wearing off.

"Oh, fudge-monkey-bat-squish!" he cried out, grabbing his wound. "Harper, you little turd. I swear, you've got the gracefulness of a vertigo-stricken giraffe."

"Dude, are you okay?"

"No, I'm not okay," Kinley grimaced. "Got any of those painkillers left?"

"I do."

As Harper rifled through his pockets, Kinley tilted over to his left and leaned his head back and opened up his mouth. "Do it."

Harper dropped two capsules into Dev's mouth, then grabbed a bottle of water and poured it down Kinley's gullet.

"Oh, my Lord," Taralyn spouted. "What are you two doing?"

Harper gave her a look. "Administering pain medication."

"Well, yeah, but I'm pretty sure that pain meds can be—"

"I'm fine. Thank you," Kinley murmured as Harper helped him back upright in his seat.

"Follow her," Rowe directed. "We have about a mile to go before we get where we're going."

"Oh, thank goodness for that," Taralyn sighed as she watched Stephanie Cash pull back onto the road. "So, where is it that we're going?"

"A high school."

It took a moment for Harp's response to sink in before either of the two answered.

"Why are we going to a high school?" Tharp finally pondered aloud.

"That seems like an odd place for a meeting," Kinley agreed.

"Well, it's because it's snowing, the school is closed, and it's obviously way out of the way. Senator Cobb-Schmidt couldn't possibly take a chance being seen meeting with us in a place where there might be a risk of cameras or witnesses. If you ask me, I appreciate her doing us the favor."

Taralyn looked down at the speedometer to see that they were going just under 20 mph. When she looked back up, the snow had become so intense that she could barely see Cash's car in front of them. She briefly considered making a smart alec remark about Rowe's "doing us a favor" comment. Instead, she asked, "When's the last time either of you were in a high school?"

"Oh, gosh, I don't know," Kinley answered first. "Best of my knowledge, it was on the day that I graduated from high school. So I guess...that would have been...close to 30 years ago. What about you, Harp?"

"Funny story about my senior year in high school. You two will love this one because of its accuracy."

"Ugh." Kinley moved uncomfortably in his seat. "Here we go."

"One of the things they did for my yearbook was that they asked all the underclassmen what three words best described each senior. Some seniors got intelligent, funny, warm. Some got athletic, endearing, attractive. Others got bookworm, motivated, introverted. You get the idea."

"We get the idea," Taralyn confirmed.

"The three words they used to describe me?" Harper paused for effect. "He...Ain't...Right."

"Boy, they really hit the nail right on the top of the nail with that one, didn't they, kid?"

The right turn signal on Stephanie Cash's car began blinking.

"I think that's a school over there," Harper pointed. "Kinda hard to tell with it snowing like it is."

Cash turned right into a parking lot coated with a half-foot of snow. The lot was on a bit of an incline, so the tires on her government-issued vehicle spun and the car fishtailed wildly before finally catching traction.

"See any other cars here?"

"I can barely see the other side of the window. If anyone besides Taralyn was driving I would be panicking back here," Harper said, leaning closer to the window. "Looks like a government ride at our ten."

"I guess this is it, big boy," Kinley turned gingerly to face his partner. "Our moment of truth is arriving."

"I never thought I'd utter these words, but I'd sure feel better if Kelly were here," Harper said. "I sent her a text to contact me as soon as humanly possible."

Stephanie Cash slid her car to a stop next to the second government vehicle that Harper had alluded to. Taralyn pulled their SUV in beside the dark sedan. They were parked in front of a four-story stone and mortar building that housed the school's library, computer and tech rooms, and a few classrooms, one of six multi-storied structures that made up the campus of the New Brighton Preparatory Academy.

"You guys want me to come in with you?" Tara asked.

"It's entirely up to you," Kinley answered. "But if you do, there's no guarantee that the senator is going to want you to join the meeting."

"If you do choose to come in and be part of this, just know that you'll be signing up to be part of our next great adventure," Harper added. And there's no telling just how high the danger level on this one might reach."

"Seems to me that without your friend Kelly being here, you're already a man down on this one, and you can probably use all the help that you can get. You can count me in on this as far as I can possibly go. Besides, it's gotta be warmer in there than it is out here."

Harper pulled a very small 2-shot pistol from the suitcase that

Rob Perry had furnished for them and slid it to Taralyn.

"What do you want me to do with this?" she asked.

"Put it in your crotch. Since you're coming inside with us, you get the nomination for the one of us that gets to carry the weapon."

"And why does this honor befall one such as I?"

"Because if she has security, they are most likely men, and they *will* be a little more light-handed with the search around your crotch area than they will be with ours."

"She's running for president. Won't she have Secret Service protection?"

"Presidential candidates don't get Secret Service protection until 120 days before the national election," Kinley informed her. "Still, United States senators usually have a decent amount of government-issued security. Knowing that she is getting ready to meet up with two former government assassins in an isolated location, it just makes sense that she'll have some kind of security going on."

"I guess we're waiting on Miss Cash," Harper said.

All three of them looked over to her car to see that she was talking on her cell phone. She must have sensed their eyes upon her because she turned her head and looked back at them. She held up her right hand and extended her index finger – the international sign for "gimme a second."

"I guess we're gonna give her a second," Harper said.

They sat quietly giving her the requested moment until Kinley spoke. "So, Harper, what did you write?"

"What did I write about what?"

"When you went into Kelly's motel room. You left some sort of note or signal to Big James or Laurie as to our presence being there. Am I right?"

"I left a note to a friend...in a place where only they would know to look for it...in a language that only they would understand. Somebody else finds it, it will read as nothing more than gibberish."

Stephanie Cash was off her cell phone and out of her car. The collar on her Balmain cashmere military-style coat was turned up under her long brown hair as she made her way beneath the overhang of the building's entrance. Shaking snow off herself, she waved for Kin, Harp, and Taralyn to come join her.

"Well, here we go," Kinley muttered in pain, "the beginning of the end."

"No need to sweat it, baby. We're golden."

"Like the streets of Paradise."

Signs of Life

Jeb Crool and David Baldwin immediately jumped out of the black SUV and into the snowy, crowded parking lot. Laurie Chase and Big James were not so enthusiastic.

"When's the last time you saw snow like this?" she asked him.

"I don't know that I've *ever* seen snow like this. Heck, I don't even remember the last time I had to wear long pants." He looked apprehensively out the window at the menacing cold. "I packed all three pieces of winter clothing that I own. But in Rio, as you well know, the coldest it ever gets in winter is 18."

"18?"

"Celsius," Gray clarified. "Oh, yeah, I forgot. We're back in the good old U.S.A, the land that is too good for Celsius and the metric system."

"Is that windbreaker the heaviest coat you have?"

"It is. This windbreaker, this stocking cap, and this scarf." James zipped the windbreaker up to his chin, wrapped the scarf around his head and neck and tucked it inside his collar, then pulled his stocking cap down over his ears. "Well, I think this is as good as it's going to get for now." The big man opened his door a bit and stuck his head out into the wintry air just in time for the wind to kick up and blow a slug of snow right into his face. Recoiling back into the vehicle, he slammed the door shut.

Laurie Chase laughed as she watched him wipe off his face with his scarf.

"Bite me, Laurie Chase," he growled. "I should've just stayed in Rio and done the jail time. This is absurd."

Jeb Crool returned to the SUV and banged on the window. "You two coming along any time today?"

Gray and Chase exited their ride and followed Crool through the crowd toward Room 11 of the Aqua City Motel. Turning around, Crool said, "I talked to the AIC Todd Adams and convinced him to clear out Kelly Campbell's room for ten minutes so that the three of us could have a run at it."

"I'm sorry," Chase said, double-timing to catch up with Jeb. "Why did you do that?"

"You and the big boy there, you're friends with Harper and Kinley. I just thought that maybe the two of you might be able to find traces of them having been here or not better than anyone else possibly could."

"Yeah, that could be," Chase said. Much to her and Crool's surprise, Big James jogged right past them and into the motel room.

"Good gosh, man," Jeb said as he and Chase entered the room a few seconds later. "Did you ever stop to think that you're trouncing all over important evidence here?"

"Well," Big James said, moving closer to the room's heater, "as soon as my brain thaws out and I can have coherent thoughts again, I'll let you know."

"I'm sure they wouldn't have let us come in here if they hadn't already recovered what they were looking for," Chase said.

"Whatever. Just take a look around the room and see what you can find...if anything. Okay?"

Chase began tooling about the room, studying every inch of

the place looking for something – anything – that might be a clue as to whether or not Kinley and Harper may have been there.

"Do you need to use the bathroom?" Big James asked her.

"No, I'm fine. Why?"

"Because I do, and once I do, I'm pretty sure it won't be a suitable place for neither human nor beast to be in. I'm just trying to be congenial, is all."

"It's all yours, sir, but while you are in there, you're in charge of scouring the area for any clues of our comrades having been here. I'm pretty sure once you're through, nobody else—"

"Yeah, yeah, yeah," Gray muttered, making his way to the bathroom. "Consider the area scoured." He shut the door behind him.

Big James had known Harper Rowe long enough to know just how Harper would leave a message in the direst of situations. The big man locked the bathroom door. He turned on the shower, moving the water temp handle all the way to HOT. He then went to the sink, turned on the hot water tap, and waited for the bathroom to steam up.

Of course, some pounding came at the bathroom door, along with some screaming of, "Dude, turn the shower off! You're washing away evidence!"

Big James did not listen to them. Instead, he patiently waited for the bathroom mirror to fog up. When it did, he read the message that Harper Rowe had left:

$$G\ 2\ C\ S\ C\text{-}S$$

Gray opened the bathroom door to find an irate Jeb Crool waiting for him.

"My first instincts about you were that you were just the everyday, run-of-the-mill idiot, Mr. Gray. But I have to say that you have now completely shattered that presupposition into a million tiny shrapnel-like pieces. Your idiocy, sir, may have just reached a new high in—"

"They were here."

"What?" Laurie asked. "Are you sure?"

"Categorically so. They were here and then they left to go meet up with the senator."

"How do you know that?" Crool asked.

"Harper left me a note."

"A note? Where? Let me see it."

"It's in there," Big James gestured toward the bathroom. "On the mirror."

Jeb pushed his way past the big man and into the bathroom. He looked at the mirror, but saw nothing because the bathroom door had been opened long enough for all the steam to have escaped. All that Crool saw was his reflection staring blankly back at him.

"I don't see anything."

"Me, either," responded Chase, who had now joined them in front of the mirror. "What did it say?"

"Oh, for crying out loud," the big man shook his head. "Watch out." He crowded his way back into the bathroom, shut the door behind him, and turned on the hot water in the sink. "Jeb, turn the shower on. Turn the hot water all the way up."

The trio stood uncomfortably close as the bathroom began to steam up again. Within seconds, Harper's message reappeared.

"Gee, two, see, ess, see, hyphen, ess," Crool read out loud. He turned to James. "And just what is it that you think this means?"

"I'm hunching the *G* stands for *gone* or *going*. The *2 C* obviously means *to see*. Since he was kind enough to leave us a hyphen, and the only hyphenated words that would be germane to our current situation are *Cobb-Schmidt*, I'm going to venture a guess that the other *S* stands for *Senator*. Put it all together—"

"Going to see Senator Cobb-Schmidt," Laurie answered.

"Well, give the man a prize." Jeb smiled a rare smile as he reached into the tub and turned off the shower handle. "And open that door up. I can barely breathe in here."

As soon as Big James opened the bathroom door, the trio – along with billows of steam – came spilling back into the motel room.

Todd Adams, special agent in charge, had found his way into Room 11 just in time to see this particular scene play out. "Did you need me to come back later?" he smirked.

"We may have found something significant, Agent Adams," Crool said sternly.

"You fellas in D.C. may need to show us some of your new investigative techniques. That looks kinda fun," Adams laughed. "Seriously, though, what was that you were saying about finding something significant?"

"It seems as though both Harper Rowe and Kinley Devereaux have been here."

"Really? And how did you happen to find that out?"

"They left a note. However, the note has been destroyed."

"Destroyed? How?"

"How?" Crool asked. "It was destroyed. Wiped out. Eradicated. Retired. What does it matter how? It's gone. The important thing is that we found it and were able to get just enough off of it to know that they were here and now they're gone. Could be that Kelly Campbell is with them."

"They must have left in a hurry then for Kelly Campbell to leave all of her clothing behind. Were you able to see where it was that they were headed?"

"No."

Adams was quiet for a moment before asking the tough question, "Do you think Campbell, Rowe, and Devereaux may have killed my men before taking off to wherever it was that they went?"

Crool shrugged. "Knowing what these two are capable of, I wouldn't put it past them."

One of Adams' agents came into the room. "Sir, we were able

to get Campbell's cell phone number from the front desk. She had to give it to them when she registered. We're already pulling up her records to see who she was talking to last night and this morning."

"That's great work, agent," Adams commended her. "Any idea how long that is going to be?"

"It'll take a little time, but I would think that we will have it within the hour."

"You'll let me know as soon as you have something."

"Yessir," the agent affirmed as she left the room.

Adams turned back to Jeb Crool. "Once we get those phone records, they may give us a better idea of where they may have gone."

"Tell you what, Agent Adams. I will leave my agents here with you to help with the search. Laurie Chase, James Gray, and I are going to go grab something to eat and be back. If you find something of substance in the meantime, you have my number. Give me a call and we'll come running."

Crool, Gray, and Chase made their way out of the motel room, through the crowded parking lot and back to their ride. Along the way, Crool stopped to speak to Baldwin, instructing him to let the rest of the agents know that they were to help FBI Agent Adams in any possible way.

Once they were in the SUV, Crool pulled out of the motel parking lot and up the road.

"So glad we're going to get something to eat," Big James said happily. "This ol' tummy of mine is really rumbling."

"Well, I got bad news for ya, big guy. We ain't goin' to get something to eat. I'm getting ready to call my two agents that are tracking down Senator Cobb-Schmidt and see if they have any idea where she is."

"Aww, c'mon, Agent Crool," James protested. "Can't we just pull into a drive-thru someplace? I don't mind eatin' on the road."

"I'm kinda hungry, too," Chase concurred. "Pull in somewhere, the big guy and I will run inside and grab something while you make your call."

"Fine," Jeb acquiesced. "But don't go ordering half the menu, Mr. Gray, and taking all day long. Is Chicken Fillet okay with the two of you?" Jeb asked as he pulled into the parking lot of a Chick Fillet restaurant.

"At this juncture, you could pull into Fat Walter's Chainsaw Repair and Jelly Donut Emporium, and I would be happier than a pig in slop," Big James grinned. "So, yeah, Chicken Fillet sounds wonderful to me."

Jeb pulled into the restaurant's parking lot. The vehicle had barely stopped before Chase and Gray were on their way inside.

Crool wasted no time in getting on the phone.

"Hey, boss," Agent Nicolette Marist answered quickly.

"Where are we with locating the senator?"

"Things aren't good on this end, sir. She had a late brunch scheduled with the head of the Minnesota Cattle Farmers for 11:00 a.m. local time. But upon further investigation that seems like a bit of a hoax. No one can account for a specific place or time for the brunch."

"Seriously?" he shouted. "How does that even happen? How does the leading contender for the United States presidency just make fake plans and fall off the map unaccounted for?"

"Because the head of her security detail approves of all her travel plans and then turns them over to the rest of her staff. As you may have already assumed, the head of her security detail is also out of reach."

"Well, she has to have some sort of beacon or tracker on her phone that can pinpoint where she is. Her car or something?"

"Yes and yes, but, however, with this storm that we are having, the tracking system that she has on her is being rather obtuse as far as pinpointing just where the senator is."

Jeb shook his head. "You know she's with them right now."

"With Devereaux and Rowe?"

"Yes, with Devereaux and Rowe. Someone there knows where she is and what she's doing. You and Fielder need to find them and fast. Find out what's going on and let me know immediately. That's an order. Understood?"

"Understood, sir."

"Good. I'll look forward to hearing from you shortly." Jeb ended the call just as Chase and Gray returned to the SUV.

"So?" Big James said. "Did you find out where the senator is?"

"No. But we will soon enough. And when we do...things are gonna get hectic. So, for now, eat your food in peace. It may be the last time you get to do that for a while."

THE CATCH

She was waiting just inside the door: Senator Brenda Cobb-Schmidt accompanied by her 12 security guards.

Neither Devereaux, Rowe, nor Tharp had ever seen a picture of her. What they encountered was a woman who obviously took great pride in her appearance.

Nearly fifty years old, the senator had the complexion of a thirty-year-old. Her straight black hair contrasted starkly with her pale skin, and her diamond-blue eyes, while friendly enough, had an unsettling quality.

Senator Cobb-Schmidt's waist was trim, her wardrobe prim: a Monroe & Main black pantsuit worn under a long camel-colored cashmere coat.

"Senator?" Harper asked.

"Yes, sir. Senator Brenda Cobb-Schmidt," she smiled warmly.

"Good to meet you," Harper shook her hand.

"I must say, it's a little surreal, having the three most wanted people in the world right here in front of me. Your friend Kelly Campbell said she would deliver, and she did."

"Well, not quite," Kinley corrected. "This woman – wonderful as she is – ain't Laurie Chase."

"But don't feel bad," Harp grinned. "You're not the first person to make that mistake."

"Taralyn Tharp," Tara introduced herself, stepping forward to shake the senator's hand. "It's a pleasure."

"The pleasure is all mine. But if you don't mind me asking, where is Laurie Chase? Miss Campbell had me believing that she would be with the two of you."

"Last we knew of her, she was down in Rio," Rowe answered.

"Speaking of Kelly Campbell," Kinley said, "any word on her situation yet?"

"Mr. Devereaux, I have three of my people waiting for her to be processed and go before a judge for her bail hearing. Once all that is taken care of, I'll pay to have her released immediately. But you know how fast the 'system'"—Brenda made air quotes with her fingers— "moves sometimes. It could be thirty minutes; it could be several hours. But I assure you I will have you all reunited just as soon as humanly possible."

"So, it would seem that you have something for us, yes?" Kinley was blunt. "Something that might finally clear our names from the Paul Michaels shooting?"

"I do, indeed. But first, let's go someplace and talk. We definitely need to talk," she said, her voice taking on a sullen tone.

"What's with all the security?" Harper asked.

"Oh, sweetie, I assure you that they are here strictly for cosmetic reasons. Let's face it. I am your meal ticket back to a normal, no-looking-back, all-is-well lifestyle. Do I really think that you're going to shoot me in the head? Of course not," she laughed, the empty halls echoing the sound.

Kin looked at Harper in bewilderment.

Six members of Cobb-Schmidt's security team led the way down a long hallway while Taralyn, Kinley, Harper, and the senator walked side by side behind them. Four more security personnel brought up the rear of the procession, while Stephanie Cash and the final two guards remained stationed at the front entrance.

They walked past walls filled with pictures of former students, trophy cases celebrating victories of days gone by, and hundreds of combination lockers. The irritating squeak of Kin, Harp, and Tara's wet shoes was amplified by the spacious and void hallway.

"Of course, you'll have to forgive me for how this meeting has been set up. I would have loved to have met the three of you in a much nicer setting and in better weather. But you can only imagine the paparazzi parade that would have brought out. I had to jump through a good many hoops to guarantee the secrecy of this meeting."

"Well, I sure hope you weren't wearing those shoes when you did," Harper quipped.

The senator gave an obligatory laugh. "*Touché*, Mr. Rowe."

"So, you were saying?" Taralyn spoke up.

"Yes, I was describing the great lengths I've gone to in order to bring this meeting to fruition. I knew my life would no longer be my own once I threw my hat into the presidential ring, but sometimes it seems the only time I have to myself is when I use the restroom. And even then it can be a little touch and go. So, breaking away for two hours to meet up with all of you most certainly took some doing."

"Well, we are certainly grateful that you did, ma'am," Kinley reached over and patted her on the shoulder. He was getting ready to continue when the six security agents stopped suddenly at a door marked "Library." One of them held it open as the senator led Kinley, Harper, and Taralyn into the vast room. The security team remained in the hallway.

"Whoa," Harper called out, looking around at the massive room. "Judas Priest, my high school library was about a tenth of this size. I don't even think the school itself was this big."

The library was three stories tall and about the size of a football field. The main floor included a computer area, music listening area, and reading area filled with tables, couches, love seats, recliners, and even some gigantic bean bags. Eight-foot-wide catwalks ran around the perimeter of the second and third floors.

"This is one of the nicer private schools in the Midwest, to be certain," Brenda noted. "And as it happens, my alma mater. I donated the money to build this library."

"That would explain why you're able to come and go as you please without raising any suspicions."

"No suspicions, no snooping onlookers, nobody at all. Just us," the senator smiled, quickly scanning the trio. "Are any of you hungry? Would you like something to drink?"

"Yes," they answered simultaneously.

"Yeah, our schedule on the way here was pretty tight. We've eaten maybe twice in the last two to three days," Kinley offered.

"I can assure you that the cafeteria here has just about anything you'd like. Just say the word, and I will have it brought to us."

"Well, as far as I'm concerned," Harper went first, "there's only one way to go on a snowy day like today. And that is: a Coke, grilled cheese, and a bowl of tomato soup with some crushed up saltines."

"I couldn't agree more," the senator smiled.

"When the man makes a point, the man makes a point," Kinley said. "I'll have what he's having."

"Make that three," Taralyn chimed in.

"Excellent." The senator dialed a number on her cell phone.

"Hello, Miss Cash. Please, be a dear and go to the school cafeteria. We're going to need three grilled cheese sandwiches, three bowls of tomato soup, and three Cokes...in the largest cups that they have available. Understood?"

Without waiting for an answer, the senator disconnected the call and returned her attention to her guests.

"Nothing for you, Senator?" Harper asked.

"I had breakfast with the head of the Chicken Farmers of

Northwest America this morning, so I'm still quite full. While we wait for your food, let's find a comfortable place to sit so we can start talking about what's going to happen next."

As the three of them looked around, Kin remarked, "I have stayed in four-star hotels that weren't furnished as nice as this library."

"Over here looks good," Harper pointed, then led the way to a spot containing a couch, two recliners, a rocking chair, and a loveseat.

Tara chose one of the recliners. Harper was ready to take the other one, but he hesitated.

"Which one do you think will be more comfortable for you, Kin, with how you are? This recliner or on the couch?"

"Getting down isn't the problem as much as getting back up. I think I'll be better off on the sofa there."

Senator Cobb-Schmidt looked bewildered.

"What does that mean, 'With how you are'? How is he? Is there something I need to know?"

"I got shot yesterday," Kinley grimaced as he lowered himself onto the couch. "Nothing too serious. It was a through-and-through, so there's little to no chance of infection. Honestly, it feels worse than it looks."

"Sweet mother of mercy. You got shot? Doing what? And where? I mean, where did you get shot? Where...on your body?"

"No, no, no, no," Harper answered for Kinley as he lowered himself into the second recliner and kicked the footrest up. "It's really nothing with which to concern yourself, Senator. We patched him up, medicated the poor guy, and he's right as rain just about now."

"What were you doing that caused you to get shot?"

"It's really quite the long story," Kinley said, removing his coat and shoes and reclining on the sofa. "And if I'm reading the situation right, we don't have time to be going into too much other material than the subject at hand, yes?"

"True," the senator agreed. "But, still—"

"We really want to know what you have in your possession that is going to be able to clear our names in the matter of the Paul Michaels shooting. That's the one and only reason we're here."

"Yes, of course," Brenda replied, placing the rocking chair in the middle of the three and sitting down. "What I have that will exonerate you two, as well as DEA Agent Laurie Chase, is a series of emails from the former secretary to someone named Tara Madison, AKA Black Ice. I'm sure you know who she is."

"We do," affirmed Devereaux. "What do these emails say?"

"They say enough. Let's just say that if he was still alive, the secretary would be spending a very long time in jail because of what these emails say. I also have two signed affidavits from former employees of his. These affidavits alone would be enough to clear all of you. I also have some recordings."

"So, what's the plan?" asked Harper. "I mean, pardon my bluntness, but I'm sure you have some sort of political agenda lined up for giving us these emails and what not. So, what is it? A big press conference of some kind?"

"I'll be straight with you"—the sullen tone returned along with a dour expression— "that was the plan, yes, but…" She fell silent.

"You all right, Senator?" Taralyn asked.

"No." She took a deep breath and exhaled. "No, I'm not."

"Okay," Harp looked at Kinley, then back to the senator. "Just how not alright are you?"

"My daughter has been kidnapped, gentlemen, and I need you to get her back for me."

"What?" Devereaux asked. "Why do you need us to do it?"

"Yeah," Taralyn said, "isn't that a job best suited for the authorities?"

"Usually, yes. But this isn't a typical situation. First and most importantly, the kidnappers have made it very clear to me that I am, under no circumstances, to involve the police in any way. That is obviously the key aspect to all of this. But there is a secondary reason, as well. You see, the political platform that I am running on is a family values-based platform. You can only imagine how my opponents would use this against me if they were to ever find out. A candidate running on a family values platform, and she can't even keep her own daughter safe?"

"Yeah, I guess I can see how someone could use that to turn the tables on you. Sure. So, what happened?" asked Devereaux.

"It's not a well-kept secret that my daughter has a nasty habit of slipping her security detail to sneak off and see her friends. Whoever took her must have been watching her. Two days ago she slipped her detail while she was at home – at least, that's where her security thought she was. While she was going wherever it was that she was actually going, the kidnappers grabbed her. They called me as soon as they had her to let me know."

"Does your security team know what happened?" Harper asked.

"No, they do not. That's why they are out in the hall, and we are in here. To be honest, I'm not one hundred percent sure that one or more of them isn't in on this."

"Where do they think she is? Obviously, they must realize that she isn't around."

"I told her detail and mine that she had, once again, sneaked away. I told them that I had sent her to stay with her grandparents in Appleton, Wisconsin, for the time being, and that while she was there she would not be needing any security."

"Didn't they find that odd?"

"They work for me, Mr. Rowe. They do as I tell them, so if I tell them that she doesn't need them, they do not question it."

"Well, what about your husband? Obviously, he knows. Is he okay with all of this – you not telling your security team, your using us to get her back?" Tara asked.

"My husband is on a business trip in China. He's been there for three weeks, and he'll be there for at least one more week before he returns home."

"And that means?"

"It means he doesn't know."

"He doesn't know that you haven't told your security team, or he doesn't know that you're using us to get her back?"

"Um, Harp, I think what she means – and correct me if I'm wrong, Senator – but I think what she means is that her husband doesn't know that their daughter's been kidnapped."

"What? Really?" Harper's pitch raised.

"Yes. That is correct, Mr. Devereaux. I have not told my husband."

"But...why?"

"My husband is a very prominent man in the business world. If I told him about the kidnapping, he would leave China prematurely to come back here. If that were to happen, it would raise a lot of red flags, thus drawing quite a bit of unwanted attention to a situation that I am trying to keep under wraps. By the time he comes back next week, this will all be over. Yes, he'll be very angry at me – probably for some time – but his anger will be much easier to control than this story would be if it gets out to the press. With his anger, we might sleep in separate beds for a few nights, but if the media were to find out that my daughter has been kidnapped, my run for the presidency is finished."

The threesome let her answer sink in for a moment. Harper finally spoke up, "Yeah. I get that."

"And you're sure this isn't some kind of a hoax? Sounds like your daughter is a bit of a rebel. Are you sure this isn't some kind of a stunt that she's pulling just to get your attention?" Kinley asked.

"I'm sure."

"Absolutely?"

"Quite."

"Alright," Kinley nodded, "then besides them telling you not to involve the authorities in any way, what else did the kidnappers say? Any ransom demands?"

"They want five million dollars. And they want it tonight...at Sunset Memorial Park Cemetery. They said they would have my daughter there. The money for the girl, they said."

"Cemetery? That seems like an odd place for a ransom drop," Taralyn noted.

"It's strategic," the senator remarked. "It's out of the way, for one thing. Plus, it's gated on all four sides so there's only one way in and out of there."

"How out of the way is it?" Kinley asked.

"I'll be sure to have Miss Cash give you the directions. It's all the way out County Line Road, about twenty miles outside of the city. It's so far out that it's one of the last places to get plowed. I don't even know if you could get out there with a four-wheel drive vehicle."

"Then how do they expect us to get out there to make the exchange?"

"Snowmobiles."

Just then the library door swung open and Stephanie Cash entered pushing a food cart loaded with steaming bowls of tomato soup, saltine crackers, grilled cheese sandwiches, and three Cokes.

The quartet sat in awkward silence as they watched the cart being wheeled toward them. Harper was the first to stand up and grab his food.

"Thank you. Thank you," he repeated. Kinley and Taralyn did the same as they reached for their food.

"Thank you, Ms. Cash. That will be all."

Four sets of eyes watched Stephanie exit the library. As soon as the door clicked shut, Kinley turned to the senator. "Snowmobiles? Really?"

"Yes, I'm afraid so."

"I've never even driven one of those things before," Kin objected.

"Oh, it's not hard," Taralyn said. "I can show you."

"Not that I doubt your snowmobiling capabilities for even one minute, Taralyn, but I just don't know that going into what could amount to be one of the most dangerous moments of my life is the time for me to be learning a new skill."

"I guess your daughter's kidnappers didn't give you a call-back number, did they?" asked Harp. "We could call 'em up and tell 'em that we're not going to be able to make it tonight."

"I'm pretty sure they called from a burner phone," the senator responded. "Bottom line is this: Make the ransom drop, get my daughter back alive, and I will give you everything you need to clear your names. It's just that simple. Any questions?"

"Do you know a good snowmobile rental place?"

The Descent of Brenda Cobb-Schmidt

People get into politics for all sorts of reasons.

Usually it is to help other people, their town, or a cause that is near to their heart. Sometimes they tire of watching politicians botch things up. "If you want something done right, you gotta do it yourself," they say, and toss their hat into the ring.

Others have a lifelong ambition to run for office. This is, after all, the United States of America – the place where a person really *can* become whatever they want with the right amount of effort and hard work.

Few people enter politics with the direct intent of becoming president of the United States. That requires a combination of serendipitous events and opportunistic connections – plus a spotless political record and an unblemished past. If those tests are passed, the next hurdle is whether or not to subject the lives of everyone they have ever known to intense scrutiny from the press, political vetters, and a slew of government agencies. And even if nothing unsavory is found, it is not uncommon for the American media to "create" something checkered in the targeted individual's past. Nobody wants that. Nobody deserves that. So this usually proves to be the point of cessation for 99.9 percent of all potential presidential candidates.

Senator Brenda Cobb-Schmidt jumped on the political carousel because "If you want something done right, you gotta do it yourself." When she tired of complaining about civil servants dropping the bureaucratic ball, she decided it was time to put up or shut up. She started a grassroots movement that got her elected to the Minneapolis City Council. After two years of effective leadership there, she made the jump to the U.S. House of Representatives.

Her serendipitous event was getting a piece of school bus safety legislation passed that had been unsuccessfully run up the flagpole a dozen times before. However, on the thirteenth time, all the right people were in all the right positions to make the right votes when it counted most. Bingo, bango, and bang tango – Brenda Cobb-Schmidt had her moment. She was finally on the map, legislatively speaking.

When Cobb-Schmidt made her run for the Senate, the voters remembered her action and were quick to show their appreciation. She beat her opponent in a landslide.

Brenda Cobb-Schmidt was a brilliant, hard-working, and diligent senator. She served her state as well as anyone ever could. And she did it by sticking to her promises and her principles, which, at the time, were about as straight and narrow as anyone's principles could be.

Then came her opportunistic connection: Secretary of Defense Paul Michaels.

Brenda had caught the S.O.D.'s attention with her senatorial win. Within six months, he had invited her to join his effort to make a bid for the United States presidency. He wanted her help and in a very big way.

"How would you like to be vice president of these United States of America, Senator?" she could still remember him asking her.

He wanted her because he was perfect.

Senator Brenda Cobb-Schmidt was small-town enough to connect with rural America, but business-savvy enough to relate to Wall Street. She was assertive enough to run with the boys, yet pro-family and able to exemplify a model American parent.

Paul Michaels' background was in military and foreign affairs. Brenda Cobb-Schmidt had a staunch pro-American record. Between the two of them, they covered all the bases.

They had met several times, each meeting lasting just a few hours. As they got to know each other better, both politically and personally, each was impressed with what they saw. At their third meeting – an encounter the senator would never forget – Secretary Michaels told Brenda about an advanced technological prototype space shuttle that he had been made privy to. It was something that, if it were to come to fruition, would change the world as we know it. He told her that he had discovered where the blueprints were going to be, and he had put a plan in place to seize possession of those blueprints. A plan involving a thief named Black Ice.

Michaels assured Senator Cobb-Schmidt that once he had the shuttle blueprints and could verify their validity, the election would be theirs.

Of course, there was no way that the S.O.D., nor anyone for that matter, could have predicted the events of that fateful night – the night of the break-in at Undersecretary of Defense Doug Hopkins' house, Kinley Devereaux and Harper Rowe walking in on the break-in, and the circumstances that would set off the chain of events that would span the next 18 months and lead up to this very moment in time.

Just what was it that led Senator Brenda Cobb-Schmidt, with her impeccable record of doing good and walking the straight and narrow, to plunge headlong down a rabbit hole of corruption and malicious behavior? Who knows for sure. But plunge she did.

Most likely it was money, or power – or both.

For some people, give them just a taste of either and they get hooked like a junkie on heroin. For Senator Brenda Cobb-Schmidt, the thought of being a heartbeat away from becoming the most powerful person in the free world gave her a rush unlike anything she had ever felt. After Secretary Michaels was assassinated, Cobb-Schmidt determined to get her hands on those space shuttle blueprints and make her own presidential run.

It took some doing, but the senator did, indeed, get her hands on the blueprints. Having done so, she set the wheels in motion to obtain the power she thought she so richly deserved. Using the blueprints, she built the shuttle and managed to keep it all under wraps.

Everything was under control. Nothing would stand in her way.

Until Aimee stood in her way.

Her daughter. Dear, lovable, funny, temperamental Aimee.

If only she had not discovered that Brenda was having an affair with Aimee's high school principal, Moses Cheeks.

If she had not found out about the affair, then Brenda would not have had to find $5 million to pay Kenton McCleary's team to kidnap her.

She would not have had to find two sitting ducks in Kinley Devereaux and Harper Rowe to take the blame for it all.

She would not have had to deceive and kill Kelly Campbell to get said sitting ducks into place.

However, Aimee did find out about the affair. And with Senator Cobb-Schmidt running for president of the United States on a family values platform, if word of the affair were to get out, the senator's career would be over. And not just her hopes for the presidency. No, she could kiss all her future political aspirations goodbye. The political work she had spent her life doing would be mocked for years to come.

Brenda was not about to let everything she had achieved get flushed down the tubes because of some snot-nosed teenager – even if it was her own daughter.

She had tried reasoning with Aimee, tried throwing herself on her mercy, even tried buying the kid off. It was all to no avail. Aimee remained steadfast in her belief that her mother needed to come clean – if not to the public, then at least to her father, Todd – the man to whom Brenda had been married for the last 22 years.

Poor Todd. Off on a business trip to China, he was going to feel awful when he heard the news about Aimee. Brenda was still not sure how she was going to break it to him, or how to spin it so that he would not forever hold it against her for not telling him about Aimee's abduction sooner.

She would figure out something. She always did. She was a politician, after all. And if there was one thing that politicians knew how to do, it was spin the truth.

29

PHONE RECORDS

It was a huge break for Sam Bergman, being able to track down the cell phone number Erica Bradley had used while she worked on the top-secret Space Frequency project.

Getting a break like this was one thing, but it was a whole different ball game to make good use of the information. Sam had been down this road before working robbery and homicide – getting a great lead only to be shut down because of security protocols.

Agent Bergman typed in the phone number.

Access denied.

He let out a sigh and tried a different approach.

Access denied.

"Boss, I'm having some trouble gaining access to the phone—"

"Tony!" Wyrick shouted across the office. "Give the rook a hand, will ya?"

Agent Tony Sawyers stepped over to Sam's desk, took a quick glance at his computer screen, leaned down to the computer keyboard and punched in a 12-digit code followed by the enter key.

Access granted.

"Thank you, Agent Sawyers. I appreciate the help."

"It's all about teamwork around here, kid. It's the only way anything gets done."

Sam began looking for patterns in the numbers lining his screen.

One particular phone number seemed to be called more than the rest. Bergman took a shot and gave it a call.

No luck. Disconnected.

Sam looked the number up to see if he could at least find out who it used to belong to. Again, no luck. It appeared to be a burner phone.

"Weird," he said aloud.

"What's that?" Wyrick asked.

"Seems the number that Erica Bradley called the most from her work cell was a burner phone. Plus, she called it almost every day at the same time: right around 6:15 each evening. And it was always the last call of the day. Kinda like she was calling someone to report on the day's progress."

"Top secret project like that...I'm not surprised. By doing it that way, you don't leave a paper trail, no documents that can fall into the wrong hands or be seen by prying eyes. Quite ingenious, actually."

"Yeah, I guess."

Sam picked another number and called it.

Disconnected.

He tried three more phone numbers only to get the same outcome: disconnected burner phones.

Then he spotted a number that didn't fit the pattern. It appeared only once throughout all of Erica Bradley's phone records. And it was called at 10:32 p.m. on a Tuesday night, *after* there had been twelve calls placed to a different number between 10:25 p.m. and 10:31 p.m., with each call lasting only three to four seconds each. The calls must have gone straight to voicemail, Sam surmised.

"I may have found something here, Sandy."

"Oh, it must be something good. You just called me by my first name."

"I've got Erica Bradley calling a number repeatedly for just about seven minutes on Sunday night, December the 18th. Every call goes right to voicemail because each call is just a few seconds long. After that she must have gotten frustrated because she then places a call to what appears to be a landline. And she must have gotten through, because this particular call lasts 22 minutes."

Sam went quiet, punching a few more keys on his keyboard.

"Ah-ha! Yes, indeedy-do. This number is a landline registered to Rae Yun Kwan of 2254 Oak Valley Drive in Eden Prairie, Minnesota." Bergman entered Rae Yun Kwan's name into the CTU search engine and almost choked when the results came back. "Oh, hello, sports fans."

"Whaddaya got, Sammy?"

"What I got is"—he began reading from his computer screen— "*Mrs. Rae Yun Kwan of Eden Prairie, Minnesota, reported missing by her husband four days ago. She was last seen on Monday morning when she dropped her children off at Central Middle School in Eden Prairie around 7:15 a.m. and was believed to be heading to an 8 a.m. doctor's appointment at Fairview Family Practice. Her car was found in the Fairview Family Practice parking lot, although she never appeared for the appointment. According to the police, there was no sign of struggle and Mrs. Kwan's purse was found intact inside her car. If you have any information about* blah, blah, blah... you know the rest."

Agent Wyrick paused typing for a few seconds. "That's good work, Marlowe. Upload everything you just did there into the case logs, then go track down Mr. Kwan. Take Sarah to wherever he is and find out anything you can from him. Agent Sawyers and I will be en route to the Eden Prairie Police Department to swap notes with those fine boys in blue. And Dwight?" She looked around for Agent Dwight Guy. "Anybody know where Dwight went?"

"I think he stepped out for a quick smoke."

Wyrick shook her head. "Well, whenever he gets back in from

working on his cancer research, tell him to coordinate with all the other agencies. Give them what we've got so far and see what they can do to assist us. Be sure he tells them that this is still our case and whatever it is that gets run...gets run through us first. Am I clear?"

"Clear as a mountain stream, boss," replied Agent Sarah Beck.

Number Recognition

Laurie Chase and Big James Gray sat in the back seat of the Cadillac Escalade eating like wild savages. Jeb Crool fidgeted in the front seat, waiting for someone to call with Senator Brenda Cobb-Schmidt's whereabouts.

"You want some of this, Agent Crool?" Laurie offered him some of her Chicken Fillet. "I ordered *way* too much."

"No, I'm fine, thank you."

"I'll take it," Big James smiled. "I ordered way too much, too, but I'm still hungry."

Jeb's phone rang. He answered it on the first ring. "Whaddaya got for me, Dave?"

"We just recovered Campbell's phone records. I thought one of the calls on here might be from Rowe or Devereaux. You wanna head back this way and let Miss Chase have a look at these numbers to see if she recognizes one of them?"

"Roger that, Dave. I was hoping we might have a *twenty* on the senator by now, but no such luck. We'll head on back. If Chase doesn't recognize any of the numbers, then maybe we can just start randomly calling 'em and see if we get lucky." Crool hung up and started a quick exit from the restaurant parking lot.

"We're headed back to the motel," he said over his shoulder.

"They were able to pull Kelly Campbell's cell phone records. We're pretty certain that somewhere in her last few calls, she either placed or received a call from our boys. Since we're rather certain that Kinley Devereaux's phone doesn't work, we're thinking that Harper Rowe's number is going to be there. Miss Chase, I know you said that you never called his number before so you couldn't recall it from memory, but do you think you might recognize it if you saw it?"

"I'm not making any promises, but if it's there on the list, I feel like there's a good chance I'll recognize it."

"I know this is going to put some added pressure on you, but I'm just telling you like it is. You being able to recognize Rowe's number is going to be our best chance to expedite tracking him and Devereaux down and saving them from walking into what's probably an extremely dangerous situation. My agents are trying to find the senator's location, but apparently her ability to drop off the grid is just slightly better than our ability to track her down. I was hoping we would know where she was by now and be on our way to apprehending all three of them, and have this thing wrapped up by supper time. Since we haven't found her yet, I'm starting to think that by the time we do, Kinley and Harper will have already departed her presence."

"And what is it that you're basing all of this on?" Chase asked.

"A feeling."

"A feeling?"

"Yes, a feeling. I'm sure this will come as no surprise to you, but I'm sure that close to sixty-five percent of my work is done based on feelings and gut instinct."

"Is it usually right?"

"Usually," Crool nodded.

"Except for when it comes to catching Harper Rowe," Big James pointed out.

"My track record of gut feelings being right usually coincides with how close I am to catching someone. I have had very few, if any, gut feelings about Harper Rowe until now because I've never been this close to catching him before. I will tell you this, Mr. Gray, getting Harper Rowe, Kinley Devereaux, and Senator Cobb-Schmidt in one fell swoop is the kind of takedown that most federal agents don't even dream about. If this goes down the way we think it's going to go down, this case won't just make my career. It will end it with a Vesuvian-like fireworks display. I can hang up the badge and start planning my book, my book tour, the talk show circuit, and guest TV appearances. This case is going to make me and my men more popular than Elliot Ness and Ted Gunderson and Melvin Purvis all rolled into one. But"—he paused for dramatic effect— "that is *entirely* incumbent upon being able to find your boys still in one piece and getting the necessary evidence to bring down the senator. Bottom line? My gut is telling me the clock is ticking, and we're quickly running out of time."

Finalizing the Exchange

As it turned out, the senator *did* know a good snowmobile rental place.

"The place is called Northwest Winter Outdoor Equipment and Apparel. They've got all the top of the line stuff so you won't have any trouble finding what you need there. Feel free to pick up whatever clothing and gear that you'll need. I'll have Miss Cash escort you to the place once we've finished up our business here. She will pay for whatever you need."

"Well, that's very kind of you, Senator," Kinley said.

"Yes, thank you, ma'am," Harper resounded. "However, all that aside, I would just like to make sure that I have all the dots connected on this ransom drop, if that's okay?"

"Of course."

"So, our course of action is to get...snowmobiles? And drive them to the ransom drop at a...cemetery?"

"Yes, that's right."

"You've gotta be kidding me. I mean, this whole premise is more absurd than the plot to the TV show *Lost*."

"Harp, take it easy," Kinley said. "It's not like she has control over any of this. Bastards took her kid in an obvious attempt to sabotage her presidential run, and she needs us to help her keep them from doing that, all the while getting her daughter back unharmed.

You know better than anyone that we've been in situations much more bizarre and precarious than this one."

Harper raised his eyebrows. "Maybe we have, but none of them are coming to mind right now."

Kinley reached deep into his bag of facial expressions and pulled out one unique to him: pursed lips, locked jaw, steely gray eyes peering fiercely at his partner.

"But, hey"—Harper got the message—"I'm sure you're right. We'll get through this just like we've gotten through everything else we've encountered."

The senator looked back and forth between the two men. "You are the only hope I've got. I'm putting my entire future and the life of my daughter completely in your hands."

"As we are with you, Senator, so don't spend even one more second worrying about us holding up our end of the bargain. We're golden here," Kinley said.

"Like a Midas touch," Harper affirmed.

"Then let's get back to the rest of the plan," Cobb-Schmidt continued. "After you make the trade for my daughter, take the snowmobiles back to the rental shop. I'll have Miss Cash meet you there. She will then take you to a room that I have reserved at the Hilton Garden Inn downtown. I will meet you there with the evidence that I have to clear your names. We can go over everything, and once the two of you are satisfied, we will call the feds to come and meet us. We'll show them everything we've got, and the good Lord willing, the two of you will be back in good standing as U.S. citizens by sunrise tomorrow morning."

"I like the sound of that," Kinley smiled.

"What about the ransom money?" Harper asked. "When will you be getting that to us?"

"Well," the senator laughed, "she doesn't know it, but the money is in a briefcase in the trunk of Miss Cash's car. You will get it from her when she takes you to get the snowmobiles."

"Okay. I guess that's that then," Kin said. "I suppose you haven't gotten any sort of update with where we're at with Kelly and her release?"

"Nothing yet, but as soon as I hear *anything* at all, I will let you know immediately. Which reminds me," Brenda said, picking up her phone. "I do need to get your cell numbers from you."

Harper rattled his off first, then Taralyn. Then Kinley informed the senator of his phone's demise in Prague.

The senator punched their numbers into her phone, then texted her own number to Harp and Tara. "Any other questions?"

"Yeah," Taralyn spoke up. "What if something goes wrong at the ransom drop? I mean, what if these guys pull a double-cross, decide to keep the money and try to kill the three of us and your daughter?"

An uneasy silence fell across the room. Harper imagined that even the library books were saying to each other, "Wow. It just got *really* quiet in here."

"Do you have anything to arm yourselves with?"

"Oh, hey yeah," answered Rowe.

"While I'm not crazy about the thought of you taking weapons to this exchange, it would be wrong of me to ask you to go into it unarmed. That being said, if things should appear to be going sideways, by all means, do what you must to save yourselves and my daughter. I have no idea how many men they will have at this exchange. Could be two; could be twenty. If it's closer to the latter, then...I'll pray for you."

"Are you a righteous woman, Senator?" Harper asked.

"I like to think I am."

"Well, I like to think I can run a three-minute mile, but I probably can't. The Bible says that the prayers of a righteous man availeth much. So, for the sake of me, Kinley, Taralyn, and your daughter, I hope very much that you are as righteous as you think you are."

"Alright," Kinley said, pushing his empty dishes aside and standing, "just to recap. We are leaving here, following Miss Cash to the winter outdoors store, getting the money for and the directions to the ransom drop from her, gearing up for the trip to the ransom drop, going to the Sunset Memorial Park Cemetery to make the ransom drop, get your daughter, head back to the outfitters store to meet back up with Miss Cash, where she will take us to the hotel to meet up with you. Does that just about cover it?"

"I believe it does," the senator said, looking at her watch. "It's almost two o'clock. The drop time at the cemetery is 6:30. That's just over four and a half hours from now. Not a lot of time, so the three of you should probably be on your way."

Harper and Taralyn quickly finished their food and drinks, then joined Kinley in approaching Senator Cobb-Schmidt to shake her hand and reassure her that they would be doing their best to get her daughter back to her safely.

"If things go the way we hope, we'll be seeing you a little later tonight."

"I know I've got the best people I could possibly have on this. I have the utmost faith in the three of you," Brenda said as she walked them out of the library.

Stephanie Cash was waiting outside the door, along with members of the senator's security team. The senator instructed her agents to escort Devereaux, Rowe, and Tharp back to the front of the school and to wait there for her. Once they were out of earshot, she spoke softly to her aide. "Alright, Miss Cash, everything is going as we planned."

"They don't suspect anything?" Cash whispered.

"They were a little uneasy about having to take snowmobiles to the drop sight, and maybe a little apprehensive about the drop sight being at a cemetery, but by the time we were finished, they were all aboard with everything."

"So, what now?"

"I need you to take them to Northwest Outdoor and get them whatever they need. I don't care what it is. Whatever they ask for, just make them happy and get them on their way to the cemetery. In just about five hours the three of them and my daughter will be dead, and we'll be heroes for having brought down the two most wanted men in America. We will gain every red-blooded patriot vote for taking Rowe and Deveraux, and we'll have the sympathy vote for the death of my dear, sweet Aimee." Senator Cobb-Schmidt smiled a devilish smile. "We play this right – which we will – and, for all intents and purposes, the U.S. presidency will be mine, all mine."

51

When Answers Lead to More Questions

Erica Bradley, deceased, mother of two children and devoted wife of one husband, had been snuffed out by a car bomb. Right in her own driveway. Now Senior AIC Sandy Wyrick and her scrappy band of counter-terrorism agents had made the ominous discovery that one of Erica Bradley's co-workers may have also met with an untimely fate.

Rae Yun Kwan, missing person.

MCTU agents Sam Bergman and Sarah Beck were seated in Rae Yun Kwan's living room, drinking Rae Yun Kwan's tea, and interrogating Rae Yun Kwan's husband, Wei Yen Kwan. Even though the temperature outside was well below freezing, the heat in Mr. Kwan's house was set to Jamaica. It was so hot that both Bergman and Beck removed their coats and laid them on the back of the couch. Bergman set his fedora atop his trench coat.

"Mr. Kwan, we appreciate you taking a few moments to meet with us this morning," Agent Sarah Beck started things off. "We know that this has to be an extremely difficult time for you and your family, and I assure you that my partner and I will try to be as quick as possible with our questions."

"I understand that it is necessary." Mr. Kwan's voice was surprisingly deep, considering his slight build and youthful look betrayed by only the slightest of gray hairs around his temples.

"We understand you have already spoken with the Prairie Eden police and the Minneapolis Missing Persons Division. However, this morning some new information may have been brought to light about your wife's disappearance."

"Something new has surfaced?"

"Yes, Mr. Kwan, that's why we're here," Agent Bergman explained. "We want to share with you what we have come across and see if it might spark something in your own memory that you hadn't thought of before now."

"I'm not sure what you mean. Spark something in my own memory?"

"It's difficult to explain," Agent Beck said. "Probably best if we just tell you what we have uncovered, and if you have something to add to it then, you know...we can see what that might lead to."

Kwan looked at her skeptically. "Is this bad news?"

"It's not great," Sam said.

"Then maybe you should tell me what in the world the two of you are talking about. Because honest to goodness, I'm completely lost here."

Sarah Beck began. "Your wife...did she ever work *with* or work *for* a woman named Erica Bradley?"

The room fell silent for a moment.

Then Wei Yen Kwan answered. "Oh, please, do not tell me that the whole reason the two of you are here is because of that woman."

"Umm," Sarah asked, "why would you say that? Why would you refer to Erica Bradley as *that woman*?"

"Because, agents, if Erica Bradley had anything to do with my wife's disappearance, I can't imagine that this will end well."

"How so?"

"Oh, where to begin." Kwan squinted his eyes in recall. "For starters, Erica had become quite paranoid about things recently.

She and my wife and a couple other specialists were working on a top-secret government project for the better part of the last three years. Towards the end of it all, Mrs. Bradley was convinced that every member of the team was in danger. Rae Yun and the others tried to ignore her at first, but Erica's fears started getting to them. She was convinced that whoever they were working for had bad intentions for the lot of them."

"Do you have any idea who that was? Who it was that they were working for?"

"No, Agent Beck, I do not. Erica was the only one in contact with whomever that was, and she was under strict orders not to disclose that information to anyone. My wife tried to get it out of her a few times – especially when Erica started to become fearful of what these people might do to them after the project was over. But she told Rae Yun and the rest of the team that it was in everyone's best interest *not* to know. Then, when the project ended, everyone was paid and reassigned to new jobs, and it all just seemed to go away. Even in a recent conversation with my wife, Erica admitted that she had probably just fallen prey to the long hours and stress that came with being the team leader for such a top-secret project."

"Do you know the names of any of the other team members?"

"Yes, there were only two of them: a Dr. David Hess and an engineer from MIT named Ronald Zook."

"Ever meet them? Or do you know if they are still in the area?" Agent Bergman asked.

"No, I never met them or Erica Bradley. As far as them still being in the area, I do believe they are because my wife said something about all of them making plans to get together at some point after the New Year."

"So, your wife had talked to them on the phone just recently then?"

"Yes. I believe it was right before Christmas."

Bergman turned to Agent Beck. "Get on the horn to Wyrick.

Tell her to get a copy of Mrs. Kwan's phone records and track down the phone numbers for Dr. David Hess and Mr. Ronald Zook."

Sarah Beck walked into an adjacent room to call Sandy Wyrick while Sam Bergman continued with Mr. Kwan.

"I know this is a long shot, Mr. Kwan, but is there any chance that your wife may have kept any personal notes about the project? Maybe in a journal or a diary of some sort?"

"My wife has an office in the basement. If she had any notes about any of that, they probably would have been down there. But when the police were here yesterday, they did not find anything."

"Be that as it may, would you mind if Agent Beck and I took a quick look-see? With the new information that has recently come to light, the two of us may have a better perspective as to what to look for."

"Agent Bergman, I can appreciate your questions and wanting to do your job to the best of your ability. But you still haven't told me why you are here."

Sarah Beck walked back into the room and nodded to Sam.

"I was just getting ready to tell Mr. Kwan why we're here today," he said to Beck.

"Yes, of course," she said, resuming her seat on the couch.

Bergman and Beck looked at each other, then at Mr. Kwan. "Mr. Kwan, I'm afraid that Erica Bradley was killed yesterday morning."

Wei Yen Kwan's face went ghost white. "May...may I ask how she was killed?"

"Someone wired an explosive device to her car's ignition. If there's any upside to it...she didn't feel anything," Beck said.

And the downside is that she'll never feel anything ever again, Sam thought to himself.

"If they killed Erica like that, then I guess that there isn't much hope for my Rae Yun, is there, agents?"

"Maybe. I mean, until they find a body there's always some hope."

Mr. Kwan stood to his feet. "If you will follow me, I can show you to my wife's office. Truth is, agents, my wife is very private about her work and research. Until now I have been hesitant to go rummaging through her things because if she came back home and found out that I had, well, let's just say that she would be quite livid with me for a very long time. My wife is a very mild-mannered woman, agents, but she does know how to hold a grudge like no one I've ever met." Kwan lowered his head and stared at the living room carpet for a moment. "Now, though, I'd be all too happy to tolerate her anger for however long she decided to impose it upon me."

Sam and Sarah stood, and Kwan motioned for them to follow him to the basement.

The Senator's Goon Squad

"All right, boys and girls, Calvin and Kojak are at the cemetery with the girl." Kenton McCleary was reviewing final preparations for the ransom drop that night. "They've confirmed that the only road into the place is undrivable. That means our combatants will have to arrive via snowmobile or dogsled, and I'm pretty sure they won't have time to get the required number of dogs together to do the latter. So, just like we planned, we're going to hear them coming from a mile away. Literally. These dopes are going to reinvent the term 'sitting ducks' tonight. So all we have to do is keep our cool, do our jobs the way we've done them a hundred times before, and we're going to land ourselves a big stinkin' payday."

The members of his squad began clapping and cheering.

"AND"—McCleary raised his hand to quiet them— "And... we're going to have ourselves a United States president that will be dearly indebted to us once she takes office just about a year from now"

Again, the crew erupted in cheers.

McCleary felt his phone vibrate against his hip and hurried to a quieter room to take the call.

"Senator, I was just talking to my crew about you."

"How are things progressing on your side of the ledger, Mr. McCleary?"

"Very well. Two of my men are already at the drop site with your daughter. They've confirmed that the entire place is vacant, and they have commandeered a utility shed for us to hole up in until go-time. The rest of us will be heading out there shortly. We've got a chopper that is going to drop us just outside of the cemetery, and we'll hoof it the rest of the way in and be there within the hour."

"Be sure to check in when you do."

"Will do, Senator," Kenton responded. "So, what's going on with our patsies? Everything still on track there?"

"It is. I just finished meeting with them, and things could not have gone better. By the way, there is one small change to everything. There will be three of them, but not the three we initially thought. Rowe and Devereaux, yes. But a woman named Taralyn Tharp is with them instead of Laurie Chase. That name ring any bells?"

"Mmm, no, I can't say that it does," McCleary said. "Rattle any cages on your end?"

"I haven't had a chance to look up anything about her yet. But once I do, I'll let you know."

"Well, what are you going to do about Laurie Chase then? She is quite a loose end to have floating around out there. Did they say where she was?"

"They said somewhere in Rio. I'm not too worried about her. Once she hears that her two friends are dead, I'm sure she'll surface looking for some answers. And that's when I'll nab her. Nevertheless, our end game is the same: no survivors. Even if Rowe and Devereaux show up with the Pope and the Queen of England, you and your men are the only ones to leave that cemetery alive.

"Now, the five mil that Rowe and Devereaux will be showing up with tonight – that is your payment for this job. Once the mission is complete, you and your guys take that money and hop the first flight out of the country. It matters not to me where you're going, and I don't even want to know. Just go and stay gone. Once the dust settles, I will contact you to let you know. But even then I think that it would be in everyone's best interest that you not return to the States anytime in the near future."

"I have made it very clear to my men that this *will be* our last few hours on U.S. soil," McCleary asserted. "Senator, I know that you have a lot on your mind – including what will be taking place tonight – but my crew and I have done hundreds of jobs over the years, and I can tell you that they don't come much easier than what we will be facing tonight. Of course we realize that things can take an unexpected turn from time to time, but my team is well prepared. We're ready to handle what is going to happen in a few hours. You just be ready to handle what comes afterward, Senator...or should I say...Madam President?"

"Yes," Brenda smiled. "Yes, you should."

TRYING TO SORT THINGS OUT

The snow was falling heavier now than at any point since the trio had landed in Minneapolis. Taralyn was back behind the wheel, following Stephanie Cash to the Northwest Winter Outdoor Equipment and Apparel store. The boys were worrying themselves with other things.

"Hey, I get why I had to shut my yap when we were talking with the senator. But I'm for real sure going to say something about all this now," Harper ranted. "She must think we're dumber than a box of rocks to go along with this plan. Snowmobiles? Cemeteries? Doesn't want anyone to know about it because of her campaign? If that was my kid, I sure as days wouldn't wanna be leaving her well-being in the hands of the two men that are currently at the top of the country's most wanted list."

"Cool your jets, Harp," Kinley said. "Let's look at this from a rational point of view, okay?"

"So, now I'm irrational?"

"You're not, but your point of view is," Kin clarified.

"Oh, well, in that case, please continue."

"From a logistical standpoint, the whole snowmobile–cemetery thing is brilliant. One way in, one way out. And with us on snowmobiles, they'll hear us coming long before we get there. It's genius. As far as the senator goes, I don't blame her for doing what she's doing. Those kidnappers have her over a barrel. She's taking the two most wanted men in America – possibly the world, but I digress – to get the job done. And you know, and I know, and Taralyn knows, and I'm pretty sure the senator knows – thanks to Kelly Campbell – that we can absolutely pull this off. Realistically, how many people get to run for president of the United States and have a legitimate shot at winning?"

"I don't know," Harper started thinking. "I guess I'd ballpark it at ten to twelve people every fifty years or so."

"Pretty much," Kin agreed. "So, it seems painfully obvious to me that her political opponent is behind all this in some sort of attempt to sabotage the senator's chances at winning the election come November. Her only chance to salvage her campaign is to keep this out of the press and away from the voting public, and her only shot to do that is us. She knows, number one, that we won't go to the press or the authorities about any of this since they wouldn't believe us and would probably have us arrested. And number two, the good senator has something we need. So we are *definitely* going to play ball and do whatever she needs us to do."

"Yeah, I get that," Harper said. "When you put it that way, it does all seem to somehow make sense."

"It does, but still..." Kinley paused as he stared out the front windshield at the hypnotizing snowfall. "Do I think that this is far-fetched and insane? Yes, I do. Do I trust that the senator is being completely honest and aboveboard with us? No, I don't. Which brings me to this: Let me see your phone, Harp."

"Sure," Harp pulled his phone out of his coat pocket. "Who ya callin'?"

"I'm going to try to call the police to find out where Kelly is."

Kin took the phone from his partner. One glance at it and a sour look crossed his face. "Dude. Your phone is almost dead. I thought you just charged it on the plane?"

"I did. But I recorded the conversation with the senator. I thought there might be something on there that we could use if it came to it."

"Well...that was a good idea, but my phone currently doesn't work. And if your phone is dead, then how is Kelly going to be able to contact us once she gets freed up, ya big mook?"

Harper raised his eyebrows and shrugged. "I suppose I didn't think that far ahead."

"Good Lord, kid," Kin said in disgust, handing his phone back to Harper. "Can I see your phone, Taralyn?"

"Yeah, go ahead and grab it. It's in my coat pocket," she answered, flapping her right elbow.

Kin reached over and pulled out Tara's phone.

"What's your screen code?" he asked. Before she could answer, Harper's phone rang.

Harper looked at the readout. "It says 'Private Number.'"

"If Kelly's calling from a government line, it might come up as that. Answer it. Put it on speaker."

Harper did as instructed. "Hello."

"Harper, is that you?" asked an excited voice.

Harp was about to answer when Kinley snatched the phone out of his hand.

"Laurie! Is that you, baby?"

"Kinley? Is that really you?"

"Yes, it's me, baby. It's really me," Smiling from ear to ear, Kinley momentarily forgot about his pain. He was so happy to hear his girlfriend's voice that he didn't even mind when Harper joined in.

"I'm here, too. Taralyn's here, too. We're both almost as excited to hear from you as Kinley is."

"Kinley, I have been trying like crazy to call you. Why is your phone off at a time like this?"

"Well, I guess you could say that my phone is dead. It – and I – got shot back in Prague when we were at the orphanage rescuing—"

"You got shot?"

"Well, yeah, but don't go stressing about it, lover. I got patched up, medicated, and got plenty of sleep on the flight back to the States. I'm doing fine. Just fine. I swear to you."

"You're back in the States? Where are you guys?"

"Right now, we are in Minneapolis. We just met with that senator I was telling you about. The one that has the information we need to clear our names. And she has us doing a quick errand for her before we meet back up with her later tonight."

Kinley thought it best not to tell her the whole story. Harper Rowe thought otherwise.

"Yeah, get this Laurie: This senator broad has us going to someplace called the Sunset Memorial Park Cemetery to make a ransom drop to get her kidnapped daughter back. This place is so far out of the city that the roads aren't even plowed yet. So, we are currently following one of her people to go rent freakin' snowmobiles just so we can even get to the drop. I think the whole thing sounds outlandish, but your boyfriend, he seems to think that it's completely normal and routine. I'm glad you called because you need to talk some sense into that melon of his."

"Look, you guys, you need—"

"I didn't say it was *completely normal and routine,*" Kinley interjected. "What I said was that it was a logistically sound plan, and that these guys really know what they're doing."

"Okay, fine. But that's all the more reason we shouldn't be doing it then," Harper shot back.

"Kinley. Harper. Shut your stupid mouths and listen!" Chase yelled through the phone.

"I need you guys to stop arguing, too," Taralyn added. "Driving in this weather is tense enough without having to listen to Bobo the Clown and Coco the Chimpanzee battle back and forth like a couple of second stringers on a high school debate team."

She heard Laurie suppress a laugh on her end of the line.

Harper looked at Kinley, "To be continued."

"Definitely."

They glared at each other as Chase tried once again to deliver her warning that they were headed into a trap.

"Listen up, all three of you. I have to tell you something that is of the utmost importance to what you're getting ready to do."

"What could you possibly know about what we're getting ready to do?" asked Taralyn. "*We* barely know what we're getting ready to do."

"Okay. Let me clarify. What I'm getting ready to tell you isn't so much about *what* you're getting ready to do as much as it is about who you're getting ready to do it for."

"You mean, the senator?"

"Yes, the senator," Chase made clear. "You can't—"

Kinley and Harper looked at each other quizzically.

"We can't *what*, baby?"

Silence.

"Laurs? You still there, baby?"

Silence.

"Laurs?"

All they heard was the electronic tone signaling the death of Harper's battery.

A Break in the Case

"The police didn't take that with them?" Agent Bergman pointed to the laptop on Rae Yun Kwan's impeccably neat desk.

"I let them look at the laptop when they were here," Mr. Kwan answered. "But I insisted on a warrant if they wanted to take it with them. That was when I thought Rae Yun's return was very possible, and I didn't want her being mad at me because I let the police just take her work. Plus, some of the information on there is classified."

"Did they indicate that they would?" Sam asked. "Get themselves a warrant?"

"Not really. They read some of my wife's notes on there, but I don't think they had a clue as to what any of them meant. They just told me that if they needed to take a look at them any further, they would come back with a warrant. That was it."

"Okay if we look at it?"

"Help yourself, agents. Here's her password."

Electronic information retrieval was one of Agent Beck's specialties. She quickly set to work, her partner looking over her left shoulder.

Every time Sam saw something that looked like it had potential pop up, Sarah had already clicked on it.

"Were you going to say something, Sam?" she asked without looking up.

"No. No, you're doing good," he said.

Screen after screen after screen went by, but every heading that seemed interesting led nowhere. The two of them had been at it for nearly an hour when Beck discovered a file entitled "Space Frequency."

She clicked on it.

Pages and pages of what looked like notes appeared; notes filled with indecipherable words and phrases. Undaunted, they read on until Bergman suddenly stopped Beck from scrolling.

"Hey, do you see that?"

"You need to be a little more specific, Sam."

"Here," he pointed. "Start reading here and go to the end of the paragraph. What do you think that means?"

The paragraph Sam was pointing to began like many of the others: *blah, blah, blah, speculative theories that are neither blah, blah, blah, ending with reduced or minimal probabilities blah, blah, blah, to the degree of a reversed value of blah, blah, blah…*

But it ended in a rather peculiar fashion: *Still, as I sit here and type this, I know that I am sitting on the real answer to this entire problem.*

"What do you think that means?" Beck asked.

"If she's writing in a figurative sense, it could mean just about anything. But if she's writing in a literal sense, I think it means... you should stand up."

Overhearing their conversation from across the room, Wei Yen Kwan asked, "What? What did you find?"

Sarah Beck stood to her feet and turned to face the desk chair. She and Agent Bergman began pressing the cushion to see if they could feel anything foreign inside of it.

"Not exactly sure, Mr. Kwan, but it seems that your wife

may have just left us some sort of a clue," Agent Beck explained, continuing to press on the seat's cushion. After a minute or two, she and Bergman finally gave up.

"Maybe we need to cut it open," Sam suggested, drawing a pocketknife from his pants pocket.

"Whoa! You can't just go cutting up my wife's chair. What is it that you're looking for?"

"Well, that's just it. We don't really know *what* we're looking for." Agent Beck held up her hand. "Hang on a second, Sam. I'm with Mr. Kwan. Let's not just go slicing and dicing the furniture just yet. Let me think."

Sarah Beck looked at the seat cushion, then back to the laptop monitor: *Still, as I sit here and type this, I know that I am sitting on the real answer to this entire problem.* She looked at Mr. Kwan and Agent Bergman who were both staring back at her.

"What if..." She bent over and started feeling around underneath the seat. "Bingo."

"What?" Bergman and Kwan asked in unison.

"Hang on. There's...something...taped to the...Got it." She pulled the object free and held it up for all to see.

It was a small brown envelope about the size of a playing card. On the envelope in small, black print, it read: *Greyhound - Hawthorne Terminal.*

"What's it say?" asked Sam.

"Is there anything inside of it?"

Beck tore off the tape dangling from the tiny package and shook it.

"Well?"

"It's an envelope from the Greyhound Station on Hawthorne, Sam. And Mr. Kwan, yes, there is something inside."

She tore the envelope open and dumped its contents into her hand. A key with the number 52 etched into its round handle fell onto her palm.

"Looks like a bus locker key. Do you know anything about this, Mr. Kwan? Has your wife said anything to you about something that she may have hidden in a bus locker?"

"No, nothing. I swear." Kwan's face showed he was telling the truth. "I don't...I don't understand."

Sam took the envelope and key from Agent Beck and studied them. "Well, if what your wife wrote is true, she believes that this key can get us access to "the real answer to this entire problem." I'm going to take a car service to the Greyhound station on Hawthorne."

Sam pulled his phone out of his pocket to summon a car. "Sarah, stay here and keep searching that laptop. Give me a call when you're finished, and I'll let you know where I am and what I've found." As he headed up the stairs, he said, "I've got a good feeling about this, Sarah. I think we might be getting ready to bust this case wide open."

"Do you want me to call the boss?"

"I wouldn't just yet. For as much as I hope we're really onto something here, it could just as well be a whole lotta hullabaloo and nonsense. No need making much ado about nothing."

Sam's phone dinged, letting him know that his ride was nearby.

"My car will be here shortly, so I'm going to go up and wait outside to flag it down. Agent Beck, I will talk to you soon." Sam looked at Wei Yen Kwan. "Mr. Kwan, thank you for allowing us into your home today. You have my promise that we are going to do everything we can to find your wife and get to the bottom of this... whatever *this* is."

A Secret to Die For

She answered before the second ring, before the ringtone got to the "look away" part in the song "Dixie."

"What do you have for me?"

"We've got movement. The agents have split up. The male agent has left the residence; the other one is still inside with Mr. Kwan. I'm thinking maybe they've found something."

"Stay with the agent and let me know where he goes."

"Roger that," he answered. "Tell you this much: If they did find something, it was a secret worth dying for because myself and Miss Cash tortured that Kwan woman to death – literally – and she never gave up anything."

"That bothers me," the senator said. "Any secret worth dying for has got to be of major importance. The sooner we find out what it is, the better I am going to feel about things."

"I'll call you with any updates."

A Frustrated Chase

Laurie Chase was fit to be tied. Walking around the Aqua City Motel lobby, she was swearing under her breath. And sometimes over her breath. And sometimes quite loudly.

"Hey, will you calm down," Jeb tried to console her. "That call was great. You were great. We got the whole thing recorded, and they're going back over it now to get every detail they can possibly get out of it."

"Yeah, but I don't even know if they heard what I told them about the senator. They may still be walking headlong into certain death. How could they both have phones and neither one of them work? It's just so irritating, those two. Ahh!"

"Did you not hear what I just said about having recorded the whole conversation? Harper Rowe told us not once, but twice, where they were headed. We'll find out where that is, and we'll get there before they do. Still, Miss Chase, that phone call just proved everything you said to me was true: Rowe, Devereaux, Senator Cobb-Schmidt. I can barely believe it, but, unless you and your two confreres are pulling one whale of a con job on me, everything you said to me back in Rio really *is* true."

"Oh, well, that's just great. Not only do I find out that my boyfriend's been shot and is headed into a very unsettled condition, but now you're telling me that you think I am a liar? Really?"

Crool furrowed his brow. "Are you seriously telling me that was your takeaway from what I just said?"

Before Jeb and Laurie could continue down their path toward an impending argument, AIC Todd Adams interrupted. "We've located the Sunset Memorial Cemetery, and Harper Rowe isn't exaggerating. It's out there. Some of my guys even told me that people won't live in that area. Once they move in, and the first winter comes, they find out all too late that they're snowed in for weeks at a time. Once the roads are cleared enough for them to move somewhere else, they are outta there. So, yes, it seems very likely that a snowmobile is the only form of transportation that is going to get you to that cemetery," Adams shook his head in disbelief. "I just can't believe that Senator Brenda Cobb-Schmidt is involved in all of this, Special Agent Crool. She's the frontrunner to be the next president of the United States, for cryin' out loud."

"Believe me, Agent Adams, I know what it sounds like. When I first heard Miss Chase here tell me this crazy story, I was filled with doubt myself. Nevertheless, the further I go down this rabbit hole, the more it all seems to be quite real and quite true."

"I don't know. I mean, until you have something a little more concrete, you can consider me a skeptic about any involvement of the senator in any of this."

"How many snowmobile rental places are there in this city?" Jeb asked.

"Sheesh," Todd shrugged, "I can think of six or seven just off the top of my head, which means that there are probably two to three times that many."

"Do you think we might be able to narrow the list down based on their proximity to the cemetery?"

"I've already got a few of my people making calls to every snowmobile rental place in a 40-mile radius of the Twin Cities. We'll try to send photos of Harper Rowe and Kinley Devereaux to them directly. Like you suggested, we're starting with the ones closest to Sunset Memorial Cemetery, but there's no guarantee that we'll be able to get the info to the right shop in enough time to hold them up."

Jeb clasped his hands together on top of his shaved head and let out a long sigh, "Ahh, boy." He looked at Laurie, then to Big James, then to Agent Baldwin. "I hate to say this, but it seems that our most prudent move is going to be for us to go get some snowmobiles of our own and see if we can catch them in time."

"That's what I would do," Adams commented.

"Can I borrow a few of your guys to give us a hand? Maybe point us to the nearest winter gear place and then get us out there to the cemetery?"

"How many do you want?"

"I figure two to a sled. You and Mr. Gray on one," he said to Laurie. "Me and Dave on another." Crool paused for a moment. "Four of your agents should do. That'll be four sleds, eight people. Any more than that would probably just slow us down."

"You got it, Agent Crool." And with that AIC Todd Adams was off to round up four of his agents for the job.

"You up for this?" Laurie asked Big James.

"No, but...since I'm riding with you, I guess it'll be okay. I'm going to need you to keep me warm, though. It sounds like this is going to be a cold chore, and I already can't feel most of my nose and the majority of my toes."

"Don't worry, big boy," Jeb slapped the big man on his billboard-sized back. "I've got Uncle Sam's credit card. You can buy as many clothes as you need to keep you warm, courtesy of the American Government."

WHAT ABOUT TARALYN?

Unbeknownst to Agent Crool and the gang, the two men they desperately wanted to find were only about 20 minutes away at the Northwest Winter Outdoor Equipment and Apparel store. Taralyn, for one, was glad that they were finally there. Not only was she going blind from staring at Stephanie Cash's tail lights through the blizzard, but she was also going deaf from listening to Kinley and Harper argue with each other over whose fault it was that Harper's phone died and whether or not going through with the ransom drop was the right thing for them to do. However, for the time being, their disgruntled state seemed to have passed as the two men were giving each other a fashion show with all the winter garments and accessories that they had access to, thanks to Senator Brenda Cobb-Schmidt's $25,000 credit limit.

The sight of them loosening up eased Taralyn's tension. Not so for Stephanie Cash.

"Shouldn't they be a little more serious about things at a time like this?"

"Most people, perhaps. But these guys? No." Taralyn smiled as she tried on a pair of thermal snow goggles. "This is what they do before a dangerous job. They enjoy life while they can. Don't worry, Ms. Cash. I have seen these two in action before. There's no one better."

While Taralyn was busy convincing Stephanie Cash that Kinley Devereaux and Harper Rowe were the right men to get the senator's daughter back safely, the guys were giving each other rat tails with $300 scarves.

"Looks like the pain meds are working okay, buddy."

"Yessir, Mr. Rowe, I do believe they are." Kinley took a good look at his friend and sighed. "Come 'ere, dude."

"What? What?"

"Just get yourself over here."

Harper smiled as he walked toward Kin. When he was close enough, Devereaux reached out and put his hand on Harper's shoulder. "I don't wanna fight anymore, Skipper, but you know we have to do this. Right?"

"Yeah, I know."

"This is our only shot to get our lives back. Besides, we make it through tonight and get our good names back so that we can travel like common folk again, I'm gonna buy me, you, Laurie, and Dr. Lara...and Taralyn..." Kin paused. "Tell me again, what exactly is your relationship with Taralyn?"

Harper opened his mouth to answer, but Kin continued. "Because I know you and Dr. Lara—"

"Mercedes," Harper interjected

"Mercedes – right – have this *thing* going on. But you and Taralyn, you guys have some serious history together. Not to mention, she's smokin' hot like a firecracker, *and* she's loyal to a fault. I mean, in her time of need, she came looking for you, old buddy, old pal."

"I know."

"Now, in our time of need, here she is. Ready to go into battle with us once again. Hey, buddy, I'm no Dr. Phil, but somebody here has feelings for someone, and if it isn't you for her then it's gotta be her for you."

"Boy, those pain meds must really be working for you to be

giving me relationship advice. But be that as it may, let me answer your question in the spirit with which it was raised. I've got three good friends in this world: you, Big James, and Taralyn."

"Hey, don't forget Laurie."

"Eh, Laurie and I are friends by proxy. If she wasn't tangled up in this gigantic spider web we currently find ourselves in, and if she wasn't in deep with you, I don't really think she and I would find ourselves running in the same circles. I really don't. Nonetheless, my father used to always tell me, 'If you've got more friends than you've got fingers on your one hand then you've got too many friends.' So, right now"—Harper held up his left hand and counted off— "you, Big James, and Taralyn. That leaves two fingers. I'm hoping that Mercedes will eventually be one. And in deference to you, I am, indeed, saving the last one for Laurie Chase."

"Alright. Alright," Kin nodded.

"That being said, Taralyn and I do have a history together. And we tried the romantic thing, oh, I guess it was about a year ago. It didn't take, but we were both mature enough to realize that we could be great friends. Which we are. Which is why in *her* time of need she called me. And that is why in *our* time of need she is right here with us. She's loyal and, in the end, no matter what kind of feelings you have for the other person, it all comes down to loyalty.

"Sure, I could try to make a run at it again with her, but why take that chance and ruin one of the very few great things I have in my life? I can't do that. I *won't* do that."

Just then, one of the salespeople approached the two men. "Good afternoon, my name is Carol. Have we found what we were looking for, gentlemen?"

"Yeah, one second," Harper looked around the store until he spotted Taralyn and Stephanie Cash. He whistled to get their attention, then waved them to come over. Turning back to the saleswoman, he said, "My friend and I need a pair of gloves that are warm but not too bulky. For instance, something that will keep our hands warm but also allow us to pick frozen peas up off of the floor. Do you have something like that?"

"Yes," Carol chuckled, "I believe I can find you what you need."

Tharp and Cash approached the trio.

"We'll also need a pair for her, too," Harper pointed to Taralyn.

"What about some night vision goggles? Do you have anything like that?"

"Well, we do," Carol said hesitantly, "but they're pretty expensive."

"Oh?" Kinley raised an eyebrow. "And just what is it about us that doesn't scream 'filthy, dirty money'?"

"Oh, no, no," Carol said apologetically. "I didn't mean for it to come across that way at all, sir. I was just saying—"

"Don't mind him, ma'am," Taralyn stopped the woman short. "He got shot yesterday, and he's just a little bit cranky."

"I'm sorry. Did you say he got *shot*?"

"I sure did," Kinley said, lifting his shirt and lowering his pants just enough to reveal the bandages over his bullet wound. "Let me tell ya, it hurts like a mother."

"How...how did you get shot?" the saleswoman asked.

"Um, Carol, is it?" Stephanie Cash asked, squinting to read the woman's name tag. "Yeah, we're on a bit of a schedule here, so let me just sum this up real quick: Money's no object; these three are a trio of mercenaries. So, yeah, they get shot from time to time. Lastly, whatever they ask for? Give it to them." Stephanie's intensely blue eyes drove home her point. "Any questions?"

"Absolutely not, ma'am," Carol answered.

Cash gave the same sharp look to Kin, Harp, and Tara. "I'll be up at the counter. We need to hurry. It's 4:30 already, and we still have to rent the snowmobiles and trailer, load them up, and haul ass. Plus, I'm sure you'll need a quick crash course on how to operate those things – no pun intended."

"None taken," Harper smiled.

"Time to gear up, kids," Devereaux said with a smirk. "Destiny, she's a-knockin', and she's not taking 'Come back later' for an answer."

KENTON MCCLEARY AND AIMEE SCHMIDT

Kenton McCleary, former Green Beret and head of Senator Cobb-Schmidt's goon squad, had joined the Army right out of high school. After Basic Training in Fort Jackson, South Carolina, he had volunteered for the Special Forces X-Ray Program.

The Army sent him to Fort Mackall, Fort Bragg, Camp Rowe, and other undisclosed locations. After 44 weeks of training in survival, evasion, interrogation, weaponry, and computer skills, his class of several hundred had dwindled to just 51. Kenton was ranked number 3.

Barely had he officially donned his green beret when Kenton was given orders to join a 12-man Special Forces team stationed just outside of Sucre, the capital city of Bolivia. After finishing his four-year tour, he signed up twice more. In those 12 years, Kenton saw a lot of men come, and he saw a lot of men go. And when they went, it was usually in a body bag.

For most of those years, he worked with Chris Kojak, a Special Forces assistant operations and intelligence officer. Closer than brothers, the two had seen their fair share of death and destruction. And they had created their fair share, too, by God.

After discharge, Kenton and Chris went their separate ways, each facing private struggles in readjusting to civilian life.

One night, a man named Calvin Walters approached Kenton at an AMVETS meeting and invited him to go somewhere for a drink. Kenton was quick to accept. At the Isle of View Bar & Grille, the vets commenced drinking and talking the night away – a night that would change McCleary's life forever.

Around 1:00 a.m., Calvin brought up the topic of a group of veterans he was connected with. He told Kent about some jobs they had pulled, how much cash they were raking in, and how on the last mission they had performed, the team's munitions and firearms technician had been injured.

That was a lie, of course.

In reality, the team member had been shot in the head and killed. But those were the kind of details that you left out of a story when you were trying to recruit someone to the squad. For Kent, whose existence had been reduced to drinking until he passed out in front of his TV each night, it was an easy decision. A chance to get back in action and feel some purpose in life again.

Kent had been working with the team for just over two years when, while on a mission in Mozambique, the team leader took a blade to his femoral artery and bled out before anyone could rescue him. In a surprise unanimous vote, Kenton was made the new team leader. His first official act was to reach out to his army buddy Chris Kojak to fill the open spot on the team. It didn't take much arm twisting to get Chris to agree to come on board. Once he showed up, McCleary realized how much he had missed his friend.

That was four years ago. Ever since then, the team had become a mercenary machine, a force to be reckoned with. They had become brothers. Rich brothers.

✳   ✳   ✳

Harrison Roberts, chopper pilot, was the fourth member of McCleary's team. He had just dropped McCleary and eight other crew members in a snow-covered field several hundred yards to the west of the cemetery. It took the group just a few minutes to get from the drop zone to the large utility shed located about a quarter mile in from the graveyard's front entrance. Inside the shed, two heaters and three lanterns gave out heat and light. Senator Cobb-Schmidt's daughter lay on the floor, bound, gagged and blindfolded.

The shed was roomy – plenty big enough to accommodate the thirteen people inside. Its walls were lined with shovels, pickaxes, rakes, and weed eaters. Walters and Kojak had moved the mowers to the back to clear floor space.

"Get the girl up and make her comfortable," McCleary ordered.

✤ ✤ ✤

Kinley Devereaux, Harper Rowe, and Taralyn Tharp were due at the Sunset Memorial Park Cemetery in 90 minutes with the $5 million ransom for Senator Brenda Cobb-Schmidt's daughter, Aimee.

Aimee, who had just turned sweet sixteen. Aimee, who, thanks to her flowing brown hair, her emerald-green eyes, and her fierce determination, had been the captain of her high school cheerleading team for two years running.

Aimee, who was an accelerated learning student and on pace to graduate a year early.

Aimee, who because of her father's billion-dollar tech corporation and her mother being a very successful and influential U.S. senator, lived a very comfortable life and had a massive amount of friends, despite being moody, mouthy, opinionated, and generally difficult to tolerate.

Aimee, who had, to her disgust, discovered that her mother was having an affair with her high school principal.

Aimee, who now found herself surrounded by the mercenaries that her mother had hired to kidnap and, eventually, kill her.

"I hope you burn in hell!" she screamed as soon as her mouth was freed from the gag. "All of you!"

"Hey, look, kid, I'm trying to be nice to you," McCleary scolded. "But if you don't shut up, the gag is going back on. Besides, we're so far removed from civilization out here, no one could possibly hear you scream even if you had a bullhorn. So, why don't you just give it a rest."

"Oh, that's rich. You're trying to be nice to me? You're going to kill me in a couple of hours, you stupid asshole."

"Hey, boss, does it really matter if this little piece of crap is still alive when Rowe and Devereaux get here?" asked Kojak. "I mean, we're going to kill them all anyway, right?"

"I'm not killing the girl just yet, so get that thought right out of your head," McCleary barked. "Listen up, everybody," he addressed the room. "We've got food. So get yourself fed, get as warm as you can, and then let's start heading out and getting ourselves in position. That's an order."

"Hey, ya stupid half-ape," Aimee said to Kojak, "just wanted you to know that I am very well aware that whoever's coming here for me is probably going to get killed. But I pray that one of them will be able to get a shot off that hits you right in the balls and that you end up dying a painful, bloody death out there tonight."

Chris slapped her hard across her right cheek. "Keep runnin' your mouth, kid, because I got plenty more where that one came from."

Aimee composed herself enough to land a snap-kick straight to Kojak's groin, dropping the soldier to his knees, breathless.

McCleary rushed over and grabbed the girl, shoving her into the wall. "Sorry, *chica*, but you brought this on yourself." Pulling out his taser, he shot her in her stomach. Her limp body collapsed to the floor.

Kent re-attached the taser to his hip and turned back to his squad. "If you're going to let yourself get distracted by an idiotic snot-nosed teenager, then tonight's mission is going to be a long and deadly one...for *our* side. Stay focused, people. Now, I gave an order about thirty seconds ago. Why is everyone still standing around?"

The Hawthorne Avenue Bus Locker

Sam Bergman shuffled through falling snow in the cold Minneapolis evening air. Once inside the Hawthorne Transportation Center, he took a moment to dust off his trench coat and fedora. Flashing his badge and ID at the security checkpoint, he took a quick look around the huge establishment, trying to find the bus lockers.

No luck.

He did, however, see an information kiosk in the distance. Maneuvering as deftly as he could through the teeming crowd, Sam finally found what he was looking for: *Individual Accommodations – Bus lockers – C-3.*

After checking the color-coded map, he headed toward his destination.

It was hard to tell which was racing faster, Sam's mind or Sam's feet, as he considered the myriad of things that could be awaiting him in the locker. What if it was nothing? Or what if, heaven forbid, someone else had already gotten to it? But why would that happen? *How* would that happen?

Sam's tunnel vision for the bus lockers had made him oblivious to the fact that he had been tailed on the way to the bus station, probably because he had been busy entering his report into his tablet as Sandy Wyrick had instructed him. The tail was now seated at a bistro table barely twenty yards away, sipping on a mocha latte and eyeballing Bergman's every move.

The mystery man took his cell phone out and dialed Senator Brenda Cobb-Schmidt.

"Yeah?"

"Senator, we were right. They've found something. And I think I'm getting ready to find out exactly what it is."

Loading Up for a Big Night

Kinley, Harper, and Taralyn were suited up for the weather conditions as well as could possibly be hoped for. The total bill for their wintry apparel came to just under $8,000. Gloves, caps, scarves, coats, boots, helmets, and goggles – the very best equipment that the senator's money could buy.

The trio was standing just inside the back of the store, watching a crew load the three rented snowmobiles onto a trailer. The trailer would then be hitched to the back of the SUV that Kin, Harp, and Taralyn would be driving.

Each member of the trio had chosen the same make and model of Yamaha snowmobile, the Sidewinder SRX LE. That way, once Taralyn learned how to operate the machine, she could give just one set of instructions to the guys.

The Sidewinder was fast and light, just what they needed to travel through the unplowed roads leading to the Sunset Memorial Park Cemetery. Its heated seats were a nice plus.

While they watched the crew work, they chatted with Stephanie Cash to see how much assistance they could expect from her.

"Any chance you have a phone charger? My phone is out of juice, and I desperately need to make a call," Kinley asked.

"No, sorry," Cash frowned. "I had a car charger, but the

stupid thing just stopped working about two days ago. You know what I mean? It was working, it was working, it was working...it wasn't working."

"Crap. I really need to make that call."

"You can use my phone," Cash offered.

"That's very kind of you. Unfortunately, the number that I need is on my phone, and without getting it to turn on, I really have no way to retrieve it."

"Do you know how to get out of the city and to the road that will take us where we need to go?" Kinley asked her.

"I do," she responded. "I can tell you how to go, or you can follow me."

Taralyn, being the driver, answered the question. "All things being equal, I think I would rather follow you. It will be hard enough to drive in this crap with a loaded-down trailer attached to me. Having to look for road signs and figuring out which way to turn might just be a little more than I would care to do."

"I can take you as far as the roads will let me."

"I would assume that will be as far as the roads will take us, too. When you feel like you're getting to that point on the drive, try to find some place to pull into so that we can unload the sleds without too much of a problem."

Kinley spoke up, "If I understand the plan properly, Miss Cash, we are to meet you back here with the senator's daughter, and then you will take us all to meet the senator at the Hilton Garden Inn. Does that sound right?"

"If everything goes according to plan – and I don't know why it wouldn't – that is exactly what you will be doing," Stephanie said.

"Looks like they're just about finished up out there," Harper observed.

With that news, Taralyn pulled on her new stocking cap. Kinley and Harper followed suit, Harper adding a scarf, hood, and gloves.

"Dude," Kinley reacted.

"What?"

"We're just going to the truck." Kinley had a habit of referring to SUVs as trucks. Harper usually had a habit of correcting him, but this time he let it slide. He had another argument to make.

"I realize that, but I think it's important to get all of this stuff on so that I'm used to moving around in it. I don't want to feel all weighted down and bunglesome when we get out there tonight. You guys should do the same. Get your gear broken in."

"Oh, I'm gonna break something all right," Kinley muttered. "I can't drive with a whole lot of stuff on my upper body. It feels like my range of motion is depleted by sixty to seventy percent. And in conditions like this, I need every advantage I can get."

"Yeah, I get that," Harper said as he finished bundling up and led the way out the back of the building. As soon he cracked the door open, a gust of wind tore it free from his gloved grasp, causing it to fly open and slam into the window behind it.

"Holy crap!" Harp exclaimed.

Kinley and Taralyn put their heads down, pulled their hoods up, and made a beeline to the SUV. Stephanie Cash grabbed her keys out of her purse and sprinted through the wind and snow to her car. Harper yelled over to one of the Northwest employees, "We all good here?"

"Everything's set," came the man's reply. "I sure hope you aren't planning to do any snowmobiling tonight. This weather is insane!"

Unable to hear him, Harper gave a thumbs up and clambered into the back seat of the SUV.

Kinley turned around to speak to his partner. "Ya know, maybe putting all the gear on wasn't such a stupid idea after all."

Taralyn started the engine, cranked the heat, turned on the windshield wipers, took a deep, relaxing breath and said, "Settle in, guys. I think it's going to be a bumpy one."

"Just take your time and keep a safe distance between us and her," Kinley advised. He checked the time on his watch: 5:37 p.m.

"With it being rush hour in the big snowy city, I'm sure you'll have no other option but to take your time."

Tharp located Stephanie Cash's car some thirty yards across the parking lot and flashed her high beams to let her know they were ready to roll.

Or slide, as the case may be.

Cash led the way to the exit and carefully edged her way out into traffic.

"Ya know," Tara said with a clenched jaw, "if I hadn't liberated a bunch of helpless children from a group of crazed sex traffickers earlier this week, I'd swear this is the most intense situation that I have been involved with in a really long time." She felt the trailer start to slide, pulling the back end of the SUV to the right. Her knuckles went pale as she used a corrective steering technique. "As it turns out," she finished her thought, "this is just a Sunday morning stroll along the beach for you guys."

Kinley laughed. "Stroll along the beach, eh? Sure, sure, sure... if it's 1944 and the beach we're strolling on is in Normandy."

Zeroing In

Cole Reese had been the manager at Northwest Winter Outdoor Equipment and Apparel for a little over seven years now. He had loaded and unloaded more snowmobile trailers than he cared to remember. But one thing he was fairly certain of was that he had never done so in the extreme conditions that he had just experienced while loading up the trailer for Devereaux and company.

Now back inside, he stood at the sink in the employee's lounge splashing warm water on his face, trying to alleviate the numbness permeating his cheeks and nose.

Carol Bixby, a saleswoman, approached him.

"Mr. Reese, you have a call on line 2. Somebody claiming to be from the FBI." Her voice had a ring of skepticism to it.

"FBI?"

"Yes, sir, that's what they said. Said it was urgent."

"Whatever," Reese grabbed a nearby hand towel and patted his face dry. "What line did you say?"

"Line 2," Carol Bixby repeated.

The store manager picked up the phone. "Yello, this is Cole Reese."

"Mr. Reese, my name is Agent Steve Barlow with the Federal

Bureau of Investigation. I'll try to make this quick so I don't take up too much of your time."

"Oh, well, thank you – what was it again? Agent Barlow? – for not taking up too much of my time." Reese looked at Carol and rolled his eyes.

"The reason for my call, Mr. Reese, is that we believe two men, Kinley Devereaux and Harper Rowe, wanted for questioning in the assassination of U.S. Secretary of Defense Paul Michaels, are in the immediate Minneapolis-St. Paul area. Furthermore, we have reason to believe that they will probably be looking to rent or buy snowmobiles from an establishment such as yours, sir."

Reese's heart jumped from his chest and into his throat.

"Anybody like that been in your—"

"They were here," Reese blurted.

"What? Are you sure?"

"Two men and a woman. They bought a bunch of snowmobile apparel and rented three snowmobiles. They were with another woman. She paid for it all with a government credit card."

"Where are you located again?"

"7040 Lakeland Avenue North. We're in suite 212."

"I'm going to send some agents over right away. How long ago were they there?"

"They left less than 15 minutes ago."

"Did they say where they were going?" asked Agent Barlow.

"No, but my saleswoman, Carol, she was helping them. She's right here. Do you want to talk to her?"

"That won't be necessary. When the agents get there, I am sure they will want to ask her some questions, so please be sure that anyone working at your store stays there till then. Understood?"

"Yes sir. I absolutely do."

Steve Barlow disconnected the call and hollered out to his

boss, Agent Todd Adams. "Found 'em! They were just at a sporting goods place over on Lakeland North. Manager said they were there buying winter clothes and rented three snowmobiles. He didn't know where they were headed."

"That's great work, Agent Barlow," Adams gave him an attaboy, then pulled out his cell phone and called Agent Tobias Kane, one of the agents with Jeb Crool and company.

"What do you have for me, boss?" Kane answered.

"We tracked them down. They just left that snow apparel place over on Lakeland North. Do you know the one I'm talking about?"

"I sure do. We're just a few blocks away from there."

"I'm going to call them back. Make sure that they have four sleds loaded up and ready as soon as possible. Once you get there, get on your way. Call me with any updates."

"10-4, boss." Kane disconnected the call.

In his government-issued black Ford Expedition, Kane was in the passenger's seat while his fellow agent, Jim Grimes, was behind the wheel. In the backseat sat a very anxious Laurie Chase and a very cold Big James Gray.

"They just left that place over on Lakeland North."

"Northwest Outdoor?"

"Yeah, they left outta there about 15 minutes ago."

Hearing this news, Chase slid forward and leaned in between the two front seats. "Is that where we're headed?"

"Yes, ma'am," Kane responded. "The boss is calling over there to have four snowmos ready for us when we arrive. They may have gotten a bit of a jump on us, but not by much."

Kane grabbed a radio from the Expedition's console. "T-Storm, this is Red Viper. Copy? Over."

Within a few seconds a man's voice crackled through the radio, "Copy, Red Viper. Do you have a new sitrep? Over."

"Roger that, T-Storm. Just got word that our targets were 10-20 at Northwest Outdoor about 15 minutes ago. We are heading there now. Over."

"Roger. We're right behind you. Over."

Tobias Kane replaced the radio and turned to address Laurie and Big James. "So, can the two of you possibly give me an abridged version of just what is going on here?"

Without hesitation, Laurie and Big James answered simultaneously, "No."

Because, realistically, there was no abridged version of what was going on.

King of the Bathroom Scuffles

Sam Bergman stood in front of the bus lockers trying to locate locker #52. There it was, five rows up and two lockers to the right. Taking a deep breath, he fished the key out of his pants pocket and carefully inserted it into the lock.

"Open sesame," he whispered with a smile.

The 12-inch square door opened to reveal a rectangular package wrapped and taped tightly in a brown paper bag. From his initial look, he guessed it to be a laptop computer. Pulling the package out, his hypothesis was confirmed. It was, indeed, a laptop. As inconspicuously as possible, Sam put the package under his arm, re-locked the door, and sauntered over to one of the Traveler's Grille bistro tables. Unbeknownst to him, the man sitting just a few feet away was just as interested in the contents as Sam was.

Bergman reached into his back pocket and removed the jackknife that he had carried with him almost every day since he had gotten it on his 9th birthday as a gift from his father. Opening the four-inch blade, he began gently cutting away at the tape and brown-bag wrapping. Once he was satisfied with the opening, he carefully pulled a Dell Chromebook free of its confines.

As soon as Agent Bergman opened the laptop and powered it up, he realized that his new co-worker, Agent Sarah Beck, would be much better suited to this job. So he wisely opted to slide the laptop back into its packaging and ordered a ride back to headquarters. The 17-minute wait was a bit long, but understandable given the current weather conditions. While he waited, he decided to fill Agent Beck in on his progress.

"Did you find something?" she said, skipping her standard greeting.

"I think so," Sam replied. "I don't know what, but it's something. A laptop."

"Really? Did you open it yet?"

"Just long enough to know that you're better suited for this particular task than I am. I won't lie to ya, Agent Beck. I am to computers what the Pope is to the missionary position."

Beck suppressed a laugh. "Are you headed back to HQ?"

"I am. Just waiting on a rider to come pick me up. What about you? Did you find anything else on Dr. Kwan's computer?"

"No, I've pretty much come up empty on things since you left. I am going to wrap it up here and head on back to headquarters myself."

"Sounds good," Sam agreed. "Be careful on the drive back. It's a real mess out there."

Sam considered using the bathroom before his ride arrived, but he also needed to make one more call to Sandy Wyrick. And Sam, being the gentleman that he was, did not think it proper to talk to a woman on the phone while taking a leak. Fortunately for him, his call to the boss went directly to voicemail.

"Hey, boss, Agent Sam Bergman here. That key did, in fact, open a bus locker. I was able to retrieve a laptop. Not going to bother to look through it. Just going to bring it back to HQ and let minds more capable than mine have at it. Currently waiting on a ride to come pick my tired bones up, and I will be there shortly."

Checking the status of his ride, Sam saw that he still had nine minutes until a red Subaru would be arriving to pick him up. Plenty of time to use the facilities before heading back to headquarters. Grabbing the package that lay before him, he headed to the men's room.

In spite of the crowd at the Hawthorne Transportation Center, the men's room was completely vacant. Sam first intended to set the laptop on the sink, but upon further inspection of the area he realized that the surface was way too wet for any sort of electronic device to come out unscathed. Rather than risk a key piece of evidence being ruined because he could not hold two things at one time, Sam opted to keep the laptop with him while he did his business at one of the porcelain urinals.

That seemed to be a wise decision when, just moments later, someone came walking into the restroom. Turning his head ever so slightly to look over his shoulder, he had just caught a glimpse of the person when he felt the cold steel muzzle of an AMT Hardballer press against the base of his skull.

"Hello, me lovely," came the man's irritatingly British accent. "I'm gonna need what it is you've got there."

Sam answered in an equally irritating, pseudo-Brit accent, "Well, chap, I'm gonna need you to be a bit more specific 'cause I've got more than one thing here."

"I'm gonna need the laptop, mate," the man, pressing the gun even harder into the back of Sam's neck.

"If I give it to you, will you let me go?"

"Sure. I don't wanna kill anyone. I've just been sent here to do a job. And that job is to retrieve what you've got in your left hand."

"Yeah, I can do that," Sam said, holding the laptop up with his left hand. The second he felt the Brit's hand clasp the package, Bergman dropped to the floor and pulled his gun from his hip holster. Laying on his back, he fired two shots into his assailant's groin. Planting both feet against the tile wall under the urinal, he kicked himself away and fired two more shots into his attacker's back. The man fell forward, smacking his forehead on the porcelain latrine and slumping to the floor. Cradling the evildoer's head in his hands, Bergman asked, "I don't suppose in your final dying breath you'd care to divulge who it was that sent you, would you?"

But before Sam even finished his question, the glazed look in the Brit's eyes told him he had passed from this world to the next.

"Ah, well, it was worth a shot."

Taking a moment to collect his breath, Sam took the laptop out of the dead man's hand. Knowing he had maybe a minute before the security team would come busting through the door, he patted the perpetrator's chest. "Normally, I'm not in favor of all this violence. But since I'm pretty sure you just caused me an additional five hours of paperwork...so be it."

He rifled through the dead man's pockets looking for identification. Neither side pocket of the fellow's pea coat produced anything.

Hearing the security team heading his way and knowing he had just a moment left before he would have a lot of explaining to do, he reached desperately into the coat's breast pocket.

Jackpot. He found a cell phone, wallet, and an ID badge. Time being short, he shoved them into his trench coat and headed for the door.

As soon as he stepped out into the hallway, Bergman saw four uniformed security guards coming down the corridor toward the men's room.

"In there, officers!" he screamed. "Oh, my heavens above, you've got to get in there now."

Sam knew that the bus station's security force had rarely – if ever – seen any sort of violent crime in this place, so they were bursting at the seams to get to the scene of this one. Screaming and flailing his arms, he screamed again, "Oh, the humanity!"

The obvious thing would have been for at least one of the officers to stop and detain him. But, no, not this crew.

Sam watched as all four officers sprinted past him and into the bathroom. Ducking his head down, he made his way to the heart of the transportation center.

Just as he did, his phone alerted him that his ride was ready and waiting outside.

CRASH COURSE

"How fast is she going? Like three miles an hour?" Harper was becoming impatient.

"Close," answered an even more impatient Taralyn, who was busy maneuvering through the wintry conditions. "Like – nine miles an hour."

"She's going to make us late. And if there's two things in this world you don't want to be late for, they're a breakfast buffet with Jethro Bodine...and this," Harper said.

Kinley turned to give Harper a peculiar look. "Seems I've heard that line somewhere before."

The inside joke was completely lost on Taralyn, who was in no mood for kidding around. "You'd think this woman was from Florida the way she drives. Miss Cash! Stop hitting your brakes!"

"I can't imagine that she'll go too much further. This road is practically undrivable now as it is."

As if on cue, Stephanie Cash's blinker came on. She slowly turned right into the snowed-covered parking lot of a Super Target. The lot was huge and empty and well-lit.

"Time to bundle up, kids. Looks like a cold one out there tonight," said Harper, having already donned his Eskimo gear back at the store.

Taralyn and Kinley grabbed their bags of winter apparel and suited up. Hats, scarves, gloves and parkas were buttoned all the way up to the neck. The three took one last moment to enjoy the warmth of the vehicle.

"Y'all ready for this?" Tharp asked.

"Ready as we'll ever be. Hopefully, everything will go somewhat according to plan, and we'll be back here in an hour and a half."

"Then let's get a move on. I'm pretty sure it isn't getting any warmer out there. Or lighter."

With that, the trio left the comfort of the SUV and were greeted immediately by a blast of harsh wintry wind. Kinley and Harper untied the canvas tarp covering the snowmobiles while Taralyn lowered the tailgate. She climbed up and began pulling the cover off the sleds.

Stephanie Cash had made her way over from her car. "I tried to get as close as I could, but the cemetery is still about 15 miles away," she said over the wind.

"No, this is great," Kinley replied, catching hold of the tarp as Taralyn handed it down to him. "Watch yourself," he said to Cash as he flapped the tarp, trying to shake off the snow.

"Let me give you a hand," Cash said, grabbing a corner. She and Devereaux shook the tarp a few more times, then folded it to a manageable size.

Taralyn mounted the first snowmobile and began instructing Harper.

"The key goes here. Turn it to 'on', then hit the start button. Once it's started, here's where you put it in reverse," she pointed. "Slowly back it off the trailer. When you're ready to go forward, slide it back to forward. These things have a four-stroke engine, so they'll shift automatically. Here's your throttle...and here's your brake.

"Another cool feature of this sled is the seat. It's not only heated to keep your buns warm, but it also has an automatic cut-off switch.

So, if for some reason you get thrown from this puppy, the cut-off switch will engage and kill the motor. That way, you don't have to go chasing the snowmobile down the road after it's dumped you on your ass."

"Well, now, that is convenient," Harper agreed. "If only human relations offered that same amenity: a kill switch for your emotions after you've been dumped on your ass."

Taralyn smiled and nodded. "Okay, relationships aside, do you think you've got this?"

"I guess we'll find out soon enough."

Harper turned to see Kinley deep in conversation with Stephanie Cash. "Hey, I hate to interrupt like this, but do you think one of you can grab the helmets out of the back of the SUV?" Rowe hollered. "If I'm getting ready to kill myself on one of these goofy contraptions, I want to make sure that I take every safety precaution first."

Kin hustled over to the SUV and retrieved the bag with the helmets.

"I'm going to get out of here while I still can," Cash shouted. "Good luck to all of you. Hopefully I'll see you back at Northwest in a couple of hours."

With that, the senator's aide ducked her head into the wind and snow and returned to her car.

Kinley legged it over to the hauling trailer and tossed their helmets up to Harper and Taralyn.

"Okay, Harp, let's see what ya got, buddy. Try not to break anything...most of all yourself."

After double-checking that all the straps were free and clear, Harper hopped onto the snowmobile and started it up. He twisted the throttle and revved the engine.

"Okay! This thing's pretty loud!"

Taralyn gave him a thumbs up. "Think you can back it off of here?"

"Only one way to find out, I guess," he hollered over the noise of the motor.

Harper moved the transmission lever into reverse, then looked to Tara for approval.

She nodded and yelled, "Now, just give it a little bit of gas. Be sure to go easy because the throttles on these things are very responsive."

Harp gingerly gave it some gas and felt the sled begin to move backwards. He navigated it perfectly to the rear of the trailer and began descending the ramp. A huge gust of wind suddenly blew snow right into his face, causing his hand to jerk on the throttle. The engine gunned, and the snowmobile shot down the ramp and across the snow-covered parking lot.

"Oh, crap," Kinley muttered as he took off running after his friend. "He really *is* going to kill himself."

Much to Harper's credit, he did not give in to the impulse to jump. Remembering the kill switch in the seat, he knew that bailing out would pretty much stop the sled in its tracks, leaving him rolling around in the cold snow. Bundled up like an Eskimo or not, the thought of spending the next hour riding a snowmobile in wet clothes seemed worse than jackknifing it into a snowbank. After weighing his options for a split second, he calmly released the throttle and let the sled come to a stop.

"Dude." Kinley came running up to him.

"Did you see that? I nailed the dismount!"

"Yeah, I saw it, ya knucklehead. She told you to take it easy on the throttle. Did you think she was joking?"

"Well...I didn't *think* she was joking. Turns out...she wasn't," Harper smiled. He patted the seat. "Hop on. I'll give you a ride."

"If it's all the same, I think I'll just walk the twenty yards back."

Rowe reached down and moved the lever forward, then eased the sled back toward the trailer where Taralyn was backing the second snowmobile down onto the parking lot.

Harper shut off the sled and quickly made his way onto the trailer to get the third snowmobile.

"You sure you wanna do that?" Taralyn yelled through the wind and snow.

"Absolutely. While I'm doing this, why don't you show Kin how to operate these things. Then let's get this show on the road." He checked the time on his wristwatch. "We've got about 23 minutes until we're supposed to be there. Stephanie said we're still about 15 miles away from the cemetery, so once we're running, we'll need to make up some time."

"Well, we are certainly on the right snowmobiles for that. These are the fastest sleds on the snow. Just make sure when you hit the gas that you're holding on," Tharp warned.

They each set to their specified tasks: Harper backed the third snowmobile off the hauling trailer while Taralyn gave Kinley the same crash course she had given to Harper.

Within minutes the three of them were sitting atop their rides. Kinley started his sled up and practiced riding around the parking lot for a quick minute before pulling up next to Harper and Taralyn.

"I think I have the hang of it, I guess," Devereaux said, killing the engine.

"Just one thing left to do then"—Harper stood up and dismounted—"and that is to properly arm ourselves."

"I'll grab the coms out of the front."

They trudged their way through the snow to the SUV.

Popping open the back hatch, Harper pulled out the suitcase of weapons that Rob Perry had furnished for them. Looking over the cache of guns that were inside, he spotted two 9mm Berettas that struck his fancy. He pulled them out and fished around the container until he found several full clips.

Taralyn claimed a pair of Heckler & Koch handguns. Upon

locating the corresponding clips, she dropped one into each pocket of her white parka. Finding two daggers to her liking, one a six-inch and the other a nine-inch, she tucked them into her interior pockets. "Sure hope we don't need to use any of this stuff," she muttered.

"That would be nice," Harper agreed. "Still, better to have 'em and not need 'em—"

"Then to need them and not have them," Devereaux finished the sentence as he came around to the back of the vehicle. He handed coms to Taralyn and Harp.

"Do these things have a volume control?" Tara asked. "Probably going to need to turn them all the way up if we're going to have a chance at hearing each other over the snowmobile engines."

"I already adjusted them. Still, we'll probably need to yell just the same."

Tharp and Rowe inserted their coms while Kinley helped himself to several weapons from the suitcase.

"Gotta hand it to your buddy Rob for having the foresight to furnish us with these babies."

"By now, he's relatively familiar with our antics."

Devereaux closed the suitcase. "We good?"

"Yeah, we good."

With that, Harper slammed the hatch shut.

The trio checked and secured the weapons on their persons, made sure their coats were zipped, buttoned, fastened, and tucked, then hustled back to their respective snowmobiles.

Harper stopped suddenly. "Oh, good grief." He spun around and high-stepped it back to the SUV.

"Hey!" Taralyn yelled, watching him open the back door of the vehicle. "What are you doing?"

"I'd hate to get all the way to the ransom drop"—Harper reached into the back seat, removing the briefcase that Stephanie Cash had given them and waving it in the air— "without the ransom!"

"Oh...yeah." Kinley gave him a gloved thumbs up.

Harper brought the briefcase to Taralyn's snowmobile and used his belt to strap it to the seat behind her.

"We're down to twenty-two minutes," Devereaux noted. "I'd like to think that if we're a couple minutes late to this party, these boar's nuts won't put a bullet into the back of the senator's daughter's head. But ya never know the mental makeup of people in situations like these. We should probably not give them a reason."

"No more putting off the inevitable," Harper said, mounting his ride and affixing his goggles. He switched on the headlights, fired up the engine, then slowly accelerated through the parking lot and onto the snow-packed road. Kinley and Taralyn followed closely behind, all of them hoping for the best but on high alert for the worst.

CONFIRMATION

Jeb Crool was true to his word.

He let Big James Gray buy whatever he needed to stay warm on the upcoming snowmobile ride: a furry Yukon Trapper hat over a ski mask, a black wool scarf, an insulated parka, thermal-lined gloves, and thermal compression pants and shirt.

Laurie Chase grabbed a similar outfit to protect herself from the bone-chilling temperatures.

Adorned with her new threads, Chase was pacing back and forth like a caged animal.

"Look, Laurs, it takes time to get four of these things loaded up," Big James said, looking like he was auditioning for a role in *Ice Road Truckers*.

"How would you know how long it takes? You've never even been in the snow before, much less loaded up a snowmobile."

"Yeah, but I've loaded up cars before. I have to think that this is the same kind of deal. Ya pull 'em up on there, tie 'em down, lock 'em in place, cover 'em up, and there ya go. Just try to stay calm. I'm sure it won't be long now."

"Big James?"

"Yes?"

"Do not *ever* tell me to calm down again. Not just me. Any

woman. We do not like it, and, if anything, it makes us even more irritated than we already were."

"I don't really care about all that. If you're gonna get steamed, you're gonna get steamed. It's still not going to stop me from trying to curtail the tension that's in the room. Look, I know you're tense. We're all tense. And, yeah, I know Kinley is your boyfriend, and you care about him very much. But Harper's been one of my best and most reliable friends for years. Believe me, I'm champing at the bit right now to get going, but I'm holding my emotions inside so that I don't make this situation any more frenetic than it needs to be."

Laurie stood still. "How long have they been back there anyway?"

Special Agents Jeb Crool and David Baldwin of the NSA, and Agents Tobias Kane, Cam Hughes, and Alexis Conley from the FBI had been out back helping the store personnel load up the four snowmobiles so the octet could arrive at the cemetery in time to stop the impending bloodbath.

Agent Jim Grimes, the fourth FBI agent, was questioning the store manager and the saleswoman.

"You said the three of them bought several thousand dollars' worth of accessories and clothing, as well as snowmobile rentals, is that correct?"

"Yes," answered Bixby.

"And how did they pay for it all?"

Cole Reese spoke up. "Oh, the three of them didn't pay for any of it. There was a fourth woman with them that paid for it all with a government credit card. I think she was from Senator Cobb-Schmidt's office, wasn't she, Carol?"

"Yes, she was. Kind of an impatient woman, too."

"Really? Senator Cobb-Schmidt's office," Grimes remarked as he wrote something down in his notebook. "Hey, do you mind if I take a look at that receipt?"

"Yes, sir. Absolutely," answered Reese. "Carol, do you mind

going to—" Carol was already headed to the cash register.

"The woman that was here from the senator's office, did she buy anything for herself? Or were all of her purchases just for the other three people that she was with?"

"I'm not sure. Carol would be the one to ask about that. She was the one waiting on them."

Carol returned with the receipt and handed it to Agent Grimes. He studied it closely, then scrolled down to the signature.

Sure enough, Stephanie Marie Cash had signed for the United States Government card issued to Minnesota Senator Brenda Cobb-Schmidt.

Jim Grimes quickly pulled out his cell phone and called his boss, Agent Todd Adams.

"Whaddaya got for me, Jimmy?"

"Boss, it looks like what they've been saying about Senator Cobb-Schmidt being involved in all this is true. One of her aides – someone named Stephanie Cash – was here at Northwest Outdoor with Rowe and Devereaux. She used the senator's government credit card to rent three snowmobiles and purchase $3,000 worth of winter gear. According to the store's employees, none of it was for her or the senator."

"You've got to be kidding me."

"Afraid not, sir. I'm looking at the receipt with my own eyes."

Before either of the men could comment any further, Agent Hughes returned from the back of the store. Her face was red from the wind and her clothes were covered in snow.

"Let's wrap it up, people. We're out of here in two minutes."

"Okay, boss, looks like we're on our way."

"Be careful, Jimmy," Adams advised. "Lines are getting really blurred here."

"I'll be sure to follow protocol every step of the way, sir. As soon as anything reportable happens, I'll be on the horn to ya."

AND THE DEAD MAN IS…?

Sam yanked open the passenger's side door and toppled into the back seat.

"You okay?" the driver asked.

"Super. Really good. Thank you for coming out on a night like this, ma'am. I greatly appreciate it."

"You're going to the CTU building downtown?"

"Yes. That's where I'm headed." Bergman straightened himself up and looked out the window to see if he was being followed. The coast appeared to be clear. "Whenever you're ready, let's go."

As the driver pulled out into the night, Sam placed the laptop on the seat next to him and fished his assailant's ID out of his pocket. Using the light from his cell phone, he examined the badge. Once his eyes were able to focus, Sam did a double take.

"What in tarnation is going on here?" The dead man's identification read: Edward Garrett – United States Secret Service. "Aw, man, I shoulda stayed in homicide."

"You sure you're okay?" the driver repeated. "You seemed a little shaken back there."

"Mind if I ask you what your name is, ma'am?"

"Morena. It's Brazilian."

"It's nice to meet you, Morena. My name is Sam. Sam Bergman."

He leaned forward in his seat. "I am a federal agent, and what I am getting ready to tell you is super, super, important."

"Okay," Morena answered with a growing look of concern.

"I don't want to alarm you or distract you from your driving, but here's the thing: I have to make a very important call to my boss. And in the course of this conversation there will be highly, *highly* classified information being exchanged. Now, I could tell you not to listen to what I'm saying, but let's be honest, all that's gonna do is make you want to listen even more. So, I'm not going to waste your time and mine by doing that. Instead, I'll just tell you this: Should any of the information discussed in my upcoming conversation find its way, in any capacity, to anyone, anywhere...it won't take much for me to figure out where it came from. Do you understand what I'm telling you here?"

"Yes," she said meekly.

"I'm sorry. I didn't quite catch that."

"Yes," she repeated, this time more vociferously.

"That's what I needed to hear," Sam smiled. "Now, look, I could not be more sorry for having to put you in a situation like this, but this is a time-sensitive matter. And if I had any other choice, well, you can bet your pretty brown eyes that I'd be takin' it. So, I will promise you this, ma'am: You get me to where I need to go safely, and I'll give you a tip that'll net you more tonight than you'd probably make in an entire week. Then I'll go my way, you can go yours, and you'll forget all about any of this ever happening. Sound like a deal you can live with?"

"I swear to you, Sam, on my mother's grave. You have my word."

Bergman leaned back in his seat, got comfortable, and prepared to make what was certain to be one of the most difficult calls of his life.

Vipers

They called themselves Vipers. It was nothing official, of course. It was not like they had letterhead with 'Vipers' written across the top or a checking account "Doing Business as Vipers." It was just a name that they had adopted somewhere along the way.

The mercenary group totaled twelve in all, but it was rare that all twelve members would be used on a single mission. The type of job dictated who would be utilized on any given assignment. But since tonight's job was offering $5 million, the biggest payday the troop had ever encountered, it was all hands on deck.

With each member netting a little over $400,000, some of them had already decided that, with tonight's haul, this would be it for them. Time to stop fishing and cut bait. Goodbye, mercenary life – hello, retirement.

They were now in place, all twelve of them.

Harrison Roberts, the group's pilot, was in his chopper about a mile away, waiting to pick everyone up and fly them to safety once the operation was over.

Chris Kojak, Calvin Walters, and Russell Johnson were with McCleary and the girl at the rendezvous point. The rendezvous point was positioned roughly two hundred yards in from the Sunset Memorial Park entrance, on the main drive of the cemetery; 80 feet to the front and left of the utility shed. The same utility shed that they had been using as a base of operations for the ransom drop.

Kiyo Potts and Jay Hammers were set up behind the utility shed: Kiyo behind the left rear corner and Jay at the front right corner.

Joe Carney, the single sniper on McCleary's squad, was perched in a tree at a 45-degree angle to the left of the rendezvous point.

Lijuan Cho and Deshawn Black, squad members nine and ten, had found cover behind two very wide, very tall grave markers on either side of the main drive, halfway between the ransom drop spot and the cemetery entrance.

The final two Vipers, Melissa Ballweg and Xavier Montgomery, awaited their guests at the cemetery's main entrance gate. Each Viper was equipped with Retevis RT1 high-powered two-way radios.

"Everyone in place and ready?" McCleary asked. "Company's a-comin'."

"You see anything from your tree, Carney?" Lijuan Cho asked.

"Don't see anything, don't hear anything. Just colder than a witch's tit up here."

"Stay warm, everybody. Won't be long now and we'll be able to go to the tropics or the Caribbean or the Virgin Islands or wherever it is you want to go," Kenton said. "Stay alert and safeties off."

Dashing Through the Snow

Kin, Harp, and Taralyn rode three-across on the unplowed road, driving through the snow and wind toward the ransom drop. Their coms had been quiet so far – driving in the falling darkness took a lot of concentration with no depth perception, no tracks to follow, and only the silhouetted tree line to mark the street.

"Can you two hear me?" Devereaux finally asked, noting that they were flying along at a frigidly paced 72 mph.

"I hear ya just fine, chief," Harper affirmed.

"I read you five by five," Taralyn responded.

"Look, when we start getting close, let's pull over and shut everything down. I'm going to trek on foot until I get in sight of the cemetery. I've got my scope, so I'm going to try to see what we might be dealing with."

"You sure you're going to feel up to hiking through this stuff with that bullet wound in your hip?"

"That pain medication you gave me is working pretty good. It'll be okay."

"I can barely see anything out here," Taralyn struggled to say against the elements. "How are you going to know when we're getting close? Are we even going to have enough time to do all that?"

"Stephanie Cash said we were about fifteen miles from the cemetery when we were back at the store parking lot. According to my odometer, we've gone just over thirteen miles. I'd say we're pretty close. We've made good time. We're going to take the time we need to do the recon...whether we have it or not."

"Think we should slow down now?" asked Harp. "Quiet the engines a bit?"

"10-4 to that, partner. Let's slow it down."

Taralyn and Kinley slowly powered down. But Harper, being a novice, hit the brakes, causing the front of his ride to dig into the snow then pop back up again, shifting the weight and throwing him off balance. Attempting to hang on, Harper's glove snagged the end of the throttle, gunning the engine. The sled careened forward wildly, throwing Harper into the snow. The kill switch engaged, stopping the snowmobile. Harper's body, on the other hand, skidded wildly across the white surface.

Devereaux eased his snowmobile up to Rowe's snow-covered body.

Harper rolled over onto his back and dusted off his face. His goggles had been knocked sideways and his scarf had come unwound.

Kinley looked down at him. "You doin' alright, Festus?"

"Yeah. Golden..."

"...like freshly peed-on snow."

Kin reached down and pulled his friend back to his feet.

"What happened here?" Taralyn asked, idling over to the duo.

"Not exactly sure," Rowe shook his head. "Something, though. Definitely something."

"We can probably chalk it up to operator error, have a good laugh about it, and move on," Dev commented.

"I would laugh, but I think my teeth are frozen to my lips."

Kinley and Taralyn turned their engines off, reluctant to leave their heated seats. The frigid temps had made their bodies so stiff, it felt like they were suffering from some sort of pre-death *rigor mortis*. Kinley groaned aloud in discomfort.

"Your bullet wound acting up?"

"No, not really. I think the bullet wound is pretty-well numbed over from the medicine and the cold. I just can't *move*." He looked over at Taralyn to see if she was equally frozen stiff.

Indeed, she was.

"Oh, come on, people," Harper protested. "You're moving around like a couple of geriatric patients. We'll be lucky to make that ransom drop by Valentine's Day at this rate."

"I swear, if this seat wasn't heated, my butt would be frozen to it," Tara said, slowly lifting herself to a standing position.

"Alright, alright," Harper said. "I'm up and around. Just give me your scope and I'll go scout the scene. You two hang back and keep each other warm."

Too cold to protest, Devereaux and Tharp nodded in agreement.

Kinley retrieved the scope from his pocket and handed it over to Harper. "You remember how it works?"

"Yes, I do," Harper answered, looking it over before tucking it carefully into his front pocket. "I'll stay in touch." Pulling his goggles down and his scarf up, he trudged off into the still-falling snow.

Taralyn dragged her frozen self over to Devereaux and climbed up behind him on his sled.

"I hope you don't mind," she said, wrapping her shivering arms and legs around him.

"I won't tell if you don't." Devereaux re-started the engine and cranked the heat and blowers, doing his best to keep Taralyn warm. "Better hurry, Harp," he said into the com. "If Tara and I freeze to death like this, Laurie's gonna be pissed."

"Oh? You don't think she'd understand?" came Rowe's labored response. After only 200 yards, his lungs were already burning.

"What do you think?"

"Aww, I think she'd go all flatliners on you, boss. She'd go dead just long enough to find you in the afterlife and take a ball-peen hammer to each one of your ten little piggies."

"Yeah. That sounds about right."

"Question is," Harper panted heavily, "what kind of torture rack would she design for me for *letting* you freeze to death in the arms of another woman?"

A TOUGH CALL

"You did *what*?" Sandy Wyrick could not believe her ears.

"I had to, boss," Bergman protested. "I think the answers to what we've been looking into the last couple of days may very well be on this computer. I couldn't take a chance on those rent-a-cops getting their grubby mitts on it. Who knows if – or when – we would have ever gotten it back. I had to get it outta there, I'm tellin' ya."

"You shot and killed a man—"

"A man who was going to shoot and kill *me*," Sam interjected.

"And you just left him there?"

"Boss, whatever is on this computer is big. Big enough to kill for. Now, if you want me to go back and—"

"No, Sam," Wyrick sighed. "It's a little late to go back now. I'll make some calls and get this worked out. Did you think to grab the dead guy's ID?"

"Well, um, yeah...I did," Agent Bergman stammered.

"Are you sure? Your answer seems a bit less than convincing there, Marlowe."

"Well...I mean...that was gonna be what I was going to talk to you about next."

"Okay," Wyrick said with a fleck of impatience.

"I grabbed the guy's wallet, phone, and ID."

"And?"

"And according to his ID, his name is Edward Garrett, and he's a Secret Service agent." Sam saw Morena's eyes widen in the car's rear-view mirror.

"Oh, for God's sake," Wyrick muttered. "Why?"

"Why?"

"Why is a member of the Secret Service trying to kill you over a computer that belongs to a missing astrophysicist that worked with a murdered astrophysics engineer? A murdered astrophysics engineer who was, apparently, working on one of the most classified projects known – or maybe I should say *unknown* – to mankind for the last three years? Why?"

"This is what I'm telling you, boss. We've got more questions than answers. But this computer I've got here, it may very well hold the key to all of it. That's why I had to bolt from that crime scene. I just couldn't take a chance."

Wyrick took a few deep breaths. "You did the right thing, agent. But I kid you not, if you *ever* do that again, I will bury you in the deepest basement office this government has to offer. For now, get back here and let's try to figure out what we've gotten ourselves into."

"10-4, boss."

Sam disconnected the call and let out a breath the size of the Grand Canyon. Catching his driver's eye in the rear-view mirror, he shook his head. "I feel bad for you, Morena. I'm sure that I'm, hands-down, the most interesting passenger you've ever had in your life, and you can't even tell anyone."

"It's okay, Sam. This will be one of those fun little secrets that I take to my grave. And who knows, maybe I'll give you a ride again sometime and you can let me know how it all worked out."

"That's a deal."

Bergman felt Edward Garrett's phone vibrate. Pulling it out of his coat pocket, he realized that several calls from the same number had come in within the last few minutes. No name was displayed, but it was not a stretch to assume the caller had something to do with the attempt on his life at the bus station. For a fleeting moment, Sam thought about calling the number back to see who picked up but dismissed the idea as desperate and reckless. Besides, he was sure that he would be talking face-to-face with the mystery caller soon enough.

Cold Realization

Two things were for certain: the air was deathly cold, and the coms were highly sensitive. Kinley and Tara could hear Harper's every crunchy step and every chilly breath during the course of his frigid journey. It was almost rhythmical.

Crunch, crunch, breath.

Crunch, crunch, breath.

Crunch, crunch, breath.

Suddenly, the crunching stopped.

Kin and Tara waited for it to resume, but it did not.

"Hey, you okay, kid?" Devereaux checked.

"Yeah, why?"

"It sounded like you stopped moving."

"That's because I did stop moving."

"Do you see something?"

"Maybe."

"What do you think you *maybe* see?"

"I'm up to a spot where there are no trees on the right side of the road, and it opens up into a big clearing. Out past that, *maybe* I see the cemetery, but it's snowing so hard, it's hard to tell. I'm tucked inside the last line of trees, using your scope to see if I can get any thermal readings."

The wind was kicking up again, sometimes nearly blowing Kinley and Taralyn off the snowmobile. They hung on tightly together, trying to keep warm. Harper could hear their teeth chattering.

"Ah, Sweet Maria," he finally said. "I've got something."

"What are you seeing?"

"The heat signatures are weak, but here's what it looks like: two waiting for us at the entrance. From there – according to your scope readings – about 150 meters or so down from them, I'm seeing two more sentries posted." Harper paused. "Kinley, is there any way to switch this scope from metric to standard?"

"No, the scope was made in Europe. It only has metric readings."

"Very good. Then about 175 meters down from them, I'm seeing a cluster of people. Maybe three or four; maybe more. They're standing too close for me to differentiate."

"That sounds like an awfully big crew for just a simple ransom drop," Taralyn shivered.

"Yeah, it does," Kinley agreed.

"Well, if you think that sounds like a lot, I wasn't even finished yet. There are two more posted about thirty meters away to the right of the group, and off to the left, it looks like another one in some sort of elevated position. Maybe up in a tree, I guess."

"You mean, like a sniper?" Devereaux inquired.

"I can't be certain, but...yeah."

"Why would they need a sniper for a ransom drop?" Tharp wondered out loud.

"Why would they need a sniper? Why would they need that many people at all?" Harper asked. "Just a low-ball estimate has me seeing eight. Maybe up to eleven."

"I don't know. My brain is so cold, I can't even think straight," Kinley grumbled. "Head back this way, Harp. We'll figure out something. We always do."

"I'm on my way," Rowe remarked. Seconds later, the rhythm resumed.

Crunch, crunch, breath.

Crunch, crunch, breath.

Crunch, crunch, breath.

The Trouble with Aimee

Burner phones were mostly used by the criminal element to hide communication records such as phone calls and text messages. Senator Brenda Cobb-Schmidt was not part of the criminal element and therefore had never had occasion to employ such a device.

Until a week and a half ago.

A week and a half ago, Brenda found herself needing to travel outside the parameters of the law. She required the services of Kenton McCleary, a professional mercenary, to help with a series of illegal activities. Wanting no record of her communication, she bought her first burner phone to use for contacting McCleary.

Two days later, she garnered the aid of Edward Garrett, a former Secret Service member that often hired himself out to politicians to help them with various off-the-books jobs. Wanting no record of her communication with him either, she bought her second burner phone.

For the past 30 minutes straight, the senator had been trying unsuccessfully to reach Garrett. She didn't bother to leave a message. She needed to *talk* to him.

"Pick up your stupid phone, Garrett!" the senator shouted in frustration. *Calm down, Brenda*, she told herself. *Everything is going to be fine. Just keep it together, and everything will be just fine.*

She paced back and forth, checking her phone every few

seconds to see if Garrett had called and she had somehow missed it.

She even checked her text messages on the outside chance that he had, for some inexplicable reason, sent her a text.

But no.

A brief smile crossed her face as she realized that she was mimicking the very same actions that she had seen Aimee do time and again while awaiting a call from her most recent crush.

The senator's ringing phone jolted her into the present. She breathed a sigh of relief as she picked up.

"Well, it's about time, Edward."

Her relief was short-lived as she realized the call was coming from Kenton McCleary's burner phone instead, the one tucked in her purse on the floor next to her.

She took a quick look at the clock: 6:36 p.m.

"Kenton," she answered, "is it finished already?"

"I wish, Senator. I'm freezing my ass off out here," Kenton answered loudly. "I was calling because 6:30 has come and gone with no sign of them. Have you heard anything?"

"What? Are you kidding me? Yes, I've heard something, Mr. McCleary. I've heard it's snowing like a mother outside, and it's windy enough to blow the chrome off a trailer hitch."

"It's just that it's 6:36, and—"

"And nothing. It's six minutes. If it was sunny and not a cloud in the sky, I still wouldn't consider them late."

"Well, when *would* you consider them late?"

"If they haven't shown in an hour, call me back. Until then, stay warm and stay off the phone."

Garrett was not returning her calls. McCleary was freaking out because people were six minutes late in a snowstorm.

She could not help but feel like things were starting to come unraveled.

She was right.

Closing the Gap

Two black Ford Explorers, pulling trailers with two snowmobiles each, were the only traffic on the road.

Tobias Kane drove the first SUV, with Tim Grimes riding shotgun and Big James and Laurie Chase holding down the back seat.

"I'm not sure how much longer I'm going to be able to keep going in this mess," Agent Kane muttered into his headset. He was linked up with Alexis Conley, Cam Hughes, and Tim Grimes in the second SUV with Special Agent Jeb Crool. "We'd make better time on the snowmobiles. I can barely maintain ten miles per hour pulling these things. I'm sliding all over the place."

"You and me both," Alexis, the second driver, replied. "You okay with us pulling off and gettin' on these snowhogs, Special Agent Crool?"

"I've been kinda thinking that for the last mile or two, so, yeah," Jeb answered from the back seat.

"Well, if you want us to do something, say something. I mean, this is your goose chase you got us on. You're the one calling the shots."

"Well...nobody likes a backseat driver. And while this is my goose chase, you're the one driving. I'll make the goose chase decisions; you make the driving decisions. It's a little thing called 'knowing your role,' Agent Conley. I'm sure they taught that to you in the academy. Whether or not you learned it – hmmm – now that remains to be seen."

David Baldwin tried his best to hide a smile. Having been on the receiving end of several similar Jeb Crool tongue lashings, he knew it was just Jeb being Jeb, using his natural, God-given talent of being a complete prick to its exhaustive state. Nothing personal, Agent Conley.

Conley did her best to ignore Crool's comment as she spoke into her headset. "Let's do it then, Grimes. Should be a shopping center up here on the right. Pull in there."

"Should be?" Grimes double checked.

"To be straight, I've been concentrating so much on your taillights, I'm not a hundred percent sure which block we're on."

"Hey! Hey! On the right." Laurie Chase poked Agent Kane's shoulder. "In that parking lot over there. "Do you see it? That truck with the trailer on it? That's gotta be them, right?"

"Yeah, I see it," Kane affirmed. "Timmy, pull into there," he instructed his partner. "This Super Target lot here."

"We're pulling in here, Alex," Grimes said into the com.

"Yeah, I see that, genius. Why here?"

"That truck in the parking lot. Yeah, those are definitely snowmobile tracks I'm seeing. That's gotta be their truck, and this is where they took off from." He eased to a stop next to the abandoned SUV. Alexis followed suit

Everyone but Big James piled out into the snow.

"Come on, big boy. Let's go. We need all hands on deck here," Laurie commanded.

"I'm a big fat guy that knows nothing about these things. There's seven of you and only so much room out there to unload the snowmobiles. I would just be in the way."

"Okay," she said. "I'll come get you when it's time to move out. Get all the warmth you can. You're going to need it."

FINAL DECISION

When Harper returned, he found Kinley and Taralyn still huddled together on Kinley's snowmobile. Too exhausted to make a smart remark, he dropped to his knees and let the snowmobile's exhaust blow on his face.

"Harper. Are you crazy? You're going to kill yourself like that," Tara yelled.

"Yeah, but if he doesn't," Kinley pointed out, "it's a pretty smart way to warm up in a hurry. Kinda thinking about doing that myself."

Harper pulled his head back and started coughing violently. "Woo. I can feel my face again," he sputtered.

"All right. Catch your breath there, Captain CO-2. We need to figure out what our approach is going to be for this ransom drop."

"Yeah, yeah. Hang on a second." Harper stood up and climbed onto Kinley's snowmobile, squeezing in just behind Taralyn. Under normal circumstances, she would have resisted having her personal space compromised. But these weren't normal circumstances.

"So, what's everybody thinking?" Harper asked.

"I'm thinking that for all the clothes I have on, I'm going into this ransom drop feeling pretty naked. We are woefully unprepared for this."

"It's supposed to be a simple ransom drop. We give them the

money; they give us the girl. But I ask you this: Why bring so many people to a simple exchange?"

"Maybe because this is such a huge payoff," Tharp suggested. "How much money do we have in that bag? Five million bucks?"

"Yeah, I think that's what we're carrying."

"A big payday like that, I'd be pulling out all the stops to make sure that everything goes right. If that means bringing the starting lineup of the all-mercenary softball team, then that's what I'd be doing."

"The lady makes a decent point. Maybe we're getting all worked up over nothing."

"Maybe," Harper growled, "or maybe we're getting ready to walk right into a great big double-cross."

"Do you think they would be dumb enough to double-cross the woman who is getting ready to be the next president? I mean, why would they do that? They're going to get their money. Why would they want to make an enemy out of such a powerful person?"

"I just said we might be getting ready to walk into a double-cross. I didn't say that it was by them, necessarily."

"Then what are you saying...necessarily?" Tara asked.

"Oh, you better not be saying that you think the senator is dirty in all this."

"Dude. I have been saying that since about ten seconds after we met the woman," Harper said. "Regardless, something's just not sitting right with me. I mean, why is she using *us* for this? A woman with her kind of stroke – she could've gotten just about anybody."

"True. And let's not forget, she didn't contact *us*. She contacted Kelly Campbell, and Kelly contacted us, and now that we're here—"

"Yeah, now that we're here, all of a sudden Kelly's nowhere to be found."

"And let's not forget what Laurie said, or at least was getting ready to say."

"Believe me, I haven't forgotten. I wish there had been time to find a charger for your phone so we could have called her back, or she could have called us back. We have just been so under the gun since we've gotten here."

"Ya know, I don't want to rehash the past, but let's not forget that I was the one who said that this was a bad idea from the beginning."

"Fine. Go ahead and say it, Harper."

"Oh, you know I will." Harper paused for dramatic effect, although not as long as usual because, after all, it was incredibly cold. "I hate it when I'm right."

"Come on. You guys are scaring me," Tharp said. "Do you really think that's what's going on here?"

"It's a thought, and if we're walking into something dangerous, we need to be prepared."

"It's like they say, 'Hope for the best; prepare for the worst.' So, that's what we're doing here."

"You know, it's still not too late to just walk away from the whole thing. We can take the five million for ourselves and just disappear," Harper suggested. "Be on a plane tonight and starting new lives in the morning."

The three of them sat huddled together in the dark on top of a snowmobile in the blinding snow and the driving wind. For a few brief seconds, Harper's idea was very tempting.

"I don't know, kid," Devereaux broke the silence. "When has it ever been our style to just walk away from something? And I don't know about you, but if I were to find out that the senator's kid ended up dead because of our inaction, I'd have a pretty hard time sleeping that one off. Plus, if we ever hope to get ourselves and Laurie off the most wanted list, this is pretty much our only shot."

"What do you think, Tara?" Harper asked.

Tharp hesitated a moment. "That thing about walking away not being your style? Well, if I've learned one thing in my life, it's that style can get you killed. Nevertheless, I'm with Kinley. If our inaction ended up costing that girl her life, I'm afraid that's a pill I would never be able to swallow. So...my vote is to go get the kid."

Harper squeezed the two of them tightly. "I love you guys. Let's go get this done. We'll stay on high alert and have each other's backs as much as we can. Check your weapons and make sure they're ready to fire."

Still clutching Kinley and Taralyn tightly, he bowed his head and prayed. "Lord God, it seems as if we are getting ready to walk into the valley of the shadow of death, so please help us to fear no evil...or anything else, for that matter. Help us to watch each other's backs, and if it comes down to it, help our aim to be true and our bullets effective. Watch over us, protect us, and if this should be our final hour, remember us in our time of passing. Thank you for this chance to do some good, and thank you for these two amazing people by my side. I wouldn't be doing this with anyone else. In Jesus' name, amen."

Having ended his prayer, Harper stood up. "Let's go get this girl and get our freedom back."

Crap or Conspiracy

"Is that it?" Sarah Beck asked. "Is that the laptop from the bus station?" She had been pacing the lobby, anxious for Agent Bergman to finally walk through the front doors of CTU headquarters.

"The very one. Where do you want it?"

"Conference room. The boss is already in there with Sawyers."

Bergman followed his fellow agent to the conference room. Once they were inside, Beck took possession of the computer, set it on the conference room table, opened it up, and began to work her magic.

Before Sam could sit down, Sandy Wyrick approached him. "We'll let Sarah handle this. You and I are going to my office to have a talk."

"About what?"

Wyrick ushered Sam into the hallway. With her face uncomfortably close to Sam's, she whispered, "For one thing, your really troublesome bathroom habits. No one here – and I mean *no one* – has any knowledge of what happened in that bathroom. Let's keep it that way."

Taking him by the arm, she ushered him into her office. "You made this mess. And now you're going to help me clean it up."

"Sit," she instructed, walking around to her desk.

"Look, boss, I know I screwed up, but it's all—"

"Sam. I know you screwed up. You know you screwed up, but what's done is done. I've made some calls, and, so far, they still don't know who the dead man is. Grabbing his I.D. was smart. I also happen to know that your former homicide squad over at the 4-5 are the ones catching the case. In a little while you'll be placing a call to see what you can find out about the progress of their investigation."

There was a knock on Wyrick's office door.

"Come in."

The door swung open, and in walked a beautiful redhead. Sam courteously stood to his feet.

"It's okay, Marlowe. You can sit back down. This is Hannah McDowell. She's an electronics forensic specialist. She's going to take that phone you confiscated earlier tonight and find out everything it can tell us about...its owner."

"Okay, that's great," Sam smiled. He started patting himself down, trying to feel in which coat pocket he had put the phone. "Yeah, here we go." He handed it to the Irish woman, whose green blouse was the same color as her eyes.

"How long do you think before you might have something for us?"

McDowell looked at the phone, swiped the screen a few times, tapped it once or twice before answering. "An hour, maybe two. There's some security on here, but nothing I can't crack. I'll call you."

"Sounds good."

Wyrick watched Bergman watch McDowell leave the office.

"When you get your eyes back in your head and your tongue off my floor, I'm going to need you to walk me through the events that led up to what happened at the bus station."

"Right." Sam nervously loosened his necktie and unbuttoned

the top button of his shirt. He sat down, crossed his leg over his knee and got good and comfortable. "Well, I ain't gonna lie to you, boss, this is one wild story."

"I appreciate the fact that you're not going to lie to me, agent. While you're at it, be sure not to leave anything out, either."

Starting at the beginning, Sam described how he and Agent Beck had questioned Mr. Kwan about his wife's disappearance and how this led them to Rae Yun Kwan's home computer. He moved on to how the discovery of the bus locker key hidden under Dr. Kwan's chair led him to the Hawthorne Transportation Center, which is where he must have picked up a tail – Edward Garrett, in particular.

Just when Sam was getting to the meat of his story, a loud knock sounded on Wyrick's door. Before she could say "Come in," Sarah Beck burst into her office, laptop in hand.

"Sandy, you've got to see this. It's – it's potentially something big."

"How big?"

"The biggest. What I have found – it looks like it links Senator Brenda Cobb-Schmidt to all of this. The car bomb that killed Erica Bradley. The disappearance of Rae Yun Kwan. The Space Frequency project. All of it."

"Show me," Wyrick said, clearing a spot on her desk for the laptop.

"Rae Yun Kwan put together a file with names, dates, blueprints, payments, dossiers, you name it. She documents that Erica Bradley told her at one point that the person in charge of the whole operation was Senator Brenda Cobb-Schmidt. Later in the report she even says that Bradley was suspicious of the senator and fearful that the team might be in danger after the project was over."

"Does she say why Bradley thought that?"

"Not specifically. Whether it was because Bradley didn't know or if Bradley just didn't tell her, that part's unclear. What Rae Yun

Kwan made crystal clear was that if something were to ever happen to her or any member of the team, the investigation should start with Senator Cobb-Schmidt."

Beck pulled up the file for her boss to read.

It took Wyrick barely five minutes to get the jist of what Kwan had written.

"Assemble the team in the conference room now. We may have a lot of incriminating evidence here, but we need to find ways to verify it, and fast. If we can prove that at least some of this is accurate, it will probably be safe to assume that the whole thing is legit."

"What if it is?" Sam asked. "What are we looking at here?"

"I have given only a cursory glance to a tiny portion of this, so I can't claim even the vaguest idea of what the fallout may be. But I do know this: We have a lot of work to do. In the next few hours, I want us to find out if we have a big pile of steaming crap...or the biggest political conspiracy of this century."

The Arrival

Easing up on their collective throttles as they approached the cemetery entrance, the trio could see that Harper's recon report had been accurate. Two Vipers were waiting for them just outside the gate.

Melissa Ballweg motioned for them to kill their engines.

Kinley and Taralyn turned their keys off; Harper lifted his butt enough for the kill switch to engage, then sat back down.

Ballweg and her partner, Xavier Montgomery, trained their weapons on the three.

"You're late," Ballweg indicated.

"I was not aware we were being timed," Harper came back. "I thought – considering the traffic conditions – we made really great time."

"You have the money?" Montgomery asked.

"We have the money. You have the girl?"

"Let's see the money."

"Let's see the girl."

"She's down there," Montgomery pointed over his shoulder.

"Well, hop on," Devereaux patted the seat of his snowmobile. "We've got room for three."

"What's going on up there?" McCleary's voice chirped through Ballweg's radio.

"They want to see the girl before they show us the money."

All five of them waited for McCleary's reply.

They waited. And waited. Finally his reply came.

"Send them down."

"Want us to come on back or just stay here?"

Another hesitation. "Stay there for now."

Ballweg and Montgomery lowered their weapons. Melissa said, "Boss said go on down."

The Art of Making Plans on the Fly

Hands in the air, Harper cautiously dismounted.

"Let me see your radio," he requested of Melissa. "Please?"

"Why?"

"Because I would like to tell your boss what is getting ready to happen here."

"Forget you, ya douche bag."

"Fine. How's about I tell *you* what's getting ready to happen, then you can tell your boss. I promise it will just take a second, and if he goes along with it, you can pretend it was your idea."

Not knowing what Harper was up to, Deveraux was uneasy. Had this been a courtroom drama, he would have shouted, "I object!" Since that wasn't the case, he decided to let it play out a bit. Much to his surprise, Melissa Ballweg acquiesced to Harper's request and handed him her radio.

"Whatever, dude. Let's just go already."

"Hi," he said into the handheld device. "With whom do I have the pleasure of speaking?"

"What? Who is this?" asked McCleary.

"I asked you first."

Kenton gave a flustered sigh. "This is Kenton McCleary. Now, do you mind tell—"

"My name is Harper Rowe, Mr. McCleary, and here's what we're going to do. There are three of us up here: my associates Kinley Devereaux and Taralyn Tharp, and me. Now instead of all three of us coming down there, showing you the money, and putting the obvious control of the situation squarely in your hands"—Harper walked over to Taralyn's sled and unstrapped the briefcase full of money—"I'm going to stay up here with the money and Kinley and Taralyn are going to come down there and check out the well-being of the girl.

"You see, Mr. McCleary, we're not complete idiots. If you're telling your two comrades here to stay put, that means you have more team members down there with you. If all three of us come down there and show you the money, I'm guessing that y'all are probably going to shoot me and my team members in the head, take the money, and leave the girl to fend for herself, while you and your merry band of mercenaries make a break for it.

"When we were making our way here, I couldn't help but notice that there were, lit'rally, no tire tracks on the road. While I realize that it is snowing somewhat tempestuously, it's not enough to completely bury tracks made in the last eight to ten hours. That leaves me to assume that your clan arrived by chopper, and it is more than likely stationed nearby waiting to usher you out to a getaway plane once you've got your money.

"So, like I was saying, here's what is going to happen. Upon checking the well-being of the senator's daughter, my two cohorts are going to let me know that we're good. At that point, they will bring the girl out, and I will ride the money down to you. I think it only fair to inform you that I have placed a small incendiary device inside this briefcase. The detonator to this device is here in my pocket."

Harper placed his right hand into his coat pocket and moved it around menacingly, a maneuver designed to convince Ballweg and Montgomery that he was not bluffing.

"Ergo, if anything should befall any of them on their way out, I will detonate the device and blow your money – and all the retirement plans that go with it – straight to Kingdom Come."

The five waited once again for McCleary's reply.

"Okay, Mr. Rowe," McCleary finally answered. "Let's just say that all your suppositions are correct, and my plan was to kill you and your friends. If I let them leave, and you bring the money down here...what's to keep me from killing *you*?"

"As far as I can tell, absolutely nothing," Harper answered. "But also – as far as I can tell – you're a military man, Kenton. And being as such, you know that as long as the objective to any mission is attained, the sacrifices to do such are always acceptable."

Kenton shook his head and chuckled. "Well, you certainly have quite the sack on you, Mr. Rowe. But hey, if this is how you want to play it, fine. We'll do this your way. Send your friends down."

Without a word, Kin and Taralyn started up their rides and slowly advanced past Ballweg and Montgomery, into the cemetery and toward the meeting point.

Kinley was surprised by a few things. Number one, he was surprised that they had not bothered to check him or Taralyn for weapons. Number two, he was surprised at the audible that Harper had pulled at the last minute. And number three, he was surprised at how little resistance McCleary had put up to Harper's plan. After he and Tara had advanced about thirty yards, Kinley said, "I know you can't answer this right now, Harp, but assuming this all goes the way you hope it does, do you have a plan of how you're going to get away once you deliver the money to them?"

Indeed, Harper could not answer. But had he been able, the answer would have been a resounding *no*.

AIMEE SCHMIDT SPEAKS HER MIND

"Do you think my mom had any idea her errand boys were going to pull a stunt like that?" Amy had heard every word of the radio exchange.

"I'm pretty sure she didn't. I'm pretty sure your mom highly underestimated these errand boys...and girl. Doesn't matter. You're all going to end up dead, and – even if by some life-sized miracle you should escape – like the man said, we'll have our money and be long gone by the time your mom realizes what happened."

"Wow. It's really hard to tell where the spineless traitor in you stops and the amoral asshole begins. Seriously, you'll either kill me and let my darling mother – slithering slimy snake that she is – get elected president, or you'll just take the money and shaft my mom like a two-dollar whore.

"If you have a shred of decency left in you, you will take the latter of the two options. I'm not just appealing to you to do that because I want to live to see my seventeenth birthday. But if you still love the country that you fought so hard to honor and protect, you won't even think twice about letting my mom run this country. She'll spit and piss all over everything you have ever held dear about this great land of ours. Are you really going to let that happen? Seriously?"

Kenton smiled and started clapping his hands slowly. "Bravo, my dear. Bravo. Do you hear this girl, fellas?" he asked Kojak, Walters, and Johnson. "I mean, if this girl isn't the captain of her high school debate team, then someone at that school clearly does not recognize talent when they see it. Heck, kid, I almost saw the flag flying in the wind and heard the Harlem Boys Choir singing the Battle Hymn of the Republic when you gave that speech."

"Hey, Skipper, they're here," Kojak informed him.

Kenton turned around to see Devereaux and Tharp pulling up on their snowmobiles. He put his hand up to shield his eyes. "Hey! Do ya mind? Your headlights are boring a hole through my brain like a laser drill."

"Kill yours, Kinley," Tara said. "I'll dim mine."

"Thank you," Kenton said sarcastically.

"Well, it's a little dark down here, and given the situation, I'd like to be able to see just what's going on," Kinley said.

He eyed Aimee Schmidt. She looked scared and shaken up – and cold, dressed in only a blue windbreaker over jeans and a t-shirt. Her sneakers were covered in snow.

"You okay, kid?" Kin asked her.

"What do you think?"

"Is that all you could find for her to wear? Where'd you get that windbreaker? The local unwilling hostage lost-and-found?"

"We're not running a Holiday Inn, jackass. Just check the girl out and get her out of here. Frankly, I'm glad you're taking her off our hands. She's nothing but a foul-mouthed, crude little kid anyway. Been a pain in our rears since we took her."

Devereaux looked over to Taralyn. "You wanna do the honors?"

"You mean get up off the heated seat and walk over there? Geez, I was just getting warm," she feigned irritation.

"If it's not too much to ask." Tara stepped through the snow and over to Aimee.

Upon reaching the teenage girl, Tharp removed her scarf and gloves and put them on Aimee.

"How ya doin', sweetie? Are you bleeding anywhere?"

"You really wanna know the answer to that question?"

"Are you bleeding anywhere that will kill you?"

THE STORY OF THE PEN

During the 48 hours that McCleary and his Vipers had held Aimee captive, they had stashed her in the basement of an abandoned home.

Scrounging around in the semi-darkness there, Aimee had found a few random, useless items: an old torn rag, some rusty nails, a dusty glass bottle. But then she happened upon something very useful: an old pen. Scribbling on her shoe, she finally got it to write. Now how to get a warning note to her "rescuers"? She needed something to write on. After several hours of fruitless searching, it came to her. She would write on the palm of her hand.

But what should she write? Her hands were small – the message would have to be short. She had finally settled on five words: *They're gonna kill us all.*

"Okay, show me where it hurts." Taralyn moved closer to Aimee.

"My hand hurts a little. Nothing that I can't handle." Aimee pulled off a glove and opened her palm, showing the message to Taralyn.

"Yeah, I see that. You'll be okay."

Tara looked at Kinley. "She's good to go."

"Cool."

Ignoring McCleary, Tara put her arm around Aimee and walked her to the snowmobile. She boosted Aimee onto the seat, putting her in front so she could wrap her arms around her and help stop her from shivering.

Devereaux raised his hands and turned to McCleary. "Like my partner said, we're just gonna take the girl out of here. He's going to bring your money down. Ain't no need for anybody to get all jumpy at this point. We're getting what we came here for: the senator's daughter. You're gonna get what you came here for: your money. We straight?"

"Just tell your man that it's all good and to bring the money to us. Then we'll be straight like a knife's edge."

"The girl's good, Harp. Tara and I are bringing her out." Kinley paused momentarily before proclaiming his best friend's death sentence "Go ahead and bring the ransom money on down."

Snowmobiles Passing in the Night

Ten times in a row, Harper started his snowmobile, then imperceptibly lifted his butt just enough to engage the kill switch. On, off. On, off.

"I can't drive these things. I mean, up until tonight, I hadn't driven one of these things since I was about 14 years old. Still, we do what we must, right?"

"Just go already," Melissa snapped.

"Well, I would, but the darn thing keeps stalling out on me. Probably this daggone weather, right?" Harper chuckled as the snow continued falling from the sky. "So, are you and your little cronies taking bets on if I survive this? If so, what kind of odds am I getting?"

"Let's just say that the longer you sit here screwing around, the lower your odds are becoming."

"Mm-hmm. Yeah, I get that."

While Harper ran out of ways to postpone the inevitable, Tara and Kinley headed back toward the cemetery entrance.

"Guys, you can hear me, right?" Tara asked.

"Yeah," Kinley and Harper both answered.

"The girl just told me...they're going to kill us all."

"What? When did she tell you that?"

"Just now. When I was checking her out. She has it written on her hand, and she showed me. They're gonna kill us all."

"Well...I guess she would know. Judas Priest."

"What are we going to do?" Taralyn asked.

"As long as they think I can burn up their money, you three should have safe passage back up to the entrance. You both have those flash grenades. My suggestion is that when you get back up to the two sentries at the gate, you use the grenades to cause a diversion, and you shoot those two pinheads dead. From there, Taralyn, you hightail it back up the road as fast as you can. Get yourself and the girl to safety. Kinley, you circle back around. Use your scope to try to locate the rest of the players and try to take out as many as you can."

"What are you going to do? You know once you're close enough to them, Harper, they're going to shoot you."

"More than likely, yes. That's why once I'm close enough, I'm going to accelerate my sled for all that she's worth. I'm going to toss them the briefcase and a flash grenade as I'm flying by. I'll try to take as many of them out as I can, but there's a lot of them and only one..."

Harper cut his sentence short as they passed each other, Kinley, Taralyn, and Aimee headed up to the cemetery entrance, Harper headed down to what seemed like certain doom.

As they crossed, the sight of Harper working the throttle with one hand while holding a briefcase full of money against his head with the other made Kinley laugh. He knew Harper was counting on this crew's greed to keep him alive. Any sniper that was going to shoot him in the head would have to shoot through the money first.

They paused just long enough for Taralyn to say, "Do what you need to do, Harper Rowe. Just stay alive."

"I don't know who you are," Aimee added, "but, please...make them pay. If you can kill them all, kill them all. I know that's what my mom told them to do to us. So you've got to stay alive just so you can see the look on her face when we show up."

"Wait a second," Harper said. "Is she...are you telling us that... is she saying—"

"Look, Harp, let's just get through this. We can sort out all the details later."

"Yeah, you're right." Harper took a deep breath. "Here's hopin' that I'll see ya 'round downtown, kids."

Countdown to Action

Harper started heading back to the ransom drop, taking his hand off the throttle just long enough to reach into his parka and grab the flash grenade.

"Let us know when you're getting ready to make your move, chief," Kinley said through the com.

"Counting down from 5…"

Kinley and Taralyn retrieved their flash grenades.

"4…"

Kin set his grenade between his legs and readied his weapons.

"3…"

Taralyn pulled a handgun from her coat and handed it forward to Aimee. "You know how to use one of these?"

"2…"

"I do," Aimee answered.

"1…"

By now Kinley and Tara were ten yards from Melissa Ballweg and Xavier Montgomery. Harper was 90 feet from Kenton McCleary, Chris Kojak, Calvin Walters, and Russell Johnson.

"Let's rock and roll these filthy animals!"

Harper pulled the pin on the flash grenade, hurled the briefcase toward the quartet, then fired the grenade right behind it.

The briefcase of money got their attention, so when the flash grenade discharged, it did its job. Harper opened the throttle full-tilt and held on tightly.

The flash momentarily blinded all four men – poor Chris Kojak never saw the snowmobile coming at almost 70 miles per hour. Harper cringed ever so slightly at the feeling of Kojak's torso being ground up under the machine.

Swerving right, Harper aimed his sled at an opening between two headstones, ducking down as gunshots rang out all around him.

SHOOTING TO KILL

"Take the woman, Tara," Devereaux instructed.

Seeing the flash go off in front of McCleary's group, Ballweg and Montgomery had lifted their weapons to blow away the occupants on the two fast-approaching snowmobiles. Before they could fire, flash grenades tossed by Kinley and Tara completely blinded them. Firing wildly in all directions, their shots were way off target. Kinley's and Taralyn's were not.

Aimee and Tara fired into Melissa Ballweg's chest. Dead before her body hit the snow, the grenade's blinding flash led her into the afterlife.

Xavier Montgomery's instincts were a little better. Knowing what was coming, he dropped to the ground and tried shoulder-rolling for cover behind a marble pillar to his right. Too much snow. Next, he tried an unsuccessful scramble to safety as the first bullet ripped through his left rotator cuff. The pain was excruciating but short-lived. Devereaux's head shot killed Montgomery immediately.

Hearing gunshots at the cemetery entrance, Lijuan Cho and Deshawn Black, the Vipers stationed halfway between the cemetery entrance and the drop site, were on the move and now had Devereaux and Taralyn flanked.

Lijuan fired first.

Dev heard two shots whistle past his ears.

"Tara, ditch the sled and take cover!"

He spotted a large marble angel sitting on a bench. It was more than enough cover, but Lijuan's third shot grazed the left side of Kinley's ribcage as he jumped from the snowmobile to the monument. The bullet sent goose down feathers from his coat flying into the air.

Deshawn Black's aim was a little off as he ran to the aid of his cohorts, but he unloaded the entire clip of his Beretta M9 in Taralyn's direction, hoping that quantity would trump quality.

By the time Tara heard Kinley's order to take cover, she had already been hit twice. Her body had shielded Aimee, enabling her to climb off the snowmobile and drag Taralyn with her. They took cover behind an immense headstone.

"Lady!" she shouted, seeing Tharp's crimson blood filling in the snow around her body. "Are you okay?"

"You gotta get out of here," Tara said, struggling to sit up. "Get out of here. I'll cover you."

From Kinley's position, he could tell that Aimee and Tara had taken cover, but monuments blocked a clear view. He heard Cho and Black approaching and gunfire coming from Harper's location down near the drop site.

Kinley was never one for pessimism, but for a moment he thought to himself, *We may have bitten off more than we can chew.*

MIRACLES DO HAPPEN

"Kinley, Harper? Do you copy? Come in, please!"

Using the selfsame coms they had shared on their job in Rio, Laurie Chase and Big Jim Gray were trying frantically to sync up with Kinley and Harp's coms as they rode into range. Maybe it was a long shot, but it was better than no shot at all. In one ear, they had the synced coms with Kinley and Harper; in the other, the coms to communicate with the rest of the rescue team.

On the front snowmobile, Agents Grimes and Kane led the charge toward the Sunset Memorial Park Cemetery. Agents Hughes and Conley were second in line, with Agents Crool and Baldwin following close behind. Laurie and Big James brought up the rear.

"Oh, crap," Big James said. "Did you hear that?"

"What? What did you hear? Did you hear them?"

"No. No, I think I heard gunshots."

Chase eased up on the gas, listening intently.

He was right. The unmistakable sound of repeated gunfire. But the thing was, she wasn't hearing it in the air. She was hearing it through her com.

"James, are you hearing it through your earpiece? The gunfire?"

"Yes! Ha, I was just getting ready to ask you the same thing."

"Hello? Who is this?" asked a bewildered Kinley Devereaux.

"Who's on this frequency?"

"Oh, my gosh! Kinley?"

"What the…? Laurs?"

"Yes! It's me, baby! Can you hear me?"

"Yes, I can hear you."

"Are you at the cemetery?" Now she could hear the gunfire in the distance *and* through the com.

"We're at the cemetery. We have the girl, but the whole thing was a setup – which I think you were trying to tell us earlier. But right now, I don't know where Harper is, and Taralyn and I are pinned down. We're running out of time. And we're running out of bullets."

"Hang in there for a few more seconds," Big James jumped in. "There's eight of us on our way to you, and we are only moments away."

"Roger that," Kinley winced, feeling his latest bullet wound. "You guys need to be careful on your approach. There are a whole lot of hostiles with guns, and they aren't shy about using them."

Kin put a fresh magazine into his gun and took a quick peek to locate Lijuan Cho and Deshawn Black. He could not see them, but they could apparently see him because every time he lifted his head, gunshots rang out. Two bullets ricocheted off the concrete angel statue right in front of him.

"Tara, did you see where those gunshots came from?"

"They're about...twenty feet away...I can't...I can't get a good shot at…"

Kinley waited a moment for Tharp to finish her sentence.

"Tara, are you okay?"

"Probably not," she laughed feebly, then started coughing violently. After catching her breath, she said, "I've been hit three – maybe four – times. My left shoulder, my left kidney, my right rib cage."

"Just hang in there, girl. Help's on the way. We'll wrap this up and get you to a hospital."

Within seconds, he heard the sweet sound of snowmobiles coming in the distance. However, it was soon drowned out by fresh gunshots from Harper's location.

"Harper! What's going on down there?"

No reply.

"Harper!"

Kinley, Taralyn, Laurie, and Big James all held their breath. But the only sound to be heard was more sporadic gunfire.

From Harper Rowe, there was no reply at all.

Losing Touch

After tossing the briefcase full of money, the flash grenade, and running over Chris Kojak, Harper had sped head-down into the darkness, running the gauntlet between the two gunmen behind the utility shed to his right and the sniper in a tree to his left. Not to mention the three guys at the drop site behind him whose temporary blindness would soon clear up.

Reckoning his options, Rowe lost concentration just long enough to miss spotting the tip of a headstone poking up through the snow. The snowmobile's steering skis snapped off on contact. When the track belt in the undercarriage hit the grave marker, Harper's ride slammed to a stop, sending him flying through the air like Superman. He slammed down on a granite monument 30 feet away, his helmeted head woozy and aching.

Harper lay in the snow for a few seconds, gathering his wits before taking off his helmet and goggles and sitting up. He had to get closer to the shooters. But how?

Suddenly, he grabbed his helmet and put it back on. With his white coat, pants, and helmet, he was completely camouflaged in the snow. Pulling two handguns from his pockets, he released the safeties and began crawling toward his first target: the tree sniper.

A sudden burst of gunfire rang out from the cemetery entrance.

"What's going on up there?" Harper asked into the com. "You two okay?"

Hearing nothing from either Kinley or Taralyn, he suddenly realized he really was hearing *nothing*. Not through his com anyway.

Pulling off his glove, he reached up to adjust the earpiece.

"Oh, you gotta be kidding me," Harper murmured. His com must have gotten knocked free when his head hit the granite monument. Cut off from Kinley and Taralyn, his only hope was to take out the remaining members of McCleary's crew on his own, one by one.

He put his glove back on and retrieved his gun from the snow.

Between the blinding snow and leafless trees silhouetted against a dark, cloud-filled sky, it was tough to tell man from limb, much less figure out which tree the sniper was in. If the sniper had a decent infrared scope, it was only a matter of time before Rowe was a goner.

Then the sniper fired.

KILL SHOTS

Joe Carney could not remember a time in his life when he had been colder.

Even with his legs wrapped tightly around a thick tree branch, he felt like the gusting wind could blow him off his perch any second. Steadying his Dragunov SVD sniper rifle with both hands, his right eye peered through the scope, trying to get a lock on the back of Kinley Devereaux's head.

With the heaviest of concentration, Joe finally had the shot he wanted. He exhaled calmly and prepared to pull the trigger when his focus was broken by a commotion off to his left.

Pulling his head back, he retrained his scope on the four snowmobiles approaching the cemetery entrance.

"Hey, we've got company," Carney said into his radio.

"Where?" McCleary responded.

"Coming up on the cemetery entrance."

"Melissa? Xavier? You hear that? You've got company coming your way."

"Mel and X are dead."

"What?"

"Yeah, those little dickheads took them out about two minutes ago. Lijuan and Deshawn have them pinned down now. I was just getting ready to take out Devereaux when I saw that we had more bogeys coming at us."

"Can you handle them? Calvin, Russell, Kiyo, Jay and me are gonna go get Harper Rowe. He ran over Kojak and killed the poor S.O.B. We're gonna go track that little prick down and end this once and for all."

"Yeah, I can take care of our guests at the gate," Carney replied. "What about the money? Were you able to check the briefcase?"

"It's there. The senator held up her end of the bargain. Now it's our turn to hold up ours. Do your thing, Joe. Let's finish this and get outta here."

"Copy that, boss."

Re-attaching the radio to his hip, Carney locked his gun in on the two riders on the first snowmobile. He lined up his shot, fired twice, and less than a half a second later two 7.62x54mm rounds found their marks. The first one went through the right side of Agent Tim Grimes' helmet, passing through his brain and out the other side – taking a good chunk of his temporal lobe with it. Death was instantaneous.

For Tobias Kane, things were a bit more painful. Carney's second shot ripped through the agent's right shoulder, continuing through his chest and out through his left shoulder. The bullet missed his heart, but it did not matter. The projectile shattered both clavicles and ripped his trachea in two, leaving both arms barely attached. The impact sent his body flying from the snowmobile like a rag doll. He lay in the snow, his body in momentary shock before unimaginable pain set in. He tried to breathe, but the damage to his windpipe made it impossible. Death was a welcomed relief.

"Bail! Bail!" Jeb yelled. He and Baldwin flipped off to their left, hoping the snowmobile would offer momentary cover in case they were next to be fired upon.

They were not.

That circumstance befell Agents Alexis Conley and Cameron Hughes.

Seeing what had just happened to their fellow agents, Conley and Hughes quickly bailed from their sled. Alexis slid off the back, ducking the kill shot that was meant for her. Cam Hughes exited a half-second later, but the delay gave time for the sniper's bullet to drill in the back of her right hip and out the front of her leg, shattering her femur and clipping her femoral artery. Cam writhed in pain as the blood turned the snow around her a dark shade of red.

Alexis crawled over to her partner, grabbing her by the coat and pulling her behind their snowmobile for cover.

"Get away from the snowmobile!" Jeb yelled as he and Dave scrambled into the cemetery looking for safe haven.

Laurie Chase and Big James were right behind them.

"What part of 'We need to be cautious on our approach' didn't those two morons understand?" Chase asked, taking shelter behind a large marble headstone a few feet away from Jeb and Dave. Big James hustled right in behind her.

"I don't think they were expecting a sniper."

"Get away from the snowmobile!" Jeb repeated.

"She's been shot. She can't move."

"Then you move."

"I'm not leaving her."

Before Jeb could answer, a shot rang out and Conley and Hughes's snowmobile exploded in a daunting ball of flame. Shrapnel flew. Both women were set on fire. Through their coms, Laurie, Big James, Jeb, and Dave heard their screams of dread, agony, and torment.

"Lord have mercy," Big James whispered. They'd never know whether the shrapnel or the fire killed them, but all four of the FBI agents sent to help them were now dead.

"Laurie!" Kinley called out. "Are you all right?"

"I'm fine."

"Then who was *that*? The two that got shot and the two that just got blown up?"

"They were four FBI agents that were with us."

"You and Big James?"

"Me, Big James, Agent David Baldwin...and Agent Jeb Crool."

"Jeb Crool? Are you kidding me?"

"No," Laurie said. "But don't worry. He's on our side."

"I hope you don't mind me saying this, but I find that a little hard to believe."

"Me, too, but he is. Now's not really the time to go into it though. Where are you?"

Knowing he had nothing to lose, Kinley fired two shots into the air. "I'm right here."

"Holy crap, baby! You're only about fifty yards away from us."

"Taralyn and the senator's daughter are about sixty feet on the other side of me. Unfortunately, we've got two bad guys about twenty feet behind us. Here...watch."

Devereaux stuck his head out from behind the concrete angel, drawing several rounds of gunfire from Cho and Black.

"Yeah, I see them."

"Any chance you – or all four of yas – can do a flanking maneuver? Come up behind them and take them out?"

"Absolutely. Do you know where Harper is?"

"No, he went down to do the ransom drop. I heard a lot of commotion, but I'm not sure what happened. His com must be malfunctioning or something because I can't raise him. At least, I'm hoping that's why he's not responding."

Three more shots sounded off in the snowy night. Devereaux, Crool, and Baldwin could tell they weren't from the sniper rifle.

"Maybe that's him now," Devereaux said.

Chase turned to Jeb Crool. "Harper's down there somewhere,"

she pointed in the direction of the gunfire. "What do you think about you and Agent Baldwin heading down that way to see what you can see? James and I are going to circle back around the two shooters over there," and she pointed to the area behind Devereaux.

"Since I'm the one in charge here"—Jeb smiled— "I'll make the decisions." Turning to Baldwin, he said, "Dave, you and I are going to go down there and save Harper Rowe's dopey behind." To Chase, he said, "You and Big James circle around behind the two shooters that have Devereaux and his running mate pinned down. Take the shooters out and try not to get yourselves shot in the process. Any questions?"

"I'm not going to argue over semantics here and now, but didn't I just say that?"

"Let's get one thing straight," Jeb said. "Regardless of the situation, I am the one that's still in charge here."

"I'm just saying—"

"Hey, Laurs," Big James cut in, "you said you weren't going to argue. We need to get going before you don't have a boyfriend left to save."

"Fine," Laurie looked at Jeb. "This isn't over."

"It's kinda over." Double-checking his weapon, Jeb looked at Baldwin. "Let's go, Dave. Keep your head down." Crool looked back at Laurie and Big James. "Be careful, you two. When I write my bestseller about all this, I want it to have a happy ending."

IF A TREE SNIPER FALLS IN A CEMETERY...

The muzzle flash from Carney's sniper rifle caught Harper Rowe's eye. Eight inches long and bright yellow orange, it stood out against the gray background like a hooker at a nun's convention.

Harper started army-crawling toward the sniper's tree, a pistol in each hand. Harp knew they'd all be coming after him soon, now that the blinding effect of the flash grenade had worn off. Running full tilt toward the tree sniper was a bad idea. And crawling through snow that was almost two feet deep was cold and tiresome. However, hearing two more shots from the sniper's rifle, Rowe decided that no matter how tired, woozy, and shaky he was, he had to get to that guy. As fast as possible.

He heard unintelligible yelling coming from the cemetery entrance. Then more shots from the tree sniper, followed by a loud explosion.

"Judas Priest," Harper said in disgust. Crawling through the snow was taking too long. A mammoth statue of Jesus stood just ahead. Ten feet tall and three feet wide, it was big enough to take cover behind and close enough to the sniper's tree to get a clean shot.

Time being of the essence, Rowe stood to his feet and tried to run to the statue. As soon as he took off, the top of his body moved faster than his stiff, cold legs, and he fell face first into the snow.

Undeterred, he shook it off and tried again.

Harper finally arrived at the holy figure lightheaded, breathless, and out of time. Steadying himself against the statue, he took aim at the silhouetted figure in the tree and fired three times.

Bullet number one landed in the tree branch on which Joe Carney was perched.

Bullet number two found its way into his lower left rib cage.

Bullet number three entered Carney's upper rib cage and traveled straight into his heart. He lived long enough to land like a snow angel in the fluffy white stuff below him.

"See ya 'round downtown, tree sniper."

The five Vipers that were hot on Harper Rowe's trail now spotted his location via the same method Harper had used to suss out their sniper: muzzle flashes.

"Want one of us to go check on Joe?" Kiyo Potts asked.

McCleary said into his radio, "You still with us, Joe?"

No response.

"Joe?"

Silence.

"Joe, if you're still there, give us a sign."

No sign was given because Joe Carney was dead.

"Son of a bitch!" Jay Hammers channeled the frustration of the remaining Vipers. "Look, we know where this little jerk-off is. It's time to end him and end him now."

"Want to surround him and take him down, boss?" Calvin Walters asked. "Or do you just want us to stick together and blast away until he's dead?"

"Let's just blow him away. Semi-circle around him so there's no crossfire."

"He's hiding behind a statue of Jesus," Russell Johnson piped up.

"And?"

"And I feel a little weird shooting up a statue of Jesus."

"Are you kidding me right now?"

"No. I'm a devout Catholic, and I just feel a little weird shooting up a statue of Jesus."

"It's just a statue, Russ," Hammers said. "It's not *actually* Jesus."

"Yeah, it's just a piece of formed concrete," McCleary added. "It could be a statue of Abraham Lincoln. Would you feel bad about shooting up a statue of Abraham Lincoln?"

"But it's not a statue of Abraham Lincoln. And I know that it's not the real Jesus. But it's just what it symbolizes to me as a Catholic. I'm sorry."

"Fine. Whatever, man," Potts shook her head in disgust. "That dude behind the statue has killed two of our own. Two of our friends. He's not walking out of here alive. You don't wanna shoot at him? Then don't shoot at him. The rest of us are going to kill that little punk."

"Fire away, soldiers!" McCleary gave the order. Kiyo Potts, Jay Hammers, and Calvin Walters joined McCleary in firing as they advanced on Harper Rowe and the Jesus statue.

True to his convictions, Russell Johnson stayed behind, taking advantage of the opportunity to check on his fallen friend, Joe Carney. Just as he turned to leave, he sensed movement to his left. He immediately hit the deck, scanning the area.

Sure enough, two shadowy figures were creeping out from behind the utility shed. Well aware of the current body count, Russell was certain that the people headed his way were not friendlies. He also knew that if he did not intervene, the two strangers were going to have his four colleagues dead to rights.

Sensing them eyeing up the quartet, Russell rose to his knees and fired several shots at the dark silhouettes. He grabbed his radio as they hit the ground. "Kenton! Company on your six. Take cover."

He fired several more shots at the downed men, unsure of what or whom he was shooting, or if he was even hitting anything.

Suddenly, a cluster of gunfire rang out from up where Cho and Black had Devereaux and Tharp and the senator's daughter pinned down.

A cluster of gunfire...a blood-curdling scream...then two more gunshots.

SOMETIMES IT JUST DOES
NOT PAY TO BE NICE

Deshawn Black crouched in the snow four rows behind Kinley Devereaux. Having exchanged gunfire with him a few times, his plan was to wait for Devereaux to run out of ammo.

For Lijuan Cho it was a different story. From her spot four rows behind Taralyn Tharp and Aimee Schmidt, there had been no exchange of gunfire for a while. It was time to make her move. Getting Deshawn Black's attention, she signaled that she was going to make her approach.

Lijuan sneaked up one row to the grave marker in front of her, drawing Deveraux's fire. This, in turn, drew response fire from Deshawn Black.

"Taralyn, are you still with me?" Kinley asked.

"Barely. I think I'm in and out of consciousness. This girl here's trying to keep me awake," Taralyn said, referring to the senator's daughter. "What's going on?"

"The shooter on your side – she's sneaking up on you."

"I've got eyes on her," Big James said. "I'm not going to let her get to you."

"I've got eyes on your guy, Kin," Laurie Chase said.

Kinley was, indeed, running out of ammo. And Taralyn, barely clinging to life, was unable to defend herself. Aimee Schmidt had a gun, but up until a few minutes ago, she had never fired one before.

For Laurie Chase, sneaking from tombstone to tombstone was not a very tall order. At 110 pounds, her wiry frame easily advanced undetected.

For Big James, *sneaking* between grave plots was a rather loose term. 310 pounds at his most svelte, he moved his lumbering frame as quietly as he possibly could. Fortunately, his target, Lijuan Cho, was focused on what was in front of her and not what was approaching from behind.

Getting Deshawn Black's attention once more, Cho gave him the signal to cover her while she advanced on Deveraux.

Black rose up and began firing in Devereaux's direction while Lijuan darted to the next row of gravestones. So intense was their focus that they completely missed hearing Big James approaching Lijuan's position. By the time Deshawn Black saw the big man closing in on his cohort, all he could do was fire several inaccurate shots toward Big James.

"Lijuan! Behind you!"

Turning a split second before the giant bum-rushed her, she had no time to raise her gun before Big James' giant fist smashed her face with the force of a 98-mph fastball. Her feet left the ground and the back of her skull slammed against the marble headstone behind her. The concussive impact killed her immediately.

Deshawn Black fired two shots at Devereaux to keep him pinned down, then stood to take careful aim at Big James. However, so fixated was he on bringing the big man down, that he did not see Laurie Chase standing just five feet away. Her first shot went into Deshawn's right hand, causing him to drop his weapon. Grabbing his hand in acute pain, he turned to face Laurie Chase.

"Hi," she said, leveling the gun at his head.

"Please don't. Please."

"Kinley, you okay?" she called out to her boyfriend.

"Are we clear?" he asked.

"We're clear."

Kinley stood up. Looking over to Taralyn and Aimee, he saw Big James bending over Tara.

Laurie held her gun on Deshawn as she walked up to him to pat him down. She found two guns in his coat and a third in the waistband of his pants. She knelt down to check for any secondary and/or back-up weapons he may have had around his ankles.

What happened next was just, well, rude.

Deshawn Black had begged Laurie Chase to spare his life, and she had. So, why he decided to try to backhand her across the face while she knelt in the snow was anybody's guess.

His cheap shot connected. And when it did, Chase's knee-jerk reaction was to pull the trigger on the gun.

The gun that was currently aimed at Deshawn's crotch.

He screamed out in agonizing pain for about two seconds – the two seconds it took for Kinley to unload his final two rounds into the back of Deshawn's head.

"Kin," Big James called out. "Ya better get over here."

Seeing the look of concern on Big James' face, Kinley and Chase hustled over to Taralyn. She was lying in the snow, her face as pale as the ground around her and her mouth covered in the blood that she had been coughing up for the last few minutes.

Kinley kneeled next to her, removing her helmet and gently pulling her matted hair back away from her forehead.

"Hey, girl," he said softly.

"Is...Harper still…"

"I don't know, but I'm still hearing gunfire from down there, so I'm thinking that means he is."

"Can you...tell him…" she started coughing uncontrollably.

"Tell him," she continued, "that I love him...and tell him thank you...for giving my life true meaning these last few days." Her breathing became labored and shallow, making it almost impossible to talk. "And, thank *you*, Kinley."

"I'm going to go get him, Taralyn. You can tell him yourself. Just hang in there." But even as he said those words, he could see the life leaving her eyes.

"Be sure you...make the senator pay." She breathed one last breath, and she was gone. Everyone watched as the snowflakes fell onto her face.

Big James reached down and closed her blue eyes. Taralyn Tharp was dead.

Never Too Late to Believe

"This is insane," **Baldwin** whispered emphatically. "I mean, this is just absolutely insane."

"It is. No denyin' that," Crool answered.

Crool and Baldwin had begun their hike down through the cemetery toward Harper Rowe's vicinity. Bent low, the agents were moving at a slow jog, taking in the dangers of their surroundings. They were well to the right of the main fray, doing their best to avoid the many lines of fire they could hear in the cold and snowy night.

"Still, as insane as all this might seem, everything Chase told us back in Brazil has turned out to be true. And we are about two minutes away from being face-to-face with the man that we have been after for the last year and a half. So, yeah, I haven't killed as many people or been shot at as many times in my whole career as I have been in the last few days. But I'll take it."

The two men were approaching the utility shed where, barely an hour ago, the Vipers had been plotting out their big payday. Walking up to the side of the building, Jeb and Dave leaned their backs against the wall. They could hear shooting nearby, and a quick peek around the corner revealed four men walking side-by-side and unloading their weapons on what appeared to be a statue of Jesus.

"I'm guessing Harper Rowe must be behind the King of Kings there," Baldwin commented.

"I'd say that's a pretty good guess."

"So...are we shooting to kill or shooting to shoot here?"

"You're a crack shot, Dave. Just be effective. But, yeah, I wouldn't mind having some of these jokers left alive to testify to all this nonsense, if and when that day should ever arrive."

"Let's do this then."

Baldwin on the left, Crool on the right, guns in each hand, they walked out from behind the utility shed.

What they saw was a line of four men about twenty-five to thirty yards in front of them. They took aim on the quartet. What they didn't see was Russell Johnson standing just a few yards off to their left.

So, for as much as Crool and Baldwin had McCleary, Walters, Potts, and Hammers lined up in their sights, Russell Johnson had the two feds lined up in his.

Johnson fired first, his first shot whizzing between Jeb's and Dave's heads. The next two shots found homes in Baldwin's left ribcage and shoulder. The final shot went through the back of Crool's coat, missing all parts of his physical being by a fraction of an inch. Jeb Crool hit the ground for cover. David Baldwin hit the ground in pain.

"Oh, sweet mercy," Dave cried out in angst. "I'm hit, boss. Two times."

Crool stood to his feet and grabbed Dave by the collar of his black jacket. He pulled his injured mate through the snow and back to safe cover behind the utility shed.

"Where ya hit?"

"Gut and shoulder."

"You gonna be okay for a few? I'm going to go swiss cheese me a couple o' criminals."

"Yeah, I'm cool. Just don't forget about me. Probably not too many cabs running out here this time of night. I wouldn't wanna miss my ride back into town."

"Back in a flash, Dave. Back in a flash."

Jeb eased his way back to the corner of the shed and slowly stuck his head out to get a good view of what was going on. No longer were the four men standing side-by-side. They had scattered to different parts of the cemetery, out of immediate sight. He looked around but saw no sign of Russell Johnson.

Seeing none of the five men that he knew were out there waiting to blow him to Kingdom Come, Jeb knew that the only way to get a read on their position was to draw their fire. Hoping to pin them down long enough for him to move from the utility shed to the nearest tombstone large enough to take cover behind, he fired his gun until the clip was empty, then launched himself 12 feet through the air to land behind a statue of Mother Mary and child.

Gunfire and bullets rained down from three directions.

Jeb scooched back against the statue and loaded fresh cartridges into his guns. Then he popped up to his knees and started blasting away in the general direction of the gunfire. He had no idea whether or not his shots had any effect. He just knew that his adrenaline was running at an all-time high and the numbing Minnesota cold was no longer an issue.

Jeb recoiled behind the Mary statuary. He was not much of a religious person, but as the counter-fire whizzed and ricocheted around him, he knew that he might be in need of divine intervention. Without Agent Baldwin by his side, Crool realized he might be in over his head.

He wondered if it was too late in the game to ask the Big Guy for a miracle.

SOMETHING. ANYTHING.

Harper thought he would have more time. Under normal circumstances, he would have had plenty of time to shoot down the tree sniper, gather his wits, and relocate to a safer position before anyone from the enemy camp could track his weapon's muzzle flash.

However, his head still swimming from having been slammed against the granite monument, Harper's reaction time was not normal. Instead of heading to safety, he was currently pinned down by combatant gunfire.

Sneaking a quick peek from behind the Jesus statue, he took a cursory look at the four gunmen heading his way, firing at random in his direction. He needed a distraction. Something to make them all look one way while he went the other.

He racked his brain to try to think of anything that he could do. Something. Anything.

The thing about in-ear coms was that no one else could hear what was being said between the participants. That's why Harper and Kinley – and whomever else they worked with – used them.

The thing about group walkie-talkies was that if someone from the enemy side was close enough, they could hear both ends of the conversation.

Vipers used the latter of the two, which is why when Russell Johnson's voice chirped through McCleary's radio, "Kenton!

Company on your six. Take cover," Harper had enough wits about himself to react accordingly.

He knew that the *something anything* he was trying to think of had just happened.

He also knew that trying to figure out the *who* or the *why* of it all would be pointless. Maybe it was Kinley finally breaking free of the fray at the front gate. Or Taralyn, perhaps. Could have been a snowbird, for that matter. Pointless to try to figure it out. The fact that it had happened was all that mattered.

Rowe had been around enough to know that if a line of four men was going to "take cover," two would break right and two would break opposite. With his back to the quartet of shooters, his best offensive ploy would be to circle back and take out the assailants that would be breaking right.

In this case, the two unfortunate souls that were breaking right were Calvin Walters and Jay Hammers.

Taking a split second to verify his theory, Harper saw the two Vipers on the right obey the call to "Take cover!"

His instincts were correct.

They broke for cover.

Harper fired seven shots.

Shots one and two put Calvin Walters and Jay Hammers face down in the snow next to each other, dead before their noses had a chance to get colder than they already were.

Harper skedaddled into the darkness expecting to draw more fire from the other members of the firing line.

He was surprised when there was none. The *something-anything* that had bailed him out of his predicament was now the target of the gunfire that should have been aimed at him.

Whoever he or she was, they were now in extreme danger. Having just had his life saved, Harper felt it only proper to return the favor in kind.

REALIZATION OF A HERO

Aimee Schmidt was not much of a crier.

The only child of a traveling father and a career politician mother, Aimee had spent her childhood surrounded by everyone *but* her parents. A series of nannies toted her around to countless political events at which Brenda would dote on her darling daughter as she prattled on about family values, cleaning up television and the school system, sex in advertising, and on and on. All this so that her daughter could grow up in a world where "values were not a foreign concept." Of course, once the event was over, Aimee would be sent on her way with the babysitter of the week.

Still, Aimee remembered being happy during those days. But reality became harsher as the cute factor wore off. Instead of the actual *her*, pictures of Aimee as a cute little kid were used during her mother's family values speeches. Aimee, herself, was shuttled aside because she was no longer the tool that her mother needed to further her political career.

From that point on, Aimee Schmidt became a bitter and disappointed young lady.

Bitter and disappointed, yes. But sad? No. Sadness and sorrow were never in the mix.

Until now.

Until now, Aimee had never known anyone who was willing to put their life on the line for her safety and well-being. Sure, there had been security agents assigned to her protection duty. But even then, she wondered how many of them would have made the ultimate sacrifice for her.

Taralyn had been holding Aimee so tightly during their escape that Aimee had actually felt the impact of the bullets that Taralyn took on her behalf.

Now, sitting next to the body of the woman that had given up her own life for her, Aimee Schmidt was nothing but tears.

"I – I don't – I don't even know her."

"It's just how things go, kid," Kinley stated. "She was that kind of person. If she had it to do all over again, she wouldn't change a thing."

The senator's daughter sobbed uncontrollably, her face buried in her hands.

Big James sat down in the snow next to Aimee. Cold as he was, he took off his coat and put it around her shoulders. Looking up at Kin and Laurie, he nodded, letting them know that he would stay with the girl.

"Go get my boy," he said, "and let's get out of here. I don't know if it's bothering you two or not, but this cold weather is really starting to become a bit irksome."

Kin looked at the love of his life. "You heard the man. Let's go get his boy."

"Keep your head up, Big James," Laurie said as she double-checked her weapons. "We won't be gone long."

The Last of the Vipers

McCleary, Potts, and Johnson were the only Viper members in the cemetery that were still breathing. On their knees behind three adjacent tombstones, they were blasting away at Jeb Crool and the concrete monument behind which he was hiding.

"Let's get Harrison on the horn, figure out where he can pick us up, grab the money, and get ourselves outta here," Potts suggested.

"Forget that," McCleary answered. "We're not leaving here until that piece of windshield bird crap Harper Rowe is dead."

"Come on, Kent. Don't be stupid," Johnson added. "Let's live to fight another day. We can track that muttonhead down when he least expects it and light him up like a fireworks display. Really shove the ol' bumbershoot right into his rectum and open that thing up."

"No way, man. Out of the question. I am *not* letting that little piss-ant get the best of us."

"Swallow your pride, boss. This job has gotten away from us. We need to make a break for it while we still can."

"Hold up!" McCleary stopped firing and slowly lowered his gun. "He's either dead or out of bullets. I don't think he's returned fire for some time now."

After waiting for a good ten count, Kenton yelled, "You there! Behind the Mary statue. If you're still alive, throw out your weapons and come out with your hands up."

Jeb was very much still alive, but he was also very much out of ammo.

"If I come out peacefully, are you going to let me go?"

"Absolutely," McCleary said, shaking his head no to his teammates. "I mean, what do we care? By the time somebody gets to you, or you get to somebody, we're going to be on a chopper and a long, long way away from here."

"Okay, well, I'm pretty sure because of the cold temperatures that you probably can't feel it, but your nose is getting longer than Pinocchio's – because I'm quite confident that you're lying out both sides and the middle of your mouth," Jeb hollered.

"Ha. That's funny. You're a funny guy. You don't sound like Harper Rowe, so I am going to assume that you're Kinley Devereaux."

"Yep. Sure am."

Harper Rowe, who had sneaked to within ten feet of Crool's position, heard the entire conversation. He did not know *who* was curled up behind the Mother Mary statue, but he did know that it was not Kinley Devereaux.

Back on his belly, Harper moved ever so carefully through the snow and grave markers of the Sunset Memorial Park Cemetery. He was quite impressed with the effectiveness of his winter outfit. With the wintry precip, the mind-numbing cold, the piercing winds, and all the snow that he had crawled through, Harper was still able to feel just about every part of his body. He made a mental note to write the company a five-star review once all this craziness was over.

He had gotten to within four feet of Crool before the NSA agent finally saw him. Jeb jumped in a panic, pointing his gun at the approaching figure.

"Don't think you're going to be able to shoot me with an empty gun, smart guy." Harper got up on all fours and expeditiously finished his route to Jeb.

"Harper?" Jeb whispered.

Harper put his face up to within a few inches of the stranger. "Holy Shiite Muslims. You're Jeb Crool."

"Special Agent Jeb Crool, actually."

Harper laughed quietly. "Oh, my goodness gracious," he shook his head in disbelief. "Honestly – and I mean, stone-cold sincerity time – in all the months and months that you've been after me, did you ever think that our first face-to-face would be anything remotely close to this?"

Before Jeb could give his stone-cold sincere answer, Harper started talking again. "I mean, what in the purple haze are you even doing here? You are *here*, right? I'm not hallucinating all of this because the cold has finally turned my brain into a cherry slushy, am I?"

"No, you're not hallucinating. I'm really here. *How* I got here is quite a long story, though – but one I fully, *fully* intend to make a shipload of money off of, by the way."

"Oh, yeah? Hey, man, that's a great idea. Ya know...if you need my help with any of that, don't hesitate to ask. I mean it."

"I won't, but...I think...maybe..."

"Yeah?"

"We may need to get out of our current predicament here before we go making any future plans. Know what I mean? You don't, perchance, happen to have an extra gun or two, do ya?"

"Perchance, I do."

It was then that they realized that McCleary was still yelling and waiting on an answer.

"Mr. Devereaux?"

"Yeah!"

"What's it going to be?"

Jeb looked at Harper. "Any idea what he's asking?"

"Not a clue."

"Hey, you know my name. What's yours?" Jeb asked McCleary.

"Are you kidding me? I just told you. Now, stop fooling around, and either come out with your hands in the air, or we're going to just come get you and shoot you in the head."

"I think that's what he was asking," Harper indicated.

"Yeah, okay." Jeb hollered. "I'm throwing out my guns."

He took the two weapons that he had and flung them toward the trio of Vipers.

Harper then handed him a Glock 18 and a Glock 35.

"They're loaded and the safeties are off, so – you know – be careful."

"You're not going to leave me out there twisting in the wind, are you?"

"Nope. Whenever you're ready just say, 'Can you believe this idiotic weather?' and jump for cover. They'll start shooting at you, and that's when I'll come up firing. You come up firing, too. We'll make mincemeat out of these chumps."

"I'm counting on you," Jeb whispered as he stood up and walked out from behind the religious statue, hands in the air. He spotted a decent-sized gravestone off to his right. That would be where he would jump for cover when the time came.

"You know there are a whole lot of people looking for you, Mr. Devereaux," McCleary said. "I'm sure I could get another five million bucks just for you alone."

"*Another* five million?"

"Yeah. You know, on top of the five million that the senator sent along with you." McCleary thought it was odd that Devereaux would ask that. Crool realized that he may have inadvertently said the wrong thing, so he cut to the chase.

"Can you believe this idiotic weather?" Jeb said in a hurry. Then he dove, head first, like he was stealing second base, behind the aforementioned gravestone.

On cue, Harper stepped from behind the Mother Mary statue and commenced firing. Kenton, Kiyo, and Russell, now no longer taking cover behind the three tombstones, were all focused on Jeb, giving Rowe time to make sure his aim was true. He fired his first shot into the chest of Kenton McCleary, his second shot into Russell Johnson's head, and his third shot kneecapped Kiyo Potts. The damage was all done before Agent Jeb Crool could come up for air and fire either Glock.

Then, as if they had been waiting in the wings for the shooting to end, Kinley and Laurie came rushing onto the scene.

"Everybody okay?" Devereaux called out.

"I'm okay. You okay?" Harper replied.

"Geez, dude. I thought you were a goner. I've been hollerin' at ya for the last twenty minutes through the com. I kept hearing gunshots from down here, though, so I figured you were still alive."

"I had a bit of an accident with the snowmobile," Harper admitted. "I'm okay, but it did knock my com out, apparently."

"What about you, Agent Crool?" Laurie asked.

"Whaddaya mean?"

"For the last few minutes, I've been trying to reach you and Agent Baldwin through the com you gave me and Mr. Gray. But I haven't heard anything from either of you."

"Oh, no. Dave." Jeb suddenly took off through the snow toward the utility shed.

"Hold up, Laurs," Harper said, walking over to the three Vipers laying in the snow. One of them was dead, one was well on his way to being there soon, and one was *wishing* she was well on her way to being there. "Did you say 'Mr. Gray'? As in Big James Gray? He's here?"

"He is," Kinley answered. "He's back up by the entrance with the senator's daughter and...Taralyn."

"Why?" Now it was Harper's turn to be confused. "I don't

mean why is he back up with the senator's daughter and Taralyn. I mean why is he here? In the U.S.? And, more to the point, why is *Jeb Crool* – the man who is leading the investigation into the three of us, the man who spent the better part of the last eighteen months trying to find me so that he could have me arrested, the man—"

Harper's rant was interrupted by a scream in the night.

It was Jeb.

Kinley looked at Laurie. "You wanna go check that out? I'll stay here with Harp."

"Yeah, I'll see what's going on." Chase gave her boyfriend a sorrowful look. She knew that Kin was staying behind to tell Harper about Taralyn, a task she most certainly did not envy.

She put her gun away and went off into the night to find Jeb.

Heartbreaking Discovery

Jeb knew something was wrong the minute he rounded the corner of the utility shed. His keychain flashlight showed that Agent Baldwin was covered in blood, too much blood for the two gunshot wounds that he had sustained. David Baldwin's eyes were shut and his breathing was shallow.

"Dave?" Jeb knelt down next to his partner. "You still with me, brother?"

Dave opened his eyes. "I'm still here, boss, but I ain't feelin' too swell."

"You've lost a lot of blood." Using his little flashlight, Jeb started inspecting Dave's body, looking for the reason for all the blood loss. The wound to Dave's stomach was a minor through-and-through off to his right side, just above where his appendix would have been had he not had it removed when he was 15 years old.

Jeb then checked the wound to Agent Baldwin's shoulder. There he found the problem: The bullet had entered just below the shoulder, rupturing his brachial artery.

Jeb's heart sank. They were in the middle of nowhere, and at the rate Dave was losing blood, he was going to bleed out before help could arrive.

"I've seen that look on your face before, boss," Dave sighed. "Things aren't good, are they?"

"No, they sure aren't, pal. Not good at all."

"Well, did you see Harper Rowe?"

"I sure did," Jeb managed a sad smile. "Dumb jackass even had the audacity to save my life, of all things."

"Oh, man...I really hate that guy."

"Yeah. Well, I hate to admit it, Dave, but I don't know what to do here," Jeb said, trying to choke back the tears.

"Am I going to die?"

Jeb was silent

"Feels like I'm going to die," Dave admitted.

"Anything you want me to say to your wife? Anyone at work?"

"My wife. There's a letter in my locker. Can you make sure she gets it?"

"Absolutely."

"And make sure she's okay."

"I will. I promise."

"And make sure you're okay."

Jeb sat down in the snow next to Baldwin and put his arm around his friend. "It's been a good run, Dave." Jeb was quiet for a few moments. "You were the best agent I ever worked with." A cold, lonely tear ran down his cheek. "Thank you for always having my back."

"Anytime, boss." Dave's words were slurred. "I think I'm going to...go to sleep now."

With that, Baldwin slid lifelessly into Jeb's arms.

Crool laid his friend down in the snow and let out a blood-curdling scream.

Anger. Sadness. Frustration.

The loss of his best agent.

The loss of his best friend.

Goodbye for Now

David Baldwin was not the only one whose life was ending. Kenton McCleary was also just moments away from expiring, due to the gaping bullet wound in his chest.

Harper Rowe kneeled down next to him. "I know now is not the time for me to be a donkey butt since you're obviously on your way out. Still, if you were going to be around for a little while longer, I'd gladly point out to you at least five different things you and your crew did wrong."

Kenton wanted more than anything to tell Harper Rowe to go screw himself, but since he was unable to talk, he tried to convey it with his eyes.

"Yeah. I get that," Harper said, catching McCleary's look. "What I will say instead is that you and your team put up a good fight. You were just fighting a losing battle. If it hadn't been you, it would have been somebody else."

"Harper, what the heck are you doing? Get away from that guy, will ya? He's trying to die, for crying out loud."

"What?" Harper was annoyed. "I'm just trying to make him feel better before he dies. I would hope that someone would do the same for me when I pass."

"Well, for one, we have a live one over here. Maybe we could question her about all this, and, for number two...I kinda need to talk to you about something."

"If it's about how we're going to clean this mess up, don't worry 'bout that, buddy. I've already got it all figured out."

"No, Harper, it's not that." Kinley paused for a moment, trying to think of the best way to break the news to his partner about Taralyn.

It was so quiet. After all the yelling and the shooting and the ducking for cover, the only sound was the wind and the snow falling – and Kinley's awkward silence.

Unfortunately, he waited just a little too long before speaking again.

The sound void was broken by the ringtone of "Superwoman" by Alicia Keys on McCleary's cell phone. Harper fished through the man's pockets until he located it. Pulling it out of McCleary's jacket, he read the phone number and the identifying name that accompanied it: "The Senator."

"Good gold, it's the senator!"

"Dude, don't answer that."

"Not gonna answer it, but I'm definitely gonna hang on to this." Harper looked at Kenton, who, by now, had made his way to the afterlife. "Mind if we hold on to this? No? Fantastic. Thank you. Oh, and while I'm at it, I'm gonna grab your radio, too." Rowe looked back to Kinley. "He is fine with us holding onto this stuff."

"Cool, cool, cool. Hold on to that, for sure. But I still have to talk to you. It's about...it's about Taralyn."

Harper stood up and put McCleary's phone and radio in his pockets. He looked at his friend. "What about Taralyn?"

"When we were riding out – up to the entrance – with the senator's daughter, a couple of shooters got the drop on us from behind. Taralyn was shielding the girl, and she...she took three bullets, Harp."

"Well, good lord, man. Why are we standing around here? We need to get her to a hospital."

"No," Kinley said barely loud enough to hear. "No...we don't."

"What? What do you mean? Why not?" Harper asked the question, but he knew.

"I'm sorry, man. She held on as long as she could. She—" Harper did not stick around to hear the rest of the sentence. He took off running as fast as he could toward the cemetery entrance.

"Harper!" Kinley called after him. "Harper, wait." He put his hands on his side where he had just been shot. "Ah...never mind."

"It's okay, baby," Laurie told Kinley through the com. "There was no easy way to do that. You did your best."

"I know how bad I'm feeling about Taralyn being gone, and I wasn't even close to her. And knowing that Harper feels about her the way he does...it's going to take him a while to get over this. I can't even begin to imagine what he's going...to be going through... losing her like this. He's going to blame himself, I just know it." Kinley wiped his eyes.

"Well, unfortunately, he's not the only one to lose somebody."

"What do you mean?"

"I found Jeb. One of his men that has been with us since we left Rio didn't make it through tonight's events either."

"Are you with Agent Crool now? How is he doing?"

"I am, and I guess he's doing all right. He wants the senator just as bad as we do now. After this, I guess we all are going to want a piece of her. Question is: How are we going to do it?"

"We've got a live one here. Skinny black chick that Harper decided to kneecap. I'm gonna grab her. Let's regroup up where we were. We're going to need to come up with a plan. It's time to end this...once and for all."

✳　　✳　　✳

Big James heard footsteps coming up behind him. He pulled his weapon and turned on a dime. "Don't come any closer, or I *will* shoot! Identify yourself."

"It's me, ya big, lovable mook."

"Harper Rowe?" Big James lowered his gun. "Well get on over here and give us a hug, ya handsome devil, you."

The two men exchanged a hefty hug, then separated and shook hands.

"I need to say good-bye to my friend."

"She's right over here," Big James put his arm around his buddy and began leading him to where Taralyn's body was lying. "I can't tell you how sorry I am, chief. I didn't know her, but I knew that she was with you and Devereaux in Prague. Plus she's your friend, and I know that any friend of yours is alright in my book. I will tell you, though...she looks rough. She took quite a beating, but she kept the girl alive She died a hero."

Harper and Big James approached Taralyn's body. Aimee Schmidt was leaning up against a nearby tombstone, still weeping over the woman that had saved her life.

"I'm so sorry," she said to Harper. "This is all my fault."

Harper kneeled next to Taralyn and pulled the coat away from her face. Seeing her pale skin and closed eyes, he leaned down and kissed her forehead. Then he sat down next to her, wrapped his arms around her and pulled her onto his lap. Cradling her head in his arms, he said to Aimee, "This isn't your fault. This is one hundred percent your mother's fault. You don't need to feel any kind of bad about what happened here tonight."

"Well, if it wasn't for me finding out about what she did, none of this would have ever happened."

"If she hadn't done what she did, you wouldn't have had to find out about it and none of this would have ever happened. You blaming yourself is putting the blame on the wrong person. This was all your mom's doing."

"Are you going to kill her?" Aimee asked.

"Thinkin' about it," Harper answered, "but I think I'm going to want your mom to suffer a little bit more than just being killed by the likes of me. I think my friends and I are going to try to bring to light just what she is doing and what she has done. I want them to throw her in the deepest hole that they can find and never let her out."

"What are you going to do with me? I would do anything that you need me to so that you could get my mother. I mean it. Anything."

"Well, we're going to need you to come along with us. We will need you to testify about all of this – what you know, when you knew it, how you found out about it. It won't be easy because it's probably going to take a long, long time for all of this to go to court. And people are probably going to be mean to you. People are more than likely going to be rude to you. Some people are even going to call you names and try to make you think that you're the bad guy. Still, in the end, it will be worth it. You'll just have to be tough, is all." Harper looked up from Taralyn's body and asked with the utmost seriousness, "Are you tough, baby?"

"I can be."

"Well, I think you're tough, and I think that your toughness and your testimony will be enough to do your mom in. Would you do that for me?" Harper looked down at Tara. "Would you do it for her?"

"I will," Aimee affirmed. "Now, I know what you might be thinking. You might be thinking that I will get up there to testify, and I will get all sentimental and think about how things used to be, when they were good with my mom, and I'm going to change my mind about my testimony. Am I right?"

"I wouldn't think that about you, Ms. Schmidt. I hope that wouldn't even come up. Your getting cold feet, I mean."

"I know that what my mother was about to do to us – and is planning to do to this country – is wrong...on so many different levels. She needs to be stopped and fast. I know that I have enough on her to do just that, but if she gets another chance to kill me, she will. And she won't mess it up this time."

Aimee laughed. "I will say this: You three messed up their plan with that whole thing you did with Kinley and Taralyn coming down to get me first, and you coming down second with the money. They were going to wait for all three of you to come down all at once and give them the money. Then they were going to kill us all right there. I know, because they told me that was what they were going to do. Kill us all. And then you and your two friends were going to get blamed for kidnapping and killing me. My mom was all ready to play the victim card about my death, then play the hero card for catching and killing the three of you. She had it all planned out."

Noticing that Harper was lost in his sorrow over Taralyn, Aimee stopped her diatribe. Seeing this man so crippled by the death of his friend – it only made her want to help him and his people all the more.

Aimee Schmidt was not one for praying, but when she heard Harper begin to pray over his friend, it brought her to tears.

"Lord God, thank you for giving me the chance to know this fine woman and experience her friendship and humanity. I pray now that you will remember your fallen child at this, her time of passing, and know, dear Lord, that she died fighting for what was right and what was just. And, while I know that this is a selfish request and probably not even doable...but, if you can, just let her know that I love her, and that I will be counting the days until I can see her again."

Without trying to hide it, Harper began weeping like a small child. When the storm had passed, he composed himself enough to finish his invocation.

"Thank you, Lord." He sniffed a few times and wiped his eyes. "Thank you, sweet friend." He held her tightly for a long while. "Goodbye for now, Taralyn."

As if it were a divine harbinger, the wind and snow suddenly ceased, and a sense of calm settled around about the immediate surroundings.

It's Just a Privilege to Be Nominated

"You're gonna be okay, kid."

Harper looked up to see Kinley standing over him.

Laurie Chase had helped the wounded Kiyo Potts up to the entrance area and shoved her to the ground. "We'll get to you in a few minutes. Stay there, don't try anything cute, and you will be alright."

Now Chase was standing next to Kin, clinging to his arm. Jeb Crool was bringing up the rear with Agent David Baldwin's body laid across his shoulders in a fireman's carry.

"I don't know that anything's going to make you feel any better right now. But I think you'll find comfort in knowing her final words to me were that she loved you and to thank you for giving her life true meaning over the last few days."

Harper managed a feeble smile.

"Oh, yeah," Kin remembered. "Her very last words were, 'Make the senator pay.' So I'm thinking we probably shouldn't let her down on that front."

Laurie Chase moved close to Harper and put her hand out for him to grab. After carefully sliding Taralyn's body off his lap, he let Laurie help him to his feet. She hugged him close and tight. "I'm so sorry," she whispered, "but I'm so glad you're alive."

Pulling back, she gave him a kiss on the cheek.

"It's good to see you, too," he answered.

Jeb Crool carried Agent Baldwin's body over and carefully laid it in the snow next to Taralyn. He looked at the trio of Devereaux, Rowe, and Chase – the three people that had enveloped his life for the last eighteen months.

"It's hard to believe it – the three of you standing right in front of me, and me not wanting to cuff you and arrest you for treason. That has been the one thought that has driven me and kept me focused for the last year and a half. And now that the opportunity is here, I realize that the three of you are nothing more than a triumvirate of fall guys. Patsies in a political game of deception and power grabbing. All this time I kept telling myself that I wanted to know the truth about the assassination of Defense Secretary Michaels, and the role that the three of you played in it. I was sure I knew what the answers were. But now that all this has happened, and the truth has come to light, I realize that I've been played for just as big a fool as you three have."

"Well, it's time to set the record straight," Chase said.

"We're going to need one heck of a plan to do that," Kinley said. "I mean, look around. We're standing in one huge mess that needs to be cleaned up. On top of that, the senator is probably starting to get suspicious that she hasn't heard from her crew of thugs yet. And with each passing second that she doesn't, I'm sure it's another bag that she's packing in preparation to fly the coop. We're running out of time, and I don't have any idea where to even start with some semblance of a plan to salvage this mess."

"Then let's break it down," Harper said. "Let's take it step by step and figure it out."

"Okay," Kinley said, already beginning to run the situation through his mind, sifting through different scenarios to figure out which one would best fit this circumstance.

"I don't know what you three think," Jeb spoke up, "but I think we have more than enough evidence to go get this broad and charge her with everything from attempted murder to conspiracy to commit treason against the United States of America. With about thirty other charges in between. Let me make a call or two, and I can make sure that her picture goes out to every airport, bus station, train station, cab company, and any other means of escape that you can think of. She won't be able to show her face in her own bathroom without somebody trying to grab 'er up."

"Yeah, sure. That sounds great...if we were dealing with the head of the local P.T.A., Agent Crool. This woman is a high-ranking government official with access to private cars, private jets, private security, you name it. She gets even a whiff of something sour, and she'll be across the border and into Canada before you can say *guano*. And for every second that we're standing around here pulling our puds, that aroma is getting stronger. And it is definitely drifting her way."

"Fine. Just give me a second then. Let me think."

"Go on then, because a second is about all we have."

Everyone took a deep breath and continued looking for a quick solution to a problem that seemingly had no quick solution at all.

Then, without warning, a voice came across Kenton McCleary's radio that Harper had stashed in his parka pocket.

"Kenton." It was chopper pilot Harrison Roberts. "It's mighty quiet over there. Are you guys headed this way or what? Should I be readying the chopper?"

Harper pulled out the radio and spoke into it, "Chopper pilot?"

"Yeah," Roberts answered with extreme hesitance. "Who is this?"

"My name is Harper Rowe. I'm one of the men that Senator Cobb-Schmidt sent to retrieve her daughter. I kinda got some bad news for ya there, Chopper John, M.D. All but one of your crew is dead, and by the end of the night, the senator is going to be cooked like burnt toast on an open flame. If ever a jig was up, *now* is that time, and *this* is that jig."

"Who's still alive?" Roberts asked.

"Afram woman. Kinda on the skinny side."

"Kiyo'?" the pilot called out.

"Yeah, it's me, Choppy," Potts moaned in agonizing pain.

"It's true? Everyone's dead?"

"Yes. You need to get out of here, Chop. Now."

"Choppy is it?" Harper asked. "Choppy, let me give you a nickel's worth of free advice: You need to start the engine on that bird of yours and fly about as far away from here as fast as you can. Your friend here probably won't give you up. I'm sure she'll be using the senator's name to cut a deal. You leave now, you have a pretty good shot at making a clean getaway."

"Much obliged, friend," Roberts said amiably. "Take care of yourself, Potts."

Within a matter of seconds, the group heard Harrison Roberts' chopper start up in the distance. Moments later it lifted off and flew away out of sight.

"Think he'll call the senator to let her know what's happened here?" Jeb asked.

"No," Potts answered. "Kenton was the point man with Senator Cobb-Schmidt. He was the only one that knew how to get in touch with her."

Hearing that small tidbit of information sparked something in Harper's mind. "Hey," he blurted out, "I think I have a plan. Some semblance of one, at least. I'll lay it out, and we can tweak it until it becomes something workable."

"Well, show us what we're workin' with," Kinley answered.

"The way I see it, we've only got one play left, and that's to make the senator think that *she's* still got one play left, which – Jeb is right. Between her daughter's testimony, my recording of our meeting at the library earlier today, and...this," Harper spread his arms and did a spin to make allusion to the entire mess the cemetery ransom drop idea had turned out to be, "we've got enough on her to put her away into the next millennium. What we need to do is convince her that, in the grand scheme of things, nothing has really changed. We have what she wants: her daughter, as well as her five million dollars. And that she has what we want: the evidence to clear our names from the Paul Michaels' assassination."

Kinley looked at Aimee Schmidt and said, "Your mom was willing to kill you – and us – to keep alive her dream of being the president of the United States. Because you obviously know her better than any of us do, do you think she would go for this idea? That if we could get her to believe there's even half a chance we could fix all this in her favor, and she would come out the other side smelling clean as a whistle...do you think she'd buy in?"

"Duh," was Aimee's immediate and irreverent response. "You practically just said it yourself. She has and will do anything to be president. I swear to you on everything that I have and ever will have, she would definitely buy in."

"Then that's what we'll do. We'll call her from McCleary's phone. When she answers, we let her know that her group of mercenaries are dead, we have her daughter and her money, but that we're still after the one thing we came here for...our freedom. We convince her that we want that just as much as she wants to be president."

"That sounds great," agreed Laurie. "But convincing her of our sincerity is just half the battle. The other half is convincing her that we can clean up this catastrophe before anyone finds out about it. The other half of that really *is* cleaning up this fiasco before anyone finds out about it. We just don't have enough time or people."

"Actually," Jeb spoke up, "we do."

"We do?"

"You do realize that I work for the NSA, don't you? Making messes disappear without a trace is what we do best. All you guys have to do is convince the senator that you have someone at your disposal that can actually pull the job off. I mean, we can't go telling her that federal agents are aware of what's going on. Kinda defeats the purpose."

"So, you'll stay here and handle the clean-up? Aren't you going to have to tell Agent Adams about his people getting killed?" Chase asked.

"I will, but I can buy a little time. Not much, but some."

"How much?" Harper inquired.

"A few hours. That's about it, but...if I promise him a piece of the action – bring him in on taking down the senator, he might keep a lid on things for a while longer."

"That sounds proper."

"Who's going to make the call to the senator then?" Big James asked.

"I will," Kinley volunteered. "Harper, sometimes your mouth gets ahead of your brain, and you say things before you actually think them through."

"Good point," Rowe agreed.

"Laurs, the senator doesn't even know that you're with us. So, at this point, that would definitely set off some red flags. Big James, same thing. So, that leaves me. I'll make the call. I'll convince her that she's still in control."

Harper retrieved Kenton's cell phone from his pants pocket, pulled up the last incoming call, and hit the call-back button. He tossed the phone to Devereaux. "It's showtime, champ."

Kinley put the phone up to his ear and waited for the senator to answer.

He did not have to wait long. Halfway through the second ring, Brenda answered.

"Kenton, thank God. I thought I'd never hear from you. What's going on?"

"Good evening, Senator. This is Kinley Devereaux. I'm afraid your boy McDreary and all of his crew members are dead."

"Oh, godda—"

"Hey, hey, hey. No need for all that. Obviously, we know exactly what's going on, what your plan was for us and your daughter, and I'm sure you're thinking right about now that your world as you hoped to know it is over. Yes?"

"Pretty much," Brenda mumbled. "Why are you even bothering to call?"

"Well, I can assure you that I'm not calling to wish you a belated Happy New Year, Senator. I'm calling to let you know that despite your best – and worst – efforts to eradicate us from the global scene, that, as far as Harper Rowe and I are concerned, the end game has not changed. We've got your daughter and your money. You've got the evidence to clear our names. You still want to be president? Well, we still want a chance to live our lives without having to look over our shoulders every twenty minutes. Do you understand what I'm saying to you?"

"I think so. Yes." The senator's mood was beginning to brighten.

"Don't think. *Know*." Kinley was adamant.

"Okay, okay. I *know*. You want your names cleared."

"Precisely. But here's the caveat: We're playing by our rules now. First thing that changes is that your home-field advantage is over. I don't care what you have to do, Senator, but you have twenty-four hours to get to the Lincoln Memorial in D.C. We're going back to where it all began. At 7:30 Eastern Time tomorrow night, Harper Rowe, Laurie Chase, your daughter and I will be in front of the Lincoln Memorial. We'll have Aimee and your five million dollars. You bring everything you have about Paul Michaels. We make the trade in an open and public place. You go your way, and we'll go ours. So, whatever it is that you have to do to get there, you do it, and you get there."

"How do I know I can trust you? If you know that I just tried to have you killed then why in the world would you want to still help me? On top of that, I can only imagine the mess you must have left at the cemetery. Something like that doesn't just go away."

"Senator, you sent us into an inescapable death trap that we were able to escape – lives intact. I will make one phone call, and the mess you made gets swept under the rug. Those guys laying dead in the cemetery are mercenaries. They aren't going to have family members snooping around and looking for them. The only people that are going to miss them are each other, and they're all dead. And as far as trusting us? When you wake up tomorrow morning, and a shootout at the Sunset Memorial Park Cemetery *isn't* the lead headline, you'll know that we cleaned up *your* mess, and you'll know that you can trust us. Besides, this goes off without a hitch, and you get elected president, it will be nice to have the most powerful person in the world owing us a favor. And make no mistake about it, Senator Cobb-Schmidt, you will owe us...big time. Understand?"

"I understand."

"Then say it: 'I will owe Kinley Devereaux, Harper Rowe, and Laurie Chase *big time*.'"

"Fine. I *will* owe Kinley Devereaux, Harper Rowe, and Laurie Chase big time," she begrudgingly repeated.

"I think I've laid everything out perfectly clear. But just in case, I don't want there to be any misgivings about what's going on here. We're talking about your freedom just as much as we're talking about ours." He let those words hang in the air for a bit. "Any questions?"

"Twenty-four hours, Lincoln Memorial. I bring your evidence, you bring my daughter and my money. Make the trade and go our separate ways, and I owe you a huge debt of gratitude. Sound about right?"

"Come alone. And if you try anything to the contrary, deal's off, and you'll be living in Screwed Land, population: you."

"I'll see you tomorrow night," confirmed the senator.

Kinley disconnected the call.

Harper started clapping his hands. "Ladies and gentlemen, the Oscar for the most convincing performance on a phone call to an evil politician goes to...Kinley Felix Devereaux."

"Yeah, even I was starting to buy into your performance," Big James laughed. "Quick question, though. Why D.C.?"

"Number one, it's home. Number two, it's warmer. Number three, I have this OCD thing about making everything come full circle. This all started, Big James, because a crooked politician, former Defense Secretary Paul Michaels, decided that he could get the better of Harper, Laurie, and me by playing us for patsies. We took care of him at the Lincoln Memorial. Now, a year and a half later, we find out he had a partner in on the whole thing. Just seems poetic that we end it at the same place where it all began."

Laurie Chase looked at Jeb. "Twenty-four hours, Agent Crool. I expect that you'll be in D.C., too?"

"Of course. I've gotta be there for my happy ending." Crool looked at his fallen friend and fellow agent, David Baldwin. "If for no other reason than I owe it to him."

"What about Taralyn?" Kinley asked Harper. "What do you want to do with her?"

Harper turned to Agent Crool. "If you give me your phone number, agent. I'll text you the information with what to do with her body. I can trust you to do that?"

"You can trust me. I'll take care of your friend. You have my word." Crool walked over to Harper and shook his hand. "We're all in this together now."

MEANWHILE BACK AT CTU

Sandy Wyrick's team members sat in silence, poring over their copies of the Space Frequency files from Rae Yun Kwan's laptop. Wyrick, Bergman, Agents Sarah Beck, Tony Sawyers, and Dwight Guy had locked themselves in the conference room for the past hour, trying to figure out just what Space Frequency was. The files on the laptop contained a plethora of blueprints, a myriad of scientific and mathematical equations, in-depth directions for assembly and fabrication, and notes upon notes about the reticulation of lightweight alloy and fiber amalgamations that comprised the body of a new breed of space shuttle powered by a state-of-the-art fuel.

The CTU agents would have had nary a clue as to what made Space Frequency so unique had it not been for the summary that Dr. Rae Yun Kwan had written in relative layman's terms and appended to the file:

"In essence, due to the lightweight shell of the craft and the synthesized fuel that will burn longer and weigh less than a composition of helium and hydrogen, and an engine made of lithium metal, Space Frequency should be able to maintain speeds three times faster than that of a regular space shuttle. For example, a trip to the moon will take less than a day, as opposed to the three days it currently takes."

"This has to be real, right?" Sawyers asked. "I don't think a renowned doctor like Rae Yun Kwan is just going to sit down and write a piece of fiction like this on a laptop and then hide it in a bus locker."

"These blueprints are so detailed. There's no way that someone could have just made them up out of pure imagination."

"It really is hard to fathom, but it would seem that Senator Brenda Cobb-Schmidt assembled herself a team of astrophysicists, engineers, and mechanics that managed to create an invention the likes of which the world has never known," Sawyers said.

"It's a rocket ship, correct?" Bergman asked.

"Not just a rocket ship, Sam. A space shuttle...a space shuttle that, it would appear, will go to the moon and back like you drive your car to the market for milk," Sandy Wyrick replied. "What we need is to get a NASA engineer in here to confirm that the specifications of this thing are truly accurate. Anyone have any NASA connections?"

After an awkward silence, Tony Sawyers stood up and left the room, only to return a few moments later.

Giving a thumbs up, Tony said, "George Tate knows the secretary of one of the higher-ups over there at NASA. He's going to make a few calls. Said he'll have someone here within the hour."

"Thank you, Tony," the boss nodded.

"Here's the next million-dollar question: If the senator really has had this thing built, then where on God's green earth is it?"

"Where is it," Beck reiterated, "and why is she killing everyone that helped her make it?"

"I saw four names that Dr. Kwan kept mentioning: herself, Bradley, and two other guys. Those four had to be strictly the logistics part of this thing. There must be another entire group that did the hands-on assembly. The senator had to have kept the hands-on crew completely separate from the planning crew, because Kwan never even mentions anything about them," Sandy answered.

"Maybe there isn't a separate assembly crew," Bergman suggested. "Maybe this thing hasn't been put together yet."

"Oh, this thing has been put together already, for sure," Wyrick said.

"And what makes you say that?" Dwight Guy asked.

"Because if it wasn't, she wouldn't be killing off her logistics team. I mean, what if something had gone wrong halfway through the assembly process? She would have needed her blueprint people around to make sure that everything went the way it was supposed to."

"True," Dwight Guy admitted. "This is just – hands down – one of the most unreal things I have ever seen, read, or encountered. I am at a complete loss for words."

"Alright, people," Wyrick rose to her feet. "This has officially gotten to the point of being too big for just us. Time to bring in some other agencies. Sounds like we've got someone from NASA on their way here. I have a good friend over at the Bureau named Todd Adams. I'm going to give him a call and get them involved. And Sam, I want you and Tony to find out where the good senator is. I don't care what she's doing, I don't care where she's doing it, and I don't care who she is doing it with – bring her in. If you two have to call the president himself to get it done then, by God, you do it."

Looking back at her computer, Sandy began searching through the text screen.

"Agent Beck," she said to Sarah, "the two other men that were on the Space Frequency team, Dr. David Hess and Ronald Zook – find out where they are and get them in here. Again, I don't care what you have to do to get the job done. If they are still alive, we'll need to get them a protection detail, asap."

Sandy turned to look at all the members of the CTU squad. "Most importantly, above all else, keep this quiet. No one, and I mean *no one*, can know what we're doing here."

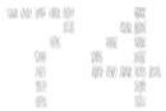

DREAMS OF BETTER THINGS

"Jeb, I've sent a couple of addresses to your phone," Harper informed the agent.

"I see that. Perhaps, you should assign a designation to them."

"The first one is where Taralyn Tharp's body is to be sent. You can still make that happen, yes?"

"Yes."

"The second one – the White Marsh, Maryland, address – that is where I want you to meet up with the five of us tomorrow before our meeting with the senator."

"Got it."

"Actually," Big James joined in, "albeit against every fiber of good sense I have in my body – although, for the record, I think every fiber of good sense I have in my body is currently frozen senseless – I think I'm going to stay with Agent Crool and give him a hand with the afterparty clean-up."

"What?" Chase was the first to react. "No."

"I've been mulling it over for the last ten minutes, so, yeah. I find if I think about something for more than ten minutes, then it falls into the category of *overthinking* something. Besides, the only reason I'm here and not sitting in a Rio prison cell is because Agent Crool convinced Tenente Aline Rapido that he needed me to testify against the senator more than she needed me to pad her arrest statistics. Plus, if I'm here, I can help ensure that he makes it to D.C. in time for tomorrow's festivities. Something tells me that—"

"Wait," Harper interrupted. "Why would *you* be testifying against the senator? I mean, how do you even *know* about the senator in the first place?"

"Oh, you didn't tell them yet?" Jeb looked at Laurie.

"Tell us what?"

"There's a lot that I haven't had a chance to tell them because... somebody doesn't know how to keep their phone charged," Chase shot a glare at Harper.

"Well, I didn't think that recording our meeting with the senator this afternoon was going to use up all my juice like it did."

"Hold on," Crool spoke up. "I heard you say something about a recording earlier. What is it that you recorded?"

"Our meeting with the senator today where she told us all about what we would be doing tonight."

"You serious?"

"As a librarian, Agent Crool."

"Then, tell me again, *why* are you going to meet with her in D.C. tomorrow? It would seem that we already have more than enough to put her away for the rest of her natural born days."

"It's like we said before, Agent Crool. Things haven't changed in the last ten minutes. If we don't show tomorrow, she bolts. And you and your boys spend the next one to two years trying to track her down and get her back here to stand trial for all the wrongs that she has done. That's also another one to two years that she's out there roaming free with an opportunity to take us out so that we can't testify against her once she *does* get extradited. I'd just as soon she try to kill us tomorrow, let us nab her butt once and for all and just get it over with already."

"Unless, Agent Crool," Kinley spoke up, "you don't think that you and your boys can give us the proper protection that we'll be needing at the meeting with the good senator tomorrow night."

"Me and my boys will do everything we can, but you have to understand that nothing is ever a guarantee. There're a lot of underlying factors that cannot be controlled. Everybody here knows that...with the exception of you," he nodded toward Aimee Schmidt. "But now you know, too."

"I feel enlightened," the youngster retorted.

"So, that being said," Crool continued, "you're really putting your lives on the line meeting up with her tomorrow night. You have to know she won't be coming alone either."

"Way I see it?" Harper shrugged. "It's just another charge to throw into the shopping cart before we get her into the judicial checkout line."

"Is that the real reason you're staying behind, big man?" Aimee asked Big James. "The danger factor?"

"I'm staying behind for the reasons I stated earlier. Frankly, the danger factor never really entered my mind. Stuff like that usually comes up around the eleventh minute of pondering matters. That's why I don't think about things for too long. Second guessing and self-doubt will eventually start creeping in. I don't need that. Ain't nobody 'at needs that."

"Fine," Harper looked at his three mates. "Kin, Laurie, Aimee... any of yas having second thoughts about meeting up with the senator tomorrow night?"

"Not even."

"Absolutely not."

"You couldn't keep me away," Chase was the last to answer.

"Then it's settled. I'll call Rob Perry and have him set up a private flight to D.C. for us in a couple of hours. We've a date with a senator tomorrow night."

"You've got calls to make. I've got calls to make. Best we get to it," Jeb suggested, extending his hand.

Kinley was the first to shake it. "Kinda surreal – the four of us working together after all this time."

"I don't know about surreal," Jeb smiled. "It's definitely ironic. I think surreal will hit when we're all sitting next to each on the set of *Good Morning, America*, talking about how we toppled the greatest U.S. conspiracy of all time."

"No offense, Jeb," Harper said as he shook the agent's hand, "but I'm going to need my own airtime. So while the lot of yas are doing *Good Morning, America*, I'm going to be on the set of *Good Morning, Britain* telling Charlotte Hawking all about the wonders of me."

"Charlotte Hawkins?" Big James suddenly perked up. "Oh, yeah, I'm with Harp on this one. That woman...yeah...she's definitely... mm-hmm...absolutely."

"Well, everyone just keep your thoughts of stardom and reality TV fame in check for a little while longer," Laurie Chase said as she, too, shook Jeb Crool's hand. "There's still a lot of work to be done."

COMPARING SOMETHING BIG

Sandy Wyrick had known FBI Agent Todd Adams since their years at the academy together. Having worked on a few joint task force operations over the years, they even dated briefly before realizing that their jobs and duty to country took up most of their waking hours. It was an amicable break-up, and they had remained good friends through the years. Wyrick knew that the FBI had to be brought in on this case, so she did not hesitate to give Todd a call.

Wyrick's number was programmed into Adams' phone, so he was quick to answer when her name popped up on the screen, "Sandy Wyrick. To what do I owe the pleasure?"

"You owe the pleasure of being brought in on something big that my team and I have stumbled upon. I need you and anyone that you can spare to come to my office and check it out immediately."

"Any chance it can wait? I am up to my eyeballs in something pretty big, too. We've got two missing DOJ agents and a former NSA handler named Kelly Campbell that seems to have vanished, as well."

"That does sound important, but I'm pretty sure that my something big beats your something big—"

"Well, wait, I'm not done yet. Earlier this morning, two NSA agents showed up. They had two civilians with them. And while we were not formally introduced, I recognized one of the civilians as Laurie Chase."

"Laurie Chase? The former DEA agent that everyone thought was dead for the last year or so until just a few days ago?"

"One and the same."

"Okay, then. Sounds like your something big might be growing a bit," Wyrick admitted.

"And I'm still not done yet. If you think that's something, then hang on to your hat for this: The two NSA agents, the two civilians, and four of my crew took off a few hours ago to go roundup none other than Kinley Devereaux and Harper Rowe."

"Rowe and Devereaux are back in the States?"

"Yes – and get this – they're apparently involved in some sort of ransom drop for Aimee Schmidt, the daughter of our beloved senator, Brenda Cobb-Schmidt."

"Whoa, whoa, whoa, whoa...whoa!"

"I know, right? I told you it was big."

"No, not just that, Todd," Wyrick said. "My big *also* involves our beloved senator. Except once you see what we have, you may not find her so beloved anymore."

"So, I've told you mine. Now, you tell me yours."

"Okay, but now it's *your* turn to hang on to your hat. We've got files from what we believe to be a very reliable source, and these files tell a story, Todd. They tell a story about our senator putting together a team of NASA engineers and having a state-of-the-art space shuttle built, and then, in order to keep it a secret...it looks like she may have had two members of her team murdered. And when I say *may have*, I mean, *most definitely did*."

She heard Agent Adams stifle a laugh. "Sandy, you know April first isn't for another few months, right?"

"Yeah, hey, I know it sounds like complete caca. But Todd,

when have you ever known me to be the joking type? Especially when it comes to work."

"You're serious about this? You've got hard evidence—"

"Hard evidence."

"That says the senator of the state of Minnesota—"

"Yes."

"The front runner to be the next president of the United States—"

"Correct."

"Had a secret space shuttle built and then committed a double homicide to cover it up?"

"Is what I'm saying."

Todd was silent for a good ten count.

"I'll see you in twenty minutes."

Story Time with Laurie Chase

Kinley, Harper, Laurie, and Aimee spent the next few hours riding back to the hauling trailer, reloading the snowmobiles, and returning them to the sporting goods store.

Harper had already called his good friend Rob Perry and made the necessary arrangements for a private flight to Washington, D.C. Once they dropped off the snowmobiles, they drove straight to the airfield to catch their flight to Maryland. Harper had also asked Rob to arrange for a nurse to treat Kinley's gunshot wounds, old and new, and to set each of them up with a fresh set of duds for the trip back east.

They packed all the weapons they had used at the graveyard shootout back into the suitcase that Perry had provided for them. The guns would eventually make their way back to Rob's possession. He would then dispose of them properly so that they could never be linked back to the events that had taken place at the cemetery.

Once aboard the plane, Aimee found a nice white leather couch, a pillow, and a blanket. She slept while Kinley, Harper, and Laurie Chase sat around a table talking.

"Okay, Laurs, you want to walk us through just how it came to pass that we're now working *with* Jeb Crool and the NSA on all of this?" Kinley asked.

"Well," she leaned forward, put her elbows on the table and clasped her hands under her chin. "I guess it all started when we stopped the terrorist attack at that club in Rio. Our faces got plastered all over the internet which led the NSA straight to us. Just about the time you two left town with Taralyn to go to Prague, Jeb and his crew showed up looking for us. Big James, Diego, and I tracked Tito del Fuento and his family to one of their safe houses after they returned to Rio."

"Yeah, I remember. I talked to you on the phone right before you and James were getting ready to take that place," Kinley recalled.

"Exactly right. So, the three of us are getting ready to raid the place and finally take care of Tito once and for all, when Jeb and Agent Baldwin show up from out of nowhere. They had sniffed out where we were. So, we tell them why we're there, and what we're doing, and they agree to help us – which was good because we were completely outmanned and outgunned at this safe house.

"Anyway, we take the safe house. And when we do, Tito del Fuento spills the beans about the drug raid in Mexico City. Seems he had set up a deal with two members of the U.S. government that, in return for financial favors, they would help his drug trade business flourish in the U.S.A. The two government officials: Secretary of Defense Paul Michaels and Senator Brenda Cobb-Schmidt.

"Well, I recognized the senator's name because when we were talking on the phone, you told me that Kelly Campbell had set up a meeting with the senator because she had the evidence that would clear our names. When Jeb hears the senator's name, he of course recognizes it because he knows that she's running for president. Meanwhile, I'm trying to call you," Laurie looked at Kinley, "and I'm freaking out because I can't get in touch with you.

"So, at some point, I make a deal with Jeb that I can get him to you two and the senator in exchange for keeping Big James out of jail and getting us back here to the States. He agrees, which, obviously, was a good thing because it was the only way I could think of to get to you and warn you in time that you all were walking into a trap. Plus, the flight back from Rio gave me a chance to tell Jeb the *real* story about what happened with Paul Michaels and Mexico City. After that, he was hip to what was really going on. And he was onboard from there."

"And the truth shall set you free," Kinley quoted.

"I'm guessing Big James was there when Tito dropped the dime on the senator?" Harper asked.

"He was."

"And that's what he was talking about when he said Jeb kept him out of prison in exchange for his testimony against the senator?"

"You got it," Chase smiled. "Okay, so here is my question: Do we know why the senator wants her daughter dead so badly?"

"Yeah, yeah, we do. Seems that Senator Cobb-Schmidt is running on a family values platform, which there's nothing wrong with that, except that the senator had an affair of some sort...and her daughter found out about it."

"You're kidding, right?"

"A lot of times, yes. This time, no," Harper said.

"You're saying that instead of dropping out of the race or just coming clean about it, she thought it best to just kill her daughter?"

"Kill her daughter, kill us, frame us for it all. Yeah, when it comes to the senator, I certainly wouldn't want to see her coming down my chimney on Christmas Eve."

"The funny thing is," Kinley shook his head, "she's probably going to give a repeat performance tomorrow night when we all meet up with her again."

Harper Rowe's cell phone suddenly rang. It was Jeb Crool.

"Hello, Jeb. Calling to give us an update on things?"

"Kinda, I guess. Had some guys out here within an hour of the four of you leaving. Clean up's just about done."

"Sounds good. So, you and Big James will be—"

"That's not really why I was calling, Harper."

"Okay."

"See, Todd Adams is the head of the FBI team that is looking into your friend Kelly Campbell's disappearance. Those four federal agents that bought the farm earlier tonight...those were his people."

"Right. I understand that. Does this have something to do with why—"

"He was calling my phone, once – maybe twice – an hour. He was wondering what was going on. I didn't answer, of course."

"Of course."

"But then, all of a sudden, he starts calling...over and over and over again. Just relentless, ya know? Just non-stop."

"Okay."

"So, I figure that I've held him off for as long as I can...time to answer the phone."

"Did you?"

"Yes," Jeb answered flatly. "I did."

"And?"

"And he didn't beat around the bush. He got right to it."

"Meaning?"

"You're going to answer this question one of two ways: You're either going to say 'yes,' or you're going to laugh hysterically at me because of the insanity of this question."

"Okay."

"Do either of the three of you know...anything...about a secret state-of-the-art...space shuttle?"

Harper started to laugh hysterically.

Then, after about ten seconds, he abruptly stopped and said, "Yes."

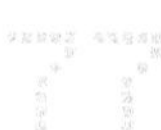

THE CLOAKED EXPLOSIVES SPECIALIST

While his current address was 2484 White Hook Road in Minneapolis, Minnesota, Ralph Finnegan was an Irishman through and through.

He even pronounced his first name like an Irishman. To look at it in print, a person might think that Ralph's name was pronounced *ralf*, but Ralph pronounced it the Irish way, which was *rayf*.

He was born in Ireland, raised in Ireland, and became part of the Irish Republic Army at age 18. He gave them the best 27 years of his life. Then, at the age of 45, he asked to walk away.

He asked. They let him. With the understanding that, once a member of the IRA, always a member of the IRA. If they called him and needed to take advantage of his special skills, he would certainly oblige.

Because Ralph, no doubt, had special skills.

He was an expert at what he did. And once an expert, always an expert. Sure, they might get old and lose their mind a bit, maybe get a tremor in their hands with some sort of neurological disease like Parkinson's or multiple sclerosis, and not be the expert they once were. But Ralph's mind was fine, and his hands were steady as a surgeon's.

Ralph was also a huge contributor to Senator Brenda Cobb-Schmidt's campaign. He had met her quite a few times along the early stages of her campaign trail and told her that if there was ever *anything* that she needed, he would be more than happy to help out.

Sensing that Ralph was not the typical campaign contributor, Brenda looked him up online one day to find out just what Ralph was an expert at doing.

On this early January night, Brenda realized that Ralph's specialty was just what she needed to take out Kinley Devereaux, Harper Rowe, Laurie Chase, and her very own daughter, Aimee Schmidt. She did not hesitate to reach out to him in this, her time of need.

She reached out. Ralph did not let her down.

Ralph's specialty: explosives. But not just any kind of explosives. No, Finnegan specialized in making explosives that looked like ordinary, everyday objects such as a key fob, or a necklace, or a TV remote, or a tampon. Whatever the client wanted it to look like, Ralph Finnegan could deliver.

For the senator, Finnegan delivered a very specific-looking bomb – a device that she could, literally, hand over to Devereaux, Rowe, and Chase, and they would look right at it and still not have a clue as to what it was.

Too smart to show up at Finnegan's place in person, Cobb-Schmidt sent Stephanie Cash to pick up the package that Ralph had ready and waiting.

After Stephanie had retrieved the package and all the necessary instructions on how to use it, she was careful to put two slugs into the back of Finnegan's head when his back was turned. From there, she brought the package to the senator's private jet. She boarded the plane and handed the package off to the senator.

"Looks kinda small," Steph commented.

"Oh, I assure you, it is just the perfect size, Ms. Cash."

Stephanie chuckled quietly. "It sounds like you've said that line before."

"I have. I absolutely have. Only difference is that this time...I actually mean it."

Brenda unwrapped the package to reveal an exact replica of one of her campaign pins: *Vote Cobb-Schmidt for President*. Reaching down next to her seat, she retrieved a large brown leather messenger bag that was covered with dozens of the very same pin. She placed the explosive pin on the bag amidst all the others.

"What do you think?" she asked, holding the bag up for Cash to inspect.

Cash raised an eyebrow. "I must say that if I didn't know which pin was the bomb...I wouldn't know which pin was the bomb."

"The three of them wanted the proof that was going to clear their names? Well," Cobb-Schmidt returned the bag to the floor, "be careful what you wish for. Right, Steph?"

Home. Home Again.

The plane touched down at a private airfield in the small town of Dublin, Maryland. About 40 minutes north of White Marsh, it was the hometown of one Harper Rowe.

On the plane ride in, Harper reactivated one of his rideshare accounts and put it to good use by having a ride waiting for them when they landed.

Stepping off the plane, Kinley and Harper were relieved to finally see no snow. A cool wind blew across the open airfield as Harper took a glance at his watch.

3:12 a.m. local time.

As Devereaux, Rowe, Chase, and Aimee Schmidt descended the steps of the private jet, a pair of headlights could be seen pulling up in the distance.

"Is that our ride?" Devereaux asked.

"At this time of night in this Podunk town? I sure hope so."

The vehicle's driver flashed his lights to let them know that he was, indeed, their ride.

Carrying just a few garment bags, a briefcase packed with five million dollars, and Kinley's infrared scope, the four of them hustled across the grassy field to the parking lot where a black GMC Yukon awaited them.

Kin tapped on the driver's window. "Okay if the kid rides in the back?"

"Sure thing." The driver popped the back hatch of the Yukon. Aimee hopped into the back while the rest of them piled into the back seat.

"Hey, gang, I'm Jeff," the driver introduced himself. "Don't think I've ever picked anyone up here before. Heck, I didn't know they still landed planes here, for that matter."

"Well, Jeff, they do tonight. You know where we're going?" Kin asked.

"2311 Laurel Lane in White Marsh?"

Kin and Laurie looked at Harper.

"Yes, that's right," Rowe affirmed.

"You got it, boss," Jeff replied as he put the SUV in reverse and started backing out of the airfield parking lot.

"And where – slash – what is 2311 Laurel Lane in White Marsh?" Kin asked.

"It's where I live," Harper answered, looking at Kinley as if the man had suddenly grown a second head.

"Where you live?"

"Yeah, where I live. My house."

"Wait. Are you talking about the house you bought just before we ended up in Mexico City?"

"One and the same, my good man."

"How? You've been gone for a year and a half."

"Yeah," Laurie Chase spoke up, "how have you been able to make your house payments? Also, how have you been able to keep up the maintenance on it? Your front yard must look like a wilderness after all this time."

"I've been wiring my house payments through an untraceable account to my neighbor, Regina. She has been making sure that the place is kept in good shape."

"You're kidding." Deveraux shook his head. "Geez, when I lived back here, I couldn't even get my neighbor to mow his own grass, much less mine."

"Yeah, well, Regina's great. I guess, to be honest, Regina technically owns my house. I sold it to her in a private sale. It just makes things a lot easier having the house in her name – not to mention the tax write-off. But, yeah, she sends me pictures and everything. I am blessed to have her around," Harper nodded his head a few times. "Anyway, since I only had the place for five days before the Mexico City debacle, you two will be my first house guests."

"Since you were there for such a short time, do you even have furniture? More importantly, do you have beds we can sleep in once we get there?"

"Well," Harper hesitated for a moment, "truth be told, I actually bought most of the furniture *after* Mexico City. So, while I have seen it in the pictures that Regina has sent, I haven't actually seen it in person. Still, to answer your question – yes, I have furniture and beds."

"Hold up," Devereaux said. "You mean to tell me that after Mexico City, while we were out there trying to avoid Interpol, the CIA, the FBI, the NSA, and every other initialed organization you can think of, you were on the IKEA website picking out matching love seats for a house you may have never seen again?"

"Oh, I felt very sure that I was going to see it again."

"Then your faith in things is a lot stronger than mine, brother."

"Well, there ya go. I don't have faith in *things*. I have faith in God. Plus, if it had turned out that we never made it back home again, I assure you that a house with matching love seats is a heck of a lot easier to sell than a house that's been sitting empty and dormant for over a year," Harper smiled.

"Can you believe this guy?" Kinley asked Laurs, who was sitting up tight against her boyfriend. Kinley had one arm around her shoulder while he held her hand with the other. "We're traipsing all over the globe, trying to stay alive, and this guy"—Kin smacked Harper's shoulder— "is playing Henry Homemaker and looking up cookie recipes."

"Ya know what? Good for him," Laurie patted Rowe on the knee. "Because in about twenty minutes, my lover, you and I are going to be extremely grateful for his actions." Laurie leaned in to Kinley, pressing her lips to his.

At some point Jeff, the rideshare driver, spoke up. "Hey, if it's all right to ask...just who are you guys? I mean, you all look really familiar, but I can't for the life of me place where I know you from."

"Well, Jeff, I'm sure you've probably had someone say to you, jokingly, 'I'd tell you, but then I'd have to kill you.' Am I right?"

"Yeah – like – a hundred times. It's practically the oldest line in the book."

"Well, let me assure you that when I say to you, 'I'd tell you, but then I'd have to kill you,' I am serious as a heart attack. But remember our faces, my friend. Because in some form or another, you'll be seeing them again in the next twenty-four hours."

"You're not terrorists, are you? That are, like, going to kill me when I drop you at your destination?"

"Terrorists? Oh, good gosh, no," Harper laughed. "Terrorists would've killed you back at the airfield and taken your SUV and gone about their business. We didn't do that because we're not terrorists. No, Jeff, we're the good guys. And if things go according to plan, by this time tomorrow night we're going to be the most famous people on the planet. At least, we'll have our fifteen minutes until the next Hollywood Me Too movement scandal happens and the four of us get bumped back to page four."

A few miles later, Jeff started up again. "No offense to your lady friend there, but I do get tired of all that politically-correct crap. Sure, some of it's legit, but anymore most of it just seems so nit-picky, like, any little thing that could possibly be taken the wrong way. They're taking it and making it a national crisis, and a lot of them – like you said before – it's for their fifteen minutes of fame."

Having successfully changed the subject, Harper engaged the driver in a conversation about the pros and cons of the Me Too Movement for the rest of the trip to Harper Rowe's residence.

It was nearly 4 a.m. by the time they bid Jeff farewell.

"Do you have a key to the place?" Kin asked as the foursome approached the front door.

Without saying a word, Harper made his way to a small metal panel next to the front door. Sliding the panel up, he punched in a code. A mechanized female voice said, "Welcome home, Harper."

"Whoa. What the—"

"We are home," Harper smiled as the front door opened. "Lights on, living room." An overhead chandelier lit up the area. "Come on in and make yourselves at home."

Kin and Laurie walked in and took a look around.

"Holy hail, Harp," Chase said. "This is...not what I expected."

"Wow," Kinley smiled. "This is genuinely nice, dude."

Even Aimee Schmidt seemed impressed. "Ya know...this place doesn't suck as much as I thought it would."

"I absolutely love the high ceilings and – is that a loft up there?" Laurie asked.

"I think it is, yes."

"Where're the facilities, chief?" Kin asked. "My bladder's been playing *Wheel of Fortune* and wanting to take a 'P' since just before our flight landed."

Harper gave him a blank look. "I...do not remember," he shrugged. "Let's go see if we can find one. Lights on, entire house."

Harper shut the front door, then he and Aimee headed left through the spacious living room. Kinley and Laurie chose to explore a hallway to the right. The first door led to the basement. The second doorway opened into a well-equipped laundry room. The third door opened onto a capacious bedroom furnished with a king size bed, enormous flatscreen TV, and custom black furniture set against walls of periwinkle. Of most interest was the door on the far side that led to an en suite bathroom.

"Finally," Kinley breathed a sigh of relief.

"Do you think this is *his* bedroom?" Laurie whispered, taking a seat on the bed.

"I don't think you need to worry about whispering, love," Kinley said, opening the bathroom door. "This house is so big, you'd need a bullhorn just to be heard at the other end of the hallway."

"However, you might want to whisper if I'm standing right here, and you don't want me to hear you."

Laurie turned to see Harper standing in the bedroom doorway.

"And, no, this isn't my bedroom. This is the guest quarters, or should I say *Kinley's and your bedroom* – at least for the next little while until you two can figure out what you're going to be doing."

"Really? You wouldn't mind us staying here for a little bit?"

"Absolutely not. I mean, what's the point in having a big house like this if your friends can't hang out for a sleepover?"

"I gotta tell ya, Harp, I love this room. Did you really pick out all of this stuff yourself? The color and the design?"

Before Rowe could answer, Kinley came out of the bathroom and asked, "What did you do with the kid?"

"We found another bathroom upstairs, so she's getting cleaned up. I gave her a t-shirt and sweatpants to sleep in. They're a little big, but they'll do for now."

"A shower and some sleep sounds wonderful to me," Chase said wistfully.

"Towels and face cloths are in the linen closet. I'll bring down some clothes for you to sleep—" Harper stopped himself short. "Check that. I'll bring down some clothes for you to put on when you wake up."

Just then, the relative calm was broken by the sound of a doorbell chiming.

The trio exchanged curious looks.

"Expecting someone at this early hour of the morning?" Kin asked.

"Um, that would be a big, fat no," Harp said. "Let's see if this works...ODISS, who's at the front door?"

"ODISS?" Kinley mouthed to Laurs, who replied with a shrug.

The female voice that had welcomed Harper Rowe home now answered his question. "Using facial recognition, the internet, and legal records, I am able to say with 94% accuracy that the person at the front door is Regina Leigh Rickenbach of 2313 Laurel Drive in White Marsh, Maryland. She is not carrying any firearms and does not appear to be a threat."

"Thank you, ODISS. You may let her in."

As the trio headed for the front door, Kinley said, "Harp, I got two questions for ya: Number one, what exactly is ODISS? And number two, is that *the* Regina Rickenbach?"

"ODISS stands for Online Defense Integration Security System. It uses everything from heat sensors that give a virtual pat down, to DMV records, to Instagram, to Google, to facial recognition to find out who is at the door and what kind of threat level they pose. With the kind of work we do, I had it installed when I bought the house. Now, with everything that we've been through, I can't help but think that it was a sound investment."

By now they were at the front door. Standing there was a woman that Kinley Devereaux did indeed recognize as *the* Regina Rickenbach.

"Oh, sweet Lord, it's true!" she squealed, stepping excitedly toward Harper and giving him a massive hug. "You're really back!"

"I really am," Harper answered, pulling back.

"I know it's late, but I had to come and see it for myself." She took a step back and ran her hands through her raven black hair as she looked Harper up and down. "Wow, I didn't think I was ever going to see you again. So when you messaged me that you were coming home after all this time, well—" She commenced a second hug.

"I told you I'd be home one day...and that one day is today."

Harper pulled back again and began introductions.

"Regina, these are my friends and partners in crime. Kinley Devereaux..." Harper motioned toward Kinley.

Rickenbach shook his hand. "Nice to meet you."

"Yeah," Kinley replied, trying not to look starstruck. "Good to know ya."

"And this is Laurie Chase."

Rickenbach reached for Laurie's hand, then threw her arms around her neck instead. "Aw, I just gotta hug you." Pulling away from Laurie, she moved back to Kinley for a big squeeze. "I feel like I know you both!"

"Yeah, she's a hugger," Harper muttered.

"How is it that you feel like you know us?" Laurie asked.

"Well, whenever Harper would send me his house payments or maintenance money he would give me updates on what was going on. He talked about you two all the time. And these past several days have been plain ol' crazy. To know that the rest of the world just found out this past week that you two were still alive – and here I've known it for a while now."

Chase and Devereaux flashed Harper angry looks. "You told her we were still alive?"

"She wasn't going to tell anybody."

"How long was she your neighbor before Mexico City? Five days?"

"Well, that's true," Regina admitted, "but I've known Harp since high school. We go way back."

"Wait," Chase said to Harper. "You went to school with Regina

Rickenbach, one of the most famous and richest women in the world, and you never told us this?"

"Well, geez, I'm sorry...but the topic of old school chums never came up while we were running for our lives over the last several months. Perhaps I should also tell you that Donald Trump's accountant and my accountant are the same guy."

"Hold on. I think we're losing sight of the real point here, and that is Harper told somebody that we were still alive. You shouldn't have told *anyone* that we were still alive. You could have put our lives into serious danger, Harper."

"Okay, number one, Regina was the only one I told outside of our immediate circle of friends. Number two, your lives were never in serious danger up until about a week ago when *everyone* found out that you were, indeed, still alive. The only one whose life was in serious danger the whole time was – wait for it...wait for it – yeah, me. My life. Believe me, if I thought for even a nano-second that Regina was a threat to tell anyone that you two were still alive, I would have never said a word. I knew your secret was safe with her."

"Aww, Harper," the statuesque beauty said as she walked over and gave Rowe yet another hug. She then turned to Kinley and Laurie. "I would never betray Harper's confidence in me. You may have your doubts because you don't know me, but I was very aware of the danger that the three of you were in. I would never put anyone in harm's way like that."

Somehow, hearing the assurance coming from Regina Rickenbach seemed to carry more weight than it did coming from the man that they had just been through the equivalent of several small wars with.

"Oh, okay," Kin said agreeably.

"If you say so," smiled Laurie.

"How's my boy?" Harper asked Regina.

"Oh, he's great. He's always outside, rain or shine, playing in his little pond or wandering around between yards in the neighborhood. Everybody loves him. And of course I spoil him like crazy. Once you get settled in, maybe we can talk about getting him a Mrs. Fudd Duck."

"Oh," Kinley and Laurie said simultaneously. "The duck."

"I'll bring him over later on today. For now, I just had to come over and see you. I know you all must be tired, so I am going to get out of your hair," Regina laughed.

She turned to Harper and gave him yet another hug.

"See you guys a little later on," she gave Kin and Laurs a wave before letting herself out.

Kinley and Laurie waited a moment to be sure that Rickenbach was out of earshot. "Dude! What was that?"

"What?" asked Harper.

"What?" they replied in unison. "That!" Kinley said pointing toward the door that Regina Rickenbach had just exited.

"Why are you not with her?" Chase asked in exasperation.

"Ya know, Laurie," Harper said, a bit upset, "when Kinley wasn't with you, and he was hanging out with me, I didn't go out of my way to point out every attractive woman to him. No. Instead, I told him how good the two of you were together. How the two of you should be a couple. I did that."

"What's your point?" Chase asked.

"My point is: I like Mercedes. I really do. Yet, somehow, whenever you and your boyfriend here get a chance, you always seem to take the time to point out to me how I can do better. I just need ya to stop, is all I'm trying to say."

"Yeah. Okay. Right. Sure."

"Hey, we have a big day coming up today. I'm beat. I'll bring you guys down some clothes and lay them on your bed," Harper said as he broke up the awkward moment.

"Sounds good, dude. Thank you." Kinley looked at his friend and smiled. "Wake us up when you get up."

WHERE IN THE WORLD IS

BRENDA COBB-SCHMIDT

FBI Agent Todd Adams finished his first read-through of the Space Frequency files as Sandy Wyrick looked over his shoulder. Snapping his laptop shut, he excused himself and went out to the hall to call Agent Jeb Crool. An hour later, he returned to his seat across from Wyrick's desk.

"Do you think that any of this is true?" Todd asked.

"We have one of NASA's top guys here looking over everything as we speak. Judging from his facial expressions alone, it looks like at least some of this is true. So, I guess it's kinda like the Bible – if you think any of it's true, ya kinda have to believe it's all true."

"You a Bible believer, Sandy?"

"Kinda hard not to be, considering who wrote it. That's why my team and I think that all of this is true. Seems hard to believe that someone as respected as Dr. Rae Yun Kwan would invent such an in-depth and detailed story like this and then go to such great lengths to hide it from everyone."

"Yes, but it also seems hard to believe that someone like Senator Cobb-Schmidt is capable of doing such things. She has done so much good for so many people. She's running for president of the

United States, for crying out loud. To think that she has committed multiple murders – and this space shuttle nonsense."

"Didn't you say that some of your people were with some NSA agents and someone you thought to be Laurie Chase headed to do a ransom drop for the senator's daughter? Is that who you were just talking to?"

"It was, yes. The Agent-in-Charge is from the NSA. Guy named Jeb Crool."

"And?"

"And he was kinda sketchy on some of the details."

"Sketchy bunch of bastards, those NSA types."

"I told him about what I just read – about the senator and the space shuttle."

"And he was kinda sketchy about that?"

"Said he needed to make a phone call."

"Did he say anything about your people?"

"Just that it was a real mess and that he was in the middle of trying to clean it up."

"Did he give you *any* answers about *anything*?" Sandy asked, raising one eyebrow.

"He said he was going to call me right back."

"I see."

"One thing we need to do in the meantime," Todd said, "is to find out where Senator Cobb-Schmidt is right now."

"The Secret Service would have that info, right?"

"I believe they would."

Todd's cell phone rang. He pulled it off his hip and checked the readout screen.

"Ah, NSA Agent Crool. I'm going to step out and take this."

"Yep," Wyrick answered for no apparent reason, as Adams was already out the door. She buzzed Agent Guy.

"Yes, drill sergeant?" he answered.

"I need someone from the Secret Service to give me a call, asap."

"Can I tell them what it's about?"

"I need to know the whereabouts of Senator Brenda Cobb-Schmidt."

"Can I tell them why?"

"Yes, you can tell them that she is a pretentious albatross, a soon-to-be erstwhile politician, and I need to talk to her yesterday. Other than that, tell them it's classified and for me to know and them to find out."

"Really?" Dwight Guy asked flatly. "You sure I can't give them the 'I'm rubber, you're glue' reasoning? I find that one to be much more effective with the Secret Service types."

"Like I said...asap."

"Yes, drill sergeant, as sarcastically as possible."

Sandy Wyrick looked at Dr. Rae Yun Kwan's files one more time. The blueprints. The notes. The summation. The seeming incrimination.

Several minutes later, Agent Todd Adams returned looking rather pale. Sitting down, he let out a long sigh.

"How did CTU get tasked with this case?" he asked.

"I tried to give it away, but nobody seemed to want it. So...I took it. With the car bomb that killed Erica Bradley, it's definitely a terroristic action. That falls into our purview. Started our investigation into Erica Bradley's murder which led us to the disappearance of Dr. Rae Yun Kwan which led us to this computer which led me to call you. Next thing ya know, Old Jed's a millionaire." Sandy tapped twice on her desk and then leaned back in her seat. "What did your NSA guy have to say?"

"Quite a bit, actually. For one thing, Senator Cobb-Schmidt is looking guilty as sin in all of this. According to Agent Crool, the ransom drop that he went to – the one to get back the senator's daughter, the one with Laurie Chase, Harper Rowe, Kinley Devereaux, and four of my agents – it was a bloodbath. Sixteen fatalities."

"What? Sixteen? That's...*sixteen*?"

"And we're going to need to pack a bag and head to D.C. because that's where we're going to find Senator Cobb-Schmidt."

"D.C.? Wait, go back to the sixteen fatalities at the ransom drop for the senator's daughter. How do you end up with sixteen fatalities at a freakin' ransom drop?"

"First of all, the ransom drop was a setup. The senator was trying to stage a scene with her daughter being killed along with Chase, Rowe, and Devereaux. And then, from what I was told by Agent Crool, she was going to pin the whole mess on the latter three."

"All three of them?"

"Along with a woman named Taralyn Tharp. Have you ever heard of her before?"

"I think I remember a couple of mentions of her name in the Harper Rowe file, but nothing that really sticks out."

"She was with Rowe and Devereaux. And apparently, they compose a pretty formidable team. For a while it was just the three of them against a twelve-man mercenary team that the senator had hired to take out Rowe, Devereaux, Taralyn Tharp, and the senator's daughter. Crool and his guy, Laurie Chase and the other civilian that was with her, and four of my agents showed up just long enough to get Crool's guy, my agents, and Taralyn Tharp killed. Ten of the twelve-man mercenary group bought the farm to fill out the rest of the dead guys' scorecard. Crool has the eleventh member with him, and the twelfth merc was the chopper pilot that flew them in and would've flown them out again, but he wasn't even on-scene for any of the real fireworks."

"What you're telling me is that Senator Cobb-Schmidt hired a mercenary team to kill her own daughter as well as Harper Rowe and Kinley Devereaux."

"Is what I'm being told," Todd Adams replied.

"On top of killing Erica Bradley and, seemingly, Dr. Rae Yun Kwan."

"Has anyone on your team been able to track down the other two guys that were part of the space shuttle assembly team? What were their names, Cook and Hess?"

"No...and yes."

"Technically, I think we can probably pin all sixteen deaths at the ransom drop on her. Plus Bradley and Kwan, and maybe even Cook and Hess. Good golly, she's really got quite the body count racking up against her...and that's just the ones that we know about."

"Why are we going to D.C.?" Wyrick queried.

"Oh, right. Okay, so Harper Rowe and Kinley Devereaux have the senator's daughter. The senator, from what I can understand, has some kind of evidence that can exonerate Rowe, Devereaux, and Chase of former S.O.D. Paul Michael's death from two summers ago. They somehow have the senator convinced that she can still get away with everything – that they'll keep their mouths shut and give her back her daughter to do with what she will in exchange for the evidence that will clear their names."

"They're not really going to do that, are they?"

"No, yet somehow the senator seems to be the only one who doesn't know this. Anyway, Rowe and Devereaux have this exchange going down – in what I believe to be a beautiful stroke of irony – at the Lincoln Memorial at around 7:30 tonight. You do see the irony in that, right?"

"I do believe that was where the S.O.D. was shot. They're not planning on shooting her, too, are they?"

"No, no, no. Agent Crool said that Rowe and Devereaux are going there to get their evidence – which Agent Crool says they don't even need at this point; it's just more of a formality. Then they're going to give some sort of signal and the NSA is going to swoop in and pick her up. He says if we want our shot at her, we're going to need to go there. He's got a whole different angle that he's going to be coming at her with. You've got this whole space shuttle scenario that you'll be using to nail her. And me, I'm just along for the ride on both counts."

"So, who's flying? CTU or the FBI?"

"I'll put this on my dime. You just make sure that my name goes in the report when all this does eventually go down."

"Sounds good. Make room on the plane for me." Sandy paused to think for a minute. "And Agent Bergman. He's done most of the legwork on this case. He'll be good to have in the room with me when I question the senator."

"You already know where we fly out of. We'll go wheels up at 13:30 hours."

FBI Agent Todd Adams stood to his feet and was on his cell phone before he was even out of Wyrick's office.

Sandy buzzed Agent Bergman's line.

"Yeah, boss," he answered.

"Sammy, I need you to go home and get some sleep. When you get up, pack a bag for an overnighter in D.C. I will text you the address where we will be catching our flight. The flight leaves at 1:30 this afternoon, so be sure to get there by 1:15."

"Private flight, boss?"

"FBI flight."

"Okay. I'll see you there at 1:15."

The next person to knock on Wyrick's office door was Ted Sidelinger, the specialist that NASA had sent over.

"It's open," she said.

Sidelinger, a large bald-headed, bearded man, entered the office and shut the door behind him.

"So? What's your verdict?" she asked.

"I will choose my words carefully so as to not sound grandiose or grandiloquent on the matter."

Wyrick waited patiently.

"Okay," the specialist finally spoke. "What I just saw on that computer is probably the most inspired piece of sheer genius I have ever had the privilege of being affiliated with. Not only that, but speaking from a national security point of view, what you just showed me needs to be guarded like it was the single most important piece of intelligence ever created...because that is *exactly* what it is."

"And you're saying this without an ounce of grandiosity or grandiloquence? That what's on that computer in there is, indeed, a realistic probability?"

"Not a probability. An actuality. A scientific certitude."

"Next question. If the math and science are legitimate, then how long do you think it would take to put it all into motion?"

"With the right team and access to what you would need to assemble it, I would say that it could be accomplished in less than two years. Again, taking into consideration that an undertaking of this sort has never been attempted, that is just an educated guess."

"I appreciate your time, Ted."

FUDD DUCK

Harper Rowe finally rolled out of bed a little after 1:00 p.m. He had not planned on sleeping that long, but since he wouldn't be on the clock until around 7:30 p.m., and after the week that he had been through – from Johannesburg, to Atlanta, to Rio, to Prague, to Minneapolis, and now back home to White Marsh – he had let his body wake up when it was ready. On his way downstairs, he peeked into the room where Aimee Schmidt had been sleeping. Empty.

Down in his kitchen, he found breakfast burrito wrappers littering the island. Traipsing through to the living room, he found Aimee sprawled out across the couch watching TV and munching the burritos.

"Holy crap, I love this house," she said without averting her eyes from the screen. "It's like you told me last night: Just say out loud what you want, and it will do it for me. I told the microwave to cook two frozen burritos, and it knew exactly how long to cook them...and they were perfect."

"Oh, yeah?" Harp raised his eyebrows. "Well, I'm glad that works. Goodness knows I paid through the nose for the 'smart' microwave. I'd've been a bit unhappy if it didn't work like they said."

"Yeah, and the same thing with the TV. I just said, 'Turn on the TV to Lifetime Movie Channel,' and the TV came on and went to the Lifetime Movie Channel. I never want to leave this place."

"So you've said," Harper laughed.

"No, I'm serious. If things go the way we think they'll go tonight, they're going to arrest my mom, right?"

"Yeah, I think so."

"Well, I'm only sixteen. They won't let me stay by myself, so can't I just stay here for a little while?"

"You have a dad. I think he's going to want you to stay with him."

"Yeah, but he travels all the time. If I go to stay with him, he'll just leave me alone again. Plus, if I'm where the media can get at me, they are just going to try to turn my life into a circus. If I'm here, at least I can have some privacy while I try to regain my bearings after all this."

"What about school and your friends? Plus, I'll be real straight with ya, Aimee. After tonight the media circus is going to be out in full force, and this house will probably be ground zero. If you want privacy and to be out of the spotlight, your best bet might be to go with your dad on one of his trips out of the country."

"Will you, at least, think about it?"

"Think about what?" Laurie Chase asked as she meandered into the living room.

"Aimee wants to stay here after tonight."

"That's not the worst idea I've ever heard," Chase commented, finding her way to one of the leather loveseats.

"She wants to stay out of the media spotlight, and I told her I'm just not sure that this is the place to do it."

"Yeah, but if she's here, we can at least protect her. You send her back home, she might be a sitting duck. Doesn't her father travel a lot? If he's not around, who's going to be there to protect her from those media savages? Even if her mom is in lock-up, it's not like Aimee's still going to be completely out of danger. Who knows what her mother might be able to pull off from behind bars. The woman is a savage."

Harper let out a long groan. "Stop making so much sense, Laurie."

"Hey, the way things are is the way things are. We rescued her from one jackpot. It wouldn't be right to put her back into another one."

Before any more could be said on the subject, the front doorbell rang.

"ODISS," Harper said, "who's at the front door now?"

"Using facial recognition, I am able to say with 94% accuracy that the person at the front door is Regina Leigh Rickenbach of 2313 Laurel Drive in White Marsh, Maryland. She does not have any firearms, however there is a drake with her."

"A drake?"

"A drake is the term for a male duck," ODISS replied.

"Thank you, ODISS. You may let them in."

The front door opened and Regina and Fudd walked in. Regina was wearing the same black turtleneck and blue jeans that she was sporting earlier this morning, but now her raven hair was pulled back into a ponytail.

"Hey, everybody," Regina smiled warmly. "I brought a friend."

"Fudd!" Harper's mood took a sudden upswing.

The duck waddled straight to Harper. Picking the bird up in his arms, Harp placed his forehead against the back of its head. "I sure have missed you, Fudd. I'm so happy to see you again, buddy."

"It looks like he missed you, too," Rickenbach said.

"This is the coolest thing I've ever seen," Chase beamed. "I can't believe he still remembers you after all this time."

"Well, you know what they say about ducks," Harper placed Fudd back on the floor. "A duck never forgets."

"I'm pretty sure that's an elephant," Chase said.

"An elephant? What? Are you blind? This is obviously a duck."

The front doorbell rang again.

"ODISS, who's at the front door?"

"There are two men at the front door. Using facial recognition, I am 85% sure that the first man is Jebediah Amos Crool of 2416 Hartland Court in Washington, D.C. He is carrying two weapons. The first is a Sig Sauer P226 that is in a shoulder holster on his left side. The second is a Glock 27 that he is wearing in an ankle holster on his right ankle. The second man is not recognizable at this time. He is unarmed and does not appear to be a threat."

"Thank you, ODISS. You may let them in."

The front door opened, and Jeb Crool and Big James Gray walked in and looked around in fascination.

"Hey, who was that telling you what weapons I have and where I have them?"

"That was my house. Well, its security system, I should say."

"No kidding." Jeb was impressed. "How did it do that?"

"It's called a virtual pat down. You can't see them, but there are hundreds of built-in sensors just outside the front door that read your every facial expression, examine all of your clothes and accessories, and even interpret the way you're standing – casual, guarded, aggressive, etc. It also has X-ray capabilities that can tell if you have change in your wallet or a gun on your ankle."

"Are you serious?" Crool asked. "How much does something like that cost?"

"Close to six."

"Six? Six thousand dollars?"

"Six figures."

Jeb shook his head. "It would certainly seem that the *killer* business pays a lot more than the *catching the killer* business does."

"Yeah, they pay us a ton of money," Kinley Devereaux said as he emerged from the hallway. "What's the good word, Agent Crool?"

Kinley gave Agent Crool a quick pat on the shoulder, then

walked up to Big James and gave him a hearty handshake. "Good to see you again, big boy."

"Well, you'll be happy to know the good word is that the clean-up operation at the cemetery was a success," Jeb said. "The other good word is that we're all ready to go for tonight. I'll have men all around the rendezvous point. They'll be pulled way back so that there's no chance she'll be able to get the drop on us or you."

"I don't know if she's going to try to get the drop on us or not. She already tried to get the drop on us at the cemetery, and we all know how that worked out," Kinley said. "Besides, we're running the same playbook on her that we ran on Paul Michaels, just that it's going to be your guys securing the scene and not me. No, I think she's going to try to get us. But I just don't think it's going to be with snipers."

"Well, if she does, we'll be ready."

"Hey, why don't you give him your scope," Harper suggested. "That thing picks up heat signatures, right?"

"Yes."

"Might pick up any explosives she might try sneaking into the scenario."

"Ya know, that's not a bad idea, kid."

"Whatever's going to keep us alive. I know it seems like we have the upper hand going into this thing, but it only takes a second for us to lose focus and everything to go spiraling out of control. We would be foolish to go into tonight thinking that she is not going to try something to take us out for good."

Kinley excused himself and headed back to the bedroom to retrieve his infrared scope.

Fudd Duck had made his way into the kitchen on an apparent quest to find something to eat. Unsuccessful, he now waddled back into the living room and quacked vociferously at his long-lost owner.

"Great day!" exclaimed Jeb Crool. "Who let the duck in?"

"He lives here. He's my pet duck, Fudd." Hearing his duck's request for assistance, Harper addressed the bird. "Is it lunchtime, bud?"

"I've been feeding him the duck feed you told me about," Regina said. "He also likes to eat a lot of nuts and fruits. I just bought a big bag of the feed. I'll go get it and bring it over."

Jeb turned to the woman. "I'm sure you get this a lot, but, wow, you look an awful lot like Regina Rickenbach."

"Dang, I was thinkin' the same thing," Big James chimed in.

"Aw, thank you. I'll take that as a huge compliment," Rickenbach smiled as she headed out the front door.

Harper, Aimee, and Laurie all smiled.

"What?" Big James asked. "What did I miss?"

"I have a feeling that we have been played," Jeb explained.

"That woman that you just said looks an awful lot like Regina Rickenbach...is Regina Rickenbach," Laurie laughed.

"Well, smack my ass and call me Franklin," Jeb smiled. "You have a duck that lives with you, a hot celebrity neighbor, and a house that does invisible searches on anyone that dares enter. Now I know why you wanted to come back home so badly."

"If we can all survive the night, this will certainly make for a happy homecoming, that's for sure."

Kinley returned with his scope and gave Jeb a quick tutorial on how to use it.

Crool ran through the steps and tried it out a couple of times. Satisfied that he was ready to use it, he addressed the room. "Okay, troop, I'm going to leave the big guy here with you. I've got agents from other agencies flying here in just a few hours that I have to pick up. I've got to meet with some members of the DOJ before then, and around six this evening I'll be meeting up with my own guys to do a quick coordination before they deploy at 6:30. Gonna be a full afternoon. What do you guys have on your docket for today?"

"Um, I think we'll probably be going out to do some clothes shopping."

Fudd quacked loudly.

"And some food shopping."

"Oh, real quick, before I forget," Kinley handed Jeb an ear com. "This is to stay in contact with us tonight. Keep it in your ear and keep it on. At some point – probably around 7:00 – you'll hear our voices coming through it."

"I will look forward to hearing from all of you at that point," Jeb said, securing the com in his shirt pocket. "Until then."

Pieces Moving Into Place

The plane carrying Sandy Wyrick, Sam Bergman, and Todd Adams touched down at BWI just as Jeb Crool pulled his SUV onto the tarmac.

"Welcome to town," Jeb said, greeting them each with a firm handshake as the trio deplaned. "Toss your bags in the back. I'll give you a sitrep while we're driving. We've got plenty to do and not a whole lot of time to do it.

"Agent Adams, I want to let you know how sorry I am about the lives of your four agents. We have already contacted their next of kin, and proper arrangements are being made for their funeral services. I figure they were under my watch at the time of their demise, so it's only right that it falls on me to take care of their final ceremonies."

"Thank you, Agent Crool. I very much appreciate that."

"Buckle up for safety," Jeb said once everyone was inside the vehicle. "We have a little less than two hours before everything goes down. I've got a team of agents waiting for us – about twenty of them spread out around the perimeter of the Lincoln Memorial to make sure the senator doesn't have any rabbits up her sleeve. And when I say rabbits, I mean snipers. I'll have a team of five agents in close proximity to the meeting place in front of the Lincoln Memorial. They will be ready to move in once the signal is given."

"And who will be giving the signal to move in?"

"Either Harper Rowe, Kinley Devereaux, or Laurie Chase," Jeb answered.

"I'm sorry. Who?" Sam Bergman asked. "I think I must have misunderstood you."

"I said it will be either Harper Rowe...Kinley Devereaux...or Laurie Chase," Crool repeated.

"You're kidding, right?"

"Nope. They're the bait, and we are the trap."

Sam looked over at Sandy. "Did you know about this, boss?"

"It was brought to my attention, but I'm not really sure how it came to pass. Mind filling us in on all of that, Agent Crool?"

"I'm sure you are well aware that Harper Rowe has been the subject of a worldwide manhunt for the last year and a half in connection with the assassination of former Secretary of Defense Paul Michaels. Yours truly was the one leading that manhunt. It goes without saying – of course, I'll say it anyway – we were unable to catch him. Then about a week ago, we found out that Kinley Devereaux – whom we believed had been killed in Mexico City – was still alive. We were able to track them to Rio, but by the time we got there Rowe and Devereaux were gone.

"However, what we did find – or rather, I should say – *who* we did find – was former DEA Agent Laurie Chase, also believed to have been killed in Mexico City, and a big-time arms dealer named James Gray. The two of them led us to a major drug kingpin named Tito del Fuento. It was del Fuento who dropped the names of both Paul Michaels *and* Brenda Cobb-Schmidt."

"Dropped their names in what way?"

"In a way that would burn any politician and their political hopes down to ashes. As it turned out, Paul Michaels and Brenda Cobb-Schmidt had made a deal with Tito del Fuento. The kind of deal that had the two of them helping him move his drugs into the

U.S. in return for kickbacks from his drug sales. To make that happen, the Secretary of Defense and the senator tipped del Fuento off to a DEA drug raid that was getting ready to happen at one of his places in Mexico City. When the DEA team showed up for the raid, they were slaughtered like lambs to the lions. The only member of the DEA team that survived? Laurie Chase.

"In the meantime," Jeb continued, "the Secretary of Defense hired Black Ice, the world's most notorious thief, to break into his undersecretary's house and steal a thumb drive. What happens when she does? Harper Rowe and Kinley Devereaux, as their lucky stars would have it, walk in on her in the middle of the break-in. When Michael's people move in to pick up the thief upon her getaway, Rowe and Devereaux think they're with Black Ice and kill them all. Black Ice, realizing she's been Michaels' pawn, decides to sell the thumb drive on the black market. And of all places, where does she go? Mexico City.

"Now the Secretary of Defense has a problem or two. First of all, he's got a powder keg on the loose in Black Ice, and secondly, there's supposed to be a DEA team in place down there in Mexico City...and there isn't.

"Meanwhile Harper Rowe and Kinley Devereaux, as it turns out, are the first two people on record to actually see the face of Black Ice and know what she looks like. So, Michaels tells his underlings that this fact is why Rowe and Devereaux should be sent after the thief. And that they can hook up with the DEA team that's in place down there...the DEA team that he knows good and well is no longer down there anymore because they're all dead with the exception of Laurie Chase.

"What happens next is Michaels calls Laurie Chase and tells her that her country is counting on her to help Rowe and Devereaux find Black Ice and get that thumb drive back from her. Do it for God and country, young lady!

"Eventually, the three of them figure out what is going on, they *do* get the thumb drive back in, from what I understand, spectacular fashion, and figure out that Paul Michaels is a power-hungry despot. They were involved in the assassination of the secretary and the ruination of the thumb drive and what was on it. But exactly what role they played and to what extent...the waters are still a little murky in that area. Harper Rowe was actually with the secretary when he got shot, which means he didn't pull the trigger. At this point in the story, Devereaux and Chase are believed to be dead, so who knows what their involvement may have been.

"We do know that at some point Laurie Chase ends up in Rio de Janeiro where she tracks down Tito del Fuento, the man she believes is responsible for wiping out her DEA team. She's down there for over a year doing recon work on this guy. And then, about a week ago, Harper Rowe, Kinley Devereaux, James Gray the arms dealer, Tito's former right-hand man and cousin Diego, and four former Delta Force operatives join up with her in Rio and commence obliterating del Fuento's entire drug compound. His crops, his soldiers, his storage buildings, his home, his money, everything...except for del Fuento himself.

"Now, here's where things get really bizarre."

"I don't know, Agent Crool. This whole thing sounds pretty bizarre already," Wyrick said.

"Then get a load of this: The whole lot of 'em...they manage to walk right into some sort of terrorist attack on a night club down there. They ended up putting those guys down in their tracks."

"Wait a second. The terrorist attempt on that club down in Rio? That was them that stopped it?"

"Sure enough. And people had their camera phones recording the whole thing. And boy, did *that* ever go viral. It's how I figured out where they were. And how we tracked them to Rio."

"And now we've come full circle, back to where your story

started," Bergman noted. "But I'm still not clear on why Rowe, Devereaux, and Chase are meeting up with the senator."

"Well, let me fill in a couple of blanks to answer your question. The thumb drive that Black Ice stole contained the blueprints that Senator Cobb-Schmidt used to build her space shuttle – the one that your Dr. Rae Yun Kwan described in her tell-all expose. Because of her association with Paul Michaels, Senator Cobb-Schmidt has the evidence that will clear Rowe, Devereaux, and Chase of any wrongdoing in the S.O.D.'s death. Those three have her convinced that they are still in dire need of the aforementioned evidence."

"Do you really think that she'll be fool enough to show up?"

"She will because she wants her daughter. Plus, she knows that if she doesn't, the three of them have enough on her to ruin any hope she has of becoming president. Of course, when she does show up, things aren't going to get real nice for her, either." Jeb paused for a few seconds. "I have a com they gave me that will allow me to hear both sides of the conversation when she meets the three of them. Once they feel they've gotten what they need from her, they'll give us the okay to move in. And then...*we* can get what we need from her."

"Where will we be in proximity to the five of them?"

"I will be about a mile away and about 550 feet high. I will need to have a vantage point where I can see everything and everyone that will be coming and going throughout the rendezvous zone. So I am going to park myself at the top of the Washington Monument. Any of you that care to join me are more than welcome, but if you want to be closer to the action, I certainly understand."

"Sounds like the place to be is with you, Agent Crool – watching all the action take place, having a live listen-in to all that's being said," Agent Bergman answered. He turned to Sandy Wyrick. "What do you think, boss?"

"I think I am going to want to stay as close as I can to the action. I want to make sure there are no mistakes made on the ground. I want to nail this woman more than I have wanted to nail anyone in my entire career. Even if it is just to see what blind arrogance looks like in person. Still, I don't mind if you stay with Agent Crool. You can keep me posted on what you guys are seeing and hearing."

"I think I'll stay close to the rendezvous point with Agent Wyrick," Agent Todd Adams said.

Jeb turned into the Fort Meade military installation – headquarters of the NSA, as well as a handful of other federal agencies – and pulled up to the security gate. After clearing their badges and IDs, the guard waved them on through.

"Time to get this party started," Jeb said.

Prelude to a Rendezvous

Against his will, Big James was made to stay behind at Harper Rowe's house. There was a good reason for this decision. Just in case things went sideways at the Lincoln Memorial and something tragic befell Kinley, Harper, and Laurie, they left specific instructions with their friend as to where their last wills and testaments, insurance policies and burial plans could be found. The lovable behemoth did not want to hear any of it, but he did understand the need for the plan. So, stay behind is exactly what Big James did.

✴   ✴   ✴

Most of the D.C. traffic had dissipated by 7:00 p.m. when Kinley, Harper, Laurie, and Aimee arrived at the Kennedy Center parking lot, a ten-minute walk from the Lincoln Memorial.

The crew had consumed their afternoon parading around White Marsh Mall. Kin, Laurs, and Aimee dropped huge amounts of money at Aeropostale, Macy's, Vans, Foot Locker, and a couple of other stores in search of a quick, fashionable, wardrobe.

After they had fulfilled their wardrobe needs, they joined Harper to hit the food court – Bistro Sensations, to be specific.

Once they were seated, Kin was the first to speak up. "I gotta tell ya. Man, it feels good to be back home again."

"You ain't just whistlin' Dixie there, my friend. For the first time in a long time, I find myself not constantly looking over my shoulder for whomever might be coming for me next," Harper replied.

"And speaking of home, Harper," Laurie began, "have you given any thought to the possibility of Aimee staying with us after tonight?"

Looking pensive, Harper took his time before answering. "I guess it will be okay. For now, at least." Rowe gave the girl a stern look. "That's only if you promise to do as I say. Can you agree to those terms?"

"Yes." the teenager could barely contain her enthusiasm. "Yes. I promise to do whatever you say."

"That applies to whatever Mr. Deveraux and Miss Chase tell you, as well. We straight?"

"Absolutely," she beamed.

"Do you have a driver's license?"

"I don't, but I was working on getting my permit when all of this stuff happened with my mom."

"Well, you'll be getting your license. I'm not going to play chauffeur to a sixteen-year-old girl. The three of us will do our best to shelter you from the press, but everything else...you're on your own. You're sixteen. You're plenty old enough to take care of yourself."

Kinley lifted his head back from chowing down on his food and said, "Good mighty, Harp, you just sounded exactly like my father did when I was sixteen. That's a scary thought."

"And, yet...here we are," Harp said sardonically.

"Okay. Now that that's out of the way," Chase said, "I think we need to go over our agenda for tonight's meeting with the senator."

"Agent Crool will be able to hear everything that's being said as long as he has activated the com we gave him. I figure we get the senator to talk as much as we can, confess to as much as she will. And once she does, we'll say the safe word, and the feds will move in and scoop her up."

"I sure hope everything goes that smoothly," Devereaux sighed. "Because we are going to be exposed to anything and everything while we're standing out there."

"Yeah, there's no doubt that this is going to be a little bit dangerous. But once we clear this last hurdle, we'll be golden."

"Like boxing gloves."

*   *   *

The mood was a bit more somber as the quartet walked briskly through the cool D.C. night air several hours later.

"I know things are supposed to go okay here," Aimee said, "but I also know what my mother is capable of, and I'm scared."

"I feel for ya, kid," Harper put his arm around her. "We've only known your mom for about two days, and we really think she sucks. So I can't imagine what it's been like having to put up with her for sixteen years."

"She wasn't always like this," Aimee sighed.

"Whatever she was before, it apparently didn't take," Devereaux said. "Because what she is now is a top-flight villain, hellbent on killing whoever she deems to be in the way of her path to the White House. Hate to say it, kid, but your mom is one bad dude."

"It's okay to be scared," Harper told her. "See, courage isn't so much about not being scared, but knowing that some things are more important than being scared. Brave people may not live forever, but people who live their life in fear...never really live their life at all. We'll get through this just like we've gotten through the last week: We've got each other, and we've got each other's backs."

"No reason to change a winning formula," Chase reached out her arms to embrace the group as they walked.

"Looking at this group portrait, you'd never know that we kill people for a living," Devereaux laughed as he grabbed Rowe by the shoulder and gave him a squeeze.

✳   ✳   ✳

While Devereaux and company readied themselves for the meeting, the senator and Stephanie Cash sat in a D.C. hotel room making their own preparations for the evening's epic engagement.

"Are you sure you don't want me to make the swap in your stead?" Cash asked. "I just can't shake the feeling that this whole thing is one big trap that you're getting ready to walk into, Senator."

"I don't think so. These three want to clear their names too badly to do anything stupid. However, on the outside chance that you're right, you've got the detonator. If things start looking a little shady or suspect, you send me the signal, I'll bolt, and you blow everything into tiny little pieces."

"If that does end up happening, we're going to have a lot of explaining to do."

Brenda laughed. "You worry too much, Steph. Let's face it, if they were going to get the authorities involved, I'm sure we would know by now. When the authorities are involved, you can't just kill an entire squad of mercenaries at a cemetery and sweep it under the rug like it never happened. No, if they were going to contact the cops or the feds, we would have heard about it by now."

"I wish I had your confidence, Senator," Cash said.

"Once they have my bag in their possession, it will be game over for them. Just make sure that I am clear of the blast zone before detonating the explosive."

"Any idea how big the blast area will be?"

"Give me a hundred yards or so. I believe that will be sufficient. When I'm ready for you to blow it, I'll text you. It'll be quick though, like a number or a letter. Okay?"

"I understand – a number or a letter. Got it. So, after you have your daughter, and Devereaux, Rowe, and Chase are finally out of the picture, what's your next move?"

"We'll spin it. Tell the press that our three stooges kidnapped my daughter and tried to take me out during the exchange. And that"—the senator affected an exaggerated damsel-in-distress tone— "it's only by the grace of God that we're still alive."

"And you're convinced that the American people will buy into what you're saying?"

"Steph, if we've learned anything through all our years in office, it's that the American public is more gullible than a bimbo after two appletinis."

"Good Lord, isn't that the truth," Cash laughed. "Do you mind if I ask you a question, Madam Senator?"

"Please do."

"What are you going to do with your daughter once she's back in your possession?"

"It's not what *I'm* going to do with her. It's what she's going to do to herself."

"Which is?"

"After all the stress of being kidnapped, nearly being killed, and the subsequent fallout from all of it, she'll try to kill herself. Of course, we won't allow that to happen to the poor dear, but we will do the next best thing...we'll have her put into a mental facility where I will pay to have her so heavily sedated that she won't know reality from real estate."

The senator's laugh made Stephanie uneasy. If the senator was willing to do this to her own daughter, who knew what she was capable of doing to non-family members.

Steph did a quick check of her watch.

"I think it's getting to be about that time, Senator."

"It is. Time to go mop up this mess and get back on the campaign trail. We'll take separate vehicles. You know where to go and what to do."

✳ ✳ ✳

"You reading us, Agent Crool?" Devereaux asked.

"I'm reading you. And once again, just as a friendly public service announcement, there is still time to back out of this nonsense. Sure, I have a ton of agents in place and most of them are on overtime, but if you wanted to back out of this needless meeting with Senator Cobb-Schmidt, nobody'd blame ya."

"We'd blame us," Harper said. "What's your 20?"

"Up high in the sky keeping watch over my flock by night. I'm a mile away at the top of the Washington Monument. Got a bird's eye view of everything from here."

"Seems kinda far away from the action."

"Like I said, gang, there's a boatload of agents all around the area. As soon as you give me the signal, her ass is grass and my people are landscapers. We'll pick her up faster than a firefly can twinkle."

"And just to be sure that we're all on the same page, the go-phrase is 'We're looking forward to having a friend in such an influential position.' We say that, and you give your team the green light to move in."

"That's absolutely correct."

"Lotta people up there with you in the monument?" Chase queried.

"Naw, I had the attraction shut down for this special occasion. Only one up here with me is Counter-Terrorist Agent Sam Bergman."

"Counter-Terrorist agent? What did we do to draw the likes of them to the party?"

"Well, don't go getting all full of yourselves now. You guys didn't do anything to get the CTU involved. That honor would once again befall our good fiend, Senator Brenda Cobb-Schmidt. Seems the three of you aren't the only ones to have made her hit list."

"Ya don't say," Laurie Chase did say. "Who else made the guest list?"

"Harper, you remember when we were talking about the space shuttle blueprints that Secretary of State Paul Michaels was trying to get his hands on?"

"I do recall that, yes."

"The senator really *did* get her hands on those. She then proceeded to put a team together to assemble the darn thing. After that, to keep it all as hush-hush as possible, she apparently started killing off some of the higher ups of that team."

"Apparently?"

"We know one is dead. Another one is missing and presumed dead. There are two more that we really don't have any information on at the present time. But needless to say, we're fearing the worst. Anyway, the one that we know is dead was killed by a car bomb, and that was long before anyone knew anything about the space shuttle, the senator, or any of that. It just looked like a car bomb was used to kill a high-ranking NASA employee with high-level security clearance. On the surface, it looked like a potential act of terrorism. Hence, CTU was put on the case. And that is why I have one of their finest with me right here."

"Any signs of the senator yet?"

"Not yet, but rest assured, as soon as I see her, you'll be the first to know."

Suddenly, a thought occurred to Harper. He pulled out his cell phone and started fidgeting around with it.

"Agent Crool," he said, "I'm getting ready to send you a picture of a woman named Stephanie Cash. She seems to be the senator's flunky. She was with her when we met up with the senator yesterday morning. And she was there yesterday evening right before we went to the cemetery to retrieve the senator's daughter." Harper sent the picture off to Jeb. "I have a feeling that when the senator does finally make her appearance, Stephanie Cash will be lurking somewhere in the nearby shadows."

"Got it," Crool verified. "Hmm, attractive woman."

He showed the photo to Bergman who was scanning the D.C. crowd with high powered binoculars. "BOLO for this woman, Agent Bergman."

"10-4, Agent Crool," Sam said after having studied the picture carefully.

"Just to affirm, I do have eyes on the four of you," Jeb said.

"Well, let's just give your view a good test run then. How many fingers do I have up?" Devereaux asked.

"That would be one finger...one middle finger...pointing way up in the air," Crool muttered. "Does that sound accurate?"

"That's a bullseye, boss."

"And Agent Crool, just so ya know...the views and opinions expressed by the right hand of the person that has flipped you off are solely that of the owner of said right hand and do not represent the opinion of any entities who have ever been, are now, or ever shall be affiliated with the owner of that particular middle finger," Harper smiled.

"All right, gang, now that the disclaimers are out of the way, it's showtime. I have the senator in my sights. She's on your six, about three hundred yards out, coming up from Constitution Avenue. She's wearing a long, hooded burgundy wool coat with a white scarf and a pair of tall black dress boots that – I'm not gonna lie to ya – really complete the ensemble nicely."

"At least she'll look good for her mugshot," Chase cracked wise.

"My people on the ground," Agent Crool addressed his agents, "stand to and let me know who has eyes on her."

"I've got her, boss," Agent Luke Mathis announced.

"I have just sent out a photo to everyone of a woman named Stephanie Cash. If any of you see her, confirm and let me know where she is. Do not move on her; just observe and report."

"Okay, Agent Crool," Kinley said, "we're set. The four of us are just going to wait for her to come to us now. Do you have my infrared scope at the ready?"

"I do. As soon as she breaks free from the crowd and I have a better angle of her, I will use it to see what I can see."

"Agent Crool," Sam nudged the NSA specialist. "Looks like she's got a bag of some sort that she's carrying."

"We were expecting her to be carrying a bag, right, gang?" Crool checked with the others.

"Yeah, that seems plausible. She should be carrying *something* that has the evidence in it to clear our names."

"Ah, for cryin' out loud," Harper said, a bit frustrated.

"What's wrong?"

He sighed and shook his head. "I gotta pee."

Meeting at the Lincoln Memorial

The evening air was becoming quite chilly as Kinley, Harper, Laurie, and Aimee awaited Senator Brenda Cobb-Schmidt's arrival. The steam from their breath was quickly carried away by a vigorous northeast breeze – a breeze that seemed to cut right through the layers of clothes, gloves, stocking caps, and scarves that the four were sporting.

The Lincoln Memorial was brightly lit, as were the streets and sidewalks that surrounded it. And despite the cold temperatures and the time of night, a fair amount of people were circulating through the area.

Kinley and Laurie were warming each other by standing close and holding hands. Harper and Aimee were doing the same thing – minus the holding hands part. What Harper was holding, however, was the briefcase containing the five million dollars that previously had been earmarked as ransom money for Aimee Schmidt.

"Look alive, boys and girls, she's in the circle and getting ready to make the turn to head your way," Jeb Crool growled through their ear coms.

"We have her in our sights, Agent Crool. You using that infrared scope yet?" asked Devereaux.

"I'm looking through it now. Hey, this thing's pretty cool."

"Seeing anything out of sorts?"

"Nothing that I can see on her person, but I can only see one side of the bag that she is carrying. So when she hands it to you, be sure to turn it so I can get a good look at the opposite side."

"Will do."

"Good luck, troop."

As the senator drew nearer, the foursome tried their best to shake their apprehension. But it was a task easier said than done.

"Good evening, all," Senator Cobb-Schmidt smiled as she approached. "Chilly one, wouldn't you say?"

Laurie Chase thought she was going to vomit. The woman that 24 hours ago had sent these men into a death trap now had the gall to talk to them about the weather? Chase looked at her boyfriend, who had the same repulsed look on his face.

But not Harper. No, Harper Rowe, repulsed or not, was just as amiable as could be.

"Colder than moonlight on a tombstone, as a friend of mine used to say." That had been one of Taralyn Tharp's favorite sayings.

"Hello, Aimee," Brenda's greeting to her daughter was so cold that it made the frigid nighttime air feel almost tropical. "It's ever so good to see you again."

Aimee took a moment to calculate her response. "Bite me, Brenda."

"Now, sweetie, is that any way to talk to your mother?"

Before Aimee could keep the icy conversation going, Harper stepped in. "You don't mind if I pat you down, do ya, Senator? We really don't want to take a chance that some federal agency has you mic'd up in an attempt to entrap us in some sort of government sting operation."

"Oh, nice move, Mr. Rowe," Jeb Crool approved.

"What? You want to pat *me* down?"

"Is what I was saying, yes."

"I would think if any of us would be wearing a wire, it would be one of you," she said indignantly.

"Fine. I'll pat you down, and then you can pat us down. Fair enough?"

"Fair enough."

And pat each other down they did.

Once everyone was satisfied that there were no outside sets of ears listening in, the exchange continued.

"You'll find in this bag everything that you will need to clear your names: emails, recorded phone calls, a complete rundown of what the former Secretary of Defense was up to, as well as two sworn affidavits from former employees that used to work under the Secretary at the time all of this was going down."

Kinley took the messenger bag from the senator.

"Give that thing a little turn there, Devereaux," Crool instructed Kinley.

He did as he was told. Turning the bag so that Jeb could get a good look at the other side, he set it down on the ground and began rifling through its contents.

Meanwhile, Harper had a few questions for the senator.

"So, what are ya gonna do with the kid here after we hand her over to you?"

"You really want me to answer that?"

"Well, I did ask."

"Some questions are best left *un*asked, Mr. Rowe...like me asking you what you did with all the bodies at the cemetery."

"Heh heh heh, well, they were dead, and we *were* at a cemetery, so you can do the math on that one."

"Just as long as those bodies *stay* buried," she laughed.

"The bodies will stay buried, and our mouths will stay shut just as long as we don't catch wind of you trying to stab us in the back somewhere down the road."

"It hurts me just a bit that you feel like I would do something like that to you. Then again, I guess I did try to kill you and Mr. Devereaux yesterday, and I'm sure that memory is still fresh in your mind...and I am sorry."

"Sorry that you tried to kill us or sorry that you underestimated us?"

"A little bit of both, actually. Although you three have taught me a valuable lesson. And that is to *never* underrate my opponent. Still, I just want you to know that bygones are bygones, and I am hopeful that in the future we can build a relationship that is mutually beneficial."

She looked from Harper to Kinley, then to Laurie. "Hey, wait a minute. You're not Taralyn." Brenda looked back to Harp. "Where's Taralyn?"

"We didn't exactly make it through killing all your guys at the cemetery unscathed," Rowe said.

"Oh. I see." The senator's complexion took on a shade of white not found in any Crayola Crayon Deluxe Packs. "I'm sorry."

Ignoring her apology, Harper moved along to his next question. "Once you're president, can we count on you to be this dirty and underhanded when you're dealing with North Korea and Russia and China and all the other countries that desire to see the U.S. obliterated from the face of the earth?"

The senator answered Harper's question, but neither he nor Kinley nor Laurie heard what she said because Agent Jeb Crool began speaking at that very moment.

"Devereaux, I need you to lift the bag back up. When you set it down on the ground, my view became obstructed, and now I can't get a good look at it."

"Right," Kinley muttered. He lifted the bag as if he were checking it for leaks. "That's a lot of campaign pins on this sucker, Senator."

"Hand 'em out to your friends. Let 'em know that a vote for me is a vote for—"

The rest of what she said was interrupted by Jeb Crool once again. "Great day in the morning! We got something hot on the side of that bag." Crool pulled the infrared scope away from his eye and grabbed his binoculars.

"It's...it's one of those pins, Devercaux. Toward the middle of the bag."

Laurie and Harper tried to hide their terror as they glanced over at the bag.

Kinley put his hand over one of the pins. "These are some nice pins, Senator."

Jeb put the infrared scope back up to his eye. He could still see the heat signature. "No, not that one," he said. "More toward the middle and lower."

Kin moved his hand to the next pin and covered it. "I would hate to see them go to waste. I mean…"

"No, next one over," Jeb said.

"...all my friends are right here, so maybe you should take some of these back." He moved his hand to the next pin and covered it.

"Son of a b-stinkin'-itch!" Jeb was getting frustrated. He could still see the heat signature. "Up one."

Devereaux moved his hand up one.

"Fu schnickens!" the NSA agent growled in frustration. "Up one more."

Kinley moved his hand up to the next pin and waited.

The heat signature disappeared. "That's the one, amigo."

Harper and Laurie let out a quiet sigh of relief.

"And these pins are made with such care and craftsmanship," Kin continued as he carefully removed the designated pin. "Especially... this one." The assassin held up the explosive pin.

The shade of color in the senator's face went from an albino-mime white to fire-engine red.

"What can you tell us about this particular pin here, Senator?"

"I – I'm not sure what you mean," Brenda stammered.

"You sure about that?" Dev asked as he flipped the explosive pin to her.

Any doubt that Brenda did not know what the pin was were completely removed by her reaction to Kinley's throw. Her eyes grew wide, her mouth went agape, and she used both hands to gingerly catch the pin like it was a tiny baby.

"Judas Priest, dude!" Harper cried out. "That was a bit reckless, wasn't it?"

"You know that was a bit reckless, Harper, because you know what that pin is. I just needed to verify that she knew what it was, too...and I did."

"What was that you were saying a few seconds ago, Senator? You learned to never underestimate your opponent?" Laurie mocked.

"I know what this looks like," she said nervously, "but I assure you, all of this is strictly business. Nothing personal."

Kinley took the messenger bag and handed it to Laurie. He then turned to Brenda Cobb-Schmidt and said, "I hate to be contentious, Senator, but my friend and I are in the killing business. So we're rather familiar with what it looks like. What you're doing isn't business. It's self-serving politics. Plain and simple. I'm sure at this point I already know the answer to this question, but I'll ask it anyway: Is Kelly Campbell still alive, or was she just someone else that got in the way of your political machine?"

"I'm afraid so," admitted Brenda.

"Unbelievable," Jeb said to Bergman. "She just confessed to killing Rowe and Devereaux's handler, Kelly Campbell."

"Hey, ya know if she's confessing to killing people, you should see if they can get her to confess to killing Dr. Erica Bradley and Dr. Rae Yun Kwan, too."

"Sure thing," Jeb obliged. "Hey, fellas, Agent Bergman requests that you ask the senator about a Dr. Erica Bradley and a Dr. Rae Yun

Kwan. They worked on the space shuttle project."

"I'm sorry, Mr. Devereaux," Senator Cobb-Schmidt continued, "but sometimes lives have to be sacrificed for the greater good. It's just the price of doing business, that's all. I know it's not what you want to hear. But in the end, we'll all get what we want. You and your friends will get your names cleared and be looked at as the heroes you really are. And I'll get to be president of the most powerful nation in the world. Sometimes you have to lose a little to gain a lot."

"What about Dr. Bradley and Dr. Kwan? Were they part of the little losses, too?"

The senator hesitated a bit before asking, "How do you know about Dr. Bradley and Dr. Kwan?"

"Senator, eventually you're going to figure out that you're not just dealing with two former government wetwork guys. Maybe that's all we were a year and a half ago, but being on the run for eighteen months has taught us to be ever diligent with whomever we're dealing. Make no mistake, ma'am...we know everything," Harper said.

The senator started to laugh. "Oh my, you are going to be one fantastic asset, Mr. Rowe. All three of you, for that matter. You don't know the lengths that I went to in order to cover my tracks through all of this, and here the three of you are, walking-talking compendiums of all my dirty little secrets."

A few random passersby were within earshot of the quintet, so the senator lowered her voice to barely a whisper. "That space shuttle project is my ace in the hole to get elected. If anyone were to find out about it beforehand, and knowledge of that craft were to find its way into the wrong hands...I shudder to think what could happen."

"Well, then, by all means, we should definitely be thanking our lucky stars above that it's in the hands of you, upright citizen that you are," Devereaux scoffed.

"You can ridicule me if you want, but you have no idea of the potential benefits that this thing has for our country. And you also have no clue about the potential devastation it could bring if our enemies were to get their hands on it."

"Seriously? You don't think we know?" Devereaux said in a harsh whisper, his temper beginning to get the better of him. "Baby, we've known all along the damage this thing could bring. Why do you think we tried to destroy it all those months ago? It's because we knew that the capacity of destruction that this contraption could cause far outweighed any possible benefits that it might render. So believe me, Madam Senator, we most definitely have an idea of what inherent dangers this thing could create. It cost the three of us the last year and a half of our lives. It cost others more than that."

"If that's the case then you obviously understand why I had to take care of Dr. Bradley the way I did. She wanted to go public with it, and I just couldn't let that happen. I did what I did for the good of the country."

"Oh, I think that's gonna just about do it, gang. I've heard every-thing that I needed to hear," Jeb spoke through their coms. "Whenever you all are ready to wrap this production up, I'm good with it."

"I absolutely understand your actions, Senator Cobb-Schmidt," Laurie Chase said, "and you're 100% right. Sometimes we have to get our hands a little dirty if we want things handled properly. I, for one, am extremely glad that we're going to have a president like you running this country."

"Here, here," seconded Harper. "We're looking forward to having a friend in such an influential position."

"All right, Alpha Team, we're a *go!*" Jeb notified his NSA team members on the ground. "Move in slow. Take your time and get it right. We do not want any slip-ups."

"They're moving in, boss," Bergman told Wyrick.

"We're right behind them," Sandy said.

"Well, Senator Cobb-Schmidt, if you're finished trying to kill us, I guess we're finished here."

Brenda was suspicious of a couple of things. For one, how could Kinley Devereaux have figured out which pin was the explosive one. It was practically identical to the other ones. Yet not only was he able to figure out which one it was, but he was able to figure it out quite quickly. Second of all, how *did* they know about Dr. Erica Bradley, Dr. Rae Yun Kwan, and the space shuttle? Senator Cobb-Schmidt was absolutely certain she had covered her tracks on all of that. The only way they could have possibly known anything about the matter was if the laptop from the bus station really did contain evidence of the Space Frequency project and had somehow found its way into the hands of Kinley and Harper. A wave of uneasiness suddenly blanketed the senator. Then, in an instant, Brenda went from thinking she knew what was going on to knowing exactly what was going on.

Problem was, they were two different things.

She went from thinking that Harper, Kinley, and Laurie were so desperate to get the evidence they needed to clear their names that they would not dare involve the authorities...to knowing that involving the authorities was exactly what the trio had done.

She saw it coming.

The *it* she saw coming was not just the band of federal agents that were stealthily moving in her direction. The *it* she also saw coming was her future – a future in which she was not the president. In fact, she was not a politician at all. In the future that she was seeing, she was an embarrassed criminal whose every secret and indiscretion had been completely exposed. It was a future where she was locked up for life. In short, it was a future that had no future at all.

As far as she was concerned, the senator saw only one way out of this mess. She just needed to buy herself a little bit of time. So she started to run. As she did, she grabbed her phone out of her coat pocket and pulled up Stephanie Cash's cell phone number. She texted the number "1."

Kinley Devereaux saw what she was doing.

He actually thought that the senator was detonating the explosive herself, but, regardless, he realized correctly what the end result would be and acted accordingly.

"Agent Crool!" he yelled. "Pull your people back! Pull your agents back now!"

Devereaux turned, wrapped his right arm around Laurie, his left arm around Harper and tackled them both to the ground.

On his way down, Harper reached out, grabbed Aimee, and pulled her to the ground, as well.

A moment later, the explosive detonated.

Kin felt the concussive effect of the blast move violently through the air above him. After hearing the deafening noise of the blast, he then heard nothing but an intense ringing sound vibrating in his ears. He could barely lift his head off the ground as he checked on Laurie.

She was laying on her back and her eyes were open but glazed over and unfocused.

"Baby," he said, but the ringing in his ears was so loud that he could not even hear himself talk. He squeezed her shoulder and shook her.

It had no effect.

He was having a hard time focusing, too, as he was trying to see if Chase was even breathing.

Suddenly, he saw Harper crawl over to her and start lightly smacking her cheek.

Harp had a distressed look on his face. He said something to Kin, but Devereaux could not hear him at all. That was when he saw Harper starting to perform CPR on Chase. Kinley managed to pull himself up to all fours, but then everything went black.

Devereaux fell to the ground unconscious.

FALLOUT

In all, the blast took the lives of nine people, including Senator Brenda Cobb-Schmidt. Also killed were a young married couple from Lincoln, Nebraska, who were in town visiting relatives; two friends from George Washington University who were out for an evening run; and four NSA agents that were unable to get far enough away before the explosive was detonated.

The number of people injured from the tragic event was 28. All of them were transported to Georgetown University Hospital.

One of those transported was Kinley Devereaux. When he finally regained consciousness some 16 hours later, his head ached, his thoughts were clouded, and his memory was vague, at best. His vision was blurry, too, but he was able to make out the figure of Harper Rowe sitting next to him.

"Welcome back, babe," Rowe said in a quiet voice. "How ya feelin'?"

"My head...hurts," Dev mumbled. "Where am I?"

"You're at Georgetown University Hospital. I'm gonna go see if I can flag down a nurse or a doctor."

"Wait," the aching man slurred. "Why am I...how did I get here?"

"What's the last thing you remember?"

"I don't – I don't remember," he said in frustration. "And my mouth is dry as the Sahara."

"Oh, here," Harper grabbed a cup of water from a nearby tray. "Drink this."

He helped Kinley guide the drinking straw into his mouth. In his thirst, Kinley took in a little more than his throat was able to handle. He began coughing violently which, in turn, caused his head to feel like a beaten piñata about to rupture.

Harper pulled the cup away and helped his friend sit up. "You okay, champ?"

"Are you sure I'm not dead?"

"If you were dead, you'd probably be feeling better."

"You make a valid point," Kin admitted. "So, why am I in here?"

"Do you have any memory of meeting Senator Brenda Cobb-Schmidt at the Lincoln Memorial? We were there under the premise of getting the evidence to clear our names off the most wanted list."

"What were we really there for?"

"We were really there to entrap her for the NSA and Agent Jeb Crool to arrest her. Do you have any memory of being at a cemetery in Minnesota? It was cold...lotta snow...people trying to kill us?"

"We were there for the senator's daughter, right?"

"Yes, right. The senator sent us there to pay a ransom to get her daughter back."

"But we were set up, right? And – and we killed a lot of people," Dev said as a look of remembrance filled his beaten face.

"Yeah, yeah, now you're gettin' it, Big Shooter."

Kinley squinted his eyes. "Oh, and I got shot."

"Yes."

"Again."

"Yes. Again."

"Then, umm...hmm...well, then we came to – we came back home." Kinley slowly nodded his aching head. "To entrap the senator...and get the evidence to clear our names...which we didn't really need for some reason."

"Now, we're getting somewhere. Do you remember the meeting? Do you remember what happened?"

Devereaux was quiet for quite a while as he tried again to recall what happened at the meeting with the senator. A wave of nausea suddenly washed over him. His skin became clammy and he broke out into a cold sweat.

"Laurie." Kinley looked at Harper. "Where is she?"

"Calm down, Kin."

"Where is she, Harper? What happened to her?"

"For the record, she's good, but for a few there, she was kinda touch-and-go. I don't usually toot my own horn, but—"

"My memory might be somewhat compromised, but I remember enough to know that you don't just toot your own horn. You're like an entire brass section."

"I had to do CPR on her until the paramedics arrived. I mean, anybody else would've done the same thing in my position, but would they have been able to maintain compressions effective enough to sustain her life for as long as I did? Who knows. But that, my good man, is why I keep my temple," and Harper thumped his chest twice, "in tip-top condition."

"Wait a second, wait a second," Kinley winced, "if Laurie almost died, and I'm in the shape that I'm in, how is it you're be-boppin' around and playing Captain America? Weren't we all together?"

"Indeed, we were, but when the senator decided to blow her top, so to speak, you saw what was getting ready to happen, and you tackled me and Laurie. When we hit the ground, your 185-pound carcass landed on top of my head, thus shielding me from the harmful effects of the explosion. In all seriousness, if you hadn't landed on my head and caused me to keep my faculties...your significant other would more than likely be a goner right about now. Your selfless act of heroism combined with my quick reaction time to keep her alive until help arrived is what saved the day...and her life."

Devereaux mustered a weak smile. "Quite the team, me and you."

"No doubt, but I for one am ready to take a break. Not from us, mind you," Harper clarified, "but in the last ten days we've survived about two lifetimes' worth of adventures. And, suck dangit, I need a nap."

"I'm with ya on that. I don't want to get on another airplane, fire another weapon, get shot at by another person, run toward or away from imminent danger, or be a hero of any sort...ever again."

"I'm sure Chase feels the same way," laughed Harper.

"So, where is Laurie? How is she doing?"

"She's in the ICU right now, but that's strictly for precautionary reasons. They'll probably move her to a regular room later today. And hopefully the two of you will be able to get out of here tomorrow."

"Where will we go then?"

"My house. Do you not remember being at my house?"

"I'm having parts of memories kinda flash into my mind like the reflecting light of a disco ball, so bear with me if I ask what will probably seem like stupid questions."

"You mean like I've been doing for the better part of our friendship?"

"I'll be glad to get out of here. I hate hospitals. I do remember that," Kinley made a sour face. "It'll be good to be somewhere where we can all get some rest. Will it be okay if Laurie and I stay with you for a minute till we can figure out our next move?"

"It'll come back to ya," Harper assured, "but we already covered this. The two of you can stay with me as long as you want. I've got plenty of room. Getting rest, however...that might be a harder calf to rope."

"Oh, yeah?"

"See, while you've been down for the count, the FBI, the CTU, and the NSA have been sifting through the chaos and mayhem that Senator Brenda Cobb-Schmidt left behind. Our buddy Agent Jeb Crool has held up his end of the bargain and is getting our names cleared of any wrongdoing in the death of Paul Michaels. Needless to say, the press has been champing at the bit to get our side of the story in all of this. There's actually a guard outside of your room to keep them at bay until you're back on your feet. But once the doctors clear you and Laurie to be released from here, we'll be on our own."

"Have you talked to anyone yet? Press-wise, I mean?"

"No. I've been here with you for the most part, and when I haven't been here, I've been busy keeping Aimee Schmidt hidden away from the media mongrels."

"Aimee Schmidt? The senator's daughter?" Kin asked. "How's she doing?"

"When you pulled me down, I grabbed her and pulled her down with me. She kinda got the old double crunch from us both landing on her. But as it turned out, she came out of it all pretty much unscathed. Maybe it helped that she landed on the money bag."

"So, we ended up hurting her more than the actual explosion? Geez, I hope she doesn't come back later and sue us." Kin mustered a painful smile.

"Yeah, couple scratches and bruises from being tackled so hard, but she's been checked out and released," Harp said. "Tell ya what, boss. I'm going to go retrieve some medical personnel, have them come in and give you a thorough going over, and when they're finished up, I'll come back in and catch you up to speed on all things forgotten and recalled."

"Hey, you mentioned something about Aimee landing on a money bag?"

"Right. So, what you aren't remembering is that along with the senator's daughter, we were also supposed to hand over the five mil in cash that the senator had given us for the ransom drop. Well, in all the confusion and hullabaloo after the explosion, I put the bag out of sight until I could sneak it away from the scene. I figured after everything we've been through, that money would go to our daily expenses and hourly wage fund."

"So...we're five million dollars richer?"

"We sure are," Harper smiled as he turned to leave the room.

"Good enough." Kinley said as he laid his head back on his pillow and closed his eyes. He was asleep before Harper reached the door on his way out.

And Now They Know...the

Rest of the Story

At a few minutes past two that afternoon, Harper shuffled back into Kinley's hospital room. Devereaux was sitting up, finishing off the last spoonful of his chocolate pudding. The color had returned to his face. His eyes were alert and had lost their glazed, far-away look.

"What did they give you for lunch?"

"I ordered the soup – chicken noodle – and a chicken Caesar wrap. Plus, I got the pudding and a Coke. I figured, at the very least, they wouldn't screw up the Coke."

"So, how was it?"

"Well...let's just say they didn't screw up the Coke. But I was so hungry that I ate it all anyway," he shrugged.

"What did the doctors have to say?" Harp asked, pulling up a chair and sitting down next to his friend's bed.

"Eh, my gunshot wound from Prague is infected, but my gunshot wound from Minnesota seems to be healing quite nicely. They said I have a grade two concussion from last night, but I'm already starting to remember pretty much everything that happened, so that's good news."

"Heck, yeah, it is," Rowe grinned. "I have some good news for you, as well. They're getting ready to move Laurie out of the ICU and into a regular room. So, I talked them into moving her in here with you."

"Seriously?" Devereaux smiled.

"Serious as a librarian at a funeral."

"Dude...thank you," Kin nodded. "Hey, you said that there's a guard outside my door to keep the press out. Are they here? Like – in the hospital?"

"Well, they aren't actually letting them loiter around inside the hospital building itself, but there's a slew of reporters out in the parking lot just a-waitin' for one of us to emerge. I sneaked Aimee Schmidt out of here last night and back to my place – there were maybe ten or fifteen of them out there then. But by the time I came back here early this morning, the parking lot looked like a news convention. Right now, the four of us – you, me, Laurie, and Aimee – are the hottest *get* in town."

"Did you leave Aimee at your house alone?"

"No, Big James is there with her."

"Oh, Big James is at your house? Did I know that?"

"You did," affirmed Harper. "You do."

"You should go talk to those reporters, man. Maybe if you give them what they want, they'll leave us alone for a while. I don't think I've ever given an interview to a news reporter in my entire life. I'm not a real big fan of the American press...or any press, for that matter."

"I'm kind of enjoying listening to them yammer on about the three of us being heroes, and how we persevered 'against all odds' to clear our names and expose the 'evil senator from Minnesota' and how we may have saved the country from making one of the most 'disastrous and calamitous' errors in judgment in the history of our nation."

"What?" Kin laughed painfully. "They're really saying all that?"

"Oh, yeah, buddy. Here." Harper grabbed the remote and turned on the television. "Check it out for yourself."

Harper flipped the channel to CNN just in time for them to hear, "...a chain of events that can only be described as tragic, heroic, and shocking all at the same time. The nation is reeling from the tragic death of nine people outside of the Lincoln Memorial last night from an explosion that seems to have been caused by one of the victims, Minnesota Senator and presidential front-runner Brenda Cobb-Schmidt. The number of victims would have been much higher if not for the brave and heroic actions of Kinley Devereaux and Harper Rowe. Yes, you heard that right...Harper Rowe, the man that was at or near the top of several worldwide law enforcement most-wanted lists, and Kinley Devereaux, who up until just about a week ago was believed to have been killed over a year and a half ago in Mexico City. We are trying to stay ahead of this – what can only be described as beyond bizarre – news story, but new details seem to be coming in almost every five minutes..."

Harper flipped to MSNBC.

"...and we received word just about an hour ago from NSA Special Agent Jeb Crool – who had been leading the investigation into the assassination of former Secretary of Defense Paul Michaels – that the men who were wanted for questioning in the matter, Harper Rowe and Kinley Devereaux, have been cleared of any wrongdoing. And that these two men, along with a former DEA agent named Laurie Chase, are responsible for exposing Minnesota Senator Brenda Cobb-Schmidt's involvement in multiple crimes – a list of crimes that seems to be growing by the hour. Agent Crool is telling us that Rowe, Chase, and Devereaux are nothing short of American heroes of the highest caliber."

Harper flipped the station to FOX News, where the host had just started an interview with right-wing conservative lawyer Laura Ingraham.

"Laura, you've spoken to NSA Agent Jeb Crool several times over the last year and a half in regard to the assassination of former Secretary of Defense Paul Michaels. Agent Crool now says that Harper Rowe, Kinley Devereaux, and Laurie Chase have been cleared of any wrongdoing in the matter. My question to you is this: Isn't faking your own death, which Kinley Devereaux and Laurie Chase obviously did, a crime in and of itself?"

"Well, Bill, that's true. It is...unless there are extenuating circumstances, which in this case there most definitely are. Circumstances that Harper, Kinley, and Laurie were well aware of a year and a half ago but are just now being made known to us, the general public, over the last several hours," Ingraham explained. "I know Agent Jeb Crool very well. He is a no-nonsense, by-the-book NSA agent, and if he says that these three have done nothing wrong, you better believe he's completed a thorough investigation to come to that conclusion."

"I gotta tell ya, Harp," Kinley beamed, "even though I feel like complete and utter smoosh, this is easily the greatest day of my life. I could watch this stuff every day for the rest of my days here on Earth and never grow tired of it."

"Amen to that, brother. Redemption is finally ours."

A knock on the door brought them both back to reality.

"It's open," Harper said.

A short, chubby nurse poked her head into the room. "It looks like you're getting a roommate, Mr. Devereaux." She disappeared, then reappeared seconds later pushing Laurie Chase in a wheelchair.

Chase's long hair was disheveled, and her overall appearance was wan and weak. But when she saw Kinley, a small smile made its way across her lips.

"Hello, gorgeous," she said.

"Hello, beautiful," he smiled back.

The nurse rolled Laurie to her bed by the window. As they

passed Harper, Laurie reached out and touched his arm. "I hear I owe you the biggest of thank yous."

"Oh, it was nothing, really. I just turned on the Harper Rowe charm and convinced the charge nurse to put you in here with Kin."

"No, not that, silly. I mean, I owe you a big thank you for my being here."

"Oh, that. Well, I may have resuscitated you back from the land of the dead, but none of that would have even been possible if not for Kin laying on top of me and shielding me from the blast. Without that, I may very well have suffered a similar – if not the exact same – fate as the two of you did."

The nurse helped Laurie out of her wheelchair and into the bed.

"Wait." Chase shot a cutting look at Kinley. "You shielded *him* from the explosion and not *me*?"

"Baby, come on. That's Harper Rowe saying that stuff. You know you can't believe a word that comes out of that guy's mouth."

Laurie managed to muster a smile. "I'm just bustin' your chops, Devereaux. I don't care how it happened. All I know is that I am truly grateful and happy that the three of us are alive and together."

"And free," added Harper.

"What?" Chase asked.

"Yes, we have officially been cleared of any and all wrongdoing," Kinley said. "Harper was just giving me the grand tour of all the cable news channels, and we are on every one of them."

"Really?" Laurie laid back while the nurse tucked blankets around her. "What are they saying?"

"What *aren't* they saying. They're calling us heroes. Saying that we saved America from its biggest mistake in the history of the nation. It's crazy."

"Yeah, Agent Crool has let everyone know that we're the heroes and not the goats," Harper added. "He called and told me that with all the lies that Senator Cobb-Schmidt told, the one thing that she was straight about was what was in that bag she gave us at the Lincoln Memorial. Crool said that even if he didn't already know what he knew, the materials in that bag were more than enough to exonerate us."

"Wow," Laurie looked over at her boyfriend and started crying. "We did it, baby. We're home, and we don't have to spend the rest of our lives on the run and constantly looking back over our shoulders."

"I am going to leave you all to get some well-deserved rest," the nurse said. "My name is Lupita. I am your nurse, assigned to this room only. So if you need anything, just let me know and I will come running. And I just want to say that I could not be prouder to be able to take care of the two of you. We have been watching the news all morning at the nurse's station, and you all really are heroes. So, just beep if you need me."

"Thank you, Lupita," Laurie smiled.

"I'm going to head out of here, too," Harper said, standing up. "I'm going to go meet up with somebody."

"Who?" Kinley asked.

Harper went over to Laurie and gave her a gentle hug. He then turned to Kinley. "I'll tell ya later." He patted his partner's shoulder. "You two enjoy each other and the news. I'll stop back by later tonight and fill you in. Get some rest."

And with that, Harper walked out of the hospital room.

It's Good to See You Again

He sneaked out through the service entrance to avoid the press staked out in the parking lot. Then he took a cab to where he had parked his car, just to make sure he was not being followed. Once safely in his car, he gave her a call.

"Hey, Harper. How are you feeling?"

"Pretty good. I'm on my way back to my house. Should be there in about thirty minutes. Where are you?"

"Well, according to my GPS, I'm about twenty minutes from your house. But I think I'll stop for gas before I get there, so we should arrive about the same time."

"Excellent. However, if you do get there before me, just wait in your car, if you don't mind."

"I don't mind. I'm excited to see you."

"Won't be long now."

The drive up I-95 to White Marsh was congested. But Harper was in a hurry, so he did some of his best driving – even if some of it was illegal. As it worked out, he pulled into his driveway first, then she pulled in right behind him.

He had not seen her since Rio. While it seemed like that had been forever ago, it had really been less than a week. They got out of their cars at the same time and threw their arms around each other and began to kiss.

Finally, a momentary stop.

"Hi, Harp," she breathed.

"Hello, Mercedes."

They might have kissed all night had it not been for Big James's voice booming from the front door. "You two better get on in here. Ya'll gonna catch your death out there in this cold."

Dr. Lara pulled back from the kiss.

"You didn't tell me Big James was here!"

"Oh...well...surprise! Big James is here. When we talked last night, I tried to hit on all the major talking points: The senator tried to kill us, we rescued the senator's daughter, the senator blew herself up trying to kill us *again*, we got our names cleared and are back in the States to stay. I feel bad that Big James didn't make the headlines."

"Hey, before we go in, can you help me with my bags? I have two suitcases. One has my clothes. The other is loaded with cash from the Rio job – cash for you, Kinley, and Laurie."

"Wow, you are the perfect woman: You kiss first and ask questions later, and you bring large amounts of unsolicited cash for me and my friends."

"Then you better treat me right, Harper Rowe. Besides, if you don't, I know three guys that won't hesitate to give you a decent beat down."

"Speaking of the guys"—Harper began walking with Mercedes toward her car— "were they okay with you leaving at a moment's notice to come here?"

"Are you kidding? You three are like rock stars to them. They've been following all the news stories since last night. They, much like myself, can't believe everything you guys have been through. You all just never gave up, even in the face of such insurmountable odds. You ever want to know how to gain their utmost respect? That's how:

never giving up, never backing down, no matter what."

She opened the trunk and pointed to the two suitcases. "This one's mine, and that one is yours."

Mercedes grabbed hers while Harper hoisted the money bag. As they lugged the suitcases into the house, Harper pointed out, "The news stories tell a lot, but the press doesn't even know about what happened at the cemetery in Minneapolis. Hopefully, it will stay that way."

Big James was waiting just inside the door. Aimee Schmidt was asleep on the couch, watching TV with her eyes closed.

"Good to see you again, Doc," Gray said to Mercedes Lara. "Get on over here and let the big man give ya a hug."

"Try not to break her, big guy," Harper said as he walked over to check on Aimee. "She seem to be doing all right?"

"Yeah, sleeping a lot. We've just been eating like a couple of college freshmen and watching MTV all day. I'd say for all that she's been through, she's been doing about as well as can be expected."

"Is she talking about any of it?"

"Yep. We've been talking about stuff. She's been unburdening herself to me. Telling me about her home life, her mom and dad, school."

"Good. That's good. It's probably not healthy for someone who's been through what she's been through to keep all that stuff bottled up. I appreciate you being here, buddy."

"Who knows, big guy"—Mercedes patted his billboard-sized back— "if you ever give up your arms dealer business, you might have a career as a high school guidance counselor waiting for ya."

"She makes a good point, James. Although, I think a high school guidance counselor might make slightly less than an arms dealer. On the other hand, however, I hear the benefits package for a high school guidance counselor is nothing to sneeze at. Health and dental insurance...401K...summers off...access to the teacher's lounge."

"And all the single moms one man could ever hope to date," Dr. Lara added.

"Well, heck, I'm sold," Big James smiled. "So, what do you two have planned for the night?"

"I am taking the lady to my favorite restaurant, The Greek Village. Then we'll probably head back down to the hospital to check in on Kin and Laurie."

"How are they doing?" Gray asked.

"They moved Laurie out of the ICU and into a regular room. Just so happens to be the one that is currently occupied by one Mr. Kinley Devereaux."

"Aww. That's good that it could work out that way."

"And Kin?" James asked. "Is he recovering anymore of his memory?"

"Seems to be," Harper looked at Mercedes. "You hungry?"

"Famished. I don't like to eat while I'm driving, and it was a fourteen-hour drive here, so—"

"Dang, Doc! You drove that far just to see all of us?"

"I did." She looked at Harper. "Some more than others. Still, I knew that once Kinley and Laurie were released from the hospital – the kind of damage their bodies took from the explosion – they're going to need some looking after for a little bit."

"James, do you mind running her bags upstairs? We're going to get out of here."

"Don't mind at all. You two have a good time. Give my best to Kin and Laurs, and we'll see you later on tonight."

"Till then, *mi amigo*."

CASH NEEDS CASH

The damp January wind blowing off the Potomac numbed Stephanie Cash's bones.

Under any other circumstances, she would never have stood on the shoreline on a night like this. However, tonight's circumstances were unlike anything she had ever encountered.

Thanks to Senator Cobb-Schmidt leaving her high and dry, Stephanie needed to disappear, which took money – the kind of money that she did not have. But someone had reached out to her. In exchange for information that only she had, they were willing to pay her the kind of money that it would take for her to properly disappear. To be off the grid permanently.

Her plan was to head to Caracas and reappear as someone brand new. Someone with no past. Someone with a bright and beautiful future.

Watching the twinkling headlights on the Francis Scott Key Bridge, she pulled her coat up around her neck. She had been waiting for almost twenty minutes and was beginning to wonder if her money man was going to show up at all when a shadowy figure finally emerged from the darkness. As he approached, she could see an attaché case in his left hand.

"Miss Cash," he called out.

"Yes, hello. I was beginning to wonder if you were going to make it."

"I apologize for my tardiness. We'll make this quick so that we can both be on our way to someplace warmer."

"Sounds good to me," Cash agreed.

"So, my first question is this: Who else knows where this space shuttle is?"

"Just me. Anyone else who knew is dead, and I should know... because I killed most of them myself."

"Really?"

"Really. The senator wasn't one to get her own hands dirty with things like that. The only other ones who knew of the shuttle location were Dr. Erica Bradley, Dr. Rae Yun Kwan, Dr. David Hess, Mr. Ronald Zook, and the senator. Well, you know what happened to the senator. I personally killed Kwan, Hess, and Zook myself, and I put the bomb in Erica Bradley's car that killed her."

"So, why kill the other three but use a bomb for Dr. Bradley?"

"Hess and Zook didn't have any family, so no one was going to ask questions about them. Dr. Kwan just had a husband – who I was also supposed to kill, but every time I went to do the job, one thing or another just did not go according to plan and I was not able to get things done.

"Dr. Bradley, though, she had a husband, kids, people that would ask questions and push the issue. A car bomb throws suspicion on a whole different cast of characters: a mob hit, a terrorist attack, someone with a vendetta against the woman…you get the idea. So, that's why we went that way with her."

"Sounds like the senator kept you busy with all her dirty work."

"Oh, yeah, and I'm not even going into the two agents from the Department of Justice and that woman, Kelly Campbell, and a bomb maker named Ralph Finnegan."

"Well, I certainly understand why you need to disappear. There's

1.3 million dollars in this case. You give me the location of that space shuttle and your word that you will take that secret with you to the grave, and we're good to go here."

"If you don't mind me asking, how did you find out about the shuttle? It was a pretty well-kept secret."

"It's been my experience that a secret between two people is only a secret if one of them is dead. People talk. Unfortunately, the people that knew of the shuttle's existence had no idea where it was being kept. That's where you come in."

Stephanie Cash reached into her coat pocket and produced a piece of paper and handed it to the man. He, in turn, handed over the attaché case.

Stephanie opened the case just enough to thumb through the bundles to ensure that they were all legitimate $100 bills. She was so focused on the task that she never saw the money man stick a handgun under her chin and pull the trigger.

Cash's lifeless body fell to the ground.

The man quickly closed the attaché case and transferred the gloves – women's size small – from his own hands onto Stephanie Cash's. He took her own gloves out of her pockets, then placed the gun next to Stephanie's body exactly where it would have landed if she had killed herself.

Satisfied with the staged scene, the man grabbed the case and made his way the quarter mile back to his car. He opened the trunk and tossed in the attaché, gloves, and his blood-spattered coat. Once back in the driver's seat, he turned to the woman passenger.

"Ugh, I do so apologize again for this. I just completely forgot that I had to drop a package off to a dude. I hate that you had to wait like that."

"Oh, please, Harper. Think nothing of it. I was texting with John while you were gone. He told me to tell you 'hey.'"

"Sweet. Be sure to return my regards in kind the next time

you talk to him. So, I guess I should have asked you...do you like Greek food?"

"Oh, gosh, I love it. I absolutely love it. Where's your coat, babe?"

"I tell ya, the one thing I hate about winter is wearing bulky coats. It's just really uncomfortable when I fasten my seatbelt and I feel like I'm stuck in a straitjacket."

"Oh, yes. Yes."

"So, I just threw it in the trunk. Besides," Harper winked, "you'll keep me warm, I'm sure."

Mercedes took Harper's hand, smiling. "It's going to be a good night, Harper Rowe."

"Mmm, baby," he squeezed her hand. "It already has been."

THE END

EPILOGUE

It was the year that was.

In January, Senator Brenda Cobb-Schmidt blew herself up in front of the Lincoln Memorial in Washington, D.C.

In May, a very short hearing took place to consider charges against Harper Rowe, Kinley Devereaux, and Laurie Chase in the death of Secretary of Defense Paul Michaels. Thanks to the contents of the messenger bag that Brenda Cobb-Schmidt had provided when she met with the trio at the Lincoln Memorial, all charges were dropped.

By early December, Jeb Crool's long-awaited book *If I Write One Book the Rest of My Life, It Will Be This One* was released. It immediately rose to the top of the New York Times Bestseller list. In it, Crool spilled all the details of how he worked with the three most-wanted people in the world to topple the biggest U.S. presidential conspiracy of all time.

A lot had happened in the 345 days between the death of the senator and the publication of Jeb's book.

JEB CROOL

Before Agent Crool wrote one word of his tell-all book, he did two things: he resigned from his position at the NSA, and he paid a visit to Dave Baldwin's widow, Maddie.

Jeb visited Maddie Baldwin a few days after Dave's funeral, taking the letter Dave had told him about – the one in his work locker – to her. The envelope contained a personal letter to Maddie, as well as the information about Dave's auxiliary life insurance policy.

Once Jeb made sure that Maddie was taken care of, he started in on his book. He ate, slept, and breathed it 24/7 until it was perfect. Then he shopped it around to the highest bidder. Jeb was going to make sure that he was taken care of, too.

Jeb hit paydirt with a major publishing company out of Los Angeles to the tune of $3.7 million smackaroos. They sent Jeb on a three-month talk show promo tour that took him to North and South America and most of Europe. He even appeared with Harper Rowe and Big James Gray on *Good Morning, Britain*, to be interviewed by none other than Charlotte Hawkins. The show's ratings hit an all-time high that morning.

"BIG TIME" JAMES GRAY

James was certainly excited to ride the coattails of America's newest heroes. And why shouldn't he be a recipient of some of the accolades? He was certainly as much a part of Senator Cobb-Schmidt's takedown as anybody else was. Plus, Big James had a made-for-television personality. He loved the spotlight, and the spotlight loved him.

Soon Big James had a slew of offers for a book deal of his own. Then came the product endorsement offers. As he told Harper Rowe, "They're coming in faster than I can turn them down."

"Well, Big Time, with a personality like yours, what did you expect? The people have spoken and they want more Big James Gray. Advertisers aren't stupid. They know that sex sells, and you, my friend, are one big sexy beast."

"Aww, now, I don't know about all that."

"Well, I do. I knew from that first interview we did together that people were just going to eat you up. They can't get enough of you. What kind of endorsement offers are you getting?"

"Automobile ads, cigar ads, cereal commercials...like I said, I can't even keep 'em all straight."

"Get yourself an agent, chief," Harper suggested. "They'll make your fifteen minutes of fame a lot easier to navigate."

Big James took Harper's advice. Before he knew it, he had nailed a book deal and was doing commercials for American Express, Herrera Estelí Brazilian Cigars, Mercedes Benz, and DXL Big and Tall Men's Clothes.

James did have to retire from the arms dealing business, but for the time being he was making a heck of a lot more money cashing in on his 15 minutes of fame. Plus, Big Time knew that if he invested wisely, he would never have to worry about money again.

HARPER ROWE, DR. MERCEDES LARA, AND AIMEE SCHMIDT

After January's events at the Lincoln Memorial, Harper Rowe was true to his word and allowed Aimee Schmidt, the senator's daughter, to stay with him indefinitely. While he went on the talk show circuit, Harper always made sure the spotlight stayed on him and away from the girl.

Once the charges against Harper were dropped, Aimee's father signed all legal guardianship rights over to Harper Rowe. Two weeks later, Todd Schmidt went on a business trip to Costa Rica and was never heard from again.

After the media hype surrounding Kinley, Harper, and Laurie

died down, Harper continued his long-distance relationship with Dr. Mercedes Lara, while spending more time at home with Aimee and his pet duck, Fudd.

Domestic life seemed to fit Harper well. When it became apparent that Aimee's father was gone from the picture for good, Harp began the legal proceedings to adopt Aimee as his own daughter.

KINLEY DEVEREAUX AND LAURIE CHASE

"A Real Schmidt Show." That's what the press jokingly called Senator Cobb-Schmidt's political catastrophe. Of all the parties involved, only Kinley Devereaux and Laurie Chase went out of their way to avoid the media circus that ensued. Sure, they granted an interview here and there, but for the most part, the couple quietly hid out at Harper's house for a few weeks until they found their own place.

Using their share of the haul from Dr. Mercedes Lara, Kin and Laurs purchased a nearby townhome just the way they wanted it: quick, quiet, and cash.

On their first night in their home, all they had was an air mattress, a lamp, and two laptop computers. Sitting cross legged on the floor, Chase was pointing and clicking away on her laptop.

"What are you doing?" Kinley asked.

"I'm trying to find a livestream of *The Ingraham Angle*. Jeb is supposed to be on there touting his new book."

"I'm going to order some food. What are you in the mood for?"

"China Hut. You know, my usual."

"Sounds like a good way to spend the first night in our new house," Devereaux smiled. "Me, you, China Hut, and *The Ingraham Angle*."

"I can't think of a more perfect way to spend an evening with the man I love," she smiled up at him.

"Maybe one other thing."

"Oh, yeah? What would that be?"

"This." Kinley reached into his pocket and pulled out a small velvet box. Getting down on one knee, he opened the lid to reveal the most beautiful diamond ring Laurie had ever seen.

"Laurie Chase?" He looked into her eyes – eyes that were now starting to well up with tears. "I was wondering if you would do me the honor of making me the happiest man in town and be my wife for the rest of my life and all eternity?"

Her mouth agape, she tried to answer yes but nothing came out. Instead, she nodded her head fervently like a bobblehead doll in an earthquake.

Kinley took the ring from the box and slipped it on her ring finger.

She looked at it adoringly. "I love it. I absolutely love it."

"It looks good on you."

"I'm never taking it off. I will go to my grave wearing this."

"I love you, baby." Kinley said.

"I am so happy right now. I am, literally, the happiest woman in the world. And you have made me feel this way. I just have one question."

"Okay."

"Do you have a date in mind?"

"For the wedding?"

"Yes, a date for the wedding."

"Well...you."

Laurie stared at him. "Don't make me hurt you on such a joyous occasion."

Devereaux laughed, then leaned in for a kiss.

Taking her hands in his, he said, "Christmas."

"Christmas?"

"Yes, Christmas. It's the day when we celebrate the greatest gift that has ever been given to mankind. And you, Laurie Chase, are by far the greatest gift that has ever been given to me. So, what better day to celebrate that gift than Christmas. This Christmas."

"Okay, Santa," she smiled. "I will marry you this Christmas. Now go put in our order and let's see what's in our fortune cookies."

A WORD FROM DOC

Thank you for reading *Chasing Redemption*.
I hope you enjoyed it.

Please read on, because I've included an excerpt from my
Dragon's Men series: *Dragon's Men: Domestic*.

I occasionally send newsletters with details on new
releases, special offers, Christmas stories, and other bits
of news relating to my characters. If you would like to
sign up to the mailing list, please go to:

www.goldenalleypress.com/boom-killers-series

I love hearing from my readers. Here's my email address:
doc@docephraimbates.com.

You can make a difference . . .

Reviews are the most powerful weapon I have when it
comes to getting my books noticed. Your honest review
will help bring them to the attention of other readers.
If you've enjoyed this book, please consider leaving a
review on Amazon.com.

Doc

If you enjoyed *Chasing Redemption*,
please keep reading for an exciting preview of

DRAGON'S MEN: DOMESTIC

Dragon's Men Series

Doc Ephraim Bates

Available in print and ebook
from Golden Alley Press

Big Bang Boom

The morning sidewalks of White Pines were teeming with pedestrians in a last-minute hustle to make it to work on time.

It was 8:39 a.m. on a chilly February Monday, as bright sunshine and clear blue skies played backdrop to another scenic day in this picturesque town.

Harry Bragantz was one of the many folks walking down Del Rey Avenue. Except that, unlike most of these people, Harry was not on his way to work. He was on his way to a mailbox.

Harry was doing his best not to look like an out-of-towner, even though that's exactly what he was. He had foregone his usual button-down and blue jeans for an Armani three-piece just so that he would not stick out like a sore thumb among the well-dressed citizens of White Pines. Bragantz needed to remain as discreet as possible because he was getting ready to commit a crime, and not a smash-n-grab job at the corner Exxon.

Head down and hands in his pockets, Henry walked another block before finding what he was looking for. He casually approached the mailbox, pulled out a small brown envelope and slipped it inside.

Blending carefully back into the crowd, he reached into his left coat pocket and removed a detonator. Once he had distanced himself enough, he activated the detonator and exploded the bomb.

The blue metal mailbox instantaneously transformed into a killing machine, propelling shards of inch-thick steel through the unlucky pedestrians that happened to be within the blast radius.

The final tally would be 54: 19 dead. 35 injured.

And this was just the beginning.

OF COURSE, IT'S MONDAY

Mondays were usually slow at the Dragon's Men Protection Agency. There was no rhyme or reason to it; it was just the way it ended up working out. If the four of them were not already working on an assignment that had rolled over into a Monday, then it usually ended up being a free day. This particular Monday was just that.

Daniel Sloane had opted to spend his Monday morning at the gym.

Dr. Mercedes Lara had chosen to spend her free time sleeping in.

Samuel Hawkins had decided to spend his Monday morning shopping at J. McLaughlin's Clothiers. As it turned out, McLaughlin's was located about three blocks up from Del Rey Avenue where the mailbox bombing had occurred. Not only had Sam heard the blast, but he now stood just a block away looking at all the chaos. The bodies. The blood. The damage to all the surrounding buildings.

Hawk was so taken by the scene that he did not even notice that he was still wearing a pair of Parker Pants that he had been trying on.

"What in the world happened here?" he asked a fellow onlooker.

"I think the blue mailbox that was on the corner there, I think...I think it exploded."

"Exploded? How the...I mean—"

"I think it was a bomb," the onlooker said. "I was just walking to work down at Duvall & Sons, and all of a sudden, it just blew up."

Hawkins could hear sirens in the distance, cop cars, fire trucks, and ambulances on their way to the location. Soon he saw the flashing lights from the emergency vehicles as they made their way to the tragic scene.

Reaching for his cell phone to call John, he realized that he was wearing the store's pants and that his pants – along with his cell phone – were still inside the department store. He sprinted back to the store only to find absolutely no one there. Everyone – patrons and store personnel alike – was outside gawking at the catastrophe. He returned to the dressing room, fished his phone out of his pants pocket and called John Watkins.

John answered on the second ring. "What's goin' on, Samuel?"

"Yo, John, my man. You gotta get Doc and Danny and get yourselves down here to Del Rey and Standish. Looks like there's been some kinda bomb or somethin' set off."

"How long ago did this happen?"

"Not long. Five minutes. Maybe less."

"Okay. Doc's here with me. Danny's at the gym. I'll give him a call and we'll be there in about thirty. Find out what you can in the meantime."

"See y'all within the hour," Hawk confirmed.

John, who had been working on the agency's finances, pressed an intercom button on his desk. "Merc, are you up?"

"Only if I have to be," came the groggy response.

"I wouldn't be bothering you otherwise," John said as he turned on the TV in the office. "We need to be out of here in five."

"Okay," he heard her sigh. "I'll be down as soon as I can get the optic ocelots out of my eyes."

"Very good."

Watkins flipped through the local news channels until he got to one that was not in commercial. It was the Channel 3 news, and he recognized the news anchor as Endora Varma, a middle Eastern woman with whom John had a bit of a past. He tuned in just in time to catch her saying "...and as soon as we have someone on the scene, we will go to them for a live update. Once again, if you are just joining us, there has been an explosion of some sort in downtown White Pines on the corner of Del Rey Avenue and Standish Boulevard. Police, Medevac units, firefighting personnel, and paramedics are on the scene as there have been multiple reports of injuries."

John grabbed the handset from his desk phone and punched in Daniel Sloane's cell number.

A breathless Sloane answered on the third ring. "I had a feeling I'd be hearing from you."

"So, I take it that you've seen what's going on?"

"Yeah, pretty much everybody has stopped working out here and we are all huddled around the TVs. You wanting to meet up?"

"Samuel's already there. Merc and I are getting ready to head out that way now."

"I'll give you a call when I'm close and find out where to meet up with everybody."

"Be safe. Talk to you then."

No sooner had Watkins ended the call than Dr. Mercedes Lara stepped off the elevator. For someone who had been awakened just a few moments ago, she looked remarkably put together. Her long blond ponytail was pulled through the back of her Jacksonville Jaguars ball cap. A black wool coat over a teal fleece top, black yoga pants, and black sneakers completed the outfit.

"I'll let you drive," she said, never breaking stride as she headed to the front door.

John grabbed his jacket from the back of his chair and was out the door right behind her.

Discovering the Worst Is Yet to Come

Lieutenant Jack Thompson arrived at the bomb scene about twenty minutes after the detonation. By the time he had gotten there, two ambos, two squad cars, and a fire truck were already present. So far, no members of the media had shown up, but he knew that it would just be a matter of time before they did. Patrolmen Brian Wescott and Tammy Bell had set a perimeter around the crime scene and were making sure no unauthorized personnel traipsed through and contaminated the blast area.

As Thompson made his way through the scene, he could see a myriad of rescue staff tending to the injured. Walking past at least five bodies covered with white sheets, he could not believe his eyes. He had seen nothing like this since his military days in Kandahar.

"Lieutenant!" he heard a voice call out to him.

Thompson turned to see Officer Pete Curry hurrying up to him. "Got ourselves a heck of a mess here, sir. Initial interviews are saying that the postal box that was there," Curry pointed to the spot where the blue mailbox used to be, "exploded and sent shrapnel into pretty much anybody that was within about a thirty-foot radius of the blast zone. Those closest to the explosion are either dead or well on their way."

"Any of the witnesses see anything useful?"

"That would be a big, fat negatory, sir." Curry replied. "However, we are just getting started, so we may get lucky yet."

"Thank you, Officer Curry," Jack said just as two more ambulances and another squad car pulled up.

He was taking in the harrowing scenc that surrounded him when he heard the familiar voice of Samuel Hawkins from behind him. "Say, hey, Cap'n Jack. Looks like ya got your hands full with this one."

"What's going on, Sam?" Thompson reached out and shook the man's hand amiably.

When it came to the Dragon's Men Protection Agency, the White Pines police force was more or less split down the middle on how they felt about the foursome. Some of the cops felt like Dragon's Men got away with a little too much. Some of the cops felt like the former military quartet did their jobs for them. Others, Jack Thompson included, appreciated the service that Dragon's Men offered the good people of White Pines. Were it not for the former Delta Force crew, crime would be a lot higher in this ritzy town. Lieutenant Jack Thompson often found himself as a go-between, with John Watkins and his crew on one side, and the White Pines police and governing administration on the other.

"I was just down the road doin' a bitta shopping when I heard all the commotion," Sam began. "Gave John Boy a call so's he and Doc and Danny could get down here and survey all the wreckage."

"How long ago was that?"

"Maybe fifteen, twenty minutes ago. John and Doc should be together. Sloane, he's at the gym. He'll be along shortly," Hawk spoke quickly. "So, what do ya make of all this?"

"Hard to say at this point. I do know this much: If the bomb that caused all this really was in a mailbox, that'll make this a federal case which means we can be expecting some boys from Washington D.C. before too long. That's just what we'll need to make this go from bad to worse."

"Well, one good thing, Lieutenant," Hawkins smiled, "At least, you'll have those reporters off ya back about your man Officer Hoffman having shot that little kid that was wieldin' a BB pistol."

"Yeah, because this is exactly what I wanted to have happen to make all that go away."

"Lieutenant!" Officer Curry hollered. "Can these two come through?"

Lieutenant Thompson saw John Watkins and Dr. Mercedes Lara standing next to Officer Pete Curry.

"Yeah, let 'em in, officer."

Curry lifted the yellow police tape. John and Mercedes ducked underneath it and made their way over to Lieutenant Thompson.

"I'd ask how you're doing, Jack, but I feel that would be a waste of my breath and your time," John Watkins said. "So, instead, I will just ask you if you know what happened."

"Preliminary reports are that somebody put a bomb in the mailbox and set it off. Turned the whole thing into a big blue hand grenade."

"Mailbox, huh? Guess our terrorist wanted to deal with the feds instead of the local boys, huh?"

"Seemingly."

"Forensics been here yet?"

"So far, ain't nobody been here yet."

"Mind if Merc gives it a quick look?"

"Can she give it a look without touching anything?" Thompson asked.

John looked over at Mercedes, who was still half asleep. "Can you do that?

"I can do that," Dr. Lara confirmed. "I can, and I will."

With that, Dr. Lara, her hands in her coat pockets and her head down to protect her face from the cold, walked over to where the mailbox had previously been. Removing a forensics kit from her coat pocket, she knelt down to analyze the ground. She took a few samples of soil from the ground and placed them in her kit.

While she was doing that, John Watkins spoke with the lieutenant.

"Will the chief be making an appearance out here today?"

"I don't believe he will, John. He's back at the station, and it's my understanding that he will be giving a press conference in about an hour. He sent me out here to see what kind of answers I could scrounge up. He's waiting to hear from me."

"Any ransom demands from whomever did this?"

"Nothing. All quiet on that front."

With that, the barrage of news vans began showing up.

"Hey!" Jack Thompson yelled out to his patrolmen. "Keep them back, and let them know that Chief Barksdale will be giving a presser at the station in about an hour."

While John was looking around the area, he saw that Mercedes had left the blast site and was now speaking in earnest to some of the paramedics and injured pedestrians. She gave John a very concerned look.

"I have a feeling if you want to scrounge up some answers, we should go talk to Merc. She's got a look on her face that I've seen before – many times, actually – and for the most part it means that she's found something not so great."

"Well, let's go find out the bad news, I guess," the lieutenant shook his head.

"Did I hear somebody say 'bad news'?" Daniel Sloane asked, showing up seemingly out of nowhere.

"See Merc over there talking to the paramedics?" John asked Sloane.

Daniel scanned the tragic scene until he saw his teammate talking to an EMT he knew as Vaughn Rogers. He, too, saw the look of concern on Mercedes' face. A look that, much like John, he knew to be bad news.

Just as the three of them were getting ready to head her way, Merc started over to them. While they waited for her to pass through the maze of dead and injured, Sloane asked what seemed to be the most popular question of the morning, "Anybody taking credit for this mess yet?"

"No one yet."

"I wonder if whatever group is responsible for this is going to have political demands or financial demands? I figure they coulda hit any city for political favors. I gotta feeling it's not an accident that this happened in one of the richest towns in the country. Heck, in the world, for that matter."

Mercedes approached the trio. "So, which do you want first, the bad news or the really bad news?"

"Just give the news to us in whichever order makes the most sense," John suggested.

"It's military explosives that they used—"

"Don't you mean military *grade* explosives?" Lieutenant Thompson interrupted.

"If I meant military grade explosives, I would have said military grade explosives. I meant military explosives, so I said military explosives," Mercedes stated with all the cynicism she could muster. "Except that the military that uses this kind of explosive device is the Russian military."

"So, we're dealing with Russian terrorists?"

"Not necessarily. Anybody could use it, but I just happen to know that it's the Russians that are doing the latest research and development with it. Like, third generation stuff.

"Okay," Thompson said, "then is that the bad news or the really bad news?"

"That's the bad news. The really bad news is that this type of bomb is thermobaric. Oxygenated."

"And what exactly does that mean?"

"It means that this particular type of bomb is based on how much oxygen is around it. It's a double detonation device. The first detonator pops open a container of accelerant – like fuel, for instance. The fuel is released, and then the second detonator ignites the fuel. And the amount of oxygen it has at its disposal will determine how big the blast radius is. Here's the thing about a thermobaric weapon: those nearest the ignition point are obliterated. Those at the fringe are likely to suffer many internal, and thus invisible injuries, including burst eardrums and crushed inner ear organs, severe concussions, ruptured lungs and internal organs, and possibly blindness. That's what I was talking to the paramedic about – to find out if he was seeing this kind of injury in the people that had survived the blast. He told me that was *exactly* what he was seeing. That very kind of injury."

"So, if I understand what you're saying," John said, "if this bomb hadn't been in that mailbox where it had very little oxygen with which to work, we'd be looking at a lot more dead and a lot more injured?"

"And a lot more structural damage to the buildings around it?" Sloane added.

"Precisely."

The four of them looked at each other with a great deal of apprehension before John finally said what they were all thinking. "Whoever did this is sending us a message: This is just the beginning, and we can expect a lot worse to come."

ACKNOWLEDGEMENTS

So, here it is, *Chasing Redemption*, the fourth and final book in the Boom!!...Killers. series. To say that there are more people to thank than I can remember would be a huge understatement. Nevertheless, here is my bold attempt to do just that: my thank yous to everyone that helped make this dream of mine a reality.

Thank you to my friends and family that knew me when I was just a boy and were there when this dream originated: Michael J. and Susan Hoffman, Mark Rose, Anne Rose, the Jenkins family, Derek Cooke, Brian Holbrook, Mike Watkins, Greg and Kenny Smith, Laura Montgomery, Claudette Fischer, Taralyn Tharp-Kohler, David Baldwin, Dawn Shek, John Ballweg, Melissa Ballweg, Chuck Purnell, Donnie Dell, and Carole Grimsley. Thank you for your faith in me and never letting me forget nor take for granted the God-given talent that was bestowed upon me.

Next, I would like to thank those that inspired me and helped me to keep aspiring for greatness: Kimmy Michael, Jessica Devine-Daugherty, Danielle Zawodny, Elke Griffin, Rob Perry, Andy Kyle, Jay Hood, Nash Villers, Julia Austin-Marolf, Jennifer VanSciver, Lindsay Wagner, Rachael Sites Hadsell, Robin Browning, Minnie Driver, Christine Caples, AnnA Ruillere, Candace, Lacy Glenn, Erica Bradley, and Tia Bell.

Here is a special thanks to my good friend Brenda Cobb-Schmidt. In real life, she is the complete 180 to the character of Brenda Cobb-Schmidt portrayed in *Chasing Redemption*. Although Brenda has her own physical hardships, she always goes out of her way to check on my well-being. She's a true friend, a wonderful mother, a fantastic daughter, and a great wife. I appreciate her volunteering to be the bad guy in this book and allowing me to have free rein to make her the "baddest" bad guy of all the villains in this series. My readers are going to love to hate your character, Bren-Bren.

I am sure that we all have, at one point or another, had that person in our life that was the perfect boss who made even the worst job in the world worth getting up for every day. For me, that person was Michael "Big Mike" Perrera, and that job was working in the shipping department at Worthington Steel in Baltimore, Maryland. Big Mike left us way too soon on January 29, 2020, and this world has been just a little bit darker ever since. Thank you for always having my back (especially the time I blew the weight on that Valeo job and should have, no doubt, been sacked on the spot had it not been for you interceding on my behalf). Thank you for all the jokes, stories, and memories that you gave us to tide us over until we can see you again one day soon. Rest in peace, Big Mike, and know that the light that you shed on this world will be carried on through the lives of everyone that had the privilege of knowing you during your time here on Earth. You were one of a kind, and I am and ever shall be eternally grateful for having known you.

Now to say thank you to the one person that has made these books possible – the one person that has taken my "very good" and made it light years better: Nancy J. Sayre. Thank you for your kindness, insight, and intelligence. You are a Godsend. I very much look forward to working with you in the future.

Finally, to the one true love of my life, Donna Somerville: there is no me without you, and there is no world that spins if you are not in it. Thank you for being the female version of me. Thank you for never giving up on us when it seems like it would be the easiest thing in the world to do. I love you. Now and forever.

ABOUT THE AUTHOR

Doc Ephraim Bates is the author of the popular
Boom!!...Killers. series.

He has been writing comedic action thrillers since age
fourteen. The youngest of seven sons, Doc mastered
the three skills most valuable to his assassin characters:
maintaining a sense of humor, learning how to take a
beating, and the art of not getting caught.

Connect with Doc on Facebook at
www.facebook.com/DocEphraimBates.

Send him an email at
doc@docephraimbates.com.

Sign up for his newsletter at
www.goldenalleypress.com/boom-killers-series